MW01170498

The Lost Bloodline Book 1

M. Tress

ROYAL GUARD

Chapter One

THERE WAS SOMETHING SO VERY SOOTHING ABOUT being out in nature. Above him, the trees spread welcoming shade as shelter from the harsh sun. It was something to relish after long days spent working outside.

The clean scent of the mountain air combined with the occasional whiff of wildflowers or the scent of hot stone was such a bracing change from the rank scent of the city. The smell of green things replaced the stink of exhaust, and the air itself felt lighter against his skin.

Koda took a deep breath of the warm air and let it out slowly in a sigh. It was good to be away from the city for a while.

Finding time to get away from it all and just relax was getting harder and harder. It wasn't that his life was changing. The lack of change was actually part of the issue. Instead, it was that he was slowly wearing down to a nub from exhaustion.

Construction was not an easy sort of job, but it paid the bills. Only having a GED prevented him from getting into a better-paying field, but at least he didn't have student loan debt to deal with.

"Small mercy," Koda muttered, rolling his shoulders and turning back to the trail now that he had caught his breath.

The path he was following was a well-maintained trail that wound amongst the evergreens of the Rocky Mountains. It was one of his favorites to take on the rare afternoons that he had the time and energy for hiking anymore, but that wasn't saying much. There were a lot of trails that Koda thought of as favorites.

Focusing on the stone-studded earth in front of him, Koda let the scent of spruce trees wrap around him and fill his senses.

The chirp and buzz of insects swirled around him like a cloak, carried by the steady breeze that trickled down into the canyon from the ridge above. A breeze that helped the dappled shade of the trees keep him cool.

Wonder if the foreman is going to swap me over to another group or not? Been getting on well with the framing guys. They are at least letting me help, rather than just carry shit, Koda thought with a sigh.

Despite the splendor of the world around him, full of rich green and brown hues, and a blue sky free of clouds overhead, thoughts of his problems would not fade.

Before it was the plumbing guys, and then before that it was the electricians. What's he going to do now? Put me back with the concrete guys?

Koda had signed on with Dockett Construction under the premise that he'd work as general labor and a gopher until a slot opened up for an apprentice with a team, and then he'd move into that.

It had been nearly three years now, and he'd yet to be given a slot. Koda had a sinking sensation that the foreman was just keeping him around as cheap general labor at this point. Even some of the old hands had pointed it out to him.

There wasn't much to do, though. He just had to keep plugging away. It wasn't as if he could move back in with his parents at this point.

It'd been most of a decade since he'd talked to either of his parents, after finally giving up and walking out of his father's house after a last-straw argument to try to guilt him into siding with the other man against Koda's mother.

His parents had divorced when he was eight and then proceeded to use custody of him as a club to beat each other. Koda'd had enough and just left the entire thing.

Living on the street for a year until he got the emancipation sorted and found work was rough, but he'd done it. Focusing on trying to find his own way in the world helped get him out of that situation.

The sudden cessation of noise from the bugs and the birds twigged Koda's danger sense and drew him out of his melancholy thoughts. Glancing around, he looked for something that might have caused the sudden drop in noise.

The undergrowth beneath the trees was all the sort of greenery that clung low to the rocks, with the occasional patch of spiky yucca or fuzzy mullein that sprouted up where the sun snuck through the trees. So, there wasn't anywhere for a predator to hide. It wasn't as if this ravine that the trail followed was very large either, and steep stone cliffs rose on either side.

Scanning the upper branches of the trees as well, just to make sure that there wasn't something like a mountain lion watching him from above, Koda sighed and shook his head.

"Whatev—" Koda started, about to brush the sensation off, when a loud crack of breaking stone echoed down the ravine from farther along the cliff wall. "What the fuck?" he swore, head whipping around to peer between the trees toward the sound.

The noise had been thunderous but singular. Just a loud crack of rock breaking and nothing else. No rumble of falling stone or scatter of pebbles tumbling down the steep slope.

Overwhelmed with a curiosity that banished his previous melancholy, Koda started up the path at a trot. He only had the bare basics in a small pack on his back, so there wasn't all that much to weigh him down as he jogged up the uneven trail.

Koda had made it almost a quarter-mile up the slope before he spotted what he guessed was the source of the sound from earlier.

Because the ravine was so steep-sided, there were a fair number of large boulders scattered around the base of the cliffs. Boulders that had laid where they rested for a very long time, just baking in the blistering sun. But one, apparently, had baked for a bit too long.

The boulder, which looked easily as large as a queen-sized bed leaned upright, had split in half right down the middle.

It was the fresh, dark interior of the rock that caught his eye and Koda slid to a stop, peering through the trees at the broken boulder. He thought he could see something in the shadows of the cliff just behind the split boulder.

So, with a shrug, Koda stepped off the trail and around a cluster of low, ball-shaped cacti, then headed up between the trees to inspect the boulder.

His estimations of the size of the thing were a bit off. The boulder turned out to be more like the size of his old pickup as he got closer. The rock had been roughly oval-shaped before the split and was now sitting on its side. The split had caused it to fall into nearly equal halves.

Stepping closer, Koda was now sure that he could see a shadow behind the rock. A shadow that looked like the entrance of a cave.

"Wonder what's in there?" Koda muttered, stepping closer to the broken stone and peering into the deep shadows that pooled there.

The rock itself radiated heat from having sat in the sun, enough that he did not want to touch the stone if he could help it. It honestly felt far hotter than it should have for the cool morning despite being in direct sunlight. It felt more like the rock had been baking all day in the middle of summer.

Around him, the air remained still. The sound of the bugs and the birds had not yet returned. That was making Koda more nervous as the moments slipped by.

However, the more he looked at the cave behind the split stone, the surer he was that there was no way that anything had been living in it. The opening was narrow, barely wider than the split from the boulder. It had been totally blocked until the rock had broken.

Fishing his phone out of his jeans, Koda flicked on the flash-light app and crawled into the split in the hot rock, careful not to touch it with his bare skin.

The fissure was narrow enough that he had to shrug off his backpack in order to fit into the split without brushing the sides. The heat from the rock roasted him like standing in front of an open oven.

When Koda emerged on the other side, the temperature dropped abruptly as soon as he stepped into the cool shade of the cave.

Playing the light from his phone around, it surprised him to find that the cave quickly wound deeper into the cliffside, angling slightly down and away from him.

The tunnel widened enough after a few feet that he could stretch his arms out to either side and not touch the edges. Overhead, he had a good foot of clearance as well.

An overwhelming desire to explore rose in his gut, and Koda had to ruthlessly stomp on it as his common sense asserted itself.

"Running off into a random cave is dumb and definitely not safe. There is no telling if this is stable, especially after whatever happened that broke the rock at the front," Koda grumbled, preparing to turn back.

As he was turning his back on the tunnel, the distant echo of a feminine shout rolled out of the darkness, and he felt every hair on his body stand up and dance.

The noise hadn't been an excited shout or a playful one done to listen to the echoes. It had been a fearful shout of surprise. A wordless exclamation of fear.

Without hesitating, Koda wheeled back to the tunnel and hurried down it, phone held high to shed light as far as he could.

"Hello? Are you okay?" he called down the tunnel, his voice

echoing oddly at the words. "Even if you are, please call out so I know!"

He listened as he shuffled down the rapidly steepening slope of the tunnel, his mind whirling. Had someone else been on the trail ahead of him and already delved into the cave? Had someone gotten lost or hurt? He knew that it would have been far smarter to step out of the cave and try to call the local ranger station for help, especially as this was an unexplored cave.

No guarantee I'd get a signal in that ravine. The mountains play hell with cell phones, he reminded himself, heart racing as he worried about whoever was also in here with him.

Koda was getting ready to call out again as he came around a curve in the tunnel when his foot slipped on something, and he fell backwards.

Yelping in surprise, Koda landed hard before the steep slope sent him tumbling into a roll.

In an effort to shield his skull and neck, he threw his arms up and tried to wrap them around his head as he skittered down the sloped tunnel.

Several times, Koda rebounded off a wall or bounced around a corner in the headlong fall. He fought the urge to try to grab onto something to stop his descent, knowing that it would likely end up giving him a broken arm rather than actually helping.

Finally, the slope lessened. Moments later, Koda rolled to a stop, head pounding and ears roaring from the adrenaline.

While he'd kept hold of his cell phone during the tumble, his backpack had gotten hooked on something and yanked off his shoulder, leaving him with just the dimly lit cell phone and what he had in his pockets.

"God damn it," Koda cursed, hissing in pain as he gingerly got to his knees.

His entire body hurt more than it had in several years, ever since one of the concrete guys had talked him into unloading a flatbed full of bagged concrete by hand. The asshole had lied about the forklift being broken, wanting to just get him in trouble and slack off instead of helping.

Stretching slowly, Koda took in his surroundings.

Behind him, the sloped length of the tunnel wound away into the darkness. He was fairly certain that he could scramble back up if he had to. The walls crowded close in around him, looming like a threat held close.

Turning to check the other half of the room, the last thing that he expected to find himself in was the entrance to a large limestone cave. The native rock of the mountains was granite, so finding the yellow-white rock here was surprising.

Long stalactites hung from the ceiling, while stalagmites mounded up around the back half of the cave. A pool of pitch-black water sat in front of him, easily a good six feet across and deep enough that his flashlight could not find the bottom. He'd tumbled down the slope and slid to a stop only a couple feet away from ending up directly in that pool.

Staring at the water in surprise, Koda abruptly remembered the feminine scream that had drawn him deeper into the cave. He immediately scanned the room again to see if someone had possibly tumbled down ahead of him but couldn't see any signs. Even the floor underfoot was pristine, except where his boots were leaving dusty prints on the yellow-white stone. The air in the cave was heavy and oppressive, and Koda swore he could feel the weight of the tons of stone hanging above him.

"This is just way too creepy..." he muttered.

Koda glanced around the cave again before the shimmer of light on the water drew his attention to the pool once more.

Something urged him closer to the edge, and he peered toward the dark water curiously. Koda didn't know what it was, but something told him to approach and wait, to be patient for just a moment longer despite his racing heart.

The edge of the pool was slick with moisture. Koda had to be careful not to slip and fall into the water as he approached. Once he was close enough to lean over it, Koda stared down into the darkness.

The edge of the pool sloped sharply under the water before abruptly cutting away, and the center of the pool was dark.

Playing his phone's light over it, Koda wrinkled his forehead for a long moment as he concentrated. Again, he felt that tugging sensation that was drawing him forward, but he refused to do something as dumb as step into the water. Especially after ignoring his instincts and coming into the cave, which led to his fall.

The depths of the pool seemed to ripple, and suddenly, the water was not depthless anymore.

Koda blinked in surprise when he could see the bottom and squinted. It looked like the water had abruptly decided to show a reflection of the ceiling of the cave, when before it had simply been a pool of darkness.

Glancing up, he checked before looking down once more into the pool. It looked roughly the same, but not exactly. Maybe he was seeing the bottom of the pool instead?

It looked like someone had been here before. Because, as he studied the depths of the subterranean well, he saw what looked like a statue of a woman standing directly across from him, but reversed as if the pool was a mirror.

9

"Huh... that is cool. I wonder what tribe built this?" he muttered while thinking.

The most likely source was an indigenous tribe back before 'civilization' had come to the land. Koda was just talking out loud to reassure himself. It wasn't as if he expected anyone to respond.

He sure as hell did not expect the *statue* to shift, let alone speak.

"The Ivory Spear clan carved out this cave initially. At least the half that I stand in."

The voice was throaty, feminine, and a bit hoarse. Like someone who had not spoken in a long time.

The statue of the woman shifted, her bone-pale skin shimmering as she kneeled to stare up at him in reverse, as if the water was nothing more than a bit of glass, and the forces of gravity were reversed on the far side.

What he had taken as shadows around her head turned out to be a mass of lustrous, black curls that hung about her shoulders in defiance of her orientation and gravity. Koda couldn't help but be envious of that mane of curls.

His own black hair was straight as a rod, and he'd given up on doing anything with it other than tying it back.

The woman watched him curiously with eyes that glinted silver in the light of his phone.

"Who? What?" Koda stumbled through the words as he fought to figure out what had just happened while swaying and nearly falling over in surprise.

His mind flashed over different possibilities in rapid succession. Had he hit his head on the fall, and this was a hallucination? A gas pocket in the long-sealed cave? Was he losing his mind?

"You are not losing your mind, Koda Burke," the woman said gently, peering up at him without blinking.

Koda swore he saw a faint, spotted pattern in the silky mass of curls that hung about her pale face.

"I think I am. I'm talking to a beautiful woman who is hiding in a pool of water."

The woman's full lips twisted into a broad smile that revealed pearl-white teeth. Pearl-white teeth that were pointed like a hunting cat's, rather than those of a normal human.

Okay, definitely crazy, he thought, heart racing.

"No, you are not crazy. I promise that much," the woman reassured him, laughing low in her throat.

The motion sent a ripple through her body that dragged Koda's attention away from her teeth to more interesting parts of her anatomy, and he took in her outfit again.

Kneeling before him, the dark-haired stranger wore a short, wrap-style skirt made of fur-on leather in a dark brown that fell to mid-thigh. The angle and reversed position showed a great deal of her creamy inner thigh, but no more than that. A simple chest wrap also made of fur hugged full breasts that looked like they were at that delicious point where they were just over a handful. Around her shoulders was a cape of leather lined with dark-brown fur as well.

"Well, if I am not crazy? What the hell is happening right now?" Koda demanded, his voice growing higher in pitch as he took a tentative step back from the pool.

The woman's amused look immediately shifted to one of fear, and she held out a hand towards him, beckoning him to stop.

The sight of her beautiful features twisting in fear punched Koda in the gut, and a wave of guilt immediately washed over him. This gave him a handle to get a hold of his rising panic, though, and he reined it in.

"I am sorry for scaring you, Koda. It was—" the woman started, but he interrupted her.

"How do you know my name?"

The black-haired woman frowned for a moment and glanced to one side as if checking something in her version of the cave. After a moment, she looked back at him. Her gaze was distant as if she could see right through him.

"I know it because I know you. Or I know... of you. Your blood calls to me, and I recognize its line. It is why I drew you here, so I could ask something of you," the woman spoke slowly, weighing her words carefully.

"How?"

"How do I know you?" The woman tilted her head to one side in a fashion that reminded him of a curious dog.

The gesture oddly reassured him. Koda felt his racing heart slow a bit as he studied the beautiful woman speaking from the other side of a pool of water.

"An ancestor of yours was once a follower of mine. I had thought calamity had taken her bloodline from me forever. Like so many others. But it appears she escaped the ruination of my world."

A glimmer that Koda thought might have been a tear formed

at the corner of one of her silver eyes, but the woman rubbed it away quickly.

"Your world? Ruination?"

Koda couldn't look away from the beautiful woman. He was now sure that there was some sort of spotted pattern to her curly hair as the shimmer of the light reflected on it showed differently.

Before he realized it, Koda was kneeling by the side of the pool again, leaning over so that he looked directly down at the woman.

The woman's features darkened, and her concerned expression morphed into one of barely restrained rage that Koda was thankful wasn't directed at him.

"Monsters, foes greater than any could have suspected, ravaged my world. They drove my people from their homes —those they did not outright slaughter. *Your forebears* were driven from their homes."

Spitting out that last statement, the woman mastered her anger, but Koda could see it still boiling behind her silver eyes like faint embers in a low-burning fire.

"Those who promised me aid declined to give it. They did not think the threat was grave enough to *waste the resources*." Her lips twisted in a snarl now that revealed those sharp teeth once more, but Koda was not afraid. Instead, he felt an echo of her righteous fury in his heart.

"What became of them?" The question fell from his lips before Koda could think, but the woman did not take offense.

"My people... your people, fled. Those who could escape scattered to the other worlds. Some fought and lived on, but most all of them died. I was carried by the few remaining of my faithful to a place of safety, after using all but the last dregs of my power to strike down those who betrayed us."

A leonine growl emanated from the woman's slender throat, and Koda felt a thrill run up his spine. Not of fear, but of awe.

"What then?"

The woman deflated at his question, slumping forward onto her hands, her long hair falling to shade her face. "By the time I woke, those of my clergy were gone. Either dead to threats in the new world or murdered by our enemies."

Koda felt the word 'clergy' ring in his head. His senses felt distorted as he stared into the pond, and idly, the thought that this might just be a hallucination while he died of a head injury ran through his mind.

"Or so I thought. I hadn't expected to find one of the bloodline so close to one of the old speaking wells. Let alone one that was connected to my hiding place."

"Why are you hiding?" Koda wanted to ask for more about the bloodlines, about the history that this strange woman seemed to know of his family, but a strange concern was filling him for her safety.

"Because I am not welcome in the lands I live in now. The powers tolerate my former people because they give lip service to new gods, but this leaves my faithful without the proper protections I should be able to offer them. Without a priest or a champion to claim sites of power for me, I am a mere shadow of what I could be." The woman scowled again, and Koda swore her silver eyes took on a hint of madness for just a moment.

"Why did you speak to me? Why call to me? What does this 'bloodline' you mentioned *mean*?" The questions poured out of Koda like water from a cracked bowl the second she paused to breathe.

The woman stared at him for a long moment, her raven-dark eyebrows furrowing as she studied him. It took the better part of a minute before she responded.

"I need you, Koda Burke. I need a priest. A champion. In my despair, I had given up hope until this moment. I peered into this ancient well in hopes of glimpsing my ancient domain one last time before the returning calamity wiped my people out. When I saw you..." She trailed off and studied him before nodding once, resolve firming her features.

"I can offer you power, riches, immortality, and more. Women or men to sate your appetites, and all the luxuries of life. I need you to help me save my people. If they vanish, then so will I. It may take time to gather the power to give you everything, but I will make good on it."

The woman's voice took on a hint of desperation as she continued, rambling as she explained herself. People in danger, places of power that she needed help to reclaim, and all of it being possible because of some ancient ties to an ancestor he didn't even know of.

The entire idea sounded so bizarre to Koda. This felt like something that would happen in a movie or a storybook. But he felt something in his body, his very blood, responding to the request this woman was making—nearly begging—of him. If her earlier words meant what he thought, the request that this *goddess* was making of him.

"Revenge is not my only motivator. I truly want to help my people. And, if you accept and help them, I am sure my faithful will shower you with riches and honor as well." The goddess had continued with trying to sway him as thoughts drifted through Koda's cloudy mind. If anything, her desperation made his decisions easy.

"No."

The one-word statement from Koda caused all the hope to fall from the woman's face. The distraught expression tore at his heart like a physical blow. Koda raced to explain, trying to bring back that hope he'd seen shining in her silver eyes as resignation took its place.

"No, I don't need to be showered in riches, women, or whatever." Koda shook his head fiercely to clear it of the distracting fog and grimaced before punching his own thigh sharply, grunting in pain at the sensation.

The blow helped him to focus, driving away the clouds that hung around his mind and made it wander.

When he looked at her once more, the goddess's silver eyes glimmered with tears, and the hope was back once more. The sight of it made his heart soar.

"You said people need help? My people?" Try as he might, Koda could not keep the desperate longing from his voice as he said: 'my people'.

Ever since his parents' marriage had collapsed, and doubly so after he fled to escape the toxic space that was their homes, Koda had wanted a real, loving family. He'd wanted to belong once more. The hope of starting his own family as soon as his income was stable had kept him going until now, seeing that as the first step toward reclaiming those familial bonds. But, with how the foreman at work was jerking him around, that hope was turning into a distant dream.

"Yes. My people are your people, Koda. They need my help, and I cannot give it without an agent. Long ago, I bound my power to the bloodline of my clergy. With that tie, and the power that flows in your veins, I can actually help them again." Hope turned to determination. It glimmered in her eyes, rang in her voice, and trembled in the shoulders of the beautiful, fur-clad woman before him. "You'll help?"

"Yes."

The decision took less than a heartbeat to make. There was nothing left for him here but a dead-end job. Koda mused for just a moment that there were a few people on the worksite that he might miss, but with what this strange woman was offering him?

Well, he would be a fool to pass this up.

And if you are lying there with a broken skull in a cave, like the idiot you are, there is no harm in playing along and enjoying the distraction while you die, right? Koda thought with morbid amusement.

With his decision made, and the benefit of the focus that provided, both the vague fear and the last of the brain-fog from earlier vanished.

"Then I need you to come to me, quickly. I will empower you to be my agent, my champion, and the first of my new clergy. Help me save our people, Koda. Help us find our way back home."

The raven-haired woman held her hand out and leaned forward like she was about to dive forward into the reversed surface of the pool.

Koda watched in astonishment as her hand touched the clear surface and sank into, then *through* the water's surface.

A delicate, alabaster hand rose from within the pool, held out to him in supplication.

"Take my hand, Koda Burke. Though you are of the blood of my people, and your line served me once, you still have the freedom to choose. All creatures should run free beneath the open sky."

The last part of her sentence rang like the words were striking a glass bell within his skull.

A rush of sensations whirled past him. The sensation of wind on his face, soft grass under bare feet, the warmth of a fire against his side, and the soft touch of a mate tucked to his chest. They were there and gone in a single instant, and his heart ached with longing to feel them once more.

Without hesitation, Koda reached out and took the pale hand.

The goddess smiled at him, her fang-filled mouth curving into an expression of both affection and relief. Her eyes danced for a moment before her expression firmed into one of determination.

"Come to me, my champion. I will anoint you with a weapon, and then you must save our people from an imminent threat. They may not understand at first, but they will come to love you for the sacrifices you make." As she spoke, the goddess pulled Koda forward and down into the pond.

When his hand touched the water of the pool, Koda felt something cool and hard wrap around his fingertips before flowing up his arm.

A gauntlet made of leather and bone, studded with teeth and sharp stones, slowly wrapped around his arm as the goddess drew him into the pool. Sharp talons made of carefully carved bones tipped the fingers, but he could still feel the soft warmth of her skin against his palm despite the presence of the gauntlet. The construct flowed over his skin as it passed through the surface of the water.

"What is your name?" Koda asked as he teetered on the edge of losing his balance and tipping fully into the water.

The raven-haired woman smiled at him, her back arching proudly in such a way that her breasts bounced in their fur wrap as she spoke with a flourish.

"When I was at the height of my power, my titles were the Pack Lady or Ivorycrown. But before even that, I was Thera, Queen of Beasts."

Thera gave him one last tug, and Koda willingly fell forward into the pool.

His cell phone fell from his left hand to land on the limestone at the edge of the water with a clatter.

The light continued to illuminate the cave, even as the image in the pond faded, and the pool returned to a bottomless, black hole that vanished deep into the earth.

Chapter Two

WATER STRUCK HIS FACE WITH THE SENSATION OF pushing through a gauzy curtain. It pushed against Koda's skin for a brief moment before parting and allowing him through. No sensation of wetness clung to him, just that gentle tugging sensation accompanied by the stronger pull of the grip on his hand.

The grip gave him a firm yank, and Koda popped through with a gasp, expecting to swallow water but finding himself standing on the edge of another deep pool. He teetered for a moment, but the hand that still held his arm steadied him until his awareness returned, and the woman in front of him captured his attention once more.

Blinking rapidly, Koda glanced around the small cave that mirrored the one he had just left.

Mirrored it, except for the woman who stood in front of him with a smile on her delicate lips.

"Welcome back, Koda Burke. I would love to give you the full welcome that you deserve, but our time is short." Thera's voice was throaty and full, sounding like there might be the hint of a purr in it.

The words caressed Koda's ears like fine velvet, and he felt a shiver run down his spine. That was until their meaning sank in, and his spine firmed up.

He reached out with his right hand to steady himself against the wall and spotted the primitive gauntlet wrapping his limb, which made him freeze again for a moment.

Flexing his fingers, Koda watched as the leather and bone articulated. The dim light emanating from Thera reflected off the polished stone that decorated it.

The gauntlet ran all the way up to cover his elbow and a few inches beyond. Thick leg bones guarded his forearm, while polished stones and the fangs of great predators decorated the spaces in between. The leather felt both supple and soft against his skin, yet hard enough to match metal on the outside. Sharp claws of carved bone tipped each of his fingers and hooked forward like razor-edged threats, while smaller bones guarded his individual fingers.

Shaking off his distraction, Koda turned his eyes back to the woman in front of him and nodded.

"How can I help?"

The four words, so simple to utter but filled with conviction, made the dark-haired woman smile even wider.

Thera bit her lower lip delicately for a moment, her sharp teeth denting the flesh there but not piercing it before she nodded once.

"The last of those who know of my survival fight for their lives outside the cave we are inside. If things continue the way they are, enemies will wipe my people out. Then I will fade. Their belief in me over the centuries is the last of what allows me to survive. I might have lived another hundred years as the faintest hint of a ghost, but I have given you what power I could spare. It will empower your weapon and strengthen you to be far more than you appear."

Thera gestured to the gauntlet that wrapped Koda's right hand. He flexed his fingers once more, the bone claws clicking together quietly. He could feel the soft leather playing under his grip, and Koda instinctively knew the claws were not just for decoration and would be far more deadly than one might expect.

Looking up from the gauntlet, Koda flinched at the sight of Thera now. While she had been pale when he first emerged from the pool of water, she now looked sickly and translucent.

"Thera, tell me quickly. How can I help you?" he rushed to demand, even as the goddess who had called him to this world grew fainter, fading out like a mist struck by the sun.

"Defend my people. As long as those who believe in me survive, I will as well. I sacrificed my last totem to make your weapon, so actions you take in my name will give me strength. Find holy sites to claim in my name, and that will empower me further. Seek out places of power in the natural world and anoint them with the lost bloodline that has returned."

As Thera spoke aloud, threads of her form frayed at the edges, spinning free to be drawn into the gauntlet on his right arm even as she grew fainter.

"Save the people, and find places of power in the world to claim. Got it. Hang on, Thera. You promised me a family again. I'm going to hold you to that," Koda recounted in a decisive tone.

Thera's fading lips twisted into a relieved smile, and she nodded before the last of her form faded away. The light died with it, leaving him wrapped in shadows.

Surrounded by darkness, Koda should have felt panicked and alone. He should have been terrified of being abandoned like this.

Instead, he felt empowered.

Instead, he felt determined.

Instead, he could see a faint trickle of light coming from off to his left, and he strode determinedly toward it.

The light grew quickly and revealed rough walls formed by simple tools that narrowed tightly before slipping out from behind a large stone to emerge into what looked like a mineshaft.

Walls and ceiling of granite supported by ancient timbers surrounded him. A smoking torch burned on the wall beside him, casting thick shadows over the passage he had just emerged from.

Taking a few steps away from the torch, Koda glanced over his shoulder. If he hadn't just emerged from the concealed passage, he would have walked right past it. The light of the torch threw wavering shadows that made the passage look like nothing more than a small divot in the wall.

Swallowing once, Koda squared his shoulders and nodded, resolute.

A quick look around confirmed his thoughts that this had to have been a mine at some point. He could see the ancient scars on the wall and floor from tools, though nothing remained of whatever ore was being carved out. A single passage curved away, and he could see more light coming from that direction.

"Let's see if we can find the exit," Koda muttered. "Thera said our people need help, after all." A thrill ran through him at saying *our people*.

He moved into a slow trot, keeping an eye on his feet as he worked to avoid tripping on the uneven floor.

Koda worked his right arm as he moved, stretching it and rolling his shoulder to get used to the weight of the primitive gauntlet he now wore.

Thera had told him it was a weapon. Her last totem given a new form. He could feel a slight warmth emanating from the leather and bone construction. In fact, he swore he could feel the squeezing sensation of someone gripping his hand like when Thera had pulled him through the pool.

Turning a corner, Koda saw a burst of light ahead and to his right where the tunnel branched, so he picked up speed.

The sounds of shouting echoed oddly down the tunnel, and he increased his pace once more. A moment later, he felt a breeze on his face and emerged into dazzling sunlight.

Blinking furiously to clear his watering eyes, Koda batted at his face with his left hand in an attempt to scatter the glare from his vision.

Through watering eyes, he could see his destination ahead of him. While minutes before, the valley he had entered the cave from had been narrow, and a large split boulder blocked the entrance to the cave, this valley spread out before him unobstructed.

He stood high on a ridge that overlooked a sprawling valley that cupped several winding rivers. Those rivers cavorted amongst pine and oak trees before diving over cliffs and down ravines to hurry out into the flatlands that rolled away into the distance. A brilliant blue sky studded with soft clouds hung overhead like the memory of a dream.

But what was most concerning was the village that lay just below the cave mouth, barely a hundred yards away. Smoke rose from several buildings, and the air was torn by the sounds of screams accompanying the echoes of clashing combat as people fought for their lives. People dressed in odd clothes raced back and forth, screaming, fighting, and in some places, dying. Monsters were attacking the village. Monsters that looked eerily similar to the people of the village.

Surveying the battle in progress, Koda could see that the village's defenders fought in scattered groups and would likely fall shortly, overwhelmed by the gangling monsters that besieged the rustic settlement.

The shrieks of the injured mixed with screams of fury from the embattled as warriors clashed against the threats.

As he watched, a muscled warrior-woman with a short, mottled, red-black mop of hair drove a broad-bladed spear through the torso of a man who had three arms and a misshapen spine.

The blow drove the man-creature to one side as it tried to claw at the face of a villager who lay sprawled on the road at the spearwoman's feet.

"Back, monster!" the redheaded woman roared before kicking the creature hard enough to send it sailing into the street. "Up, Ula. Get to the square! Get everyone to the square! The hunters will buy you time!"

"Thank you, huntress!" The woman who had been about to have her eyes gouged out by the creature panted in thanks before scrambling to her feet.

The villager raced down the street, clutching at the simple wool dress she wore to keep it out of the way, dodging past several bodies that already cluttered the packed earth of the road.

Blowing a breath out through his nose, Koda watched as the spear-wielder drove the wide iron blade into the back of the downed man-monster's neck to end its thrashing and screeching.

That done, she whirled to race down another narrow alley towards the sound of more fighting. Something long and red trailed behind her, a sash of some kind, but she was gone before he could make it out.

Breaking into a jog, Koda hurried down the narrow road from the cliff to follow her. If she was some kind of protector for the village, then it made sense to help her. It meant that he would be sure that he only fought the right people.

Glancing down at the dead, misshapen, half-naked man as he passed, he suppressed a shudder.

Not like it would be hard to tell, if that is how the monsters all look. Thera, I would have appreciated more guidance besides 'drive off the invaders', he thought as he navigated the tight confines between buildings.

Emerging onto another road, Koda immediately spotted his target. The redheaded woman was engaged with four of the crooked people, three males and a female. He could tell that one was a female because her sagging breasts hung exposed to the air within a tattered dress—all five of them.

The creatures lashed at the woman with crude weapons that looked like farm implements someone had twisted into tools of war. They moved with unnatural speed and had joints that seemed to refuse to follow the expected rules for what direction they were meant to flex or how far.

Crouching just behind the redheaded warrior woman was a pair of children, likely no older than five or six.

The spearwoman's sash danced and flicked as she moved, fending the monsters off with her spear but not able to score a decisive blow as they harried her. She couldn't maneuver without exposing the children to danger, and they remained paralyzed in fear behind her.

The fact the woman was fighting what looked like a losing battle, but to defend children, galvanized Koda out of his disgust at the gnarled monsters.

Focused on their prey and the woman, the four monsters fought with single-minded purpose. They were unaware of his approach as three fought to trap the spear, so the other could kill the woman.

So focused were they that when Koda hit the group of bent monsters from behind in a shoulder tackle, he swept two of the four off their feet and threw them into a wall to land in a squalling heap.

The female monster spun on him with a shriek of fury. The shriek came from a mouth that opened not only horizontally like a mouth normally would but with her chin splitting in half to reveal hundreds of ragged teeth like a horror-movie version of a grasshopper.

Before the female monster could act, a shower of gore erupted from her bare chest as the tip of the redhead's spear burst through. The redheaded woman had seen the opportunity when the monster turned and struck.

Not taking a chance, Koda slapped out with the clawed fingers of his gauntlet. The blow opened the female monster's throat.

A moment later, the warrior woman kicked the monster off the spear and whirled to club the last standing monster in the side with the haft.

Koda turned to the two downed monsters, who were struggling with each other to get free. Their many-jointed limbs, previously an advantage but now only getting in the way, flailed about, kicking up the dust of the road.

Stomping down hard with one boot, Koda pinned the arm of one of the two to the road with his entire weight, intending to go for this one's throat as well. The crunch of breaking bone surprised him, but it only slowed him for the barest of moments.

The bone-clawed tips of his gauntlet sunk into the creature's neck, and he ripped downwards, opening the chest as well. His taloned gauntlet sliced cleanly through the creature's ribs as if they were not there. The monster gave one last weak thrash before going still.

Behind him, Koda heard a meaty *shunk* noise that he was willing to bet was the redhead spearing her opponent, given that the shrieks of the last standing monster died off into a gargle.

Good, nothing at my back now besides an ally, right? he thought quickly while he shifted clear of the dead body.

Not wanting to take a chance with the last of the downed monsters, Koda drop-kicked it in the side to a cacophony of breaking ribs. The power that Thera had promised him as a champion showed itself then as his kick lifted the beast off the ground and bounced it off the wall again, its chest caving inwards from the blow.

As the last of the monsters wheezed on the ground, clutching its chest in pain, Koda wound up for another kick, this time at its head. The blow snapped the creature's neck, and it went limp.

Turning to check on the warrior woman and her two youthful wards, he came face to spear-tip and froze.

"Who are you!?" snarled the warrior, her eyes flashing while her sash flapped in the wind behind her. A wind that also stirred at her short hair, too.

"I'm here to help you. We need to drive these creatures off," Koda snapped back, nodding to the dead in front of them.

The warrior-woman studied him for a long moment, her eyes dropping to his bloody gauntlet before bouncing back up to his face. The front of her shirt flapped in the slight breeze, revealing the barest curve of her chest. She looked like she'd dressed in haste, with the tail of her shirt untucked from the close-fitting pants she wore.

Koda did his best to not think about the fact that he'd killed several creatures. Right now, he needed to focus on saving people. He could freak out about having to kill later. His determination to do the right thing helped him from losing it entirely in the moment. That and the distraction of the beautiful woman in front of him.

"All right, but you will explain more later, stranger," the spear-toting warrior woman said finally.

"Koda."

"What?"

"I'm not 'stranger.' My name is Koda."

"Fine, Koda. Help me evacuate as many people to the center of the village as we can," the woman urged before snapping her spear to one side.

The motion flicked the blood clear of the wide blade. She kept the weapon held out to one side while crouching next to the scared children to talk to them, speaking quickly in a low tone. Koda wanted to listen in, but the furtive movement and the second to think allowed him to spot something else that distracted him instead.

What he had thought was a sash that hung from her waist was not actually a sash.

It was a tail.

A long, red-and-brown speckled tail that was flicking ever so slightly as the woman spoke. The stirring motion also drew his attention to her short hair, and Koda spotted a pair of pointed canine ears emerging from the top of her head.

Huh... fox? No, the fur pattern isn't right. Almost looks like a red wolf, Koda thought as the woman rose to turn her glare back at him.

"Lead the way, miss."

"Sienna!" the woman snapped. "Not miss. I am a warrior!"

Koda nodded in understanding and hurried after her, leaving behind the bloody corpses of four enemies in their wake. As he followed after the animal-featured woman, he could feel the thrumming pulse of the goddess's approval in the gauntlet he wore.

Chapter Three

Sienna was an able guide and led the way deeper into the village for Koda without hesitation.

They clashed twice more with the gnarled creatures, and Koda gave as good as he got with the clawed gauntlet. He could feel something guiding him as he fought, a sensation of someone watching over his shoulder and helping slide him into the right position, directing him so that his strikes would find their mark.

He blocked with the bone-reinforced forearm of the gauntlet. The knapped stones and thick femurs armoring it handily deflected the gnarled blades of his enemies without showing even a crack or a nick. The slapping motion needed to make the most of the claws on the gauntlet slowly became natural as he fought and killed.

They took down another half-dozen of the monsters and saved three more people on their way into the center of the village.

Emerging into the village square, he and the redheaded

spearwoman hit another group of monsters from behind like a pair of rampaging bulls.

The shrieking monsters were driven onto the spears and arrows of the other warriors who guarded the huddled forms of the villagers, grinding against them until none remained alive.

In the echoing silence that followed Sienna hacking the head off the last of the attackers, Koda stared around him in grim horror.

Dead lay piled everywhere. But for every dead villager or warrior, four of the crooked monsters lay still. The only sound he could hear beside the thunder of his own heartbeat was the sobbing and moaning of the wounded.

Then again, that wasn't entirely true. Distantly, he could hear faint cries and cackling laughter that drifted away on the wind that he guessed came from fighting in other parts of the village.

"Get a count on how many are here. We need to find out if the Crooked took anyone, and how many that is," Sienna snapped to one of the bloodied village guardians, a rail-thin man with dark-gray ears and a bushy tail of the same color. "Tend to the wounded. Any injury needs to be seen to so that their hurts do not fester. The last thing I trust a Crooked to do is fight cleanly." Several more nods followed her orders from the other fighters.

Koda grimaced at the mention of cleanliness and looked down at himself. Blood spattered his jeans and shirt, and there were a few rips in the cloth now where the chipped fingernails of the enemies he'd taken down had caught and tore them.

Enemies I killed. The thought wandered through Koda's

mind, and he felt his skin crawl at the wet sensation of blood on him before he shook it off.

No, they threatened Thera's people. They threatened those who she promised were my people, too. Clinging to that thought, Koda could push the bile back down his throat and fight off the urge to vomit.

"And you! Explain yourself. Who are you, and where the hell did you come from? I'd accuse you of being one of the Crooked, but your body does not show the twisted growth that they do."

The sharp demand for information from Sienna brought Koda's head up, and he stared at her in surprise. The suspicion in her tone hurt, even after they had fought side by side for the last few minutes. He guessed that 'Crooked' was the name of the monsters, given how Sienna had used it so far, and he was glad that she at least knew he wasn't one of them.

Thera's words before echoed in his mind.

They may not understand at first, but they will come to love you for the sacrifice you make.

Shoving his irritation away, Koda met the woman's eyes with a straight spine. The pair of canine ears on top of her head flicked once as she watched him suspiciously, but Koda refused to be distracted.

"I'm the one who came here to help you. My name is Koda, and I was sen—" The sensation of a hand on his throat, not clenching or crushing but resting there, interrupted what he was about to say.

Does Thera not want me stating it out loud? he thought silently, looking down at his armored right hand.

No answer was forthcoming from the ghostly sensations that emanated from his gauntlet, or those pressed against his neck, but he felt that it was the right message.

Looking back up, Koda found Sienna watching him while other beastfolk from several different animal types moved back and forth to help the injured. The sharp wariness was still in her blue-green eyes, but she wasn't menacing him with the spear again at least, so he'd take that as a good sign.

"I heard the fighting and came to help. You did need the help, didn't you?" Koda said, changing his story with a shrug, not trying to expand on it this time while gesturing to the injured around them.

"Fine. Thank you for your assistance. I apologize if I come off as harsh, but monsters have raided my home and slaughtered or captured my friends. You can understand my lack of trust at the moment," Sienna replied a moment later, the iron leaving her voice though she continued to stare at him curiously. Her slender features twisted into an expression of suppressed anger as she talked about the people harmed by the attack, but Koda could tell she did not direct it at him.

"What is the plan, then?" Koda's question brought the wolf woman up short, and she glanced at him in confusion.

"What do you mean?"

"I mean, what is the next step?" Koda gestured to their surroundings, including the damaged buildings, injured villagers, dead monsters, and the upright hunters. "You gave orders to tend to the wounded and count folks. But clearly you all still need help. What is the next thing you need help with?"

Sienna opened her mouth to speak, but an older, male hunter with the brighter red and black fur pattern of a fox interrupted her.

"Nothing, stranger. We don't need your help," the fox-eared man yipped, his voice surprisingly high for his size, though his features were hard with anger.

Whirling on the man, Sienna snarled at him in irritation, her lips peeling back in a canine threat that would have been more effective if she had fangs to match.

Several others among the hunters, both men and women, jumped into the argument a moment later, and the squabbling sounded to Koda like a pack of foxes arguing with a couple of dogs intermixed with words.

"We need to find those taken."

"Don't need the help of an outsider!"

"We need to set up guards."

"Don't trust him...

"Too convenient, I say."

Koda sighed and pinched at the bridge of his nose with one hand. The squishing sensation of cooling blood against his face made his stomach roll. He grimaced when he realized that he'd used his gauntleted right hand to touch his face.

The one covered in blood from the fighting.

Well, at least I didn't cut myself on the claws, he thought with a sigh.

Glancing around, Koda spotted one of the gnarled men nearby who was wearing a ragged tunic, and he walked over to wipe his clawed gauntlet off on that fabric.

The cloth of the tunic was a mottled gray-blue. It looked like someone had attempted to do a tie-dye pattern on it, but somehow, they had ended up with a most bizarre fractal of stains and color.

Koda's instincts told him not to let the odd cloth touch his face. So, when he finished wiping his gauntlet off, he used the edge of his shirt to get as much of the blood off his face as he could instead. The garment was already stained with blood, so a bit more wouldn't hurt it.

A shout cutting through the argument nearby drew his attention back to the hunters just as Sienna looked to be trying to establish control over the situation.

"Look! The most important thing right now is dealing with the threat of the Crooked! We drove them back, but we didn't eliminate them. As long as they lurk in our woods, they are a threat to the village and all of us!" barked the redheaded spearwoman.

As if they had been waiting for a break in the argument, a short woman dressed in forest-colored clothes with a bow raced out of an alley nearby, shouting Sienna's name.

The spearwoman whirled to the speaker and hurried over to talk to her. From the expression on their faces during the brief exchange, Koda knew it wasn't good news.

Slipping closer, Koda listened to the discussion as Sienna relayed what she'd been told while the female hunter hurried off to check on something else.

"The Crooked made off with over a dozen people. The tanner and his family, the Oslo girls and their father, and a few others. They've taken them east," Sienna said in a voice that trembled with fury.

Sienna's grim words sparked another shouting match amongst the hunters as they all demanded the opportunity to be the first to speak.

The redheaded huntress grimaced as she fought to argue back with the half-dozen people complaining, even as the sounds of the injured and scared continued to rage in the background. The entire situation grated on Koda's nerves, and he chafed at the desire to do something.

"Are you lot going to continue arguing, or are you going after them?"

Koda's sharp statement brought silence to the group. Sienna shot him a confused, but grateful, look. Unfortunately, the more vocal of the arguers had a new target now and tore into Koda.

"Who are you to demand things from us?!" snapped the same fox-eared man who had barked at him initially. He yelped a moment later when Sienna cuffed him on the back of the head with an open hand.

"He has a point! You know what the Crooked do to captives. We need to launch a rescue mission—as I've been saying!" Sienna scowled down at the man, but another spoke up before she could continue.

"But we don't know how many of them there are! We might be racing into a trap—"

This was a signal for the entire group to once again dissolve into an argument over what to do next.

Sienna scowled and looked about ready to start laying around herself with the haft of her spear, but she restrained herself and began arguing for a rescue operation.

This is stupid, Koda thought to himself. *They are so panicked that they don't know what to do next. Whoever is supposed to be leading them is obviously not here. I had thought Sienna was their leader, but she's only got a small handful of the hunters listening to her. How terrifying are these 'Crooked' that folk whose life should have hardened are so scared?*

Koda glanced down at the corpse he'd used to wipe his claws off.

The dead man's head sat on a neck so twisted by malformed growth that he actually looked in reverse. In addition, either the fight had broken his back and spun him about or his knees were also reversed to match his head.

"Okay fair, that is a good reason to be freaked out." Koda chuckled darkly. The rolling nausea at the sight combined with the faint sensation of blood on his face again rose up, but he throttled it with a grimace. "I don't have time to be sick. I can break down later. People need help. My people," Koda muttered to himself, reminding himself of what Thera had promised him. Of what had driven him to choose to believe her words from the cave.

He repeated the chant two or three more times before his stomach calmed. Glancing to one side, he saw the verbal sparring raging still, though Sienna had managed to talk a few more onto her side of things.

By the time they decide anything, it might be too late, Koda thought grimly.

He caught Sienna's eyes and nodded to her before turning and striding down the road away from the square and its squabbling and screaming.

He knew that he could have stayed and helped tend to the wounded, but the weight of the blade-fingered gauntlet on his hand pulled him into pursuing the enemy.

People needed help, needed protecting, and he was going to give it to them. He'd just have to be careful about it.

Sienna watched the strangely dressed man leave, his long, straight, black hair billowing slightly as he stomped down the road, heading to the east.

Something about him tugged at her. A desire to follow after him in his decisive action. Those who would come with her would come. Those too afraid or confused would stay behind where they were safe.

Her tail bounced slightly, wagging at the thought before distractions intruded once more.

"Look at him go. Even this supposed 'helpful stranger' is fleeing."

Sienna whirled to confront the sneering speaker with a snarl of her own, but one pointed ear remained tracking the stranger, this 'Koda.'

Chapter Four

FINDING THE PATH LEFT BY THE MONSTERS WASN'T hard. They hadn't exactly been trying to be subtle in their flight. Koda followed the road that the female hunter who had reported to Sienna came in on, then looked for signs of struggle.

The blood trail and drag marks made it easy to follow along, as well as the number of bodies having passed through the undergrowth.

He stopped only once as he passed through a small orchard of blooming trees, using the well that was on the property to get the last of the blood from his face and rinse it out of his gauntlet.

Koda wasn't sure if it was the material of the gauntlet, Thera's blessing and magic, or just that he was washing it quickly, but none of the blood from the fight stained any part of his primal weapon. The claws still gleamed, the pale white of bone remained unmarred, and the leather and fur underneath bore no discoloration.

It's a magic gauntlet. Of course it's going to be stain-resistant, Koda thought wryly when he realized that he'd let himself get distracted. *Focus. You need to find the people taken and figure out if you can do anything to help them. Hopefully, Sienna and her group will follow soon. That way I don't have to do this alone.*

The gnawing worry sat heavy in his gut, but Koda did his best to push it away. He would do his best, just as he promised Thera. He tried not to dwell on the fact that today he had taken lives. Or the fact that he knew he would have to kill again.

Focusing on moving as silently as he could, Koda crept through the damaged brush.

The passage of the Crooked and their captives actually made following after them easier for him, since many of the small branches and twigs that he might have stepped on had already suffered that fate. Winding through the trees, Koda kept an ear out while he walked, his bladed gauntlet at the ready.

The forest, which normally felt so welcoming to him, felt stuffy and oppressive now. The air felt as though it refused to move, only stirring in his passage like he was walking through thick honey. No breeze stirred the branches of the trees overhead.

Shade that had welcomed him only an hour before in the mountains of Colorado now felt oppressive and threatening. Only the cool weight of his totemic gauntlet kept Koda moving, a gentle reminder of the promise he'd made.

After nearly half an hour of trotting along at a steady pace, the trees thinned, and Koda slowed down, crouching to ensure his silhouette did not stand out easily against the sky or the tree line. The thinning trees and what brush remained would help break up his outline, but the last thing he needed was to be spotted before he knew the threat he faced.

The tree line gave way to a ridge of rock. Stopping on the edge of the trees, he could detect the distant jabbering of words from the other side of the outcropping of gray stone, accompanied by the rattle of movement.

Peering around a tree, Koda listened closely for several long moments.

He could hear talking, though he couldn't understand the words being spoken. The language sounded like someone had taken Russian and run it through several AI translation filters before having it spit out in English. Individual words felt familiar but sounded mangled and twisted, ensuring that none of them really made sense. Through all of that jabbering, he could hear the quiet sobbing of those he guessed were the captives, joined by the clatter of metal on metal or metal on wood.

Growling deep in his throat, Koda crept forward carefully to ensure he did not alert any sentries that might be around the camp he could hear.

Approaching the large, flat-topped stone, Koda discovered that the path the kidnappers had taken wound around both sides of the immense rock.

Edging to one side, the stone revealed that it was obscuring a small hollow in the earth. The little valley wasn't deep— maybe twenty feet at its center and about two hundred across—but the low section was enough to easily hide the camp from casual view.

Though this does give me a decent vantage point to watch them from, Koda thought wryly as he peeked around the edge of the stone.

He'd played enough first-person shooters to know that one of the easiest things for someone on watch to spot was an irregularity against the sky. So Koda made sure to keep his head low to ensure that the blue sky did not outline him while he darted glances around the side of the stone.

What lay before him was simultaneously familiar and disturbing in the same ragged breath.

The camp sprawled out in a jagged formation that roughly approximated regular rows. But somehow, none of the lines in the camp were parallel to each other. The only thing that was regular and reliable about the camp in front of him was the fact that *nothing* was orderly.

Tents constructed of the same dappled and stained canvas as the clothes the monsters wore sat in mottled, haphazard arrangements that tried to be rows. Roughly in the middle of the camp was a wide tent that had seven sides and was almost forty feet across by itself. The large tent sat slightly off-center, and none of its poles were straight or the same height.

A cloud of smoke hung over the entire camp from a trio of large fires that burned in shared spaces where a handful of tents were clumped together. Gross banners hung irregularly amongst the tents, displaying a pitchfork with bent tines crossed with a sword that vaguely resembled a kukri based on how bent its blade was, but the weapon had the look of a regular arming sword with edges on both sides.

Stumbling amongst the tent were more of the bent and twisted people. Many of them wore rags or the rough approximations of clothing, none of them in good repair.

A man with his left knee reversed and his right regular hobbled over and began talking in the garbled tongue with another man who had two arms, both growing from his right

46

shoulder. Nearby, a woman with two mouths, one on her face and another in her neck, stirred a bubbling cauldron by one of the smoky fires while tossing in large hunks of meat with the bones still in them.

A cackling laugh drew Koda's attention farther back into the camp. He saw another bent figure jabbing a broken stick at someone who was wearing actual clothes, though torn and tattered.

"Away from us, beast!" snarled the old man, his white beard swinging as he batted at the offending weapon with his wrinkled hands while a matted tail of the same color hung limp behind him. "Can't you leave us alone?! Why torture us now? You'll have plenty of time to do it later, freak!"

The prancing, crooked man jabbered again in that distorted tongue. Koda thought he caught something about 'broken toys' before another of the Crooked emerged from a nearby tent and cuffed the one with the stick. The second Crooked was larger, though his muscles flared in bizarre proportions, leaving his biceps thin but his forearms swollen. The swollen one barked at the stick-wielder and pointed at the old man.

Whining, the one with the stick dropped his toy and nodded before going back to herding the old man into what Koda now recognized as a corral. It was hard to see at this angle, but from the splashes of normal, unfaded colors that he saw, Koda guessed that was where the other villagers were being kept.

The pen was near the center of the camp, with only a single row of tents between it and the larger main tent. Two rows of tents encircled the other sides of the corral, though. That would make it harder for those inside it to escape, even if there weren't guards walking around at random intervals.

Watching, Koda counted as many of the gnarled men and women in the camp that he could. He noted that there were usually three or four of the Crooked hanging around the pen of people at any given time, ensuring there was always a watcher present, though they did not pay particularly close attention.

While Sienna and he had taken down a dozen or more between them, those had been in smaller groups. There were easily thirty or more of the crude tents, and because of the way no one of the Crooked looked like the others, he had a feeling that the count of about fifty or sixty of them still in the camp was accurate.

As Koda watched, another handful of Crooked stumbled into camp from the far side, dragging a deer behind them that had three bent spears sticking out of it. One hunter was also dragging the gored body of another Crooked.

The deer was hauled to one of the cook-fires, while the dead Crooked ended up dragged into the central tent by its feet. For what purpose, Koda had no idea.

"This is going to be difficult," Koda muttered under his breath, the clawed tips of his totemic gauntlet tapping against the stone in front of him. "How do I get the villagers away from them without alerting the entire camp? I might sneak in under cover of night, but that is no guarantee I can get them out. How can I even the odds?"

A scream split the air of the camp, and Koda had to fight the urge to leap to his feet. The scream originated from the large, seven-cornered tent where the Crooked had dragged their dead companion.

A second and then third scream split the air, the noise gurgling and distorted like a badly tuned amp. A pulse of energy echoed through the air a moment later, causing a stirring in the lingering smoke that hung in the valley from the fires. The pulse hit the stone walls of the little valley but did not escape it.

Unable to tear his eyes away, Koda watched in morbid fascination as the flap of the tent stirred a moment later, and the Crooked who had dragged his dead companion past a moment earlier shoved that same companion out ahead of him.

A companion that was now walking upright with blood still staining his thin chest from where the deer's antlers had torn him open. A wound that was now a mass of scarred, sealed flesh.

"Disturbing, isn't it?"

The voice in Koda's ear made his heart jump. He whirled to find Sienna crouched only inches away from him, her spear held low and to one side.

Arrayed behind her were a dozen of the leather-clad hunters from the village with bows, spears, and clubs at the ready. He only could pick them out from the trees because they would move on occasion to dart a glance at him or past him at the camp, and the movement revealed them briefly.

Every single one of the hunters shared features with some kind of animal. He saw many with the ears and tails of wolves, foxes, cats, and one large man who had rounded ears that vaguely reminded him of a bear. Two bore feathers in the place of hair and had the piercing eyes of hawks.

"More than you can imagine," Koda panted, keeping his voice low as he met the serious gaze of the redhead. Of all the others, she was the only one who had approached within twenty feet of him.

"I can imagine quite a bit. Crooked are the stuff of nightmares. Then again, you've seen them. You can see how easy it is for them to inhabit that particular sphere." Sienna's voice was low and tense as she spoke.

Koda watched her warily. She did have a habit of sticking that spear into his face at a moment's notice, after all. The blue-green shimmer of her eyes, like a polished bit of jade, distracted him as they both studied each other.

"Pretty sure I saw one raised from the dead," Koda said warily.

Sienna just nodded, her expression stony.

They stared at each other for another handful of seconds before Sienna tilted her head to one side, causing her pointed red-black ears to flop slightly. The gesture softened her harsh appearance and actually looked quite adorable, though he ruthlessly quashed that reaction for now. He had more important things to think about besides how cute the wolf woman in front of him was.

Or wondering if the fur on her ears and tail is as soft as it looks. Stop it, Koda!

"Why are you here... Koda? I believe that was the name you gave us?" Sienna's question came in a whisper, but there was the ring of iron determination in her voice.

Koda had a feeling that if she didn't like his answer, that spear might end up in his face, again.

"I'm not going to abandon someone in need of help, and it didn't look like you were going to be able to talk the others into helping in time," Koda said after a moment of thought.

Sienna blinked once, a single, slow gesture with her eyes before she tilted her head the other way, causing her ears to flop again. A slight movement behind her caught his attention and drew Koda's eyes to the mottled red-black mass of her tail, which wagged slowly.

"So you decided to hare off by yourself to try to lend a hand?" Sienna's tone was neutral, but he thought he saw a twinkle of amused curiosity in her eyes.

"Better than sitting around and being yelled at," Koda said with a shrug and got a nod in return.

"You will help us?" she asked again as if she didn't believe him.

"I said before"—Koda fought to keep irritation out of his tone at her question— "I'm not going to abandon someone in need of help."

Chapter Five

"So, what is the plan, Sienna?" the bear-featured man said once Koda and Sienna had crept back into the trees so that the other hunters could talk to them more easily.

The group crowded around, though none besides Sienna got within arm's reach of Koda.

"I don't think they've started twisting any of the captives. Probably still recovering from being pushed back from the village and mending their own injuries." Sienna leaned on her spear with the butt planted firmly in the ground, chewing on her bottom lip thoughtfully after she spoke.

Koda stood to one side of the redheaded woman, keeping his back to a tree while he watched the others. While none of them had menaced or insulted him, Koda thought it best to return their wariness. This also allowed him to keep an eye on the enemy camp in case anyone came out of it toward them.

"What I don't get is how they managed to get this close to the village without anyone seeing them. The Crooked aren't cunning enough to be this sneaky," groused one of the hawk-featured hunters, a woman from the sharp lines of her cheekbones and her figure.

"Enough, Netta. We can worry about how they got there once we have eliminated the threat. Until we deal with that, there are more pressing concerns." Sienna's words got a huff of irritation from the feathered woman, but she nodded in understanding.

"We need to save those taken captive. I don't think I could live with myself if we let the Crooked have them," grumbled one of the fox-featured men. A series of nods circled the group.

"Obviously. But how do we go about it? We don't have the numbers to just raid their camp," Netta said, her feather-hair ruffling in irritation.

"You lot are hunters, aren't you?" Koda interjected, getting a glare from a few, and speculative looks from the others. "Hunt them then," he continued. "Harass them when they leave camp. Pick off those that you see the opportunity to. I just saw a group of them return with a deer, so they don't remain confined to the camp. See if you can't tempt some into the trees where you can kill them. If we thin their numbers enough, without raising the alarm, we might stand a better chance."

"That's not a bad idea," Sienna mumbled, shooting him a glance. "I've been thinking about this too much as a stand-up fight. If we have the opportunity to pick away at them, we should."

"And if one of us gets caught? Do we just leave them to be slaughtered?" The growling question came from one of the others with wolf features, this one with gray fur.

"Clearly we help them," Koda growled back, his irritation rising. "Why are you acting like a fool? If they spot someone, then those seen should try to drag as many of the Crooked as possible into chasing them away from the camp. This will allow those who remain to have a better chance of getting the captives out. Baiting the enemy alone like that wouldn't be smart unless one of you has a death wish, but it can make the most of a dangerous situation. And if you look out for those near you, then you can try to lend aid to help the spotted one escape."

The odd looks he got from the hunters irritated Koda. This was a basic strategy that he'd seen in video games back home, as well as in war documentaries. A small force pokes the larger one, provoking them into chasing after them and into a trap.

A trap... Koda paused to think for a moment. He could feel Sienna's gaze boring into the side of his face. This group didn't have time to dig holes and build pit traps, but there might be something nearby that could work.

"Is there a swamp or a fast-moving river nearby?" Koda's question broke the quiet argument that had picked up between the hunters over the merits of his idea. Sienna had been silently watching him though and was quick to answer.

"Lodestone is the fastest-moving river in the area. Its spring is high in the mountains and splits into several branches in the valley. It's about a mile that way." She gestured to his left with one hand, towards the east. "As far as marshes? Not really on that front."

"What about ravines?" Koda asked intently.

"There are a few mountain clefts to the north," suggested Netta immediately, her dark eyes widening. "If you didn't

55

know about them though, you might run right off a cliff into one, since the trees come right up to the edge!"

"That's a thought then. If we have to prod them from one side to draw them off or if you get spotted, go either north or east. See if you can't draw them into the river or to fall into a ravine. Hunters trap game all the time, right? We don't have time to dig pits or build elaborate traps, but use what you have." Koda saw comprehension dawning on the hunters' faces, and a few bore wicked smiles now.

"We could see about bringing a few fallen logs to the edge of their camp to throw down on them."

"Boulders would work, too. Don't need to be big to cause havoc with how heavy they get."

"Deadfalls and rope traps would slow them down."

The ideas flew thick and fast as the hunters chattered quietly until Sienna brought them to a stop with a wave of her hands. Her tail was bouncing happily back and forth behind her, distracting Koda with both the movement and how cute it looked on her. She'd taken the time to do up her shirt and organize her appearance, so she looked far more professional, save for that waving bit of fluff.

"Okay, Koda has some good points. I want us to split into four... no, five teams. Three-person hunting parties. I'll go with Koda as the smaller team. Each party takes a direction. Begin laying traps and preparing surprises. If you find a patrol or a sentry outside their camp, eliminate them. Take down any stragglers or wanderers that you are confident on, but focus on ensuring you can fall back. Cause trouble if you need to. Use natural features if you can, even if it's just a field with gopher holes to break ankles. Koda is right. We need to approach this as hunters, not as warriors. Koda and I will roam and move to support anyone spotted or strike at larger groups. Got it?"

Hearing her encouragement, as well as being credited for the ideas, sent a thrill down Koda's spine, and a warmth settled into his gut. He waited and watched as the hunters settled into teams of three and then vanished into the trees.

Soon, it was just him and the redheaded spearwoman crouched there in the bushes. Sienna turned to shoot him a speculative glance before her gaze fell again to the totemic gauntlet he was wearing.

"I know there is more going on here than you just stumbling upon our village, Koda." Sienna's words were slow and measured. When Koda opened his mouth to answer her, she held up one slim hand. "No, not now. When we deal with this problem, we can talk then. I am taking you at your word, though. Something tells me that I can trust you." Sienna's eyes darted to the gauntlet again before returning to his face, the question obvious in her eyes.

"You can." The words slipped out of Koda's mouth before he could stop them. He grimaced at how eager he sounded. Sienna just smiled.

"Show me."

The hunters set to work with a fervor while Koda and Sienna patrolled in a long loop around the valley camp.

More than once, Koda stumbled across a dead sentry stashed in a bush or stopped at Sienna's direction so she could point out a laid trap in the form of a tripwire made of a sapling or something similar.

They paused to help carefully carry three different logs close to the edge of the short cliffs that helped conceal the camp, preparing them to be rolled down onto the tents below. Koda even helped heft a boulder the size of an oil drum into place, grunting only slightly at the weight while the others watched on in surprise.

Thera's blessing is again showing its worth, he thought as he settled the stone into place just a short distance back from the lip.

Sienna darted forward to wedge some smaller rocks into place around the boulder's base to keep it in position. With that done, they hurried back into the trees.

"How is it that they are dumb enough to not set better sentries when they have to *know* that we could follow them back from the village?" he asked Sienna after they had finished helping one hunting party take down a group of three Crooked who were dragging a dead doe towards the camp.

"Overconfidence maybe?" Sienna shrugged before continuing. "The Crooked do not think along the same lines as the rest of us. Like their bodies, the dark powers they serve have twisted their minds. Their actions are illogical and should not lead to success, but they do. Likely, they expect to raid us again in the morning or even tonight, counting on the fear and terror to make us cower in our homes. It's a tactic that works all too well."

"Why did it not work on you all, then?" Koda's question was blunt, but Sienna smirked at him, rather than becoming offended.

"Because a loudmouthed outsider provoked a few of us into taking a chance, then got us thinking along a twisty bit of our minds we'd forgotten about." She shot him a wink, and Koda was glad for the thicker shadows to help hide his blush at the attractive woman's flirtations.

"Happy to be of assistance," he said carefully, doing his best to not sound too proud.

"I'm sure you are," Sienna said dryly, giving him another smile before turning and gesturing for Koda to follow.

The wolf-eared woman had donned a cloak a short while ago, pulling the hood up to cover her red hair and ears, much to Koda's disappointment. He couldn't help but watch the shifting appendages and wonder at how soft the fur there looked. The thought helped to keep the disgust at bay from having to kill, though a numbness was taking its place now in his gut.

Am I getting used to killing already? Koda thought while he carefully followed in Sienna's wake. *Has my sense of right and wrong changed? Or is it because Sienna and the others don't seem bothered by this. Is that helping me handle it?*

Koda pondered the question as they continued to circle the camp, springing surprise attacks of their own on small groups or individual sentries when they found them.

The fights were always brief and tense, with having to hide the bodies taking far longer than the actual fights.

Twice, they stumbled upon a sentry that was inspecting bloodstains where their predecessor had once been. A single time, Koda spotted one of the Crooked getting ready to sound an alarm after having found a body.

Sienna had thrown her broad-bladed spear with surprising accuracy and taken the creature down with the weight of the weapon in its guts. Koda had torn out its throat with his claws a moment later to stifle the cry of pain.

The evening was coming in quickly, and several of the hunting parties had reported minor injuries but were in good spirits so far.

Their forces had taken down at least twenty of the Crooked so far, and the camp remained unaware because of their disorganized state.

Many of the 'sentries' just wandered into the trees to poke around like they were looking for something or just stared idly into the woods before being taken down by an arrow or a dagger. Their numbers did not seem to be dwindling though, as more Crooked emerged from tents.

Koda was thinking about the fact that none of the enemies they'd faced thus far had any sort of armor on when a distant shout from the direction of the camp alerted him.

The sound was in the garbled language of the Crooked, and several others quickly followed it.

"Shit," Sienna cursed, her head whipping around to look toward the noise.

Koda saw her hood shift as her ears flicked and turned before she nodded once decisively.

"What happened?" Koda asked, wishing he could understand more of the twisted language to get an idea of what was happening.

"The north team got spotted, and a good portion of the camp is in pursuit. We should go help them. The others will take this chance to hit the camp."

Sienna started jogging but came up short when Koda caught her right arm with his left and pulled her to a stop. She whirled to him with an open-mouth snarl, about to chastise him, but Koda spoke quickly.

"Sienna, we are on the far side of the camp. Trust your hunters and their traps. If we push with the other three hunting parties, we can hit the camp from behind hard and get the villagers out," Koda urged, locking eyes with her.

Sienna growled deep in her throat but nodded a moment later.

"Fine. But as soon as the camp is cleared and secured, we have to go help. I'm not abandoning any of my hunters as bait."

"Never said you should," Koda whispered firmly, not dropping her gaze. "Now, come on. Let's make these Crooked regret taking our people." After saying his part, Koda let go of Sienna and turned to jog into the trees towards the rumbling sound of the camp and the shouts.

―――――

Sienna followed after him, staring at the black-haired man with his odd clothes and strange weapon.

Our people? she mouthed silently, confusion and curiosity warring with the worry on her face for her friends and neighbors.

Chapter Six

By the time Koda hit the edge of it, the camp was already in disarray.

The other three hunting parties had waited only moments for the group that was pursuing their fellows to exit the camp before they shoved the prepared logs and rocks over the cliff edge to crash into the tents.

Someone had even managed to get one of the large logs to land in the cooking fire, spreading burning embers into the nearby tents and setting several ablaze.

As Koda watched, two hunters shoved the large boulder he'd positioned over the edge of the cliff. It tumbled down to crush two of the Crooked as they rushed to try to put out the fires. The rock bounced and rolled, taking out three more tents before coming to a stop.

Arrows flicked down from the trees and took down more of the Crooked while the hunters used their height and angle to strike with impunity.

Crooked screamed and died, while others rallied together and pushed to hurry up the narrow paths that led to the cliffs. Still others worked to climb the cliff face itself, moving like fleshy spiders with unnatural grace.

"Block the path!" Koda called to Sienna, rushing to do just that as the first of the Crooked reached the top of the narrow animal trail.

Using the toe of his hiking boot as a scoop, Koda kicked a fistful of dirt and small rocks at the lead Crooked, who yelped in surprise as the grit got into all three of its eyes. The creature's left hands—it had two of them sized like a child's attached to its left wrist—batted at its face to clear its vision.

Seizing his opportunity, Koda brought his lead foot stomping down from the kick. The heavy leather of his hiking boot crashed down on the bare toes of the Crooked even as he straightened his fingers and drove them forward in a knife-hand position.

The Crooked opened its mouth to scream at the pain of its crushed foot, but only let out a wet gurgle as Koda's knife hand drove his claws into its throat before slashing down. Sienna was there, driving her spear into the creature's chest just to the side of its breastbone where its heart should be.

Twisting her hips, Sienna gave a grunt of effort as she used the leverage of the long weapon and her bodyweight to toss the Crooked back into those following it, sending another crashing down the narrow track and back into the little valley with a scream. The scream cut off after barely a second of falling when the duo landed with a crunch on the valley floor.

"Thanks," Koda grunted, stepping up around Sienna while she spun her spear around to reset her grip.

He met the next Crooked head-on, batting aside the spiral-bladed sword it thrust at him with the back of his gauntlet, then slamming his palm into its chest. This unbalanced the creature enough that Sienna's blow into the side of its knee also sent the monster over the edge.

The two of them worked together, Koda leading the way because of his shorter range, and Sienna slipping around him to use the length of her spear to cover his back.

Fighting his way down the ramp, Koda sent a mental prayer of thanks to Thera as he could feel *something* guiding him in the punches, slaps, slashes, and thrusts with the bladed gauntlet. Occasionally, the tug and guidance would throw him off balance, but he managed to keep his feet and was slowly beginning to expect what would come next.

Slashing his claws across the face of one of the Crooked, sending the misshapen creature to one side and directly into the thrusting path of Sienna's spear, Koda bulled forward to the bottom of the ramp. Another handful of blows and a squeal of pain from their target followed, and then a brief moment of calm opened up at the base of the ramp.

To the north and the east, Koda could see small swarms of the Crooked flowing up the ramps and into the trees. Only on their ramp did they fight through the enemy. Above him on the ledge, Koda heard the hum and snap of bowstrings while the hunters sent arrow after arrow into the ravine.

"Sienna!" Netta called out from above. "The big tent! Something is moving inside it, and I can see some of the Crooked heading for the captives!"

"Shit!" Sienna cursed, and Koda felt an odd thrill hearing the beautiful woman swear. "Okay, pick off the ones you can. We will push to try to get them free. If we can arm the captives, we can fall back."

"Maybe set fire to the tents when we exit?" Koda suggested, checking himself over during the brief lull to make sure he had taken no injuries. A pair of scratches on his left arm bled sluggishly, but other than those, he was fine as far as he could tell.

"No!" Netta called down. "We can't risk the fire getting into the forest with how spread out they are. It would only take one bit of canvas blowing into the trees, and we could burn out the mountainside. I'm already going to tear Gregor a new one for risking it with that log in the cookfire!"

"Got it." Koda nodded sharply before glancing at Sienna to check on her.

The red-haired spearwoman was in far better condition than he was. While Koda was panting for breath, Sienna looked barely winded. The only blood she wore was on the blade of her spear and a small smudge on one cheek that gave her a wild air. Her short hair hung tousled, and sweat marked her forehead from the exertion.

Their eyes met for a moment, and Koda swallowed hard as those blue-green orbs seized control of him.

"Ready?" Sienna's question broke the spell of her eyes and he blinked a few times.

"Yes"—Koda coughed a moment later—"let's do this."

Breaking into a trot, Koda rushed forward into the haphazard rows of tents, slashing at ropes and the like as he went to bring them down on any occupants that remained inside. Arrows zipped past them to clear the way as a few Crooked who had been in hiding crawled out to confront the chaos descending on their camp.

Sienna followed close behind, mirroring Koda's actions as they sabotaged tents or driving her spear into the wriggling lumps of those trapped inside the rotten canvas. They never slowed their march through the camp, though.

A rank scent, like old fat left in the sun, stained the air as they got closer to the large tent. They would have to circle around it to get to the pen where the captive villagers were. Both gagged at the smell and the acrid smoke that billowed from the firepits as they went. Koda had to stop to kick a burning log back into the firepit as they went, the flames licking at the dry grass nearby.

Twice they had a Crooked who was either hiding out of sight of their archers or playing dead attempt to ambush them. The first one got hold of Koda's foot and tried to yank him to the ground, only to have that hand hacked off by the flashing blade of Sienna's spear. The second targeted the wolf woman, but Koda had glanced back to check on her in time to see the movement in the shadows.

Whirling, he grabbed Sienna by the forearms and yanked her to him. This put her out of position for the bloody hatchet that swung through the space where her head had been heartbeats before. An arrow erupted from the monster's forehead a moment later in a spray of black blood.

Sienna did not react well to being grabbed, even by an ally, and she was mid-snarl when she heard the wet thump and gurgle from behind her.

Glancing back, her eyes widened when she saw the monster that had approached without any hint or clue. She gave him a grudging nod of thanks, and Koda thought he saw a spark of respect kindling in those depthless eyes of hers.

Fine, whatever, he thought. *If she respects me, then it'll be easier to keep her safe along with the others. She's been the nicest of the lot so far.*

Koda released her and whirled back into a jog toward their destination.

The two of them rounded the edge of the large tent in time to see three of the Crooked crawl through the bars of the fence while wielding chunky-bladed swords, baying like hunting hounds with a head cold.

The captured villagers hung back and away, though an older man and two young women stood between the others and the Crooked with grim determination etched on their features. Wolf-ears, horns, and tails like Sienna's but in a dark gray showed them as fellow beastfolk. Koda saw the old man's eyes dart to them and widen in surprise as the monsters approached.

"Help is here! Hold them back, girls!" he shouted, assuming a crude boxing stance and stepping forward to put himself first in the path of the hobbling monsters. The two sturdy farmgirls mirrored him, the wan light of the evening glinting off the fur of the ears that poked out of their hair as they prepared to defend themselves.

Bending as he ran, Koda scooped up a loose stone and hurled it at the monsters as they closed to attack range. He'd been aiming for the Crooked's head, but the stone slammed into the creature's wrist as it brought its blade down in a chopping motion.

Squealing in pain, the Crooked dropped its weapon and clutched its wrist with its right hand. One girl dove for the dropped weapon even as the other two feinted and lunged at the old man.

The corral was made of heavy logs interlocked and pinned in place with iron spikes, but gaps existed that were large enough to wiggle through if someone was careful. It rose up to Koda's breastbone and had no shade at all for the captives inside. As they approached, Koda debated whether to try to climb through a gap or over the wall.

Sienna had no hesitation at all.

As Koda slowed to jump up and begin climbing, Sienna continued moving at full speed. The part-wolf woman planted the butt of her spear into the earth and used it as a vaulting pole. This gave her the leverage to crank her body up and over the barrier and land on the far side, still in motion.

A feral snarl tore from Sienna's throat as she came crashing down on the Crooked who still clutched his hand as her weapon came around to drive into the side of another of the trio of monsters, even as the beast pulled its weapon back from a slash across the old man's forearm.

"Sienna!" Koda called as he slid to a stop and began to climb the barrier to join her.

The only warning Koda got was a brief twinge of oncoming threat before something far larger than a regular Crooked hit from the side. All he saw before he went flying was a fist the size of a watermelon coming at him before it landed.

The blow caught him in the ribs, sending him tumbling to one side across the rough ground to slam into one of the tents set up around the corral.

The impact of his body hitting the tent snapped the support poles and tore two of the strings right out of the ground with sharp twanging sounds. It drove the breath from Koda's body, and he fought to get air into lungs that were busy panicking while he fought his way free of the canvas, slashing it indiscriminately with his claws to work his way free.

What greeted Koda's eyes as he finally rolled out of the entangling mass drew a roar of anger from his throat.

A massive... *something* stood over the side of the corral.

It was easily around eight feet tall, with shoulders as broad as a barn door that were knotted with distorted muscle. Its right forearm split at the elbow into two separate, smaller forearms that were of a more normal size. Short but stout legs supported the creature's broad torso, which was capped by a lumpy head as smooth as a bowling ball and about the same size.

The creature wore only a crude kilt of mottled red-brown cloth around its hips and had in its right hand what looked like a meat-cleaver forged out of a hunk of someone's car door.

Currently, the monster had its two left hands wrapped around Sienna's throat from behind and was holding the wolf-woman aloft while it wound up with its cleaver to hack her in two.

Fury gathered in Koda's gut at the affront of this monster threatening Sienna. Instinct, or maybe Thera's hand, guided Koda to roll to all fours from his position on his side.

A kick of his feet threw him to the back of the creature, and he lashed out with a slashing motion as he threw himself past the back of the grotesque monster.

The claws on Koda's gauntlet, sharp as ever and coated in the gore of the other Crooked he'd slain, caught the creature in the wrist right as its arm swept forward and above Koda.

The blow jarred its grip, and the cuts to the tendons in its wrist sent the chopper flying through the air to crash into the side of the corral, splintering wood and driving through two logs before getting stuck in the third. A rain of black blood followed Koda as he rolled to a stop on the monster's other side.

Squealing in pain and surprise, the beast dropped Sienna

and slapped its left hands over its wounded arm, whirling to look to its right for whatever had wounded it.

Gritting his teeth, Koda fought against the grinding pain in his chest from the earlier blow. While his adrenaline was high, he couldn't tell how bad the injury was. Maybe he had a broken rib or two, but it was impossible to tell. All he knew was that he didn't have any problems breathing at the moment, and the beast in front of him needed to die for threatening Sienna.

With fury still singing in his veins, Koda lunged forward and laid a slashing blow across the back of the creature's thighs with his claws. The bladed tips were only a few inches long, but it was enough to get through the crude cloth of the monster's kilt and bite deep into its legs, taking out the hamstring on its right side.

Koda wasn't fast enough to get out of the way of its reprisal, though. The meaty right hand of the monster came around in a backhand that caught him in the right arm. Koda was alert enough to get his gauntlet up to block the blow, even though the weight of it still sent him flying to crash into the splintery logs of the corral.

"Koda!" The raspy shout of Sienna from inside the corral told him that she was okay. It added to the fire in his gut, giving him the strength needed to shake off the confusion and return his attention to the hulking monster that snarled at him from close range.

Now that he was closer, Koda could see the beast had four eyes—two where they should be, one set high on its fore-head, and the other looking out from beneath a bent nose from a socket in the wide lip above its drooling mouth.

"Man meat!" the creature howled, blowing spittle past teeth that looked like a forest of rotten stumps. "Man meat to eat!

Crooked walk, Crooked take! Crooked kill the man, then bake!"

The fact that Koda could understand the hulking monstrosity was even more disturbing than the words that it was speaking.

As it slapped out towards him with its still-bleeding right hand in another backhand motion, Koda lashed out with his gauntlet to fend it off. The blow caught the creature across the back of its hand and sent it wheeling back with a squeal of pain.

"Sienna! Get the villagers out of here, and I'll distract it!" Koda yelled over his shoulder, dodging out of the way of another wide slap. This drove him closer to where the cleaver lay buried in the logs.

"Not going to leave you behind! That is a champion!"

Both the logs between them and the ringing in Koda's ears distorted Sienna's protest. He could feel his shirt sticking to him because of the spilled blood, but whether it was his or belonged to the Crooked he'd killed, Koda wasn't sure.

"Bake and take! We walked a mile, never but a single file!" shrieked the monster. It bulled forward like an angry ape and swung both its arms overhead to bring them down in a hammer fist at Koda. The distorted rhyming of its speech made its words all the more disturbing.

Lunging to one side, Koda took the opportunity to open up the Crooked's side with a slashing blow, sending another river of blood down the creature's chest.

"Crooked come, and Crooked take! Do not let our prey escape!" the monster screamed as it whirled. The side effect of its charge missing Koda was that it had reclaimed its cleaver. It slammed the weapon into the ground threateningly before lunging at Koda.

"Go, Sienna! It's calling the others back! I can handle it!" Koda shouted, feinting to the creature's wounded side and baiting out a chopping blow with the heavy cleaver. He had to put the villagers out of his mind as Koda now had to focus entirely on the monster before him.

A champion? Well, that is appropriate since I'm Thera's champion, Koda thought wryly as he studied his enemy. He had to focus now or else he'd die, and he couldn't accept that.

For all the wounds he'd inflicted on it, the monster was still going strong. Blood dripped from its many slashes and lacerations, and a grimace of fury and hunger twisted its features, but no weakness showed in its frame.

Koda risked a glance over its shoulder to see a trickle of the Crooked beginning to flow back out of the trees to the north and start down the ramps into the camp.

Can't let this drag out. I need to finish it quick, Koda thought frantically. The monster's sheer size worked against him right now. It was bleeding and would fall eventually, but Koda couldn't risk kiting it back towards the ramps and the hunters there. He didn't know where Sienna and the villagers were.

The next lunge of the monster forced him to move before he had a plan. It swept the cleaver horizontally across the ground at Koda, who swayed back before lunging forward, only to have to throw himself into a roll as the creature reversed its swing with surprising ease.

Whistling overhead, the pitted surface of the cleaver's blade glittered with a deadly promise. Scrambling to one side, he led the lumbering and wounded creature away from the log corral. Because of his blow earlier hamstringing it, the beast moved in fitful lunges. He nearly fell himself when he tripped on a tent line, and that gave Koda an idea.

"Come on, ugly! You want to eat me, then get your skinny ass over here and eat me!" Koda yelled, yanking one of the crude tent stakes out of the ground and hurling it at the creature. The limping beast tried to dodge the flying stake, but its injuries made that difficult, and the stake bounced off its forehead, just to one side of the glaring eye set there.

Roaring in fury, the creature lunged into a stumbling run, using its left arm to help support its weight awkwardly even as Koda kicked the base of one of the tent poles to shift it backwards and then threw himself away.

The beast brought its right arm up high in an overhand chop as it surged through the tents. Koda thought for a moment that his ploy would fail, but the hulking brute yelped in pain, its left arm coming down to clutch at its stomach where blood suddenly poured out.

Protruding from it's chest was the tent pole his kick had adjusted, but the remaining lines had kept it hanging roughly at around a forty-five degree angle while making the tent look like it was flat.

And the beast had charged right onto the point of the tent pole, burying it into its guts.

A sharp snapping sound followed as the rough tent pole broke under the monster's weight, but the damage was done. In the instinctive grab for its gut with its left arms, the monster was now overbalanced by the weight of the cleaver over its head and stumbled, then fell onto its face with a thump.

Koda jinked to one side, avoiding the falling cleaver that was no longer being aimed as the groaning monster clutched at its body.

Lunging forward, Koda drove his bone talons into the back of the creature's neck and slashed down to open up both sides. The monster shifted from clutching at its guts to clutching at its neck, which gave Koda the chance to snatch up the crude cleaver from where it lay abandoned on the ground.

Turning to put the strength of his hips into it and tapping into the full boost that Thera had given to his body, Koda whirled the cleaver up before bringing it down in a chopping motion that cleaved the sickening monster's head from its shoulders with a wet *thunk*.

Silence descended in that moment, only broken by the thunder of Koda's pulse in his ears.

A stirring of movement drew his attention to his left. He turned to find Sienna with her spear out, a small mound of dead Crooked lying around her while she menaced even more that were staring with eyes wide in horror at Koda. The villagers crowded in behind Sienna, wielding weapons taken from the dead Crooked to keep the converging enemy back.

Deep in his chest, Koda felt an urge welling up. From somewhere deep in his past, a primal part of him that had been slowly growing like an ember burst into flames.

A roar of challenge tore free of his lips. Koda hefted the misshapen cleaver up one-handed to charge to Sienna's side. More enemies threatened his people, and he would have blood for it.

The Crooked, as one, screamed in fear and scrambled into a retreat with Koda in chase, wielding the bloody cleaver that had slain their champion.

Chapter Seven

KODA CHASED THE CROOKED FORCES UNTIL THEY reached the narrow paths that lead up and out of the low valley. He swung the oversized meat cleaver that the Crooked champion had once wielded like he was beating dirty rugs with it, hacking down foes with abandon.

A rage gripped his soul. All Koda saw of these gnarled and twisted monsters was the danger that they represented to *his* people. For just a moment, his anger began to wane as he cut more and more down. But then he spotted one of the Crooked that had been menacing Sienna, and the wave of protective fury rose once more.

The hunter teams did their best to help. Several with spears worked atop the cliffs to bottleneck the narrow track the Crooked ran to. They created a makeshift barricade to slow down the miniature horde of Crooked in full rout. The archers amongst the hunters sent arrow after arrow zipping into the writhing mass of fearful monsters, while Koda continued to hammer on them from behind.

As the crowd thinned, Sienna's shouting voice finally called Koda back from the red rage that had filled him.

"Koda! It's okay, the hunters have them!" The faint drawl to her speech, normally only a hint, was even more evident at the moment, underlining the exhaustion in the lithe wolf-woman's voice.

Koda turned to glance over his shoulder and found Sienna there only a few feet away, blood caking her spear and forearms, her short hair wild with sweat.

She'd been following in his wake as he hammered the enemies like a butcher chopping meat, ensuring those he hit stayed down. Behind Sienna, Koda could see the villagers, armed with what weapons they could find, watching him warily.

The old man from before had a rough bandage made from his shirt around his forearm, and he was wielding a bent short sword in his off-hand while the two girls, his daughters Koda guessed, crowded protectively around him. Silently, the graying older man gave him an approving nod, while his girls were eying Koda speculatively. All three's tails were slowly wagging, while their ears stood upright.

Behind the old farmer, Koda could see that those who were watching him warily, and those who looked on in approval, stood divided nearly evenly.

"Is everyone okay?" Koda coughed after he finished speaking, his voice hoarse and his throat aching.

Was I screaming? The thought chased itself in circles around the inside of Koda's skull. *I think I was? My throat hurts like I was.* He vaguely remembered a wordless scream of anger touching his lips, but he couldn't remember when he'd stopped.

"Yes. A few minor cuts or wounds, but no one is dying besides the Crooked," growled the older man. "What you and the others did today was the work of heroes, young man. Who are you?"

Koda grimaced and tried to swallow, his dry throat working painfully in the wake of the moment. Sienna must have seen the pain in his eyes because she produced a leather pouch corked with a bit of horn from behind her and offered it to him.

While Koda fought with the waterskin, then drank to wet his throat, Sienna turned to look at the older man.

"His name is Koda Burke. He showed up to help us push back the Crooked in the village and was the first to race off to track you all." The redheaded spearwoman's words took the tension from those still wary of Koda, and the entire group regarded him with open curiosity now.

"Either a hero or a fool." One of the young women laughed. "Since you are speaking for him, Sienna? I'd put my coin on the former. Can we get out of here?"

"No," Koda said after his throat was working once more.

He coughed once to clear his throat again and offered the leather pouch back to Sienna, grimacing at the gore on it. He hadn't realized he was so heavily coated in blood from his fight, but Koda felt like he'd swam in a river of spilled blood right now. He had left a dark hand-print on the leather and around the mouth of the waterskin.

Sienna didn't seem to mind, taking the pouch in her own blood-covered hand and drinking as well.

Turning back to the startled group of villagers, Koda explained his earlier statement. "You all need to get to safety, but stick near the hunters so they can look after you. We don't know how many of these things are still lurking in the woods. When we are sure this place is clear, we can travel as a group back to the village."

"What about you?" This time it was Sienna who spoke up as she used some of the water to wash the blood from her hands.

Now that he had better control of himself, Koda could feel the pressure of something pulling at the totemic gauntlet he was still wearing. Like someone had hold of his hand and was trying to pull him along toward the large tent.

For the moment, Koda resisted the pulling sensation and turned his attention to answer Sienna.

"I have to make sure the threat is gone. There might be more hiding, and there's something—"

"We need to deal with the dead, too. We can't leave Crooked lying around. They'll poison the land," grunted the older man, interrupting Koda. "You do what you need to, Burke. The rest of us can sort through this trash and get it piled up."

Not a single villager voiced a protest at the old man's words, just giving stern nods or understanding grimaces. Sienna glanced between them and Koda a few times before one of the old man's daughters spoke up.

"Go with him, Sienna. We will keep an eye on each other, and I know I saw Netta up there on the ridge. She'll keep us safe."

"All right, Jenna. Keep your father and the others safe, okay?"

"You do the same, Sienna. Keep our hero in one piece. Poor man looks ready to collapse." Jenna tossed a nod to Koda, not bothering to whisper as she eyed him speculatively.

Growling quietly under his breath, Koda squared himself and swung the oversized cleaver onto his shoulder. He winced when the gnarled bit of metal landed on a bruise but turned to start towards the big tent at the center of the camp.

Behind him, Koda could hear the villagers discussing something in tones low enough he couldn't pick it out, and then the grunts of people setting to work followed.

They are surprisingly resilient, Koda thought. *I would have expected them to need time to bounce back from the danger, but they are getting to work cleaning up the aftermath. How does that reflect on the lives they have to lead?* He tried not to dwell on it too much as he allowed the totemic gauntlet to draw him towards the larger tent.

Koda stopped twice to ensure that a Crooked was dead on his way to the tent. Sienna caught up to him after the first one and followed in his wake silently, her spear held ready as she kept a wary watch on their surroundings. She did not try to speak to him, content to follow in his wake for the short walk through camp until they stopped outside the structure of rotten canvas.

Rather than duck through the hanging bit of musty cloth that served as a door, Koda switched the oversized cleaver into his other hand and used the razor-sharp claws on the gauntlet to slash the door free before stepping back and waiting for a moment.

When nothing emerged from the tent after several heartbeats, he peered through the opening to search the dark interior in the waning light of the day. Sienna stuck close to his left with her spear oriented on the door while she scanned their surroundings.

Distantly, Koda could hear the hunters calling down to the villagers to check on those they knew, but he put that aside while he focused. *The hunters will watch over them. If they are talking, then no more Crooked are lingering nearby.*

The interior of the tent confused him. Poles made of crudely hacked off saplings supported the roof, while ropes and stakes crossed back and forth to pull the canvas roof taut from the inside. This left the interior something of a maze to navigate as they cluttered the walking paths.

Several large, ancient stones stood as pillars towards the center of the large, impromptu structure. These pillars still bore the dappled pattern of lichen, along with ancient-looking grooves carved into their flanks that had their sharp edges softened through time and weather.

A few rough tables crouched around the interior of the tent, supporting a mixture of crude surgeon's tools, weapons, and the half-chewed remains of a barely cooked boar. A pile of stinking furs sat in one corner, telling him that the champion he'd killed had likely slept in here, too.

Besides the dead boar, though, nothing else inhabited the tent that Koda could see. He took a slow breath. The rank scent of death and decay filled his nostrils, and he snorted in disgust.

"Yeah, doesn't smell pleasant to me either. It's preventing me from getting a good fix on if there is anyone else in there," Sienna murmured, drawing Koda's eyes to her.

Sienna was grimacing as well, glaring into the tent with an offended scowl on her face. Her tail hung limply behind her while her pointed ears lay flat in anger. Koda was about to speak, to ask her what she thought they should do next, when the gauntlet on his hand gave him another firm tug that nearly pulled him off balance.

"Son of a... Okay, Thera, cool it," Koda grumbled under his

breath, glaring down at the gauntlet. He missed the startled look Sienna shot him as he was already moving forward.

The interior of the tent was dark, only the barest bits of light coming in from the tears and holes in the rotten canvas overhead or from a hole over the juncture above the circle of standing stones.

The gauntlet resolutely pulled Koda towards that circle of stones. Sienna followed in his wake, watching Koda with brows knitted in curiosity and concern.

In silence, they navigated the maze of ropes and strings that held the ramshackle tent up.

Each of the standing stones was easily eight or more feet tall and three feet wide. In places, the gray stone bodies of the standing stones bore a crust of light brown lichen and a few bits of moss that were already drying out and dying— whether from the shade or the malignant smoke was hard to say.

The seven stones stood roughly in a circle, providing support for the center of the tent that should have made it easy for it to be constructed, but the poles and lines inside still left the entire structure lopsided. The open space at the center of the circle was filled with a round of ancient, cracked stone about six feet across. Sitting in the middle of it was a piece of nightmare.

The object looked like someone had tried to construct a stove or a chest out of bones and then stitched human skin onto it. Gnarled leg bones made up the outer frame, but the bones bent and twisted on each other before splitting grossly to cradle a discolored brass dish about the size of a cooking wok. Ribs lined the sides to give it shape, and an open space sat below for a fire. Underneath the wok in that hollow, the stone had the discoloration of ash, and the bits of charcoal from an old fire remained there.

Inside the metal dish was a pile of bones. A bundle of very small bones that Koda desperately hoped was animal bones.

Bones that were twisted from heat and something more, bent to look like a vague facsimile of a child, but with the tiny skull of a deer rather than a head.

Disgust welled up in Koda's gut, bile rising in his throat, and he reacted before thinking.

The heavy blade of the Crooked champion's cleaver came up and off his shoulder before whistling down at the bizarre altar-stove-campfire. Sienna gasped and stepped backward at the sheer *wrongness* emanating from the thing.

The blade of Koda's weapon slammed into the edge of the metal bowl and exploded with a discordant chiming noise.

Fragments of smoking iron blew out in all directions, and Koda felt a line of fire race across his left cheek.

The bones and bowl remained untouched.

The disturbing object inside the bowl didn't even shift in response to the blow or the explosion. A moment later, Koda studied the smoking handle of the cleaver in his left hand before tossing it aside.

Distantly, Koda could hear shouts of surprise coming from the hunters and Sienna swearing, asking him... *something*. He couldn't focus through the sheer disgust and desire to retch welling up in his soul.

Koda touched his cheek with his right hand. Despite the gauntlet he was wearing, he could feel the warm blood trickling from the cut on his cheek. His blood.

The disgust crystallized, and he lashed out in a slashing motion with his totemic gauntlet at the undamaged bowl in front of him. He caught sight of Sienna lurching forward to try to stop him out of the corner of his eye, fear obvious in her blue-green eyes.

The altar, Koda wasn't sure how he knew what it was but he *knew* it was one, had shrugged off the blow from the massive metal weapon earlier.

However, the second the clawed fingers of his gauntlet met the metallic bowl, the bowl parted as if constructed of smoke.

A gurgling howl, like a wolf with pneumonia, rang out from the gross construct.

In the space between seconds, Koda saw black fire flicker in the fangs studding his gauntlet before racing down and out the claws on his hand. The second the fire touched the tips of his claws, it flared a brilliant ruby-red.

That red fire consumed bone, metal, and flesh with the speed of flash paper going up before Koda's next heartbeat thundered in his chest.

The sickly keening of a wolf shifted tones mid-howl, like someone tuning in a radio to the correct frequency. As that second of forever came to an end, the ringing, primal sound was pure, high, and joyful as Koda's blow finished abolishing the Crooked altar.

Sienna crashed into Koda's side a moment later, nearly knocking him over as she dragged him backwards in response to the burst of flame. The pulse of energy that followed the disappearance of the altar threw them both flat on their asses.

The pulse also uprooted or broke many of the stakes and ropes in the tent, tearing canvas and cracking the support poles like a dozen giants popping their knuckles together.

Grunting in pain, Koda coughed and rolled onto his side as the tent shredded around them. Sienna wasn't much better, groaning in pain while fighting for breath.

One crunch came from close by, and he looked up. Koda saw one of the cracked support poles swaying ominously before falling towards Sienna, born down by the weight of the canvas tied to its top when the tent slumped and fell in on itself. The splintered and sharp end fell towards the prone wolf woman.

Sienna was entirely unaware of the falling danger, and Koda reacted again on instinct.

The blow from his gauntleted right hand batted the falling tent pole off course to slam into the ground a few inches to one side of Sienna's shoulder, rather than her chest.

Silently, Koda thanked whatever training, power, or knowledge it was that Thera had imbued in him to help him learn to use this weapon.

"Watch out!" he coughed, still fighting to get a full breath in.

Sienna nodded and rolled into a sitting position, her eyes wide as she stared at the impromptu spear that had nearly gotten her. The last shreds of the canvas settled around them, leaving a lumpy circle that bowed outwards as the walls didn't entirely collapse but also exposing them to the evening sky.

"My apologies, Champion," a familiar, throaty voice said from nearby, drawing Koda's eyes back towards the center of the standing stones.

Standing there, one hip cocked and a smile on her translucent lips, was the faintly glowing ghost of Thera.

Her fur clothing clung just as tight as ever to her pale skin. Her long, black hair shimmered in the light, the spotting pattern more visible in the odd combination of exterior sunlight and what she emanated. Poking up above her head were a pair of ears that were even more immaterial than the rest of her. A faint ripple that might have been feathers shimmered through her hair as she turned, and the ghost of a feline tail flicked on her left before switching to the right side, turning into an extremely plush fox-tail as it passed behind her.

"What the hell, Thera?" Koda demanded in a strained voice as he climbed to his feet.

Turning, he offered a hand to Sienna, who was gaping at the apparition that stood before them.

"I hadn't expected you to sanctify a holy site already, Koda. I admit, I was a bit... enthusiastic in seizing it. But you don't understand what this means to me, my champion." Thera's throaty voice was full of affection and pride as she spoke. "Not only did you destroy the profane altar of the Crooked, but you also claimed this ancient holy site in my name. Now, the ley lines beneath these stones feed me strength once more."

"Is that why you are showing up to talk to me again? I thought you said you'd be out of contact while you recovered."

Koda bent over further, waving his left hand in front of Sienna's face, making the spearwoman jump in surprise. Blushing, she accepted the hand up, but her eyes went back to Thera immediately while her mouth worked to form words that would not come.

"Indeed. They had begun collecting power in the altar you destroyed, but they had not spent it yet. I believe they were intending to use it to corrupt the villagers they had captured. When you destroyed it with an anointing of your bloodline, you claimed the power bound up within the altar for me. Which is why I'm awake once more," Thera explained, her smile growing wider and revealing her myriad fangs.

Koda considered her words, remembering the black fire that had turned the color of rubies as it hit his fingertips.

The color of blood, he thought silently before pushing it aside to deal with later.

"Glad to help, then. Would have been nice to know what sort of monsters were out there before I went after them, though," Koda said tersely, doing his best to not growl at the goddess.

Sienna shot him a horrified look for the disrespectful tone he was using, but before she could chastise him, Thera laughed.

"Ah, my champion! I wish I could have given you more warning, but I spent all the power I had left. And you have repaid that with interest! Thank you again for saving my people." Koda grunted in understanding, the ache in his body having traveled into his head now. He understood what she said, but that didn't stop the irritation he had with the ghostly woman.

"Lady Thera? Is... is that you?"

The tearful hope in Sienna's voice froze Koda in his tracks. The tone of voice that Sienna spoke in echoed in his mind like the voice of a child begging for a loving parent to reassure them that monsters weren't real, and the only thing in their closet were shadows. It shook him to his core.

Without hesitating, Koda reached out with his left hand and wrapped it around Sienna's shoulders, drawing her to his side comfortingly. She went willingly, leaning against his shoulder and clinging to him for reassurance without ever looking away from the apparition before her. He could feel her fluffy tail whipping slowly behind them, bouncing against the back of his thighs with each pass.

"Yes, daughter of my people." Tears also welled up to sparkle in the corners of Thera's luminous eyes as she turned her gaze on Sienna. "It's me... I've finally found a way back to my children."

Chapter Eight

"I CANNOT LINGER FOR LONG RIGHT NOW, MY CHILD, but I want to let you know that I have never abandoned all of you. I just couldn't rally the power to do anything like this." Thera gestured to her ghostly self, her foxy tail flicking behind her before it narrowed slightly to match Sienna's as a wolf tail.

"No! Do not apologize, Pack Lady. We knew you had spent yourself to protect our ancestors long ago, that you had given us everything already. We had believed you were gone or faded to the point you might never return..." Sienna's tears ran freely now, mirrored by a handful of crystalline drops that traced Thera's cheeks.

Turning towards him, the apparition of his black-haired goddess spoke directly to Koda. "You look after her, Koda Burke. She is the first of my children I have truly laid eyes upon in centuries." He nodded without hesitation at her demand.

Thera's words broke Sienna out of her trance, and she turned to look at Koda, their eyes nearly level as she stared up at him.

Koda turned to meet those sparkling blue-green orbs and lost himself in them for a long moment. Surprise, wonder, and hope danced in those eyes, and they tried to drink him in. How easy it was for Koda to fall into Sienna's beautiful eyes.

It wasn't until Thera spoke that he was broken free of their spell. He still struggled to look away from Sienna, but he was no longer drowning in an ocean of crystalline, blue-green light.

"I don't believe I will have to worry on that front, it seems." Thera's voice was bright with laughter now. "As much as I would love to linger and tease you two, this is draining on my limited reserves of power. Koda, my champion, there are two more war parties of Crooked that lurk within the Silverstone Vale."

The goddess's words immediately pulled both of their attention back to her. Koda felt a rippling growl start deep in his throat. Beside him, Sienna matched it perfectly only half a moment later, and he shot her a surprised glance.

The fur on Sienna's ears was bristling, and he caught sight of her tail sticking out straight behind her. The love, joy, and relief she had been wearing like a cloak was falling away, replaced by pure fury.

"They hunt for people to convert and for places of power they can claim for their profane gods. Destroy them and take those sites of power for me," Thera continued, a small smile on her lips at seeing their reaction. "Claim the two sites they are seeking to corrupt, and I can grant you a boon, Koda. I wish I could give you one now for your actions in saving the village and speedily finding this one, but—"

"No need," Koda interrupted. "You promised me a people— a family to call my own—when you called me here. What kind of man would I be to demand a reward for doing something I would have done anyway?"

Thera smiled down at them for a long second, her form growing more translucent by the second. She spoke after the moment had passed, her voice echoing from a great distance.

"I am glad to have found you, Koda. Fate has blessed both me and my children with an opportunity in you. While I cannot reward you yet, I have a feeling my children will find a way to thank you. Until we speak again."

The goddess's silhouette dissolved into a cascade of black and silver sparks that swirled three times over the center of the standing stones, spinning like a chest-high dust devil.

First, it scoured the remnants of the fire stains from the rock. The second pass left behind a pristine, tanned hide of a gray wolf. And then the third deposited a stone bowl in the center of the hide.

That done, the swirling cloud of motes scampered across the ground before diving into Koda's gauntlet, sinking into the stones and fangs that studded the back of his forearm and vanishing.

A faint pulse ran through the gauntlet. The various bits of blood and evidence of battle that had lingered on its surface vanished as if he'd dunked the weapon into a fast-moving stream.

Silence descended over the standing stones, with Koda and Sienna still holding each other as they stared down at the fur and bowl there. Both items gleamed as if new, shimmering with a glossy finish that stood in defiance to the ancient, worn stone upon which they sat.

Koda could feel the power collecting in the bowl already.

While before, the altar had felt profane and wrong, this one felt at one with the world around it and peaceful.

Sienna turned again to look at Koda, their nearly matching heights evened out further by her position tucked against his shoulder. Tear-stains still marked her cheeks, having cut through the dust, mud, and blood there, but hope glimmered in those crystalline spheres.

Sienna's lips parted like she was about to speak, but then the sounds of the rest of the world finally made it back to them.

"What the hell was that?"

"Is Sienna okay? She went into that tent before it collapsed!"

"What about the man with her? Did Koda turn on her?"

Glancing over his shoulder, Koda saw that the remnants of the tent still hung in the way, blocking an easy view of the center of the circle. He could see people moving and casting shadows on the far side of it as they hurried over to check on Sienna and him.

The pulse that had come from his destruction of the altar had mostly destroyed the big tent, but the outer edges still had enough scraps of canvas and half-standing tent poles that he and Sienna had been the only ones to see Thera when she appeared, it seemed—a thought that was disproved a moment later.

Flickering movement at the edge of his vision drew Koda's eyes to the stony ridge above. Directing his gaze up, Koda saw the awestruck face of Netta, the eagle-woman, and her two hunting partners staring down at them.

Using his gauntleted hand, Koda held one finger to his lips in the universal 'shush' gesture while locking eyes with Netta. The feathered huntress stared dumbly at him for a long second before nodding once with narrowed eyes that gave off a distinct 'you will explain later' look, to which he nodded his agreement.

"Come on, Sienna. Let's go and let the others know we are fine." Koda gave the redheaded wolf-woman a squeeze with the arm around her shoulders, and she nodded, not looking away from him.

In an effort to break the growing sensation of awkwardness from her staring, Koda continued to speak while not looking away from her glittering eyes as they had captured him again.

How do they keep doing that? Koda thought just before he spoke, unable to look away.

"Don't want your people to worry about you, you know? Besides, we can't let that old fellow and the villagers do all the work of cleaning up the mess we made. Come on, let's go."

Sienna blinked, and again, that action broke the spell of her gaze.

Koda glanced away quickly before her blue-green orbs could trap him again, though he did not release the arm around her shoulders until Sienna shifted to step back.

"You are right, Koda. We have much to do, and I am sure the village will want to celebrate the safe return of its citizens. Farmer Oslo needs to get that arm seen to by the healers as well." Sienna's tone was businesslike as she straightened her clothing and then bent at the waist to pick up her spear.

The action put the redheaded huntress's back to him. The banner that was her red-black tail was already stirring up a storm, showing she was clearly happy about something. Whether from the idea of getting back to the village, that her people were safe, or seeing the vision of Thera, Koda had no idea. But he had to fight the urge to reach out and touch that fluffy appendage to see if it was as soft as it looked.

Clearing his throat, Koda turned towards where the bulk of the voices were coming from.

"We are fine. Don't worry!" he called out, and the shouting quieted down, followed by a bit of relieved laughter from the villagers.

"Is Sienna okay?" came another voice, a female one that Koda thought might have been Jenna Oslo.

"I'm fine, Jenna," Sienna said quickly while straightening, her spear going over her shoulder. "I think the camp is clear. If there were any more of those beasties lingering around when that... thing went off, they'd have reacted, I'm sure."

Turning slightly, Sienna shot Koda a look over her shoulder, her tail still wagging away, a smile on her full lips with a quirked eyebrow. He nodded in agreement with her summation, and her smile spread further into a full-on grin.

"Let's get this done with. I really want to get clean again," Koda said, glancing meaningfully at his bloody clothes so he didn't lose himself in her eyes and make an idiot of himself. Again...

Sienna glanced down with a shared grimace. He'd managed to get some of it on her during their brief hug, but she just shrugged it off a moment later.

"Fair. I know I want to wash as well."

The group of hunters that the Crooked had spotted earlier returned a few minutes later, battered and bloody but without having lost anyone.

They'd successfully led the group following them to the northern fissures. Those that had not fallen to the traps, trip-wires, and deadfalls that the hunters had set up in the woods ended up either on the point of an arrow or down the ravines.

Two of the three-member hunting parties remained on the cliffs to watch over them as the other two hunting parties descended to help the captured villagers deal with the camp.

There had been some argument about whether to just leave the bodies there or burn them initially, but Farmer Oslo had been firm that they needed to burn the Crooked to ensure they stayed dead.

Koda had sided with the older wolf-man, given he'd watched what he guessed was the champion raising one of the Crooked from the dead just before they'd attacked. It didn't take much to convince the villagers and hunters, thankfully.

Working together, the villagers piled the dead Crooked at the far end of the little valley, where the ground was hard and stony. On top of the dead, the villagers piled the tents, bedding, and everything else the Crooked had brought with them before adding wood in several layers.

The villagers even tossed on the weapons they had claimed to defend themselves. Everything went onto the pyre. The gnarled swords and bent spears were apparently not worth keeping to the tired folk.

When all that was done, they set the whole thing alight with the embers of one of the cooking fires before kicking dirt over any cooking fires that remained.

This action resulted in a slowly growing fire and the rank scent of burning flesh spreading out from it. The smell quickly pushed everyone back to the northern end of the valley—as far from the pyre as possible.

In the end, the six hunters who had stood watch while they piled up the bodies agreed to stay at the valley to ensure the fire didn't spread while the others, Koda, and Sienna returned to the village to let them know of their success.

Sienna had spent the entire time moving from group to group, ensuring that everyone was okay and that they didn't overdo it while helping where she could. When she wasn't doing that, she followed close behind Koda to help with what he was working on.

Koda caught her talking quietly with Netta and her group several times, the four of them shooting glances at him the entire time. Netta and her friends speculatively, and Sienna with pride glowing on her face. He had to glance away quickly each time as her blue-green orbs drew him in like a magnet drew iron.

The exhaustion hit Koda as their group filed out of the valley and up one of the narrow tracks.

He'd gone up first to stand guard at the top while the others followed after in a single-file line. Once he stopped moving, though, he could feel the tiredness seeping into his bones.

Standing on the edge of the cliff, Koda squinted in the dim light of the oncoming evening as he surveyed what he could see of the little valley.

They'd been thorough in collecting anything that had belonged to the Crooked and throwing it onto the pyre. They even disassembled the corral—the splintered logs used for fuel for the blaze.

Now, by the light of that fire, Koda could see that the little valley was in much better shape, though it was not pristine. It had been stamped flat by the passage of many feet, torn from tent stakes, and the stains of blood still scarred the floor of the valley where the camp had stood. But still, Koda felt like the little valley would recover given a season or two.

A light pressure on his right hand, like someone taking it and squeezing gently, gave him the impression that Thera knew what he was thinking and agreed, which set his heart at ease. This place could recover and would, given time, he decided.

"Come on, Koda. Let's get back home," Sienna called from nearby as she crested the slope, having come up last.

Nodding to himself, Koda turned to her with a broad smile.

Arrayed behind Sienna were Netta and her two companions, as well as the other three hunters who would be escorting the captured villagers back. Said villagers stood in a group just behind the hunters, some huddling against each other, while others just took deep breaths of the clean air that the wind brought from between the trees, savoring being alive and free.

"Yes, let's head back home."

Chapter Nine

THE MARCH BACK TO THE VILLAGE THROUGH THE darkening night was difficult. All of them were exhausted, both emotionally and physically, at this point. Either from the stress of battle, capture, or emotional revelations, in Sienna's case.

The wolf beastfolk woman stuck close to Koda, studying him in the flickering light of the makeshift torches scattered amongst their group. While she didn't need the additional light, there were others amongst the villagers that were not so gifted with stronger night-sight. So, one in three people had a torch to help light the way.

Sienna turned over what had happened in the camp in her mind. Koda had overcome a Crooked champion, something that normally took a dozen or more warriors working in concert—if she believed the stories she'd heard from traveling merchants.

That or another champion. Lady Thera did call him hers, she thought while her tail flicked back and forth slowly. *And she has returned to us, with the aid of this man... Do I tell anyone? Netta agreed to keep it silent for now.*

Sienna was so lost in her thoughts that she didn't realize Koda was talking to her until he repeated the question while waving a hand to get her attention.

"I'm sorry. What was that?" she asked, her tail fluffing out in embarrassment at being distracted.

"I was asking if there is an inn or somewhere I can stay in the village? I don't exactly have much of anything, or money to pay, but I can do chores in the morning to cover the cost of a room and a bath," Koda said, fighting back annoyance that sprung more from his exhaustion than any real ill feelings towards the gorgeous wolf woman.

She's earned a rest as much as you have, idiot. Don't get mad, Koda reprimanded himself mentally while Sienna blinked at him.

"An inn? Yes, there is an inn. Given what you've done today, though, I doubt they will accept payment from you. And even if Banno asks for money to let you stay, you come to me." Sienna's words had transitioned to a growl at the end there. "Worse comes to worst? You can stay with me in the hunter's hall. It's not exactly private, with the bunk setup, but it's more economical than unmarried folks having to build and maintain a house themselves."

"Okay. Thanks, Sienna." Koda shot her a smile and got a tentative one in return.

Their brief conversation lapsed into the same sort of bone-deep exhaustion shared by the entire party. Koda spared a brief moment of concern for the other six hunters they'd left behind to watch the pyre but pushed it aside by reminding himself that they hadn't had to help dismantle the camp.

The muted conversation and grumbling from the group fell away as they finally broke free of the tree line and into the ordered rows of the orchard. No one splintered off, though Farmer Oslo and his daughters glared at the ruined front door on the large house that sat farther back from the trees, which made Koda think this must have been their home.

Probably don't want to risk staying this far from the village tonight. I wonder if the inn will even have rooms left? Koda thought while the pace of the group picked up, with folks hurrying to get home and tell family they were safe.

As they got to the edge of the collection of buildings that made up the village, several of the village's defenders, a mixture of hunters and armed citizens with rough weapons, melted out of the darkness to greet their return.

The welcoming shouts and excitement sapped the group's momentum and energy. They ground to a halt as family welcomed back family in a riot of noise and happiness.

Laughter sprung up at being spared by the Fates, while some shared tears over those the Crooked had killed rather than captured. All around him, people were hugging and chattering with each other excitedly, some even dancing impromptu jigs.

Koda stepped back from those tearful reunions, giving people the space to speak and express their grief while not being crowded by a stranger. Sienna stuck close to him, her spear over her shoulder.

More than a few villagers came up to thank Sienna, who brushed it off as the hunters just doing their duty. She turned several of them towards Koda, insisting that he helped just as much as she did—a statement reinforced by several of the freed villagers, who made no bones about the fact that Koda was the one who had taken down the Crooked champion. So the thankful groups latched onto him instead despite his best attempts to not intrude.

While the villagers had viewed him with suspicion before, that all changed now. Koda was not ready for the open and joyous thanks directed his way by the families of the rescued villagers, and those who just wanted to thank him for eliminating the threat.

He did what he could to spread the credit around, saying that without Sienna and the hunters there, it wouldn't have worked. However, after having their appreciation redirected once already by Sienna, the thankful would not accept another diversion.

Their group was able to get moving again slowly, threading through the rough streets towards the center of the village at a slow mosey, when someone mentioned drinks and food. Rejoining their families and celebrating the successes seemed to give the villagers a second wind, and a few hurried off to wake others and alert those who had not been on guard duty.

By the time the rescue party made it to the square where Koda had first decided to take his chance on his own with the rescue and head out, a party atmosphere was brewing. Their group had grown to easily four times the size it had been when they hit the edge of the village.

The square had been cleaned up since the last time he was here. No longer were wounded laid out to be tended to or makeshift barricades barring the roads. People had apparently been moved back into their homes, and the hunters or fighters of the village roamed the streets on patrol until now.

Tables were being brought out as lamps were lit to give

people light to talk and celebrate as more people flooded from their homes.

"Excuse me, yes. Pardon me. Let me through," a creaky female voice cut through the throng to his left and drew Koda's attention.

Working her way between chatting villagers, villagers that he noted mostly were beastfolk like Sienna, was an older woman dressed in well-tailored clothing. She walked with the aid of a knobby stick of pitch-black wood that ended in a spherical head, slipping between celebrating villagers as needed.

While she leaned on that walking stick, the older woman moved with a nimble grace that told Koda she likely didn't need it as much as she might appear. A pair of triangular, gray and black-striped cat's ears poked out of her neatly combed fall of gray hair, while a striped tail danced in her wake.

"Let me get by here. Yes, thank you. Good to see you all made it back. I need to speak with—" the old woman called, her weathered voice cutting through the conversation until someone backed into her while gesticulating wildly.

The older cat woman moved as quick as lightning when the hunter in question bumped into her, sidestepping to maintain her balance before thumping the man in the side with her cane, making him grunt in surprise and stumble.

"Watch where you are going, whelp!" she snapped as the hunter tripped and fell while his friends laughed.

"Sorry, Headwoman," he muttered with a quick bob of his head before his friends got him on his feet and towed him off in another direction.

"Where did he go now..." the old woman muttered before locking eyes on Koda and Sienna, where they stood at the edge of the square. "There! You, stranger! I need to talk to you. Oh, Sienna dear! I need you as well."

The older woman gestured with her staff, and the three converged in the shadow of a large wood and stone building that Koda guessed was either a common meeting house or maybe the inn that Sienna had mentioned.

Koda tried not to think about the fact he looked like a mess with his clothes tattered and stained with blood, mud, and other things while they stuck to his skin in many places. He hadn't taken more than a few bruises and a knock to the head during the fight, so he could tough this out, but he dearly wanted to wash right now. Almost every inch of his skin felt grimy and just *wrong*.

"Headwoman Kris, I'm glad you are okay." Sienna was the first to speak once the older cat lady came to a stop in front of them.

"And I am glad you are safe, pup. You and all our hunters that went with you. At least, I hope they are all safe. Where are the others?" the headwoman asked as their trio came to a stop.

The old woman planted her walking stick in front of her and rested both hands on it. For all that she had a bit of a stoop and leaned so heavily on that cane, Koda could see the faint outline of corded muscle in her forearms to show she wasn't weak by any means. That and the memory of her deft movements only seconds ago.

"We eliminated the camp where the Crooked took the captives. Koda killed their champion and destroyed the altar they had constructed out by the old standing stones," Sienna was quick to state. The headwoman's brows drew down in anger, and a feline growl built in her throat at the mention of the champion, though it relented when Sienna mentioned the altar's destruction. "The others are still back at the camp, watching over the pyre. Farmer Oslo insisted we burn the Crooked. If what Koda and I saw before the attack was true, then his insistence makes sense."

The headwoman nodded, her ears flicking slightly while she glanced between Sienna and Koda rapidly, her eyes glimmering slightly with thoughtful consideration.

"So you broke up the camp, killed their champion, destroyed the altar, and then drove them off?"

"I'm pretty sure we wiped out nearly all the Crooked in the camp, actually," Koda spoke up for the first time since the older woman had started interrogating them.

Kris's eyebrows went up, the faint wrinkles in her features smoothing as surprise took over again.

"Truly?"

"Yes. I didn't get a firm count, but we wiped out just shy of a hundred Crooked. Some ended up falling down the northern ravines when they pursued a few of the hunters out of the camp, but we caught the others in a bottleneck and picked them off relatively readily. Their camp was in a brilliant spot to hide, but it was a poor one to defend. Especially given how shoddy their patrols and guards were." Fighting back his exhaustion, Koda swayed slightly, and Sienna sidestepped to help brace him as he finished his explanation.

"You didn't get hurt, did you, young man? Sienna, is he... Is that blood?" The headwoman's voice took on a note of concern as she studied the young man in front of her, her eyes going wide as she made out the stains on his already dark clothing.

"Not mine," Koda grunted, shaking his head once in an effort to clear the exhaustion swimming in his veins.

"He's dead on his feet, Headwoman. Koda raced off ahead of our group to scout the enemy. He also accounted for a good chunk of the Crooked slain. I should have asked earlier, though, Koda. Are you hurt?" Sienna replied to the head-woman's question before turning her concern back to Koda despite him already stating the blood wasn't his.

"Bruises mostly. Just wore out like you said. Was tired when I got here the first time, but I kept pushing to protect folks," Koda answered, leaning slightly on Sienna until his head stopped swimming. Even after he got it under control, Sienna kept a hand on his back to help support him if he swayed again.

The headwoman stared at him for a long moment, her pale green eyes glinting in the torchlight as the noise in the square rose higher. She glanced between Sienna and Koda several times before a slight smile crossed her lips.

"Sienna, you should tend to our helpful stranger. He does look rather dead on his feet, and you look just as tired. The rest of these fools might be willing to party, but I know from my time serving in the army that the Crooked are like an infection. You have to ensure you fully cleanse their taint before you can truly celebrate."

Koda nodded in agreement with the headwoman's words. After a minute of consideration and a glance to make sure they weren't being overheard, he leaned in closer to her.

"I have it on good authority that there are two more Crooked camps in the area. This is the Silverstone Vale, right?" The question got an odd look from Kris and a tensing of Sienna next to him.

"Yes, young man. This is the Silverstone Vale," Kris said slowly, the question in her tone obvious: *'How do you not know this? You came here, didn't you?'* A moment later, the rest of what he said sunk in. Her eyes went wide, and her brows drew down in anger.

"I didn't want to assume. But yes, I have it on good authority that there are two other camps in the area that are doing what the first one was. Profaning ancient sites of power."

Kris's feline features turned thunderous once more, and the growl started deep in her throat while her tail bristled behind her.

"They would dare? No, I will not allow that. I will look for maps and records to see what areas they might be targeting tonight. We will find this infection and cut it from the land before it can take root. But that is a problem for tomorrow." As abruptly as it had come, her growl dropped away, and she gave Koda a rather intense look that darted to Sienna for a moment before going back to Koda. "For now, you need to rest and clean yourself up. My son's old things should fit you, so I will send someone along with them. I doubt your current outfit is salvageable. Sienna, are you taking him to the inn or to the hunter's hall?"

Sienna glanced over at the increasing crowd in the square and then up at the building behind her before sighing.

"The hunter's hall is going to be quieter, and Koda deserves to sleep after everything he's gone through," Sienna said, her ears drooping slightly.

"He deserves far more than just a night's rest for the work he's put in, if half of what I heard on my way over here is true," said the headwoman, her ears perking up while her tail flicked idly behind her in amusement. "But that is something for tomorrow when you have rested enough to think properly. Can I trust you to look after him, Sienna?"

"Of course, Headwoman. I'd rather get some rest myself than deal with a party like this. I get that people want to celebrate our successful defense, but there are still other threats we have to be on guard against. We have hunted the game, but the meat isn't smoked yet."

The way that Sienna said the last part of her statement felt like a euphemism to Koda, but he couldn't quite get his brain to focus enough to figure out what it meant. The conversation continued before he could backtrack to it.

"Good girl. Go take care of your partner there. I'll have someone bring clothes to the hunter's hall as I said, and we can meet in the morning to figure out our next steps." The headwoman's words brought a blush to Sienna's cheeks that Koda didn't quite understand. Before he could puzzle it out, Sienna nodded before shifting the hand on his back to grip his right biceps.

"Come on, Koda. You really are dead on your feet, and honestly, I'm not much better. If we are going to do anything to help out tomorrow, we need rest."

"Bath?" Koda's monosyllabic question got a laugh from Sienna and a snicker from the headwoman.

"Maybe not a full one, but the hall has a hearth, and we can heat some water to at least wipe down. The sooner we get there, the sooner you can get clean, then sleep." Sienna's voice was gentle, almost like she was trying to encourage a reluctant child to go to bed.

Koda knew he should be indignant about being treated that way, but after standing still for their conversation with the headwoman, his exhaustion was rising faster than he could combat it.

So, rather than arguing with the beautiful redhead tugging on his arm, he fell into step behind Sienna. When she realized he was following her willingly, Sienna let go of his arm and led the way around the edge of the square to avoid being stopped.

The bouncing of Sienna's fluffy, red-black tail was hypnotic to Koda. Its wagging motion nicely accented the slight sway to Sienna's hips and rear as she led him down a dark street to a promised place of rest.

Chapter Ten

Sienna led him through several side streets that Koda didn't really pay much attention to.

Instead, the swaying of her fluffy tail transfixed him, along with how her bottom bounced in counterpoint to it. His tired mind focused on those two things to the exclusion of all others.

So, he mechanically put one foot in front of the other and followed after her, trusting in his guide to get him to somewhere he could rest. Only the moon and the occasional light from a window lit their way, but he never lost sight of that flicking tail.

The hunter's hall sat back from the main square, closer to the edge of the village. The building was two stories with a thatched roof and walls made of wood with a stone base. Several shuttered windows pierced its walls, and a large double door stood guard at the top of a short pair of stone steps. The barest hints of light flickered along the bottom of the door from inside.

Not hesitating, Sienna led the way up the stairs and pushed the doors open. A pair of tin lamps on tables and the dully glowing embers of a fire in a massive stone fireplace across the room dimly illuminated the interior of the building.

Scattered around the first floor were a collection of rough tables and chairs, while bunk beds sat against the walls, intermixed with the occasional hammock hanging between the support posts of the roof.

Glancing up, Koda could see the second floor was open in the center, with rooms leading off a balcony. A set of stairs along the back wall to the right of the fire led up to the second story. Given the fact that the sleeping area was in the main room, he guessed that the upper rooms were all used for storage.

Trophies, weapons, tools, and carved figures decorated the walls and hung from the ceiling. Everything from animal skulls and horns to a tanned bear skin that looked almost twice as long as he was tall. The air inside the hall smelled of smoke, leather, oil, and just a faint hint of sweat. Where he stood right now was a slightly lower section floored in stone, but the main floor of the building sat raised on wooden planks.

"Take your boots off, Koda. No need to track mud or worse into the place." Sienna's words broke Koda out of his distracted state.

At some point, Sienna had stopped and turned around to look him over speculatively, her spear still over her shoulder, her hand on her hip.

Koda was silently grateful that she hadn't turned around while he was still distractedly following her tail and butt with his eyes. That would have likely led to him getting yelled at and losing any good impression he might have gained with the attractive wolf woman.

Get it together, idiot, he chastised himself internally.

A quiet clearing of Sienna's throat told him he was still staring, but at least at her face this time. So, Koda quickly squatted down to start working at his laces.

The change in orientation nearly made him fall over as his blood pressure adjusted, and Sienna caught him with a hand on his shoulder.

"Easy now, Koda. This is as safe as we can be, so you might as well relax," Sienna said quietly, and he just nodded without looking up, hoping that the blush would fade before he had to meet her eyes. "You get your boots off, and I'll get some water warming by the fire. I don't think you want to wait for a full bath to heat."

"I'll take what I can get and not complain. Just want to feel clean," Koda answered quietly, getting a little chuff of laughter from the woman.

"You'll get plenty, but I think you need sleep more than anything right now. We just have to make sure you don't leave a mess when you lie down." Sienna waited long enough to make sure he was stable before hurrying across the room to a corner by the fire.

Koda watched her out of the corner of his eyes as he worked at removing his boots without cutting the laces on the sharp claw-tips of his totemic gauntlet.

Sienna paused to lay her spear horizontally in a pair of hooks on the side of the top bunk of a set that he guessed was likely hers. She had already shed her boots quickly while talking to him, so she only paused to take her woodland cloak off before padding on stockinged feet through a door to one side of the fireplace.

A moment later, she returned with a metal kettle, which she hung on a hook by the fire. Sienna vanished through the door again to return with an armload of firewood held to her hip on one side, a wooden bucket of water on the other.

By the time Koda had his boots off, Sienna had laid the wood on the embers of the fire and got it burning before pouring the water into the kettle and setting it to heat.

She stood there for a moment, her curved and muscled form silhouetted alluringly by the glow of the fire. Koda took the moment to drink in her form appreciatively before forcing himself to look away again so she wouldn't turn to catch him staring.

He set his boots next to Sienna's on a rack to one side of the door before following her route out of the entryway and into the main room.

Sienna stirred from her position in front of the fire as Koda approached, glancing over her shoulder at him.

The fire threw flickering highlights into her russet-red hair and highlighted how well her outfit clung to her body. Not wanting to get caught staring again, Koda let the distracting blue-green orbs of Sienna's eyes capture his attention instead.

Coming to a stop a few feet back from where Sienna stood in front of the fire, Koda waited as the wolf beastfolk woman turned fully around, her tail flicking slowly behind her.

Sienna studied his face intently at first before letting her gaze drop to take him in once more. The spell of her gaze broke when she looked down, and Koda allowed himself the brief moment to return the favor and study her back.

When Sienna finished looking him over, she let her eyes return to his face, and she let out a slow breath.

"It's going to take time for the water to warm up," she said after a moment. "I have questions, if you have the energy to answer them?"

Yes, I'm single, Koda thought without warning. *I wish that was what she was going to ask, but I doubt it.*

Instead of voicing his thoughts, Koda nodded and glanced towards one of the nearby tables questioningly.

"Sure, mind if we sit?"

Sienna nodded, gesturing for him to take a seat. Once Koda had settled, Sienna took the rough chair next to his and leaned her elbows on the table with a relieved groan of her own.

"Ugh, I know sitting down is a mistake. It's gonna be hard to get up to wash, but I'll have to get up anyway to get to the bed," Sienna grumbled quietly, grimacing down at her bloody hands. "I haven't been this messy since I had to help Netta dress that moose she brought down over the winter."

Silence fell between them as Koda tried to imagine Sienna and the hawk-feathered woman cleaning and carving up a kill the size of a moose.

Shaking off the distraction, Koda glanced towards Sienna. He could tell that, despite stating she wanted to ask him things, Sienna was hesitating with how she bit her bottom lip and continued to stare at her hands. Since he didn't have the energy to be tactful at the moment, he prodded her gently with his words.

"What questions did you have?" Koda asked after the silence had sat long enough.

Sienna sighed gustily, propping her elbow on the table and leaning forward like she was about to rest her head on her fist. She stopped at the last moment, grimacing at the dried blood that she had already nearly forgotten, and pushed herself away to lean back in her chair.

"Everything. I have so many questions. Who are you, really? How did you get here? Why are you here? Was that really Lady Thera I saw? How did she return?" Sienna rambled, her frustration peaking at the situation.

Her tail, which had slotted through an opening in the back of the chair, thrashed behind her with as much fury as a fluffy appendage could muster, clearly trying to convey its mistress's frustration.

Koda blinked at her dumbly for a moment before a bitter laugh leaked out. This was apparently not what Sienna had expected his response to be because she jerked her head back and scowled at him.

"I wish I knew the answer to most of those," Koda said before she could snap at him. "I can answer with what I know, though. Starting in reverse then. As far as I know, yes that was Thera. Why and how I have no idea. I'm here because she asked me to help her people—my people, apparently—and I didn't have much going for me back home. The opportunity to make a difference and have a family was tempting enough to get me to decide before I really thought about it. I've been cruising on adrenaline and determination thus far, but even *I* am wondering what I got myself into." Koda glanced down at the gauntlet, still strapped firmly on his right arm.

"What is that?" Sienna's question drew his gaze back up, but she was staring at the gauntlet, apparently curious about it.

"A gift from Thera. She said that she would give me a weapon to defend myself when I came here, so I could help people."

Koda abruptly had a desire to remove the gauntlet, to separate himself from the weapon. His skin itched, and he swore he could feel the slick sensation of blood on his palm. So, he began tugging on it, searching for a catch or release to unhook it so he could take it off while fighting down the sudden nausea in his stomach.

Try as he might, though, Koda could not remove the gauntlet. Gripping the wrist and tugging on it, or any other part of the gauntlet, did nothing to dislodge the weapon. Each motion felt like he was just tugging on his own arm. And he could find no buckles or hooks to loosen its grip.

Sienna watched, clearly thinking over what he had said, for several moments before patting the table.

"Here, lay it out, and I'll see if I can find the ties. While I'm doing that, fill me in on everything that led you to being here, okay?" The previous frustration that had colored Sienna's tone was now gone. In its place was quiet understanding and acceptance.

With nothing better to do, Koda followed her instructions. At the very least, he hoped the story would allow him to push down the creeping sensation in his gut and the memory of blood.

Turning in his seat so that she had easier access, Koda laid his arm out on the table for her to inspect and fiddle with while he recounted everything that had happened on this very strange day.

Sienna was silent while he talked, her eyes focused on her hands while she worked and listened. She would make the occasional questioning noise or glance up at him as he described first Earth, then his work, and finally, his life back home that resulted in him taking Thera up on her offer to step through to help them.

The rambling story continued to the first encounter with the Crooked, the disgust of having to kill, and his determination to protect his people.

He half expected her to react negatively when he referred to both her and the others as *his people*, but she just nodded along while picking at a strap that covered his wrist.

The story wound down with the fight against the Crooked champion, what he could remember through the fury of the fight, and the adrenaline of the close calls. Koda finished it up with the act of destroying the altar and Thera's appearance.

"That's it. Everything that has happened today," Koda said with a sigh. The act of telling the tale had helped him put his whirling mind in order, and while he was still tired, he wasn't about to pass out now that he could think straight again.

Talking about it did help, he thought wryly, rubbing at his eyes with his left hand.

"Pack Lady be praised," Sienna murmured, still staring down at his gauntleted hand.

She'd stopped trying to remove the garment a while ago, instead just studying the leather and bone wrapping carefully while she listened. She traced one of the sharp claws delicately with her fingertip while she continued to speak.

"Our goddess reached across time and space to find the last of her champions to save us when we needed her. You abandoned everything you had to come here, to help people you'd never even met."

Koda shrugged, a blush creeping up to burn his face in embarrassment at her statement.

"There wasn't much to leave behind. My parents cared more about hurting each other than looking after me. My work was crap, and I had no prospects," Koda mumbled.

"But you had safety. You said your world did not have threats like the Crooked, the Risen, or Tyrantborn. No oppression to speak of either," Sienna protested.

"Dunno about those others you mentioned, but at least we didn't have Crooked. Oh, and there was oppression. Humans love to oppress others, even those of their same race and the ones they were supposed to be protecting."

"Not the same. Was there slavery in your country?" Sienna's question was sharp, and Koda grimaced, still not looking up.

"Kind of? With the costs that people had to pay to even survive, it was similar to debt slavery. But I understand your point," Koda explained. Sienna waited until he looked up at her to nod in acceptance.

"The point, Koda, is that you came here with only hopes and a desire to help. Lady Thera promised you a people to belong to and a purpose. I can guarantee you have that after today." Sienna's smile was simple and bright, joy trickling from the curve of her lips and the sparkles in her eyes as she continued. "I guarantee that if you asked the headwoman to join our village, she would leap at the opportunity. And that is before she learns that you are not just of the bloodline of the Beast Queen's priesthood but also that she has anointed you as her champion."

"Maybe... maybe we shouldn't tell her that just yet?" Koda asked, glancing down at where Sienna was lightly running her thumb over the palm of his gauntlet.

Even with the leather in the way, he could feel her fingers on his skin like he wasn't even wearing the piece of armor turned into a weapon.

"Why not?" Sienna's brow wrinkled, and she tilted her head in confusion.

"I don't want anything handed to me. I have no problem working to earn it," Koda began to explain, and Sienna held up a hand to halt his argument.

"Stop. Koda, that is not what I was saying." Sienna paused for a moment to make sure he was going to let her finish before she continued. "Headwoman Kris and her family have done all they can to keep the Beast Queen's faith alive over the years. She's told all of us stories of our homeland, sagas passed down through her family so that none will forget what the Beast Queen sacrificed to allow our escape. If her family, the Dewclaws, had been of the bloodline of the priesthood, I guarantee that we would have a temple here. But they aren't, and we have had to keep our faith secret. Lady Thera could not help us if we drew the wrong attention. That will be different with a champion of the lost bloodlines." Another genuine smile scampered across her face. "Perhaps lost no longer?"

"But I don't know how to do any of that," Koda protested weakly. Sienna just shrugged, her smile not fading.

"You can learn those skills. I'm sure that Headwoman Kris will jump for joy at the idea of being able to sanctify a temple to the Beast Queen. She can teach you all about our people's history." Sienna tilted her head to one side, the smile fading a bit. "Though I am curious... You mentioned that she said your ancestors traveled to another world and survived there. But as far as I remember from what the headwoman taught us, only those of the beastfolk were members of Thera's clergy. I wonder what breed lies in your ancestry..."

"Well, I don't have ears or a tail, so it's hard to say," Koda replied jokingly, but Sienna just nodded, a serious expression on her face.

"Indeed, it is likely quite distant in your ancestry but still strong enough that Lady Thera could find you. You fight with the ferocity of the cat folk, but you have shown the loyalty of the wolf folk like myself, and also the fury of the bear folk. I wonder..."

Sienna's words trailed off. She sat there, silently staring at Koda for several long moments.

As the awkwardness began to build again, Koda cleared his throat and shifted. The motion broke Sienna out of her reverie, and she blushed as well, a faint dusting of color on her sun-tanned cheeks.

"Ah, sorry about that. I got distracted..." Sienna said. She bit her lip, and it looked like she was about to say more when the sound of the front door opening pulled both of their attention away from each other.

"There you are. Headwoman Kris sent me with clothing for our heroic friend here," Netta said as she stepped through with a small bundle of cloth in her arms. "Come grab these from me, Sienna. I need to go make sure the boys don't get too rowdy."

Sienna shot to her feet, hurrying around Koda and towards the door.

As she passed, Sienna's tail flicked over to caress Koda's cheek as she went by. The fur of her tail was soft, and it felt vaguely like she'd smacked him in the face with a very flexible feather-duster that smelled faintly of pine and a wild, womanly scent.

Blinking, Koda stared at the table in front of him. He could hear a quiet conversation between Netta and Sienna behind him. Then the door clunked once more to herald Netta leaving.

A minute later, Sienna set the bundle of clothing on the table next to him before striding past to swing the cauldron of steaming water off the fire.

Using her sleeve to shield her hand from the hot metal, Sienna poured a portion of the hot water back into the bucket that still sat by the fire. She added a coarse cloth to it before glancing back at Koda over her shoulder.

"Water is ready. The bathing room is through there if you want to strip down in privacy." She gestured to the door that she had come in through with the kettle. Koda nodded, pushing himself to his feet with his hands on the table. His bone claws grated on the tabletop and drew Sienna's attention to the gauntlet. Sighing, she shook her head for a moment. "I couldn't figure out how to get that off you. As far as I can tell, it's stitched in place, like someone assembled it around your arm. Sorry about that."

Glancing down at the bladed claws of the gauntlet that he was stuck wearing. Koda bit back a sigh all his own.

Would be nice if I could at least sleep without having to worry about clawing myself in the night, Thera, he thought with a grimace.

There was no response from the mysterious goddess, so Koda decided to just do his best. It was a familiar position to be in.

"Thanks, Sienna. Appreciate you looking after me," Koda said, accepting the bucket and rag from her.

"Happy to, Koda." Sienna's smile lit up the room for a moment before she continued. "Get washed up and sleep. When you wake, we'll meet with the headwoman and figure out how we are going to tackle the threat of the other Crooked hunting parties in the valley before they try to raid us again—if you are up for it?"

"Got it. Where am I sleeping?" Koda asked, wondering if he'd end up with a chunk of floor by the fireplace. Given how tired he was, he wouldn't complain. Even the bare floorboards looked comfortable.

"Bunk under mine," Sienna said, nodding towards the one she intended. "No one has been using it, so it's open. If you snore, I'll suffocate you in your sleep."

Sienna said the last part with such a mixture of amusement and earnest threat that he wasn't sure how to take it. So, instead, he headed for the bathing room she had indicated with the bucket in one hand.

It wasn't until after he finished washing the blood off himself in the dim room and was standing there naked that Koda remembered his new clothes were still sitting on the table in the other room.

Chapter Eleven

TOO TIRED TO CARE THAT NIGHT, KODA HAD JUST pulled on his boxers once more and strode out of the washing room to grab his new clothes.

Sienna was already in her bunk asleep, apparently having washed out here while he was in the other room. So he just set the bundle of his soiled clothes on a small table by the bottom bunk and crawled into bed, intent on dealing with the clean clothes when he woke the next day.

He'd fallen asleep almost as soon as his head touched the pillow.

The next thing that Koda felt was the soft sensation of someone poking him in the cheek. It came lightly at first, just a general pressure, and then a more insistent prodding.

His first instinct was to wave off whoever it was, but the question of who the heck would be poking him this early in the morning hit, and Koda's eyes snapped open. Had someone snuck into his apartment? He had made sure to get the spare key back from Rhiannon after they broke up, so it couldn't be her.

Moving on instinct, he sat bolt upright and promptly saw stars when his forehead hit something hard right above him.

"Ouch. Easy there, Koda," a familiar voice said, the faint country burr coloring it as Koda winced and rubbed at his aching head.

"Sienna?" Koda's voice was thick and gravelly from sleep, but the blow to his head had forcibly brought back his memories of the events leading up to this early morning wake-up.

"Hopefully. If not, she's going to be rather upset that I'm wearing her clothes," Sienna replied wryly.

The blurry form that stood over Koda was slowly resolving into the redheaded huntress. Her pointed red-black ears flicked from within the short mop of hair. Her tail played back and forth in a slow, amused wag while she watched him struggle to sit upright.

"What time is it?"

"Time to be awake. The sun is up, and the day has begun. You and I have a lot to get done. The sooner we get started, the better. The headwoman sent over those clothes last night with Netta, remember? You should get changed so we can head over."

Sienna continued to grin down at Koda in his spot on the narrow bunk, her tail's movement slowly picking up speed as she watched him rub at his forehead.

The rough sensation of leather on his face finally made it through the pain and confusion of his sudden wake up.

Pulling his hand back, Koda realized that he'd been rubbing his face with the hand still wearing his totemic gauntlet. Somehow, despite the sharp edges of the bone claws that tipped his fingers, he hadn't cut himself.

Thank god for that, Koda thought wryly before looking back up at Sienna.

"You gonna give me space so I can stand?"

Sienna rolled her eyes and took a step back from the bunk so he could get up.

Today, Sienna was wearing an outfit similar to the one she'd had on the previous day. A pair of dark brown close-fitting pants that tucked into sturdy leather boots in a dark brown, and a simple shirt with short sleeves in a light tan under a leather jerkin that hung to mid-thigh. The jerkin had a number of small pockets, and Koda saw the shape of a quiver poking out from behind one hip. She had cinched the whole thing in with a thick leather belt that had a pair of small pouches hanging from it, as well as a short knife strapped to her thigh.

All in all, Sienna looked quite ready for the day and very capable. Something that Koda *decidedly* did not feel or look sitting there in the bed with just the totemic gauntlet and his boxers on.

Deciding to remedy what he could of the problem, Koda sat up more carefully this time and tossed aside his blanket. Rotating, he set his feet on the floor and pushed himself upright to stretch.

Koda had half expected his muscles to feel extra stiff after the long day previous, and sleeping without a proper bath to soak in, but he felt fine. There was a bit of a crick in his back from the simple bed, but it wasn't anything to really complain about, considering what he'd done the previous day.

Sienna's reaction to his sudden surge upright was unexpected, though. She'd jumped back another few steps, her face flaming red while she yanked her gaze away from him.

She darted another look at Koda and then looked away once more. This happened several times before he glanced down at himself.

"What?" Koda asked pointedly, trying to figure out what was bothering the normally brash woman.

"You are naked!" Sienna protested, her voice pitching up a notch. Her tail was standing out straight behind her, fluffed out like a brush.

"No... if I was naked then certain bits of my anatomy would be swinging in the wind. Also, I'm pretty sure you'd be blushing more," Koda replied dryly, getting an even more furious burst of color on Sienna's tanned face. "Come on, this can't be the first time you've seen a man partially dressed?" He gestured down at his boxers meaningfully. Which, of course, dragged Sienna's gaze down to his lower half once more.

It was about then that Koda realized that, while he was comfortable standing there in just his boxers, there was a certain regular event shaping his anatomy that occurred for all men in the morning.

"Ahem... so those clothes?" Koda said after a moment, a faint blush residing on his own cheeks, but he refused to back down now that he was in this position.

Sienna pointed at a stack of clothes on the table, right where he remembered seeing them the night before.

That blow to the head must have knocked more than just the sleep out of me, Koda thought wryly and strode past Sienna to grab the clothing. She skipped back another step to give him space as he went by, acting like his skin was red hot.

"I'll meet you out front?" Koda offered to give Sienna a way out of her embarrassment.

She fled, only pausing to snatch her spear off the rack as she went by, her tail flapping behind her as she went.

It took Koda a few minutes to figure out how to get the clothing in place since it didn't use buttons or zippers like he was used to.

Thankfully, Kris had a good eye for fitting since the clothing actually sat relatively well on him.

The waist of the pants buttoned farther to the side than he was used to, and the shirt was loose on him. Most importantly, they didn't bind up when he moved. Both were in a mottled tan caused by either age and washing or intentional dyeing to break up his outline in the forest. Which it was, Koda wasn't sure.

Rolling the sleeves up as he exited the hunter's hall, Koda found Sienna waiting for him on the front steps. Her blush had abated somewhat since she had run away, but it flared for a brief moment when she caught sight of him trying to roll up his left sleeve without tearing holes in it with his claws.

"Here, let me do that," Sienna insisted in a no-nonsense tone. She immediately stepped forward, swatting lightly at the back of his gauntleted hand.

Not wanting to argue, Koda turned and let her work. Sienna's nimble fingers made quick work of the task, neatly cuffing the sleeve just above his elbow. That done, she then stepped around him to straighten the cuff on his right arm. She let her spear fall into the crook of her arm while she worked, and Koda took the opportunity to study her wolf ears at the closer proximity while she was distracted.

The furred triangles flicked and rotated slightly, each moving independently of the other, seemingly with a mind of their own. He could vaguely remember the soft sensation of her tail from the day before, and Koda couldn't help but wonder if her ears were as soft as her tail had been.

"Okay, looks at least decent for now. We should hurry to meet with the headwoman. I'm sure she's already up and waiting for us," Sienna said at last, stepping back and hefting her spear once more.

"Lead on, my lady," Koda replied with a yawn.

Through squinted eyes, Koda thought he saw a surprised look and the increased speed of Sienna's tail at his words, but by the time he finished the jaw-cracking yawn, she was once more wearing a neutral expression and gestured for him to follow her.

Did I actually see that? Koda thought, fighting back another yawn before he shrugged it off for now.

They threaded back through the streets, their path lit by the morning sun. There were several other people already out and about, mostly picking through leftover food on the tables in the square or ambling along the cobbled roads, looking like they were nursing hangovers. Anyone not haunting the bones of the previous night's party had the look of trades-people returning to their workshops to get a start on their work for the day or one of the hunters patrolling the city.

There weren't that many beds in the hunter's hall, Koda thought as they walked, trying to remember how many people he'd seen still asleep there while dressing. *I wonder how many people in fighting condition they have? I haven't seen or heard anything about a city guard, just the hunters. How tribal is this village?*

He was lost in thought, considering the implications of trying to protect these people without a standing fighting force, when Sienna led him up the steps of one of the smaller buildings off the side of the square.

The building was built mostly of wood with a stone foundation and base to the walls that was made up of river stones mortared into place. Unlike the other buildings around the square, it didn't have a shop shingle hanging out front or the large porch of what he guessed was the inn, so he assumed this had to be the headwoman's house.

That assumption was proved correct a moment later when Sienna rapped on the bottom of the door with the butt of her staff before swinging it open.

"Headwoman? It's Sienna and Koda. You said you wanted to speak with us early?"

"Yes, yes, come in! I've been going over the old maps and scrolls for most of the night to find what we are looking for. Close the door, too. I don't want the rest of the village hearing this. Those who can sleep in should," came the creaky reply from deeper inside the home.

Sienna glanced over her shoulder at Koda and gestured for him to head in with a nod while she stepped to the side just inside the doorway.

The interior of the house was much like the outside, made primarily of aged wood with stone accents where it made sense. The door opened into a large main room with a stone fireplace set into one wall.

A scattering of stools and chairs surrounded a large table on one side of the room, while a smaller collection of three chairs backed in leather with cushions sat closer to the fire. A set of doors in the back of the room, just to one side of the fireplace, led deeper into the building. It was through those doors that the headwoman emerged.

Just as he'd seen the previous day, Headwoman Kris had a look of affected frailty to her. She moved steadily, but slowly, with the help of her knobbly cane of age-blackened wood.

She wore the same long dress that she'd had on the night before and clutched a bundle of scrolls to her chest with her free hand.

"Open up a few windows, Sienna dear," the old woman ordered, nodding to them while she made for the table against the wall.

Sienna moved quickly to do so, throwing open the windows at the front of the building to let the morning light in and dispel more of the shadows in the room.

Koda moved to help the woman, but by the time he'd thought to do something, Sienna had already finished the task.

"Come on over here, young man," the older woman ordered brusquely while flapping a hand at Koda.

He hurried over to join her at the table as the older woman dumped her burden onto its top. Four large scrolls flapped loudly as they landed on the scrubbed wood of the table. Glancing up at the headwoman, Koda received a nod of approval, so he took one of them and carefully unrolled it.

Whoever had made it had actually written the scroll on some type of thin leather that crinkled quietly with age as he unrolled it. Sienna arrived a moment later with a squat brass lamp that she'd lit from the embers of the fire and set on the table as well.

"Set it out here, young man." The headwoman patted the table lightly with one wrinkled hand, so Koda did as instructed.

The bundle turned out to be a very old map, drawn on the leather in ink that had faded over time. It detailed what he guessed to be the shape of the valley they were in, with the village marked out and several rivers drawn in. A few other marks on the leather were hard to discern, but Koda studied it carefully.

"This is one of the oldest maps we have of the vale by our tribe. The other three are the same—maps of the area made over the years. Some have details that were not copied over when a new one was drafted. I think I have an idea of where the other Crooked would be congregating," the headwoman explained, smoothing the leather out with one hand before pointing at a spot along the bend of the river to the south of the valley.

"That's Last Fang Cave, right?" Sienna asked, peeking over Koda's shoulder, apparently deciding it was better to crowd him rather than the headwoman to be able to see.

"Yes. Stories tell that it was the den of a great bear in times long past. Some of the old records state that she was a guardian sent to protect us when our people fled our homes centuries ago. As far as a place of significance, that is one of three that I know of in the valley, and it is the first one that came to mind when you mentioned that they are seeking to profane sites of power." The headwoman's wrinkles deepened with a scowl as she spoke.

"What makes you so sure that they'd target it? If the bear died so long ago?" Koda asked.

"Guardian? I never heard that story," Sienna muttered from behind him, her voice confused as she focused on a different part of what Kris had said. "I just know it's part of the hunter's initiation to travel there and make an offering to the spirits."

"The answer to both your questions is the legend that surrounds the cave. The great bear was the last line of defense we had. She denned in a cave overlooking the pass that holds the primary road down into the flatlands. She was our gatekeeper while she lived. Since her passing centuries ago, the hunters have taken up that role. Her existence isn't talked about as much because, with her passing, the last physical tie we had to our... past was gone."

Koda could sense there was more to the headwoman's words, and he remembered Sienna's statement the previous night. How the headwoman had been forced to step in and do what she could to keep the stories of Thera alive. But not being a member of the priesthood, she was limited in what she was able to do.

Why is she being so cagey? Is it because she still believes me to be an outsider? Koda thought before deciding that was likely the reason.

"And the other two?" he said aloud, weighing in his mind if he should reveal the information on Thera to the woman in front of him yet. He didn't feel like Thera was pushing him one way or another currently, so he just considered the thought himself.

"The second is the old mine. There were two of them established, both mithril mines. The one above the village is still producing a trickle of ore, but the other one is over here."

The older woman's wrinkled fingers traced over the leather map to indicate a small square that Koda had missed. It was east and slightly north of the village on the other side of the vale.

"That mine hasn't produced ore for decades, if I remember the miners grumbling. Why would the Crooked think it's anything important?" Sienna was the one to speak up.

"It and the mine above the village are the entire reason our tribe was successful at inhabiting this valley. They represent the lifeblood of the village, for all that they are mostly played out. It's a long bet, though. If you are sure there are only two other war parties?" The headwoman directed the question at Koda, who nodded firmly in answer. "Then I believe the Windwalker's Retreat is the more likely target than the old mine."

The headwoman's wrinkled finger shifted farther north, up into the ridged marks of the cliffs. It circled over a section of mountains before she pulled another map from the pile and unrolled it to lie beside the other. The section she had indicated had a circle with another smaller circle inside it that she tapped.

"This stone valley has significance as well. In the past, hunters fought and killed a wendigo that came down out of the high mountains there. The land has long since reclaimed the monster's bones, but there is a monument to those who fell in the battle. It was possibly the greatest predator our people have taken since we settled in the Silverstone Vale."

The three of them regarded the maps silently for several long moments before Koda broke the silence. However, it wasn't to weigh in on the subject in front of them. Instead, it was to address a question that had bothered him since he'd first come into the village.

"Why is it that there isn't a wall around the village?" Both women turned surprised looks toward Koda, but the headwoman was the one to answer.

"Simply put, we never needed one before. We are far from the war front and have never had issues with raiders from the plains before. Complacency that we regret now. It is something I plan to rectify. Though it will be too late to help with the current threat."

"Better to resolve it for the future than ignore it at least," Koda said with a nod before looking back down at the maps.

He could feel something tugging at him, pulling him to that cave that Kris had mentioned. The same kind of tugging sensation that had guided him to the disturbing altar the previous day.

Lifting his right hand, the one wrapped in the totemic gauntlet, he felt as though someone was pulling his hand towards that lone shape on the map.

"There." His single-word answer got a curious look from both women in the room.

One clawed finger had extended to point to Last Fang Cave.

"What makes you so sure, Koda?" Sienna asked, curiosity and something else coloring her tone. Headwoman Kris glanced between them for a moment, the question obvious in her eyes.

"She wants me to go there. I can feel it," Koda answered with certainty.

"Who?" asked the headwoman.

"Thera," Koda answered, lifting his eyes from the leather map in front of him to meet the headwoman's wide eyes. "She's found a way back to you. Those she calls her children. I'm here to do what I can to help protect you for her. And it starts there."

The clawed tip of Koda's totemic gauntlet had continued to be drawn to the map as he spoke until the sharp tip of the extended finger sank into the ancient leather right over the cave drawing.

Chapter Twelve

KODA SIGHED. "I DON'T LIKE THAT THERE ARE ONLY TWO of us going."

"It makes sense, though. There are only so many hunters available." Sienna's tone told him that she agreed with him but knew there was no point in complaining. "We have to confirm the presence of Crooked so we can plan from there."

"They are at the cave."

"I know that. You know that. But you heard the headwoman. We don't have the people to do this without leaving the village stripped bare. We need to scout them while we can, then report back with what we see. While we are doing that, she's going to get as many fighters ready as possible and hopefully meet us on the route there."

The discussion had been going back and forth for the last few hours while they walked. While the vale itself wasn't huge, it still would take the better part of a day to cross the length of it due to the rougher terrain.

Koda and Sienna had set out as soon as they finished their conversation with the headwoman earlier that day.

Sienna insisted that she knew a way to the cave that would allow them to get there without risking the main road. All three of them agreed that it was entirely too likely that the Crooked had set up some kind of ambush along that road, in order to keep the village cut off in case there were any who had escaped. So they had to work around that.

Traveling overland through the vale was a lot like the pleasure hikes that Koda had taken in his free time. Lots of fresh air, trees, and interesting animal sounds.

A lot of interesting animal sounds.

Everything from strange bird calls he didn't recognize to the chirrup and buzz of various insects, then a distant whooping call that sounded like some kind of monkey that shouldn't exist in a pine forest like the one they were in.

Sienna remained quiet for the first part of the trip, clearly preoccupied. She only spoke up when Koda asked her a question or to warn him of something as they made their way overland while following a series of animal trails that wound through the forest.

When the newness of the animal calls wore off, Koda lost himself in his own thoughts.

He had a lot to think about after having to explain the entire situation to Sienna first, and then again to Kris when the headwoman demanded a more complete explanation of his earlier statement. The headwoman had actually gone as pale as a ghost and looked rather afraid when he mentioned Thera's name, but when Sienna had spoken up and backed him as well, her color had started to return.

The idea that the goddess her family had been doing their absolute best to safeguard for the last several centuries was finally returning to them gave the older cat woman a burst of life and energy that took decades off her lined face when she finally had all her questions answered.

Kris had nearly refused to let Koda leave when he explained his claim about Thera having brought him there to help them, mentioning his status as one of the ancient bloodlines. But the older woman finally caved when she realized she couldn't do anything to actually stop him.

He and Sienna only remained long enough to give Kris the basics before they had to get on their way if they stood any chance of getting to scout the Last Fang Cave before night fell. It was something that Sienna insisted on doing, as the Crooked had stories of their unpredictability, and they wanted to get a chance to scout and fall back if they could without having to fight the darkness of night.

The headwoman had insisted on supplying Koda with a few more basics for the trip while Sienna gathered her things to stay overnight in the woods, partially in thanks for his work the previous day and partially to ensure he would actually come back.

Now, Koda had on a proper woodsman's cloak in a mottled mix of green and brown. The cloak was thick enough to serve as a blanket if he needed, but it was not so heavy that it was getting in his way. He also had a belt knife, pouch, waterskin, and fire-starting materials.

"Koda." The single word from Sienna brought him out of his thoughts as they wended along the edge of a small meadow, keeping to the trees where they could.

"Yes?" Koda focused his attention on Sienna again as he'd been staring off over the gently waving grass of the meadow until she spoke.

"I didn't pry too much before, when you said that Thera sent you here to help us. I don't want to sound ungrateful for it..."

Sienna's sentence trailed off, and they walked for another ten yards or so before he tried to guess at the answer to her unfinished question.

"But why did I do it? Simple, because she asked me to and said people needed me. I've felt unwanted for most of my life. So, the idea that someone could actually have a *need* for me was intoxicating," he explained idly, ducking a branch.

"Wasn't quite where I was going." Sienna shot him a small smile over one shoulder.

He worried for a moment that he'd said something stupid, had somehow let something slip to lose the respect of the strong, attractive woman before him. But the smile and the slight wag of her fluffy tail told Koda that he was still safe.

"Then what was it? Sorry if I was putting words in your mouth with that. It was just what I had expected to hear you ask. It's the question I've asked myself a few times." Koda tried to act nonchalant as he followed her around a particularly old-looking stand of fir trees crusted with lichen and long beards of hanging moss.

Sienna hesitated again, her eyes going forward while her ears twitched a few times. Another minute passed before she finally spoke.

"Do you think we can do this?" Sienna asked at last, the uncertainty in her voice taking on an almost begging tone.

"Do what? Protect the village?" When she nodded, he continued. "Sure, I think we can do that. It's just going to be hard without a wall to defend. And we don't have time to get one built up around the village now."

"How do you do it?" Sienna asked, not looking back at him now.

"Do what?"

"Stay so focused? I'm half-mad with worry over the presence of so many Crooked in the vale. The other half of me is elated that the Beast Queen has finally returned to us and is sure we can do anything."

Sienna's voice was such a mixture of loss and hope that Koda didn't need the prompting tug from his totemic gauntlet to reach out and gently take her free hand with it. The slight pressure made Sienna jump and glance down before looking up at him shyly.

"I just focus on getting done what I can. Because the only option I have right now is to succeed," Koda said after a long moment of silence, staring over her shoulder in thought.

Sienna's head tilted curiously, and one of her ears flopped over cutely. He gestured for her to keep walking while they talked, fighting the urge to reach up and straighten her ear.

Letting out a slow breath, she released his hand and nodded. Silently, Sienna continued, glancing over her shoulder occasionally to check on him while they traveled, clearly thinking.

After walking for another few minutes, Koda started to explain more of what he had said earlier.

"I've been trying not to think about it ever since I got here, Sienna. But Thera never said anything about me being able to go back. Given the way she talked about the random chance of coming into contact with me, I have a strong feeling that this was a one-way trip. I've got to make it good here because I don't have any other option."

"Is that why you are so focused on helping us? Because you don't have a choice?" Sienna's question was in a neutral tone, but Koda could tell that the answer he gave was going to matter quite a bit to the canine-featured woman.

"I won't lie. That is part of it," Koda said carefully. "I don't want to lie to any of you, Sienna. Which is why I told you that, despite knowing it wouldn't exactly win me any points." Sienna grunted quietly but didn't interrupt him.

"When Thera asked for my help, she offered me a place to belong, and a people to call my own. I started to explain it last night, but there's more. If you knew anything about how I grew up, then you'd know why that means so much to me."

"Oh? Are you an orphan, too?" Sienna's question was quiet, but Koda had been listening to his companion intently, a survival mechanism from his work on the construction sites.

"Orphan? Were you...?" Koda couldn't help the question and winced when he realized how insensitive it might have come across to Sienna when he blurted it out.

Thankfully, the lithe woman didn't take his words badly. Instead, she just shrugged while using her spear to push aside a section of thorny bushes so she could get past.

"Bandits killed my parents when I was young. The village helped raise me, and I repay that debt with my work as a hunter, at least I had until recently." Sienna grimaced before continuing. "Several of the older hunters claim that I resemble my mother while at rest. Calm and collected. But when on a hunt, my father's intensity shines through. I honestly can barely remember them... but it is nice knowing that I have that connection, I guess?"

"I'm sorry for your loss." Koda frowned at how his words sounded like platitudes and was struggling to find a better way to empathize with Sienna when she waved him off.

"It's fine. Like I said, I don't really remember them much. I've heard stories and the like, but that's not the same. Anyway, what about you? I bared that bit of my history to you, so you can return the favor. I have a feeling you were about to before we got sidetracked."

"My parents separated when I was a lot younger. They fought a lot after that, mostly using custody of me as a means to make the other one suffer. Mom would either miss appointments to drop me off or go to the wrong place. Dad would fight back by promising me that Mom had agreed to do something with me, so I had these high expectations when I went back to her. Things like that."

"That sounds horrible. Why would two people who loved each other enough to have a child act like that?" There was pain in Sienna's voice as she asked the question, and Koda could only shrug.

"Don't know. They always claimed that they had their reasons, but I never got any of them. I walked away from it all as soon as I could. Dad had dropped me off somewhere for my Mom to pick me up, but either he got the time wrong by accident or did it intentionally to make her look bad. I took the opportunity to run away and seek emancipation." Sienna made a questioning noise, so he continued to explain. "It's a process from back home, to be considered an adult before the normal age. It's necessary to get work."

"And what kind of work did you do?"

"Whatever I could. But most recently, it was construction of all sorts. Everything from laying foundations to framing walls, hanging shectrock, or putting on roofs." Koda shrugged again as they continued to walk.

For the rest of their walk, Koda and Sienna traded stories of growing up, either lacking parents or with less-than-affectionate ones. They learned of the gaps that existed in both, and how there were flaws in both sides.

Koda learned about what it was like growing up being raised by the village as a whole, while Sienna asked dozens of questions about the various construction techniques that Koda knew while listening to different stories about the things he'd gotten up to while working on different job sites.

While they made their way along the back paths that Sienna knew, the sun continued its march through the sky. They only paused for a quick meal of dried meat and bread that they'd brought with them.

By the time they found the first evidence of the Crooked, any awkwardness had faded from their interaction, and the two were chatting like they'd known each other for years, having bonded over their fragmented childhoods.

"Learning how to hunt wasn't hard. It was figuring out how to properly process all the different kinds of animals that was the most difficult. The general parts stay the same: Don't puncture the intestine. Remove the organs and bleed it to preserve the meat. But how you remove and preserve the hide, as well as what other valuable parts of the animal there are, can vary a lot from beast to beast."

Koda nodded in understanding as they came around a ridge of stone to discover a large stain of blood on the pathway ahead of them. Shredded fur and hunks of meat were scattered amongst the blood, but not nearly enough to account for the amount of blood and disturbed earth.

Sienna was in the lead and froze as soon as she saw it. Koda had been following close behind her, and he had to act quickly to not just plow into the wolf-woman. He'd picked up the bad habit of watching her fluffy tail again as it slowly wagged back and forth. That distraction nearly had him collide with her.

The rotten scent of the meat and blood going bad washed over them a moment later, and Koda had to fight back a gag of distaste. Something more than just meat going off in the sun was at work here as the scent had a similar foul tang to it that reminded him of the noxious smoke of the Crooked camp.

"What is it?" Koda's question was spoken just above a whisper, and Sienna grimaced, taking a few steps closer while scanning the surrounding trees for threats.

"Not sure... Right fur color for a bear, but the leg bones are too small. I think it was a cub," she answered a moment later. "I don't see the skull or head around here anywhere, and nothing has been at the meat..."

"You remember that... thing that was in the altar, right?" Koda didn't want to remember it himself, but the memory was floating back to the surface of his mind, regardless.

A tiny body, formed of the twisted and gnarled bones of small animals in a grim parody of a baby but with the fleshless skull of a deer instead.

It had laid inside the metal bowl of the altar they had encountered before like it was sleeping, and Koda hadn't waited to see if the thing would react. He'd just smashed it along with the altar.

Something deep inside his chest had told him that, whatever it was, the thing was unnatural and wrong.

Sienna took a slow step back from the ruined carcass, her forehead wrinkling as she lowered her spear from her shoulder and held it ready in front of her. The action ended with her left shoulder pressing back into Koda's chest slowly. She obviously sought a bit of comfort in his touch but was unwilling to turn her eyes away from potential threats.

"Maybe," she said slowly. "Maybe something like that. We are close enough to the Last Fang Cave that it's possible... Other animals don't kill like this. This was messy, and just for the sake of the kill, not for the meat. Any natural creature hunts others to survive only, not for sport. Animals that hunt other animals for sport are sick, and we cull them whenever they are found."

"Odds that this was one of those animals?"

"Nearly nothing. I don't see any tracks other than bear and" —Sienna paused for a moment and stared down at the bloodstain—"there's more blood here than one cub would have. I'd put good money on the Crooked having tracked down and killed a mother *and* her cub. They likely dragged the mother's body back for meat after toying with the bear cub. Why not take both bodies back for food? I don't know..." Her voice trailed off as she continued to stare.

"Better to get off the trail then, make it a little harder to be spotted?" Koda suggested quietly. He'd been picking up bits and pieces from Sienna all day during their talks while they traveled, but he didn't need that knowledge at the moment.

His instincts screamed at him to get off the trail.

"Yes, off the trail and into the trees. We can parallel it for a while, but we should come up on a ridge in a bit that will overlook the pass. That will let us look in on where the cave is located," Sienna said without hesitation. "We need to get a feel for the numbers there. Then we can return to the village to make the report and meet up with Headwoman Kris and the hunters she's bringing." The reminder of their mission seemed to calm the woman.

Moving carefully, the two stepped into the brush and away from the game trail, all their senses tuned to high alert with the threat of Crooked once more hanging heavy in the air.

Chapter Thirteen

THE NEXT SIGN THEY FOUND OF THE CROOKED WAS JUST as ominous, but not as obvious as the corpse and bloodstains had been.

Less than ten minutes after they had left that first mess behind, Sienna spotted the twisted form of a rabbit that had been crucified against a tree.

Just beyond the rabbit, another dozen feet down the trail, hung what Koda could only describe as a macabre wind-chime created from the bones and sinews of animals, still fresh enough to glimmer with moisture from the blood and bodily fluids.

The closer that they got to the cave, the more of these strange fetishes and decorations were found hanging in the trees.

Dozens of them, some as small as Koda's outstretched palm and made of a few rabbit bones, then others large enough that they would have qualified in the 'world's grossest hula-hoop' competition. With each of them that passed, the more disgusted Koda got.

"What is the point of these?" he asked as quietly as he could while they passed another tree that had a squirrel nailed to it at the center of another strange array of bones.

"Territory markers," Sienna suggested. "Or some kind of dark magic ritual. We saw nothing like this in the area near the standing stones, but they hadn't spent long there. Maybe a day or so? This group might have spent a few days here... or maybe the raiding force that attacked the village camped here with them for a bit and helped establish this? We have to be quiet, though. No idea how many of their hunters are lurking in the forest."

Koda wanted to ask more, but he remembered just how many patrols they had picked off the previous day while dealing with the Crooked. He had no idea how big the group they were about to run into was, so it would be far better to be tactful and quiet.

That decision proved to be valuable as a brief flash of movement from the nearby pathway caught Sienna's eye. Since Koda was paying close attention to his companion, he saw her reaction and mirrored it as well. The stilling of her pointed ears and the slow easing into a crouch was all the warning that Koda needed, having seen this reaction before while they stalked sentries.

A trio of the twisted Crooked stumbled along the game trail just a few feet away from them. Two of them carried short spears that were so bent they looked more like bows. The bloody iron tips on the shafts showed exactly what they were and their deadly effectiveness. The third had a strange-looking bow that was even more gnarled than the spears were, the top half forking into two points and actually holding a pair of strings that ran to either side of the bow-staff.

Are the arrows even straight? I don't know how they make do with such bizarre weapons, but still... aerodynamics is a thing, right? Koda thought as he waited next to Sienna while the trio walked past.

Squatting down like he was, Koda was suddenly even more appreciative of the woodsman cloak that Kris had given him when they left the headwoman's house. Between the cloak and the earth-tone clothes, he was blending in fairly well, and the mottled pattern did wonders for obscuring his outline. Just how much the trio of Crooked stood out against their surroundings reinforced his desire to blend in.

The one with the bow slowed down for a moment, saying something in a guttural, phlegmy tone that made Koda think of the sort of voice someone might expect out of a clogged drain.

He couldn't make out what they were saying, but he thought he could understand a few of the words that were being spoken. Though none of them made sense in the context.

The trio laughed, and one of the spear wielders moved ahead of the bowman with a limping, rolling stride that made Koda wince as he imagined the pain it should be causing to the creature's hips.

However, the spearman didn't flinch or grumble. The group continued down the path with one spearman in the lead and one in the rear, now with the bowman standing in the center.

Leaning slowly closer to Sienna, Koda let his weight rest against her back just as she had leaned into him before. She did not react other than to slowly turn one ear around to point towards him.

"We should take them out," Koda whispered into that fuzzy, red-black triangle.

He immediately felt something stir against his leg, and he had to fight the urge to jump. A glance downwards revealed it to be Sienna's tail slowly beginning to wag.

"Why?" Sienna's question was barely a breath in volume, and there was not an ounce of judgment in her words, just curiosity.

"Every one of them we take out now is one less to deal with later, and maybe a life saved on our side," Koda muttered back into her ear. "Also, less damage they can do in the meantime."

Sienna nodded slowly after only a second of thought and gestured with her spear for him to lead the way back to the trail.

Koda glanced around and spotted a section they could get through the low-growth underbrush without making too much noise and gestured to that.

"Good call," Sienna's words came to him as he led the two of them forward. He shot her a questioning look, and she elaborated more. "The cave is maybe another five or ten minutes' walk that way. We have to be very quiet and quick to ensure they do not raise the alarm."

"I'll hit them first and try to take one down while stunning the other. Do you want to hit them from the front or back?"

"Front, I have reach, so it's better to let you sneak in." Sienna's tail flicked, clearly happy with his plan. She winked at him before stepping away from him and vanishing behind a tree.

Koda stopped and looked back. If he strained his eyes, he was fairly certain that he could catch bits of movement that had to be Sienna around branches and bushes. Once he caught the red-black flash of her tail as she crossed through an errant beam of sunlight. But it was there and gone so fast he would have missed it if he wasn't looking.

"Damn, she's good." Koda couldn't help the respect and admiration in his voice.

Work on it, and you can get that good. Going to have to if you are going to survive, Koda reminded himself. *Talking with Sienna was good. It helped center me and remind me why I stepped through. Family and a people of my own again. I need to be better to earn them.*

A warmth welled in his chest at the idea of calling Sienna family. He took just a moment to reminisce over the muscled curve of the wolf-woman's bottom, as well as her teasing glances combined with her gentle smiles that had become more and more common as they traveled through the day.

For all the strangeness of the ears and tail, Sienna was as attractive as hell to him, between her fit and full body and her cute face. That was all before he added her amusing banter and quick wit to the mix.

Shaking his head, Koda focused on what he needed to do now. They would have to work quickly to deal with the trio of Crooked, then drag them off the trail and hide them. He had to protect his new home.

Glancing down at his clawed totemic gauntlet, Koda grimaced at the memory of how bloody a weapon it was. He could appreciate the fact that wounds caused by this weapon would look like an animal attack, though.

Something to keep in mind. We need to disguise what killed them, in case the bodies are found before we get back to this place with the other hunters.

Moving alongside the trail rather than on it was a bit harder, but thankfully, the Crooked weren't marching with any determined speed.

Koda was able to get caught up to them without too much trouble. He paced them for a minute or two to ensure Sienna was in place to make her attack before he started the encounter off.

Wish we'd come up with something to signal with before I started the fight, Koda thought as he crept closer to the three Crooked from behind.

As he was thinking this, Koda saw a brief flash of movement ahead, before a quiet *crunch* of something shifting in the brush on the left side of the trail brought all three Crooked to a stop.

Shit, did Sienna go on the other side of the trail? Did they hear her?

Koda's heart leaped into his throat, and he was up and moving as the leader of the trio stepped off the trail, his head weaving on a bent neck to try to see whatever it was that had made the noise.

Moving with steady steps, Koda slid onto the trail behind the group and hurried forward, keeping low and bringing his arms out wide to either side. The archer said something in its burbling, phlegmy voice as he approached, and that covered any missteps or noise that he made.

Sliding into place behind the rearmost of the spear-wielders, who was intently peering off the trail with its companions, Koda brought his left arm around and caught a handful of the greasy mop of hair on the man's head. He used that grip to crank the Crooked's head back before slashing across its throat with the clawed fingers of his right hand.

His captured victim thrashed, dropping the bent spear on the ground and flailing wildly at Koda to get free. The scrape of the claws on the bones of his enemy's throat told Koda that the effort would be useless, though. A gushing shower of blood filled the air around the archer.

As the archer whirled in response to the warm shower that it had gotten of its companion's blood, Koda spun and threw the dying Crooked into the bushes while bringing one booted foot up and around to drive into the archer.

His aim was off, sadly. Rather than catch the Crooked archer in the chest or the head, the steel toe of Koda's boot slammed into the creature's forearm. The blow still broke the bone there with a dry *snap* and sent the creature's weapon flying into the brush.

As he continued to spin, Koda saw the unwounded spear-wielder turning to address the threat. Eyes clouded with cataracts widened in surprise at seeing him, then Koda lost track of the Crooked in his turn.

By the time he brought himself back around and lunged at the archer, Sienna had already emerged from the bushes on the right of the trail.

The red-black-furred wolf woman's face was twisted in a fierce snarl as she intercepted the Crooked with the spear, deftly batting the weapon to the side with the flat of the blade before driving her spear's broad blade into her enemy's chest.

The motion continued as she twisted to lock the blade in place and heaved to toss the Crooked to the ground in a heap while still pinned on the end of her spear, the long lever of the spear's haft aiding the maneuver.

Knowing he needed to move fast as the Crooked archer was already beginning to yell in pain, Koda lunged forward and tackled the archer to the ground, driving the wind out of its lungs in a whoosh.

Koda heard several ribs break as he landed on top of the twisted man. He immediately balled his right hand into a fist and drove it into the throat of the Crooked, forgetting the claws on the gauntlet for a moment as he rushed to silence the archer before he could call out.

The man under him had a severely misshapen face. His right eye bulged easily twice as large as his left, and the left side of his head was dented inwards like someone had taken a large melon-baller to his skull.

Despite the skinniness of the Crooked man's arms, they held a surprising amount of strength as he flailed at Koda while gagging and gasping for breath. The blows slammed into his arms and head, sending stars through Koda's vision, but he held on.

Bucking under him, the Crooked tried first to throw Koda off but only succeeded in making him miss with the second punch and connect with the ground instead. The third punch slammed into the jaw of the Crooked with a dry *snap* noise before the man went limp under him, his jaw hanging disconnected and twisted to match with the unnatural angle that his head was sitting at. His third blow had apparently also broken the creature's neck.

Koda leaned back slightly, his heart racing as he looked to check on Sienna just in time to lurch backwards as the tip of Sienna's spear slammed down in front of him and through the throat of the already dead Crooked under him.

"Better to be sure," Sienna hissed in response to the questioning look that he shot her.

Nodding, Koda pushed himself to his feet once more and went to check on the one whose throat he'd slashed earlier.

That Crooked was dead now, too, but had made quite a mess of the undergrowth near him with the arterial spray and his flailing. Grimacing, Koda considered how best to conceal the evidence of the attack.

"Drag them out of sight," Sienna muttered as she yanked the blade of her spear out of the dead abomination, gesturing towards the two Koda had taken down before hopping over to follow the same instructions with the one she'd speared initially.

Nodding in understanding, Koda set to work.

Despite the fact the Crooked had the bodies of fully grown men, Koda did not struggle as he hauled them about. He wasn't sure if it was the improved strength that Thera's blessing had given him or just that the Crooked did not weigh what a normal creature would.

It only took him a minute to pull his pair deeper into the woods and stash them behind a low log out of sight of the trail. Far enough away that, from the trail, the bodies wouldn't be easily spotted, and the scent of the death hopefully wouldn't carry until after they had dealt with the camp.

Returning to the game trail, Koda found Sienna using a leafy branch to brush at the disturbed dirt of the path. The motion helped to wipe away much of the tracks and evidence of the attack. There wasn't much that they could do about the blood on the ground and surrounding bushes, though. But, while Sienna brushed, Koda did his best to kick loose dirt over the blood to at least obscure it.

"That's good enough," Sienna said after a minute. "We can't get every sign. We aren't set up to kill them cleanly enough to do that. So, we need to quickly scout the camp, and then hurry back to meet up with the others." She tossed the broken branch into the forest on the other side of the path to further spread out the evidence before turning to look back at Koda and give him a once over.

"Everything okay?" he asked, looking down at himself.

"Just a bit surprised you avoided getting blood on yourself this time. You made it look like it was the goal to be as intimidating as possible yesterday," Sienna quipped with a small smile.

Koda returned the smile and quick examination before nodding. Sienna had succeeded in avoiding blood as well, but her weapon allowed for a lot more range in her engagements. That had worked to help keep her safe from sprays and the like.

He was briefly disappointed by the fact Sienna didn't have even a bit of blood on her that would have given him an excuse to help her clean it off.

Seriously! Focus, damn it, Koda chastised himself silently. *You can worry about flirting with the pretty lady later. Is it fucked up that you are thinking about flirting right now just minutes after killing and disposing of two... people?*

The jarring consideration about whether the Crooked were really people was enough to keep Koda from spiraling as Sienna led him off trail and back the way they had come.

This time, they kept farther from the game trail and circled a bit more to the east to get a higher vantage point as they approached the camp.

When the two of them crested the last hill, Sienna gestured for him to keep low while creeping up to the edge. Koda did exactly that while taking in the view in front of him, keeping as close to his companion as he could without stepping on her.

Ahead of him, Koda saw the main road that wound down between the trees before vanishing through a small divide in the ridgeline. He figured it would continue on the other side, just rolling downwards from there. But what he focused on lay beyond.

A vast, rolling plain disappeared off into the distance. If he squinted, Koda could pick up a thin ribbon that was either the road or a river splitting the distant green fields. The ribbon eventually met up with a larger smudge some distance off that he bet was another town or village nearby.

Dotting the vast plain in front of him were small copses of green trees, but the rest of the vast expanse was nothing but rolling grass in a blue-green color that danced under the caress of a distant breeze that made it ripple like a wind-tossed sea.

Koda thought he could see the distant shadow of another range of mountains on the edge of the horizon, but it was hard to say given the distances and height that he was looking at.

A gentle elbow in his gut drew his attention back from the horizon, and Koda glanced down to see Sienna pointing off to his right.

Following that pointing arm, he traced the bare, stony ridge along until he found an open meadow about half a mile away. To one side of the meadow was a sheer cliff face that rose up another thousand or more feet into a ragged peak.

Set into that cliff was a wide cave mouth overlooking the meadow and the pass. The stone walls on either side of the cave mouth had a rough texture to them that looked as if someone had taken a cheese-grater to both sides and run it up and down the mountain face, leaving behind grooves and trenches in the stone.

What was more concerning was the campsite that sat in the meadow under the cave. A dozen tents clumped up just before the cave, with one larger one towards the center of the bunch.

Around them, the entire meadow had been churned up. The scars left behind by other tents were also obvious in the grass and torn earth. As were the patches of scorched ground that had been used for campfires.

"Looks like our guess was right. They must have come here first, then the other groups either broke off—or at least the one that hit the village did," Sienna murmured, not moving from her position directly in front of Koda. She actually shifted slightly to lean back into him while they studied the camp, repeating her previous pose of tucking into his chest from the front.

"Not seeing a lot of movement, though." Koda shifted just slightly to help support Sienna's weight. For all her muscled form, she didn't feel like more than a gentle pressure, though Koda had a feeling Sienna was putting a good chunk of her weight into him at the moment.

"Makes me worry. Are they all out hunting? How many are left behind?"

"Possible, but I doubt it. In the other camp, they had a bunch of them loitering around, even after the attack on the village. Still not sure why they weren't more on guard, especially after being pushed back from the village. I want to believe they thought that their camp was too big to be attacked, but we proved that handily wrong."

"Yeah... they still can't have been here long. The vale is large, but not so large that the hunters would have missed a camp like this or the other for long. Wait, I think I see something... up by the cave." Sienna used the tip of her spear to indicate the direction, and Koda squinted to look.

Right at the mouth of the cave, he saw a bit of back-and-forth movement like something trying to crawl out of the cave. While he watched, Koda swore that he saw the darkness in the mouth of the cave boil slightly like the shadows were made of a liquid that had something shifting just under the surface.

A sharp tugging at his right hand nearly yanked him off balance when the totemic gauntlet reacted. Worry raced up his spine as the tugging continued and rose in strength. He swore he felt a hand crushing his and yanking him forward.

Something was going on in that cave, and Thera wanted him to move, now.

"We need to get closer and see what is going on insid—" Koda started to say when the pulling on his arm turned into a full-on jerk. The motion pulled him off balance to send him to the ground in a heap, knocking over Sienna in the process.

"Are you okay?" Sienna hissed after landing on her rump. She'd initially turned to glare at him but found Koda in such an odd pose that her anger turned to confusion.

"Thera is telling me we need to move. Like... *now*." Koda grimaced, pushing himself up onto his hands and knees while the yanking on his arm fought the motion and nearly dragged him forward.

Sienna started to argue, but a deep, bellowing roar echoed out across the meadow.

A roar of pain that made both their blood freeze.

A roar that came from the cave.

Chapter Fourteen

KODA WAS ALREADY MOVING ALONG THE RIDGE TOWARDS the cave as the echoes of the roar faded away. Sienna was right behind him, spear held at the ready.

He wanted to charge down the hill and through the camp to get to the cave, but he still hesitated, not sure if there were any other threats lurking there that might catch them in a pincer movement.

"Koda," Sienna's panting word pulled his attention back to her.

He glanced over his shoulder to find her lagging behind him, not able to keep up with the headlong charge he was making through the trees.

How? The thought ran through Koda's mind. *She's the hunter. I'm just some guy who worked construction who has a magic glove?*

"My champion, you must hurry," Thera's voice curled around him, carried on the wind. Even Sienna heard it. Koda could tell because she scowled and redoubled her pace into a dead run to catch up with Koda while he hesitated.

"What was that, Thera?" Koda demanded, beginning to slow so Sienna could catch up.

"They are committing blasphemy most foul. Please, Koda? Stop them. Do not let them take her spirit. I can't lose another one!" Thera's voice wove in and out like she was speaking through a tunnel that distorted her words.

"Go, Koda!" Sienna called as she closed with him. "I'll catch up. Just go. If the Beast Queen needs us to intercede, then we must!"

Koda glanced at his companion, taking in the beauty of her wind-blown red hair and the fluffy banner that was her long tail behind her. The close-fitting clothes hugged her firm body, while determination glimmered in her crystalline, blue-green eyes even as the late afternoon sun glinted on the broad blade of her spear where she carried it low to her side.

He absorbed the fierce beauty of his companion and her determination for a pair of heartbeats. Koda let it buoy up his heart before he spun on his heel and charged full tilt towards the cave.

They had been cutting around the edge of the tree line to keep away from the camp and avoid detection. But, with Sienna and Thera's urging, Koda threw caution to the wind and charged fully towards the cave mouth, forsaking the tree line and shelter for speed.

The route he took brought him out into the open ground along the camp. The open ground made it even easier for him to travel. Now that he was aware of it, Koda realized that each of his leaping strides was covering far more ground than it should. He flashed past the tents and a still-smoldering cooking fire in three long steps.

A tent flap opened, and something stuck its head out. Koda

was moving too fast to tell what it was, so he reacted on instinct.

Lashing out with his gauntlet, Koda raked the clawed finger-tips over the Crooked before the enemy warrior even noticed him. The blow knocked the bent man back onto his ass into the tent as blood flew through the air.

Not slowing, Koda pounded up the slope to the cave mouth where it narrowed at one side.

Halfway up, he saw a trio of the Crooked emerge from the cave with weapons held ready and shouting in their garbled language. He'd been spotted in his charge. Koda did not hesitate as his blood pounded in his ears now.

Distantly, he could hear more voices speaking, shouting, chanting, and screaming. But as he drew even with the mouth of the cave to confront them, he finally caught sight of what lay beyond.

The cave was deep and wide, easily about forty or more feet across and at least twice that deep. Now that he was closer, Koda realized that the abrasions on the walls were actually deep grooves, resembling claw marks created by something massive sharpening its natural weapons on the stone, or perhaps using them to excavate the cave.

Below him, the floor of the cave sloped slightly to one side, where a shallow stream trickled from a fissure in the back wall and ran across the cave before vanishing into another fissure in the stone. Opposite the stream was a bowl-shaped depression that looked like a massive bed—and likely had been at one time. Ancient bones sat piled in the hollow of the 'bed' space, with a large ribcage being chief amongst them, rising up to provide a bony roof to a profane ritual.

Nearly two dozen Crooked stood watching while four of

their number were holding a fifth down on top of a furry mound while it screamed hollowly.

A small bear's skull had been jammed down on top of the pinned Crooked's head, and blood ran from beneath it to show that it had been forced to fit there. On either side of the group were two more Crooked, one to each side, and they were even more bent than their companions.

The one on the right wore a long robe of stained green cloth in the same murky pattern that made it look like mildew had eaten away at the cloth and the dyes. Its long arms ended in a pair of hands on each wrist, and these hands were gesturing and drawing symbols in the air over the pinned Crooked while the chanting continued from within a deep hood. Each word sounded like something you would hear from a tortured feline rather than a human mouth.

Beside the robed one stood another of the hulking, brutish Crooked like Koda had fought and slain the previous day. Koda guessed this was another champion from its gnarled stature and over-muscled limbs.

A trio of thick legs protruded from the creature's stumpy torso, while only his right arm was the same muscle-bound mass as Koda had seen the previous champion wield. The left arm hung shriveled and close to its chest. The monster clutched a dagger in that weaker arm while the larger one had an iron-banded club.

As Koda continued his charge towards the group, he saw the great bones glow a dull, pearly white. Fragments of that glow began to detach from the bones to drift towards the pinned Crooked.

This brought another ursine roar of pain that echoed from nowhere and everywhere at once. The roar was followed pathetically by the unhappy squeals of the Crooked man who was receiving the glowing fragments in the middle of the ritual circle.

Not pausing to watch further, his disgust and fury boiling over, Koda lunged at the trio between him and the horde of Crooked surrounding the ritual.

The three carried the same style of gnarled and bent spears that he'd already dealt with. So when the closest thrust one at him, rheumy eyes rolling while his misplaced mouth snarled from its spot high on his right cheek, Koda spun into the thrust.

Using his unarmored left hand, Koda caught the spear behind its head and yanked hard, even as he brought his right around in a backhand that put all of his bodyweight behind the blow.

A wet *crunch* of shattering bones echoed as the blow lifted the first Crooked off his feet to toss him into his nearest companion, knocking both to the ground.

Koda still had hold of the spear in his left hand. The guidance coming from Thera through his totemic gauntlet had him continuing the turn fully through.

He let the shaft slide through his fingers until he gripped it halfway down. Using the length of bent wood like a crude sword, he slammed it into the elbow of the third Crooked as that one swayed back to try to stab at him.

The blow threw the lone standing Crooked off balance, causing it to drop its spear with a yelp of pain. Lunging forward, Koda drove his stolen spear into that Crooked's chest before kicking it in the lower stomach.

Again, his increased strength surprised him, and Koda sent the monster into a tumbling roll down the slight slope into the cave when he'd just been aiming to knock it down.

Not wanting to leave a threat behind him, Koda stomped down on the uninjured Crooked, who remained pinned under its fellow guard's body.

The blow broke even more bones in the duo. Koda wasn't sure who got the worst of it, but he was more focused on the fact that the eyes of all the Crooked were on him now. So he wound up and booted the ensnared duo into a tumbling roll down the hill towards the crowd.

"Hunt him down and make him cry, twist and break him while alive. Slain he has, those of ours, replace he will, born from his scars!"

The voice that spoke out over the squealing, roaring, and rumbling of the crowd cut through it like a rusty knife. It creaked and burbled. It warbled and crowed all at once as the robed figure gestured with both right hands towards Koda.

Instinct told him to duck, and he did not hesitate as a sickly yellow fog billowed out of the creature's sleeve before forming into a whip that lashed the air directly over where Koda fell.

The rising threat was obvious as the other Crooked in the room all howled and lunged to their feet to race towards him. Even the hunched champion lumbered forward from his position by the robed one, grinning maniacally from a mouth that looked like a dentist's worst nightmare combined with a bear-trap left to rust.

Glancing around, Koda searched for options to help even the playing field even as he got to his feet.

He'd succeeded the previous day because he was able to narrow the group that was attacking him down to a single file line, or two at most. The mouth of the cave was too open though and would allow the enemy to encircle him. But this was also the only high ground, and he was loath to give it up.

To buy time, Koda dug a cantaloupe-sized rock from the earth with his gauntleted right hand. He lobbed that at the front-runner of the group in an overhand throw.

The Crooked he had aimed at, a bent older woman in a patched dress and wielding a rusty hatchet with malicious glee, dodged to one side.

The stone whistled past her, missing his target entirely. Instead it crashed into the man just behind her with a solid *thunk* that sent the man screaming backwards to tangle the legs of the others charging up the slope.

Sparing a glance, Koda noted the approach of the champion. The enormous monster was covering the ground with great leaps that were assisted by its trio of legs and the sole muscular arm it had, moving like a misshapen gorilla. It charged in a fashion that was as equally dismissive of its fellows as Koda remembered from the last champion he'd fought.

A plan began to form in his mind, and Koda smiled grimly.

Koda still had the spear in his off-hand, so he swapped it over to his right and threw it as hard as he could at the charging swarm of Crooked.

He didn't wait to see if the bent spear flew true. He just kicked out with his boot to swipe dust, grit, and gravel into the air and obscure the vision of his attackers while taunting them verbally.

"Come on, you ugly bastards! Every one of you has faces only a mother could love, and even then I would doubt her sincerity!" Koda shouted before turning tail and running back down the slope out of the cave and towards the camp.

He spotted Sienna coming up the slope and made a swiping gesture towards the bushes. Sienna immediately nodded and dove out of sight, vanishing into the undergrowth along the trees like she had never been there.

The redheaded huntress had made it most of the way to him, so she was only about a dozen yards shy of the cave mouth and hidden from sight. He just had to pull them away from the cave and Sienna's hiding spot. Then she could either hit the group from behind or go and disrupt the ritual herself.

"Come on, you lot! You'd think a dozen of you and a champion would be enough to catch one man!" Koda shouted, hoping that Sienna would hear his warning and stay hidden. He charged into the clustered tents and dove down one of the oddly canted rows in a rush.

The swarm of Crooked behind him followed, baying like hounds as they chased him into their camp. The champion actually plowed right over top of two of its fellows while batting a third aside with its club. A tongue that had to be two feet long flapped from its rusty-bear-trap mouth as it panted in glee.

"Catch and take, scars make ours!" chanted the grotesque creature, its voice high pitched and chaotic like that of a child.

The difference in its build and the sound of its voice was enough that Koda actually tripped over one of the tent stakes in surprise when he snapped his head back to look at the creature.

This lucky stumble actually saved his life. Another Crooked, one who had been hiding amongst the tents apparently, lunged through the air above him with a wavy-bladed dagger clutched in one hand. The enemy landed in a heap to one side of him when it missed.

A maelstrom of noise, crunching wood, tearing fabric, and snapping rope heralded the trampling arrival of the swarm and the champion with them barely two dozen feet back.

Rolling to his feet, Koda quickly stomped on the weapon-wielding hand of the Crooked who had tried to tackle him with a crunch like he'd just stomped a bag of chips flat. He snatched the dagger from its broken fingers before ducking into the tents once more while the creature screeched in pain.

He made a beeline for the larger tent at the center of the camp, all while slashing tent ropes and sides to stir up as much chaos in his wake as possible.

A high-pitched bellow of anger, like an enraged toddler screeching into a megaphone, was enough to warn Koda to dodge. A thrown missile whistled past him to slam into the lane ahead of him. The fact that the missile itself was screaming as it flew was disturbing enough, but the brittle cracking noise of its impact with the ground when it missed made his gut turn over.

The champion had literally picked up and thrown one of its allies at him.

Guess my gamble on the champion not having much regard for its fellow monsters paid off, Koda thought with a wicked grin as he ducked into the larger tent and out of sight.

Just like before, at the standing stones, the central tent was a mottled patchwork of canvas and rope, with the interior being a maze of those taut strands holding it up, the guylines for the tent *inside* for some reason.

Unlike the previous camp, though, this one didn't sit on a group of standing stones, and there was no altar here.

Instead, there was a large table with the remains of a meal on it that made his stomach turn. Half a dozen large beds and just as many twisted chairs made of warped wood planks sat around a central fire pit that still held a small fire that billowed with sickly blue smoke.

Moving as quickly as he could through the maze of ropes, Koda slashed out with both hands to cut them while shoving at the supporting poles to upset those as well. His pursuers hit the side of the tent just as he got to the center, this time with the champion in the lead.

A whistling noise warned Koda to dodge again, throwing himself into a sideways roll to avoid the spinning length of the iron-bound club as it smashed through the support poles to crash into a bed on the far side of the tent, reducing it to kindling.

The thrown club had taken out far more of the support poles than Koda had been able to, and it triggered what he had been hoping for: the collapse of the tent.

His rolling escape had put him close enough to the edge of the tent that Koda could scramble to the side, slit the rotten canvas, and escape as the roof fell in to ensnare the Crooked champion and his companions.

Keeping his head down, Koda scurried down another row of tents, this time not cutting the ropes and the like to prevent being tracked easily.

He'd broken contact. Now, he had to flank his opponents. Koda needed to meet back up with Sienna. The two of them working together would stand a far better chance, and if they could use the cave mouth, they might survive this. Especially since Thera had pushed them into attacking the entire camp by themselves.

She has to have a good reason, Koda reminded himself. *She wouldn't have risked this if she didn't. I've gotta get back to Sienna.*

A female yelp of pain followed by another ursine roar of anguish echoed from the cave mouth. Koda's hurried jog turned into a full-on sprint for the cave mouth. Any attempt at being subtle and concealing his escape from the main tent went up in smoke as he recognized Sienna's cry of pain.

He passed three Crooked who were emerging from their own tents in that charge.

Koda didn't stop his headlong dash, lashing out with his totemic gauntlet to open bellies, slash faces, and sunder throats as he went by. Blood flew and bones shattered, but he did not pause to check on them.

He thought he heard the crackle of fire behind him, but at the moment, Koda's entire attention was on that cave mouth.

He could feel Thera urging him on to greater speed as he flew up the slope. And, oddly enough, he thought he could feel Sienna's weight against him again. The memory of their brief moment pressing into each other while surveying the camp returned to him.

Cresting the rise and entering the cave mouth, Koda charged down the other side while taking in what he could see.

His initial attack had served its purpose of drawing off the bulk of the Crooked forces. Only the robed Crooked with the many hands, his four helpers, and their pseudo-victim remained. Of those four helpers, two were dead while the other two approached Sienna with empty hands.

The previously screaming Crooked remained sprawled on the furry lump that it had been lying on earlier, but its body bulged and shifted like someone playing with a balloon animal and making different parts shrink to make others grow.

He didn't spare it more than a glance, though. Sienna took up most of his focus.

She lay sprawled on her back in the dust near the two dead Crooked, twitching and flailing as the grimy yellow whip of light had her by the foot. That whip was slowly dragging her prone form towards the robed Crooked. And Sienna thrashed like she was being actively electrocuted.

"Hey, ugly! Hands off!" Koda screamed as he continued down the slope into the cave at a full charge. Clumsily, he switched his grip on the wavy-bladed knife and threw it at the robed Crooked as hard as he could.

Unlike fighting with the gauntlet, his body, or the massive cleaver the previous day, the throw felt extremely awkward. Either that dagger had never been intended for throwing, or throwing ripple-bladed daggers was not part of the knowledge that Thera had given him.

Regardless, the dagger spun through the air and, while it missed the caster to fall short, it did slam hilt first into the chest of the prone Crooked with enough force to break a few bones—if the cracking noise was any indication.

The blow had enough force to roll the ballooning Crooked off the fuzzy object that it had been lying on, revealing what it was.

The body of a large brown bear lay folded and arranged like some sick sort of table. Blood matted its fur and wept from open wounds on it, but the bear grunted in response to the change in weight on it.

Is it still alive? Gods, is that the mother of the dead cub we found?

174

The thought galvanized Koda further as his charge got him to the edge of the ritual circle. He ducked down before leaping over top of the sick, living altar and tackling the robed Crooked to the ground with a roar of fury all his own.

Being football-tackled obviously distracted the caster enough that the unnatural lightning-whip failed, and Sienna's thrashing stopped at last. Which was Koda's entire goal at the moment.

The two remaining assistants glanced back at him, the five eyes between the two of them going wide before they reversed course and hurried back to help their robed leader.

Koda rode the caster to the ground and lashed out with the clawed fingers of his gauntlet to drive them into its throat. A heavy blow caught him in the side of the head before his attack could land and threw him off as the caster's elbow got him in the temple.

"Hands you lay on me and mine, first I will break and mend in great time. You will pay for this mistake, from your bones the meat we will rake!" shrieked the caster, the sickening voice and its bizarre rhyming cadence making Koda's stomach actively roll as it washed over him.

Still prone, the caster launched a fork of the yellow lightning at Koda, and his head swam too much from the elbow he'd taken to the temple to escape it this time.

The coiling bolt connected with his left leg and sent rippling waves of pain through Koda's body. Every joint in him locked up, while his muscles did their absolute best to flail in protest as the electricity tried to get them to dance the electric slide.

The two unarmed Crooked loomed over Koda for what felt like a moment and an eternity. They grinned evilly down at him, one reaching for his throat while the other hooked rotten fingernails into his shirt to yank it off. The two hissed something that he couldn't understand through the pain and language barrier.

Abruptly, that pain stopped without warning, and Koda could think clearly.

Rage filled him as he imagined that this was the pain that Sienna had felt only moments ago.

Lashing out with his right hand, he raked his clawed fingers up through the guts of the one going for his neck, while he brought his left fist crashing into the jaw of the one trying to rip his shirt off.

A flurry of blood sprayed into the air while a dual-toned scream of pain echoed through the cave. Both of the Crooked standing over him froze for a heart-stopping moment.

Where is that scream coming from? Koda wondered even as he brought his clawed gauntlet around to smash the off-balance Crooked aside with another fierce punch while shoving the other away from him.

As the two enemies tumbled to either side, one with a broken jaw and the other with his guts exposed to the world, Koda stared in astonishment at what he saw.

The Crooked spellcaster lay pinned, buried under the furry bulk of the mother bear that had been serving as his altar moments before.

The bear had apparently rallied the last of its strength and simply tackled the Crooked in the robes, burying him under its not inconsiderable frame while growling faintly.

As he watched, Sienna limped over, using her spear as a crutch. She swayed for a moment when she lifted the weapon up, and then she chopped downward with the blade like she was splitting wood.

A hollow *thunk* noise and a wheezing gasp was enough to convince Koda that the caster was now dead, and he felt relief flood through him.

That relief was tested a bare second later when a massive ursine bellow rocked the cave.

It invigorated Koda, washing away the pain of the electrical damage and giving him fresh conviction and motivation. Sienna even straightened, shifting from leaning heavily on the haft of her spear to gripping it properly and limping over to help him upright.

Together, the two of them ensured the last of the Crooked in the cave were dead. The most disturbing was not actually the caster, its face exposed from the cowl and disfigured from the wound of Sienna's killing blow. It was not a pleasant sight and Koda tried not to stare.

No, the most disturbing was the body of the Crooked man who had been held on the bear altar that had been doing the odd ballooning earlier.

Apparently, when Koda had hit him with the knife, the blow had rolled him down and onto the ground by one of the ancient ribs. A rib that had moved during the fight as the massive skeleton shifted as a result of the ruckus.

It had pierced the Crooked's chest and pinned it to the cave floor, finishing the job of killing it. But the body was slowly deflating, much like the balloon Koda had been comparing it to earlier losing all of its air, leaving behind a deflated skin stretched to odd proportions, with nothing inside.

"The hell?" Koda muttered before physically shaking himself. This sent a spatter of blood droplets over the ground as he hadn't been able to avoid the blood of his kills during the fight as successfully as before. "No, we need to go and deal with the others. Come on."

Sienna just grunted in agreement, falling in on his left with her spear held ready as they raced to the cave mouth to meet the rest of the Crooked force.

Chapter Fifteen

WHAT GREETED THEM WAS UNEXPECTED.

The camp was in flames.

The collapsing central tent had apparently caught fire from the central pit and gone up like the fabric had been soaked in oil. Many Crooked had been trapped in the burning canvas and either flailed blindly on the ground in pain or lay still as the tents continued to burn around them.

The champion was lumbering towards them, but from the severe burns and the limp it was sporting, the creature wasn't as much of a threat as it had been only moments before.

"I'll take the champion. You handle any of the others that try to jump me from behind." Sienna grunted her agreement with Koda's words, and the two of them charged down the hill and into the fight.

The rest of the battle was short and bloody. Koda fenced briefly with the wounded champion, but its injuries kept it from doing more than menacing him. Burn marks and several bleeding injuries from the tent collapsing on top of it kept it from being anything resembling nimble. So avoiding its reclaimed club was easy enough.

Feinting a few times, Koda got it to overextend long enough to rip his claws through the arm using the club, which he then claimed as his own and used to end the monster with a blow to the head that nearly removed the lumpy object.

Sienna hurried through the camp, quickly using her spear to take care of the Crooked that looked threatening and administering an execution to any that she doubted were dead from the fire.

After Koda finished the champion, he expected the Crooked to flee in fear like they had the last time. Unfortunately, this time the death of their champion whipped them into a frenzy.

There were roughly a half-dozen of the monsters left at that point. They immediately converged on Sienna, seeing the still-weak spearwoman as the easiest of their two targets to vent their anger upon as Koda hefted the champion's bloody club onto his shoulder and turned to check on his companion.

She did her best, but the trembling from her earlier electrocution made her normally deft movements clunky. While the spiritual pulse and the roar earlier had helped restore her, it was obvious some injury remained.

The group of six closed in on her with eerie synchronicity. They moved like a hunting pack, circling from all sides so that Sienna could not fend them all off at once. Seeing her plight, Koda threw himself forward to help.

Before Koda could get there, one threw itself onto the blade of Sienna's spear. It accepted a mortal wound to the chest in order to tie the weapon up, while two others threw themselves onto the haft to arrest the weapon.

The other three lunged at Sienna with a mixture of short-swords and axes raised high, cackling and laughing in glee at their apparent success in trapping their prey.

Rather than hold on to her weapon and be taken down, Sienna released the haft of her spear and skipped backwards, grimacing as her muscles protested the motion. She yanked a long hunting knife from her thigh-sheath with her right hand and parried away the axe blow coming at her chest.

Sienna was able to dodge the first short sword that would have taken her in the side, but the second slashed across her left arm and drew another yelp of pain from the wolf-eared warrior.

Her attacker did not escape unharmed, though. Sienna twisted and drove her knife into the Crooked's throat, ripping it to one side to send a spray of red-black blood over his fellows.

Koda roared in fury. He'd been mad before when fighting the Crooked the other day, and he'd been angry earlier when he found Sienna being tortured with that sick yellow lightning, but seeing blood flowing from the long, ragged cut on her arm, Koda felt something snap in his chest, and instinct took over.

Lunging in low, Koda dug the claws on his gauntleted hand into the earth and pulled himself forward, running on all fours like a beast, abandoning the iron-shod club on the ground as it would only slow him now.

Given how human anatomy worked, it shouldn't have been faster to run like that. It should have actually slowed him down quite a bit to run on all fours rather than how one normally would. But Koda was beginning to understand that the words of Thera, and her actions only the previous morning, had done something to him.

Made him something more than just human.

The leaping bound that Koda took forward launched him through the air like a stone launched from a sling. He covered the twenty feet between him and Sienna's attackers in a single motion and football tackled the unwounded pair she had fended off with enough force that he could hear ribs break from the impact as he carried them down.

Slamming them to the ground, Koda's body moved on autopilot as he allowed his remaining momentum to roll him forward over top of his victims and to his feet.

This resulted in him landing next to the still-gurgling sword-wielder who Sienna had gotten with her knife.

Snatching at the Crooked's weapon, he yanked the bent sword out of its hand with his left, while slamming the fist of his right into its face with a sickening crunch that stove in its skull like he'd just slammed a bowling ball down on top of it for daring to injure Sienna.

Not even waiting to see if that was enough, Koda whirled to drive the stolen sword down into the chest of the axe-wielder, who still lay sprawled on the ground. Meanwhile, he slammed his clawed fingertips into the throat of the other sword-user who had dared even *attempt* to harm Sienna.

The entire time, Koda could feel a deep, basso bellow echoing in his chest. It sounded like the challenge-roar of a grizzly bear to him, but he pushed the noise aside for now. He had to deal with the threats in front of him before he could worry about anything else.

A glance told him Sienna had fallen on her back as her legs now refused to support her, and the woman was clutching at her wounded arm while watching Koda through dazed eyes as he dismantled her attackers.

Planting himself over the two critically wounded Crooked and directly between the last two healthy ones and Sienna, Koda threw the bent sword as hard as he could at the two who were still trying to disentangle themselves from their dead fellow and Sienna's spear.

The weapon flashed and spun through the air, the blade slamming edge-first into the elbow of one of the Crooked and cleaving right through it in a spray of blood and a scream of pain.

Seeing how effective this tactic was, Koda snatched up the axe from the dying Crooked at his feet and repeated the feat. Unfortunately, he missed entirely as the bent weapon veered off to one side, its flight impeded by its bent form.

He snatched the last sword from the dying Crooked. First, he used it to ensure that these two would be no threat to Sienna, then he lunged forward to finish off the others.

It was as he was hacking into the last of the three and his anger began to bleed away that Koda realized where that deep basso roar was coming from.

It was his own throat.

The veil of red fury that had descended on him at seeing *his* Sienna injured—Koda grimaced at that thought, pushing away the possessive and protective instincts that welled up for now—was beginning to clear, and Koda could feel his lungs aching from just how empty they were in the wake of that explosion of fury.

The roar petered out then as he gasped for breath. Koda had no idea if they were safe at the moment, though. He had no idea if any other Crooked were hiding in tents or nearby, so he kicked the dead away from Sienna's spear, ripped it free of the fallen that had pinned it, and hurried over to check on his companion.

Sienna was sitting up, grimacing in pain as she applied pressure to her injury. The trembles resulting from the electrical attack were even worse now as adrenaline and shock in the wake of the fight added insult to her injury.

"Koda," Sienna mumbled, looking up at him with those wide, crystalline blue-green eyes that always devoured him whole whenever he met them.

"It's okay, I got you. Can you stand?" Koda crouched protectively over her, scanning nearby to ensure no threats were within range while setting her spear across her lap.

"No... legs don't want to work. Need to bandage my arm up," Sienna said with a grimace.

Her injured left arm shifted to grip the haft of her spear, and the presence of the weapon seemed to reassure her some as the trembling slowed.

Koda nodded and quickly scooped her knife up. A swipe of the bloody blade over the leg of his pants had it clean, and he slipped it back into the sheath before kneeling next to her.

"Gonna move you to the cave. It's more defensible there. Do you have bandages?" Sienna nodded and did not fight it when he scooped her solid form up into a princess carry as gently as he could.

Koda hurried back up the bloody slope to the cave as quickly as he dared. Sienna's injury didn't look to be fatal, but he was galvanized by how weak she looked and the occasional muscular jerk of her body still trying to fight off the damage of the lightning.

She's in shock. People can die of shock, right? The thought raced through his mind like a river overflowing its banks. *Why aren't you more heavily affected by the lightning? You got shocked, too...* That thought floated through Koda's mind, but he brushed it off. He could feel the slight trembling in his muscles and the slowly building ache that was becoming familiar after bruising combat. He would take what he could get for now.

"Can worry about that later," he growled under his breath. Koda didn't realize he was speaking aloud until Sienna made a questioning noise. "Nothing. Where are your bandages?" Koda quickly changed the subject as they topped the rise and looked down into the cave.

There were still several of the dead Crooked piled around, and the corpse of the spell-casting Crooked was buried under the still body of the mother bear. But no sound came from within the cave. Only the gusting of the wind stirring outside and the distant crackle of the slowly burning remains of the camp site.

Koda made a note that he would need to go check on the camp to make sure the fire didn't get into the trees. But for now, Sienna was his greater priority.

Seeing the crude ritual circle and the surrounding dead, Koda remembered the last time he'd seen something similar to this. The previous day, when they'd dealt with the Crooked and their camp closest to the village. He'd seen it around the sick altar. When he'd destroyed that altar, Thera had appeared. Thera had appeared and been empowered by it. Thera was a goddess and could help.

"Bandages are in my pack, Koda," Sienna croaked, her voice still shaking from the shock. He didn't stop moving at the mouth of the cave, though.

Hurrying down the slope, Koda looked around for some sign of the altar that the Crooked would have used to claim this site of power. Sienna groaned quietly, and he clutched the redheaded woman closer to his chest. He could feel the soft bouncing of her tail against his thighs as he moved. The fact that it was hanging limp bothered him quite intensely, rather than the usual happy wiggling he was used to seeing, even after only knowing Sienna for a day.

Koda spotted his target low to the ground in the shadow of an immense rib bone towards the back of the cage. The same gnarled bone structure with its brass bowl sat there with the glowing embers of a small fire underneath it.

Not hesitating, Koda hurried over and gave the bronze bowl a solid kick.

Only the steel-toes of his boots prevented him from ending up with a broken toe. The bone construct resisted the blow like he'd just tried to kick a block of marble, not shifting in the slightest.

"Gauntlet," Sienna grunted, shifting so that she was leaning more into him, her eyes fixed on the sick altar as well.

Understanding dawned on Koda, and he shifted his burden higher on his chest for a moment, dipping the claw tips into one of his many scratches to wet them with his blood. He then slapped out in a slashing motion at the bronze bowl with his totemic gauntlet before letting Sienna fall back into his arms with a slight grunt.

As before, the bowl that had been immovable before by any other means melted in response to contact with the gauntlet.

Black fire rippled down the bones that made up the reinforcement on the back of his arm. It danced amongst the stones and fangs for a space between heartbeats before transforming once more into that same blood-red fire that leaped from his clawed fingertips and consumed the altar entirely.

As the fire devoured it, the altar emitted a sickly, phlegmatic roar that transitioned into that same ursine bellow that Koda had heard minutes earlier.

While he had remembered quite a bit about the process of destroying the altar, Koda had forgotten about the pulse of energy that the altar emitted as it vanished.

The ripple blasted outwards in time with the transition of the roar, and Koda stumbled, falling back while clutching Sienna to his chest to keep her safe. Stars burst in Koda's vision as his head thunked solidly off the stone of the cave floor.

The wolf girl yelped in surprise herself and lost hold of her spear in the fall. Sienna yelped again, this time in pain, when she landed hard on Koda's chest.

The sound of Sienna's pain hurt more than when his skull hit the stone floor of the cavern, and Koda refused to let go of her, steadying her on his chest before rolling to sit up, shaking his head to clear the stars from his vision.

He could feel the same tugging sensation from the totemic gauntlet he wore a moment before a dull flash of red light lit the cave up. Koda knew that the flash was the appearance of the new altar to Thera, which should result in her appearing, or at least he hoped so.

Glancing around, he spotted the same clean fur and stone bowl combination had appeared in front of him. This time the fur looked to be a bear's pelt in a stippled black-and-white pattern like someone had brindled a polar and a black bear together.

"Thera?" Koda called, looking around for his patron.

"I am here, Champion." Thera's voice echoed from behind him.

Koda turned in his seated position to see the apparition of the goddess standing nearby. She still had the translucent animal features, shifting as she adjusted and turned. While before they had been bare ghosts, now they looked far more firm to Koda's eyes, and Thera was even more solid-looking than before.

"Can you help Sienna? She's hurt, and one of the Crooked hit her with a spell," Koda asked in a rush.

"They hit you, too," Sienna protested weakly, glaring up at him while clutching her still-bleeding arm.

Thera looked them over, and a small smile curved her lips before she shook her head. The motion made her, currently fox, ears bounce cutely before shifting into rounded bear ears.

"I could heal the injury, but it is not a critical one. Time and rest will let her heal just as well. Also, it will not tax her body as much as my healing might," Thera said gently.

Koda was about to protest and demand that she do this when Sienna spoke first.

"I appreciate it, Pack Lady. Knowing that the foul sorcery did not leave lasting damage is reassuring." Sienna turned to look up at Koda and cocked one eyebrow with a trembling smile. "Can you get those bandages and help me with this? Forearm injuries are awkward, and the more I bleed..."

"Are you sure?" Koda's question made the smile grow stronger on Sienna's lips, and she nodded. Thera spoke a moment later as well, drawing his attention to her again.

"My people are hearty, Koda. Trust in your companion. I understand that your concern over the magical effect overrode sense, otherwise I'd be chastising you for waiting to tend to her wounds." Thera's voice held a bit of recrimination in it regardless of what she actually said, and Koda winced.

"Fair, I guess I just... panicked."

"As I said, it is understandable. You are protective of your people and may one day reach the level that I am," Thera said gently. "Now, I wanted to thank you for moving so quickly to secure this place. If you had not rushed here, then something even more horrible would have happened. Something I had not foreseen or expected."

"I guess that's why you were using the gauntlet to push us into attacking without support?" Koda shifted so that Sienna was sitting comfortably in his lap, her head leaning against his shoulder. Once she was balanced, he began rifling through her pack for the bandages and a waterskin to clean the wound. When he found each item, he set them in Sienna's lap.

"Yes. They were in the midst of performing a ritual that was trying to bind the ancient bear spirit that resided in this grave to one of their own. If they had succeeded..." Koda glanced up in time to see something disturbing, the vision of a goddess shivering in both fear and disgust.

"Well, they didn't," Koda said firmly before turning back to help Sienna wash and bandage her cut.

The injury had looked a lot worse than it actually was. The slash wasn't very deep, but it was long. A bandage and something to keep it clean would ensure it was fine. While he began to unroll the bandage, Sienna fished a small bone jar of ointment out of her belt pouch and applied it to the injury. With that done, they wrapped a bandage over it, pulling it tight.

"Indeed. I have a great deal to thank you both for." Thera's voice was full of warm affection for them both, and Koda heard the quiet *pat* of her footsteps as she strode around to stand next to them and watch their work.

"It's nothing. You brought me here to do this." Koda brushed it off while he focused on ensuring the pressure was even across the bandage.

Working with Sienna in his lap made this task awkward, but even the idea of letting her move farther than touching distance away from him right now was setting off a heat in his chest. Koda could feel his anger bubbling just below the surface as well, fury still gripping him at the *audacity* of those who injured one of his.

"You blessed us with a champion to protect us, Pack Lady. Of course, your faithful will do all we can to return that gift to you. I know that I already owe Koda my life at least twice over at this point. I will have to find some way to repay him..." Sienna's voice trailed off suddenly, and he glanced up to check on her. The wolf-eared woman was blushing slightly but pointedly staring at her injury. Her pointed ears lay flat along her skull, so they were no help in trying to figure out what was on her mind.

"Well then, I will have to see what I can do to repay you both. Koda, I have an idea, but it will take some time to prepare. This influx of new power is helping me recover, and I can use that to empower you further, given time. Unfortunately, the true reward will need another infusion of power. If you can secure the vale and claim the other site of power that I told you about, then that should give me what I need. For you, though, my dear Sienna..."

Koda felt a brief shiver run through the woman on his lap and tensed up. That same surge of protective instinct burned hotter in his chest, but it calmed a moment later when Sienna leaned into him.

"I will visit you in your dreams, so we can speak privately," Thera continued to speak, either not noticing or just disregarding the tension that passed over Koda. "For now, though, I must be going after I collect my errant charge."

Thera turned away from them, the motion making her fur skirt swirl out and lightly brush over Koda's cheek, feeling like a cloud had just reached out and caressed his face. The motion was so similar to what Sienna had done with her tail the previous night that Koda just blinked in surprise and flinched.

Sienna looked up from her bandages to see what Thera did next, so Koda did the same. The goddess walked over to the nearest part of the skeleton and gently rested one hand on the bone.

"Come to me, daughter. You have languished here too long in the form of a spirit, and that risked you. Come home so we can make you whole once more."

The goddess stroked the bone gently with one pale hand. As Koda and Sienna watched, a wisp of yellow energy detached from the bone and flowed out to wrap around Thera like a hanging cloak.

Briefly, Koda thought he saw the silhouette of a woman wrapping her arms lovingly around Thera from behind before the energy faded into the goddess.

Moments later, Thera turned translucent and faded from view as well.

Chapter Sixteen

WITHOUT A BETTER OPTION, THEY DECIDED TO CAMP that night in the cave before heading back to the village to meet up with the headwoman and let her know they had secured this area.

Koda briefly kicked himself for not thinking about asking Thera which of the two potential spots held their last group of enemies, but he couldn't change it now. Hopefully, Kris would know more when they finally met back up with the headwoman.

It took Sienna getting grumpy at him for hovering over her to convince Koda that he could leave her to set up their camp in the cave.

Instead, he piled the bodies and ensured the fire in the Crooked camp did not get out of control. His boosted strength made piling those corpses together in the already burned space the large tent had occupied even easier. Especially since the fight hadn't lasted nearly as long as it had the previous day.

Once that was done, he hurried back to the cave to find Sienna carefully working to remove the hide from the mother bear that had killed the Crooked spellcaster.

"Why are you doing that?" Sienna glanced up at his question in confusion, clearly not understanding why he asked.

"Because she's already dead. Leaving the hide to rot would be disrespectful. It's damaged from how they captured her, but the tanners can still find a use for it. I'd cook some of the meat, but we have no idea if it's tainted by the Crooked and their ritual, so it's better not to risk it."

Koda considered her words before nodding and getting in there to help her.

He learned quite a few things about how to remove and begin processing a hide.

First of which was just how messy the entire process was.

Sienna coached him through the most efficient ways to make the necessary cuts and then how to scrape the hide to ensure no flesh or fat remained on it. Then they washed it and lay the hide in the coolest part of the cave to preserve it until they could get back to the village where the rest of the tanning process would be taken care of.

"It's not the best, and the hide is already a bit damaged, but with taxes being what they are..." Sienna sighed gustily before grimacing and glancing down at her injured arm.

Following her gaze, Koda was relieved to see the bandages only bore the lightest stains of blood. The salve Sienna had applied was apparently working well to help staunch the blood flow and encourage the healing process. Then his mind caught up to what Sienna had been saying.

"Taxes?"

Sienna nodded at his question and gestured for Koda to take a seat with her by the campfire that she'd set up on a small patch of dirt away from the scene of the battle. Even with the bodies disposed of, neither of them wanted to lie on blood-stained rock or dirt.

"Yes, the local baron is demanding increased taxes to deal with more raiding parties from enemy nations. Unfortunately, with the mithril mine dwindling, it is getting harder and harder to meet those taxes. We can't make up the difference with crops, the land in the vale isn't flat enough to farm. Same with furs. It would only take a few years to decimate the local populations unless we range farther into the plains." Sienna shifted slightly and pulled her fluffy red-black tail around to lie in her lap, idly stroking it with her right hand while she talked.

"Like the raiding group of Crooked?" Koda's question had points to it, but Sienna just shrugged and spoke again.

"There is only so much that the baron can do for outlying villages like ours. This is the first time in generations that the Crooked have brought this many troops to our area. We got lucky with that raiding party that was near the village. The group was made up of their weakest fighters and only a single champion. If they'd had two like this group did, accompanied by that number of their foot soldiers, then we would have lost a lot more people in that fight."

"Still! You say that you pay taxes for protection, but I didn't see any guards or any stationed soldiers to protect the village," Koda protested.

He sat down at Sienna's injured side. Close enough that, in the dim light of the fire they had going in the cave, he could check on her injury without making it obvious. She'd not snapped at him after the first time, but he respected her independent nature enough that he didn't want to crowd her.

While he sat there, Koda watched as Sienna's expression turned dark.

"There haven't been guards stationed in our village in my entire lifetime. Kris told me stories of a small group that was stationed there as the watch when she was young, but the baron pulled them out to send them somewhere where 'the need was greater.' Whenever we ask about it, they say that the different fronts need the soldiers more than our back-water village. And until recently, they were right."

"Regardless, that is wrong. I guess we are just lucky that there are enough vigorous men and women to protect it from this incursion," Koda grumbled quietly.

"So far, at least. You said that there were two remaining groups of Crooked in the vale, and we've eliminated one. I doubt the other will be this small again."

Sienna glanced up from staring into the fire, and her capti-vating eyes snared Koda again. They shared a long stare for six or seven heartbeats before Sienna glanced away, releasing him from her hypnotic gaze. Blinking, Koda replayed what she had said to try to catch back up with the conversation.

"What makes you think that it won't be just as small? One would think that they would send their largest force against the only source of opposition in the vale." Koda's brow wrin-kled as he thought it over.

"Simple. I've learned that whatever power governs fate doesn't like our little village." Sienna sighed again, the gesture making her short red hair bounce. "The mine is beginning to run out, and taxes are increasing. Now the

Crooked coming to attack our vale in force? One or two would just be life, but all three at once?"

"Maybe it's just fate trying to balance the scales?" Koda said the first thing that came to his mind. When Sienna gave him a questioning look, he hurried to continue. "I mean, your people have had it rough for a while. So has Thera, for that matter. She's been trapped right on the edge of reality for so long without someone from her chosen bloodlines to actually let her act. But this confluence of events all led to her finally getting her hands... paws? Eh, whatever. Getting her the chance to snatch me up, which is opening opportunities. At least that's the feeling I've been getting. Am I wrong?"

Sienna's gaze darted over to the far side of the cave where the ancient skeleton rested still next to the small, pristine rug of bear hide with its burden of a polished bowl.

The altar to a goddess she'd heard about all her life and actually *seen* and spoken to finally.

Something deep in her chest seemed to shift as the depression brought on by her injury, the shock of the fight, and the events of the last day or two appeared to fall away again.

"I don't know. Maybe you are right, and this should be treated as an opportunity." Sienna glanced back at Koda, and he averted his eyes to the small fire that crackled in front of them, not wanting to lose himself in her crystalline gaze again.

"I will do anything I can to help you," Koda said quietly. Because he was staring into the fire, he almost missed the blush that crossed Sienna's cheeks.

"I-I know," she stammered. This drew Koda's gaze back to her face from the fire, but Sienna had looked away already. "You've made it obvious that you would risk a great deal to help out the village. I'm sure the others will be grateful when they realize just how much. I know Kris already was grateful from before. But, with what you did today, that'll only get stronger."

"What *we* did, Sienna. You helped me just as much as I helped you."

"Psh. I got caught by that caster before I even got close enough to strike at it. Seriously, I got the two by the altar through luck. But he had me with that lightning magic before I could do anything or even consider dodging. I'd have been dead without you circling back to help me."

"And if you hadn't taken the caster's head off in the moment you had the chance, I don't know if I'd have been able to finish it. That lightning was no joke. The mother bear gave us the opportunity with her last act..." Koda countered Sienna's statement, letting his trail off as he thought back to the dead animal.

After Sienna had finished skinning it, he'd dragged the body out into the tree line, away from the camp. It had been Sienna's idea to let nature reclaim the body so that her spirit could return to the earth. He'd offered to bury it, but she had told him not to.

"True." Sienna glanced back at Koda, studying his profile in the firelight for a long moment.

In her lap, her tail began to wiggle slightly under her fingers as she studied the human in front of her. Glancing down at the errant bit of fluff, Sienna bit her lip while brooding.

"Like I said, Sienna. I'll help you out however I can. I told you before that Thera brought me here to help her people, and I intend to."

"Is it just because I'm...?" Sienna began to ask but cut the question off before she could finish giving it voice.

Koda glanced her way curiously, but the wolf beastfolk shook her head, refusing to meet his eyes while her cheeks flushed. Movement drew his eyes downwards to her fluffy tail, where it lay draped over her lap.

He could see the tip of her tail twitching rhythmically. Like it was trying to wag, but she had it pinned down. The sight warmed his heart, and Koda felt a tension in his gut slowly begin to unwind.

Admit it, you think she's cute, Koda thought in the safety of his own mind while he studied Sienna's blushing features. *She's more than cute. She's beautiful. And unless I'm blind, she might be attracted to me. I've only known her for a little over a day, though, so it's not like I can judge this.* The dull ache that formed in his chest at the idea that Sienna might not return his affection startled Koda, and he blinked furiously.

"I need to gather more firewood. I'll be back in a bit," he said quickly, pushing himself to his feet.

His sudden statement and movement yanked Sienna out of her thoughts, and she looked up at him, then back down at the fire.

"Koda, you've been going all day. You just fought in a tremendous battle *and* cleaned it up. How can you want to work more right now? You should be dead on your feet," Sienna asked, tilting her head to one side as she spoke and making her ears flop to one side.

"We need it done, and I'd rather take care of it now than when it is dark. I don't want you doing it with your injury. Before you protest, I know that you aren't an invalid just from the cut, but I'd rather you rest as much as possible. If we are *very* lucky, we'll have another minor battle in a day or two to finish this off. If we are unlucky, we have another big fight to come, and you will need all the strength you can muster for that," Koda said, his rate of speech increasing as the seconds ticked by. "I told you that I would help you however I can. Since I cannot heal your arm any faster, I will do everything else I can to enable you to recover quickly. I promised Thera I'd protect you."

Koda grimaced a bit at the last part. He hadn't meant to just spit that out. Finally, he took a deep breath and looked down at Sienna.

She stared up at him in surprise, her head still tilted slightly in questioning with her ears flopped over, but her crystalline eyes were wide and glittering. Her fluffy tail bounced in her lap more emphatically despite the weight of her hands on it, telling him that she was not unhappy with his statements.

Pointedly, Koda kept his vision locked on the tip of her nose rather than those mesmerizing eyes.

Last thing you need after that kind of declaration is to get lost staring at her and make it awkward. Now, get moving, you idiot! Koda chastised himself silently.

He then turned to hurry out of the cave, his mind turning over the surging emotions in his chest. The mixture of possessive, protective, and affectionate emotions wrestled with fears of inadequacy and the hesitation born of not knowing his prospects in the world as he went.

Sienna watched the black-haired man as he walked away. The fine strands of his long hair flowed with the movement from their spot in the simple ponytail he wore, and she wondered if his hair was as soft as it looked.

She was entirely unaware of the fact he had wondered much the same thing about the fur on her tail or ears. Fur that she was now carefully combing her fingers through while imagining doing the same with Koda's hair.

Unbidden, her thoughts turned to Thera's promise to visit her dreams and *discuss* things. The thoughts made her heart race just a bit faster while her tail continued its happy wiggling.

Chapter Seventeen

Koda made sure they had plenty of firewood, with multiple trips back and forth from the tree line near the cave. Keeping moving helped work the stiffness out of his joints from the fight, his subsequent beating, and the spell damage.

The pyre he had set for the Crooked continued to burn, but thankfully, the breeze was coming down from the higher peaks, and it blew the stinking black smoke away from the cave and their campsite—a blessing that made hunting through the trees a bit easier.

Even with the relative quiet after the battle, Koda did not relax his watch. There was a decent chance that some of the Crooked still lurked in the woods despite the destruction of the camp. They had eliminated a patrol as it went out, and there was a chance that there might be others still out there. So he was wary as he carried armload after armload of wood to the cave.

While he worked, Koda thought over the last day and a half. So far, he had been dragged through a cave spring that was actually a portal, met a goddess three separate times, and been anointed as her champion. This had resulted in him having to kill quite a few people. Despite their twisted appearance and disgusting actions, it was hard not to see the Crooked as people still. Twisted and broken people, but people, nonetheless.

And you met a beautiful woman who seems to at least be somewhat attracted to you, Koda reminded himself absent-mindedly.

He grabbed a branch he thought was loose on the forest floor to add to his stack while he thought. A yank of his hand produced a splintering crack, and he looked down to find that he had torn the branch off a fallen log hidden amongst piled leaves. The branch was as thick as his wrist at its base, and he had broken it off with no more thought than he might snap a toothpick.

And apparently got stupid strength, too. Koda snorted, adding the branch to his pile. *Whenever I get a chance to actually experiment and find out, it might be good to discover just how far this blessing Thera gave me will go.*

Regarding the fallen tree for a moment, Koda shrugged and began snapping more branches off.

The log had been laying there for some time, leaving only a pale gray trunk with no bark, so it was as brittle as it would get. But each branch he snapped off came cleanly without a problem. It was kind of fun, in a somewhat childish way, to snap and break the branches free of the tree like this. It reminded him of picking twigs off a branch during a break while hiking.

No matter what he did, Koda couldn't keep his mind from drifting back to Sienna and his growing attraction to the woman. He'd known of her for not even two days and not really *known* her for more than half a day at this point.

Their earlier conversation while hiking across the vale to the cave was the first real bonding moment that didn't require the heat of combat to promote.

And you are already smitten with her. Spunky spirit, tight body, and that cute tail as well. Does this make me a furry? Koda snorted, scooping his pile of branches up under his arm and shaking his head while he walked back to the cave. *If it does, I don't care. Sienna is a sweet gal, and if she's interested, then I'm not going to hesitate because of judgments from my old world. There's a reason I left it.*

It was only when he had enough of a pile in the cave to last them *several* days that Koda finally flopped down with a sigh, wafting his shirt to try to get some air flow to cool his skin after the exertion.

While he had worked, Sienna had gotten their bedrolls laid out and made a light soup for their dinner. The savory scent of the food made his stomach growl, reminding Koda that the last time he'd eaten had been trail food while they walked.

"No bowls," Sienna said quietly, nodding to the pot sitting to warm by the fire. "Spoon's in your bag. I already had my share. You should eat and rest, Koda. We've both done a lot today, and while camping in the cave gives us security, the proximity to the burn site as well as the enemy camp means we will have to sit up on watch."

The wolf beastfolk's words were quiet, but he could feel the care she put into them as a result, so Koda just nodded and settled in to eat. The soup was excellent—a bit heavy on the salt because of the preserved meat but still good. He hadn't realized just how tired he was until the food hit his stomach, and he began to feel better.

I've been just running on ornery for hours now, Koda thought while staring down at the half pot of liquid with its floating scraps of meat and vegetables. *The whole 'if I sit down, I'm not getting up again' kind of ornery. Used to do that a lot for work...*

While he pondered his past and let the food restore him, Koda was only vaguely aware of Sienna continuing to steal glances at him or how her nose flared cutely in response to the sharp scent of his sweat and exertion where it had cut through the other smells of their camp.

Neither of them was aware of the watchful intent directed towards them from across the cave, as Thera spied on her champion and his companion from within her altar, a small smile twisting her lips.

Koda took the first watch, urging Sienna to sleep so she could recover. The food had given him enough strength that he would be fine—at least, that was what he told her.

She'd started to argue but paused with her mouth open as something clearly occurred to her, and then she blushed.

Sienna settled into her bedroll shortly after, reminding Koda to wake her part way through the night so that he could get some sleep, too.

As Sienna's breathing evened out and the wolf-eared woman went still beside the fire, Koda became even more aware of the sounds of nature around them, as well as the silence that snuck in between those sounds.

Night had crept in while they had sat in a companionable silence by the fire. Now, Koda could hear the distant squeaking of bats as they swooped through the shadows to collect insects in the last failing light of the day. The quiet creak of crickets acted as a counterpoint to the snaps and pops of the small fire that threw dancing shadows around the cave walls.

It only took half an hour for Koda to realize the one permanent truth about standing watch, regardless of what world you did it in: it was boring.

Koda did his best to make sure he stayed as alert as possible.

Walking back and forth by the mouth of the cave, he placed his feet carefully so as not to wake Sienna.

He performed the eye-exercises he remembered hearing about from one of the semi drivers on a work site that were meant to prevent fatigue and road-hypnosis while driving long distances.

Koda even went over mental plans of how he could help fortify the village from what he'd seen so far. Without access to rebar and concrete, his options were limited unfortunately. But there might be analogues here that he wasn't aware of, so he didn't disregard any ideas yet.

Finally, he settled near the firepit and alternated between watching Sienna sleep and the flames dance. It had been several hours, but Koda knew it would be a few more before he could wake Sienna for her turn.

The lack of stimulus was making his brain foggy. Koda was just considering grabbing a stick from the pile of firewood to try to use his totemic gauntlet as a whittling tool on when the long day finally caught up with him and tugged him into a doze while sitting upright.

The first thing Koda heard was a quiet voice singing in a low tone. The voice was familiar, but with his cloudy mind, it was hard to put an exact pin on who it could be.

There was something infinitely soothing about the sound, and it tugged at the base of his heart, reminding him of a time before his parents had gone to war with each other, and when his mother would sing him lullabies as a child.

Without even considering it fully, he followed the sound through shadowed hallways made of stone. The only source of light was the occasional flickering lamp hung high on the wall, spreading just enough illumination to get him between pools of light.

As he walked, Koda strained his ears to make out the words of the song, but it always seemed just muffled enough he couldn't make them out. The tone was there, gentle with affection and care, but what the song was about eluded him time and again.

Turning one particular corner, he found the hallway ending in a large room lit by a massive marble fireplace.

There were two large, wing-backed chairs covered in soft, purple velvet sitting some distance apart, angled mostly towards the fire. Between the two was an enormous mound of fur, sprawled with its back to him and its belly towards the fire while a delicate hand stroked over a head that lay on a pillow next to the rightmost chair.

"Easy, my dear one. Rest and recover. We have much to do, but if you rush, it will only make it harder. Trust in my champion. He will bring me the strength to heal you fully." The singing voice was now recognizable as Koda paused at the entrance to the room, no longer feeling the urge to chase the sound.

"How do you—" another familiar voice started to ask, and he blinked in surprise.

"Know what she's thinking? She is my daughter, even more directly than your people are. I would be a poor mother if I did not at least have an idea of what sort of trouble my children might get up to. This one has been away from me for quite some time, but she hasn't changed that much. Have you, beloved?" Thera's voice cut the other off before turning loving as her hand rubbed behind one of the great bear's ears.

"There is a lot resting on him..." That familiar female voice that had startled him before came again from the leftmost chair. "The hopes of my entire tribe. The future of our faith. Not that many know that yet."

"He will require love and support in the future. I offered him treasure, fame, and women initially, you know? He turned it all down and demanded only family and community instead." Thera's voice was filled with laughter, and the great bear huffed a deep noise from its throat that sounded like a laugh as well. "I knew you'd like him, dear one. Be patient and trust in him." The bear grumbled again, deep in its throat.

"How can I help?"

"Simple, be there for him. Know that, if I am to succeed in my return, I will need far more than just the one champion to do so. Tying the power of my priesthood to a lineage empowered it in the past, but now it is a threat that I cannot dismiss. The only way to insulate from that threat is to expand the pool of those who carry that power. He will need support and love from many sources, if my priesthood is to recover."

A small grunt from the mound of fur drew Koda's attention to it. What he thought was a large brown bear pretending to be a rug while getting scratches shifted and turned. The thick hair that he had thought was fur shifted and fell away to reveal pale skin and bandages, along with a fur blanket that had been covering her. Sparkling yellow eyes met his from beneath that messy mane of brown hair, though they remained hooded from the gentle strokes their owner was receiving. Koda saw the curve of one large breast peeking out from beneath that thick mane of hair, and he could see wide hips and a glimpse of a muscled abdomen before the woman lying against the chair gave another quiet grunt.

Koda blinked. He wasn't sure how he knew it, but he could feel approval and interest radiating from the large woman lying on what he now recognized as a thick pad on the floor. His vision swam again, and for a moment, he saw the muzzle of a great bear before the woman's strong features returned with a sultry smile.

The only noise for the next few minutes was the popping of the fire and another low and happy groan from the large woman, who winced slightly when she tried to shift closer towards Koda, her hair falling away to reveal even more of her curves. The hand on her head stilled, and then a shuffling of movement preceded the glimmer of eyes peeking around the edge of the rightmost chair.

"Naughty, naughty. Peeking like that, Koda." Thera's eyes crinkled around the edges as she smiled just out of sight, the hand that had been stroking the bear-woman's head rising to wag a finger at him.

Another brief burst of movement drew his eyes towards the leftmost seat, and a familiar pair of red-black wolf ears perked upwards over the back of the chair. He opened his mouth to speak, but Thera made a flicking motion towards him as she spoke.

"Wake up, Koda. Let us girls continue our conversation in peace."

Koda jolted awake, blinking owlishly into the fire in front of him

It took a long moment for his mind to catch up to what had happened, but he snuck a glance over at Sienna, who was still sleeping peacefully.

A slight stirring under her blankets made him worry at first that something was about to attack her. That was until he spotted the tufted tip of her tail where it emerged from under the blanket, wiggling slowly and revealing that it was her wagging that made the motion.

What the hell was that? Koda thought with a hard swallow. *Was I seeing Thera and Sienna's conversation that the goddess promised? If so, how did I do that?*

Turning that thought over in his mind was enough to keep Koda awake for the rest of his watch shift.

Waking Sienna several hours later, Koda couldn't help but notice the blush staining the woman's cheeks even in the darkness. He didn't say anything though, just giving her a smile and falling onto his own bedroll.

Koda hadn't expected the thin pad over the packed earth of the cave floor to be so comfortable. But, even with his brief nap earlier when he'd somehow spied on Sienna and Thera, Koda was exhausted. He was out almost as soon as he got settled.

The morning dawned far too quickly, with the early rays of the morning light painting the tree tops brilliant colors. Sienna had made some sort of tea for them that emitted a warm and toasty smell from the tin mug that she set in front of him. Glancing down at the dark beverage, Koda looked back up to Sienna and quirked an eyebrow at the woman.

"Dandelion root tea. It's a habit of mine to wake up with some when I can," Sienna answered with a shrug, not meeting his eyes for longer than a second.

The wolf beastfolk woman had already tidied up the camp-site and tucked away her bedroll, so Koda took a sip of the nutty tasting beverage and smiled. While it wasn't coffee, the drink had enough crossover that it worked well for him.

Alternating between sips of the tea and working, Koda got his things packed up while Sienna extinguished the remains of the campfire.

By unspoken agreement, the two ate more of their trail rations and got on the move as soon as Koda finished his tea and packing. The night had left the world dewed in a million pearls of sparkling water that made it feel as if the passage of the night had somehow purified their surroundings.

Even the charred mound of the pyre wasn't quite as ominous as it might have been the day before. It had burned out during the night, the dew having snuffed out the last of the coals.

All that remained of the Crooked camp was a burned smudge and piles of charcoal, but Koda knew nature would reclaim that soon enough. He'd seen enough wildfires back home to know that nature always found its way back in.

Before heading out, Sienna took a quick trip around the edges of the clearing to check for tracks. She pointed out several sets that left and returned along different trails, though the largest set of them came from the road that led up through the pass and into the valley where the camp was. Exactly how many had passed through was impossible to tell, but Sienna was at least able to confirm that no other Crooked had come back to the site during the night.

"Back to the village then?" Koda asked as he settled his pack and draped his cloak over himself once more.

He'd done what he could to wash the blood from his clothes using the small stream in the cave, but the visceral fight the other day had left him speckled with the stuff, and he had waited too long. So now his clothes had several small stains on them—a state he was getting used to at this point.

Koda wondered idly how it was that so many stories never bothered to mention how bloody the fighters got when dealing with melee combat.

Most fighters probably don't claw people's throats out, though, Koda thought wryly. His stomach did a little flip but didn't protest beyond that. *Would have been nice to have a weapon with a bit more range, Thera. But I can't complain about the performance so far.*

"Yes, back home," Sienna's statement drew Koda's attention back to their surroundings. "Kris will likely have heard back from her scouts and have what fighters the village can spare mobilized. If we hurry, we can stamp out the last of these raiders." Sienna paused to glance back over her shoulder at the clearing and then the pass. "I don't like that they just came right up the road. There's another settlement we trade with farther along, and it makes me worry that they were hit as well."

"Secure our territory first. Once our home is safe, we can then reach out to help others," Koda said, and Sienna nodded in agreement.

"Yes, if we rush to help them before we are secure then both villages may fall as a result. What is the point of that?"

"Exactly. How's the wound doing, by the way?" He nodded towards her bandaged arm. Sienna flexed, rolling her wrist slowly and only wincing once in pain.

"Healing but still tender. Just glad that it didn't damage the tendons. It'll probably need stitches when we get back, though… I'll have to be careful with my spear for a bit, so I don't tear it open," she said at last, and Koda nodded in understanding.

"Makes sense. Anyway, let's get moving. If Kris is already heading this way, we want to catch her and the others before they waste too much time," Koda said with a nod, turning to begin retracing their steps.

Sienna hummed in agreement with Koda's decision and fell in behind him as he led the way back to the game trail from the day before.

She watched him as he hurried along it, moving with an effortless grace that would have surprised her if she hadn't seen him fight already.

She remembered her talk with Thera, and everything the goddess had told her. How she had invested as much of her power into Koda as she could, to make the most of this lost bloodline that had returned. Thera wished desperately for this last chance that she had to help her people to succeed.

We cannot lose his line again, Thera had told Sienna. The memory of those words warmed her heart now, just as they had the previous night, and she felt that warmth spread lower while a faint blush colored her cheeks.

Chapter Eighteen

"Koda?" Sienna's quiet voice intruded on the silence of their hike back after a few hours.

Blinking, he turned to look over his shoulder at his companion and tilted his head curiously while he waited for her to continue. When she didn't, he slowed and came to a stop along the game trail they had been following.

While they could have likely taken the road back to the village, they'd both agreed it was better to be safe. The path that the two of them were on was winding through several stands of tall pines, leaving the ground relatively free of clutter, save for the occasional fallen branch and scattering of needles. So he stepped off into the shade of one of those pine trees.

"What's up, Sienna?" he prompted when she didn't continue after a moment of waiting.

"Sorry, I was just trying to figure out how to phrase this politely." Sienna's ears fell to either side, and she grimaced in annoyance with herself.

"Just ask straight out. I think we know each other well enough that we wouldn't misunderstand each other, especially with warnings like this." Koda shrugged, glancing around to check their surroundings before leaning on a nearby pine tree, being careful to avoid the sections thick with sap.

"I guess it's in two parts? How do you know how to fight so well? And how do you handle having to kill like this?" Sienna sidled over to stand next to him, letting her spear lean on her right shoulder. She didn't look up at him but came to a stop a bare inch away from Koda, darting a glance to the side at him before looking back at the ground.

Without thinking too hard about it, Koda slung his left arm around Sienna's shoulders, pulling her against his side comfortingly. She stiffened for a moment before leaning into him more with a quiet sigh.

"I suppose I could see why you were worried about phrasing. The way you said it, I could take your words as you accusing me of being some kind of serial killer or maniac," Koda teased gently, squeezing Sienna lightly with the arm around her shoulders. "But I know that's not how you meant it, so no worries."

"Sorry," Sienna murmured anyway, her ears falling to either side again in guilt despite his reassurance. The tip of one fuzzy ear tickled the side of Koda's face, and he turned slightly to rub his cheek against it, making the appendage twitch more.

"Don't sweat it. Like I just said, I know what you meant. First, the straightforward answer. I only know the basics of how to fight, the kind of stuff you learn while growing up and having to fight bullies. Actually using this thing?" Koda held up his right hand and flexed it, the leather creaking quietly as he waved his totemic gauntlet around. "That's all

Thera. She said she would guide me in how to use it, so most of what I end up doing is instinct."

"You have messy instincts," Sienna teased lightly, her ears perking up as she shot him a sidelong glance.

"Thera has messy instincts," Koda corrected with a smirk. "I'm slowly getting the hang of it, but back in the beginning, when we fought in the village? It honestly felt like someone else was guiding the gauntlet, and I was just along for the ride."

"That must have been disconcerting."

"It was, but I'm doing a lot better now. I swear that after every fight, I feel like I'm stronger, faster, and more aware of my surroundings. More aware of how to stand, how to swing, and how best to use my bodyweight in a fight."

"All important things. I almost wish I had that kind of guidance. Most consider the spear a simple enough weapon, but mine incorporates elements of halberd fighting as well. I've studied it for years, and I know I still have many years to go before I'm a master." Sienna sighed gustily, her breath tickling Koda's nose as it whiffed past.

"I'll make sure you have the time to get there. I have a feeling you will get all the practice you could possibly want," Koda replied, squeezing her shoulders again lightly.

They stood there in silence for another few moments, Sienna just leaning into him while Koda considered the other question.

The harder question by far.

"As to killing? It's not a straightforward thing to accept. I think that if they weren't so obviously twisted, I would struggle more with killing the Crooked. The fact that they are more like a bizarre mockery of a person with the instincts of a monster makes it easier to accept," Koda said at last, staring down at the ground in front of them in thought.

"I thought I could handle killing. It's part of being a hunter. But..." Sienna trailed off and leaned a bit more heavily into him.

"But hunting deer is far different from a pitched battle?" Koda offered, getting a nod of agreement from Sienna. "Think of it this way then. What sort of threat do deer pose to you and the ones you care for?"

"None, but we need the meat and hides to survive," Sienna protested, finally lifting her gaze to meet his. Koda stared intently at the tip of her nose to avoid being lost in those crystal orbs again. The last thing he needed was to stare at Sienna, hypnotized by her beauty and the blue-green depths of her eyes.

"You hunt because you need to. That's different from having to fight and kill, though," Koda said.

Sienna made a confused noise and tilted her head to one side. This made her ears flop away from him, and the motion actually caused one to turn inside out, exposing the soft-furred inside and faint pink shell.

Koda fought down the urge to reach up and fix it, instead trying to focus on what he was saying to her, even as he worked through it in his own heart.

The weight of having to kill was something that had bothered him as well. But he had this feeling that expressing it to Sienna and helping her would also help him.

"You hunt because you have to," he repeated after a long moment of silence. "You fought and killed those Crooked to defend others, though. There are similarities to hunting, but fighting is something different."

"Like if a local predator started hunting people. We'd have to eliminate it for the safety of the village?" Sienna asked, her head still tilted as she considered his words.

"Yes, somewhat like that. You didn't seek out the Crooked to kill them because you hate them or because you enjoyed the act of killing. You did it to protect your people and rescue captives. I suppose that the difference between hunting and just fighting is that hunting has a more clean-cut purpose, while with fighting you have to constantly assess your reasons to ensure they are good ones. And you have to *trust* yourself when you decide those reasons are good."

"That sounds easier than it is to actually do," Sienna said with a sigh, her lone good ear wilting like normal while her inside-out one struggled.

"Remember why you do what you do, and who you are doing it for. It's how I have dealt with all this. Back home, the worst I'd done was a school-yard fistfight. Within an hour of coming here, I'd killed half a dozen people. Not saying it's easy, but remembering what motivates you will help keep you sane."

Koda gave her another squeeze, and Sienna nodded slowly before shifting to step away from him now that their talk was done. As he pulled his arm back over her head, he couldn't help the temptation and gently flicked her ear to turn it right-side out once more. The softness of her fur was exquisite, but he didn't dwell on it.

Sienna blinked at him in surprise for a moment, but a small smile tugged on her lips.

Nothing else needed to be said, and the two of them started along the path once more. Sienna considered what Koda had told her, while Koda did the same, but he couldn't stop thinking about how soft her fluffy ear had been under his fingers.

***

They actually made it back to the village before Kris and her group had left.

Since they weren't trying to sneak up on the Crooked camp like they had been on the way out, Sienna and Koda moved at a quicker pace than they had used before. The increased speed was what Koda attributed their better time to. That and the fact they had left with first light, so they arrived shortly after noon in the village.

While there hadn't been time for the villagers to erect walls, Koda was gratified to see that the road into the village had a decent blockade set up with a pair of wagons turned lengthwise in the road and cut logs piled in front of them, giving the defenders some shelter.

From what Koda observed on their way to the square at the center of the village, all the side streets had gotten similar fortifications to slow enemy approaches for the time being.

Need to talk to the headwoman about what sort of building technology they have. If I'm lucky, all that general contracting knowledge from working construction will help. Otherwise, it's just my fascination with history that could be useful. I think I remember how the Romans made their famous concrete, but if I remember right, they had access to quicklime and volcanic ash. No idea if Sienna's tribe has that.

Koda was lost in thought while he walked, to the point that Sienna had to say his name three times to get his attention.

"Sorry, what was that?" Koda blinked at her owlishly as Sienna snorted and rolled her eyes.

"I was saying that we should find Kris and see if she has heard yet. If they know where the last group of Crooked are, we can wrap this up and secure the vale. Also, get you that reward from Ther—" Sienna cut herself off and glanced around to make sure none of the people moving about heard her. Confirming that no one was listening in, she leaned closer and continued. "The reward from your patron, I mean."

"Thanks for keeping it quiet," Koda said with a small laugh. "But it's not that big of a deal."

"It is, though! She needs time to grow in strength enough that we can simply disregard the threat of other faiths," Sienna replied heatedly, her tail flicking in irritation.

Koda couldn't refute that, so he just nodded in agreement. "Fair point there. I forgot it wasn't just for my sake that we want to keep it quiet."

Sienna blushed and nodded, looking away quickly before her ears perked up.

"There's Kris! It looks like she's meeting with some of the hunters, likely trying to figure out how many need to be left here to guard the noncombatants."

Koda followed her pointing gesture and spotted the aged feline beastfolk on the far side of the square, standing in the shade of the inn and talking with a trio of beastfolk in the same patterned cloaks that Sienna wore.

"I can report to her if you want to get your arm seen to?" Koda offered as they hurried across the street.

"I'll be fine. The healer won't be able to do much more for it than what we have already," Sienna said while dismissively waving her left arm.

Koda wanted to protest, to insist she get her injury checked out, but he reminded himself that Sienna was her own person. She would make her own decisions after all, and he shouldn't try to force his desires where they weren't needed or wanted.

The hunters spotted them as they approached, and the pointing of one of their number drew Kris's attention to the duo. The feline-eared woman's eyes widened when she spotted them approaching, and she started to smile until she saw the bandage on Sienna's arm, then her expression turned worried.

"You two are back. And you are injured, Sienna! What happened? Tell me everything," Kris demanded, her weathered voice as firm as iron when she spoke.

"Yes, yes, we found another group and eliminated them before coming back to check with you," Sienna replied impishly, her tail wiggling happily behind her back as she came to a stop next to the four older beastfolk.

Kris apparently did not enjoy her cheek and scowled up at the wolf beastfolk, her fingers drumming on the head of her walking stick while she squinted and looked between the two of them.

Sienna wilted under that glare and started to stammer out a better explanation.

Deciding to rescue his companion from her failed joviality, Koda interrupted Sienna before she even got started in digging her hole even deeper.

"We found that group right where you expected, at the Last Fang Cave. They were performing some sort of profane ritual, which is why we attacked them rather than return for help. We didn't have a choice in the matter, Headwoman." Koda's words drew the irritated look away from Sienna and onto himself. Thankfully, Kris's gaze softened as she looked him over.

"Truly? No choice at all?" interrupted one of the hunters, a younger male with the heavy shoulders and rounded ears that showed he was of the bear clan amongst the beastfolk.

Kris shot him a withering look, which the hunter ignored, continuing to stare at Koda with suspicion.

"No, we did not. Thankfully, there weren't many, and we were able to use their natures and the location against them," Koda replied evenly. The bear-man gave him another pointed look with a judgmental snort, then turned his gaze towards Sienna.

"How many got away, Sienna?"

"Not sure. We only encountered and eliminated one hunting party, but their group was small at the camp. It's likely they were a reserve force left behind to watch the pass rather than raid or anything. As far as we know, we eliminated every one of the Crooked in that camp," Sienna answered with a shrug, clearly not as bothered by the bear-man's stare as she had been by Kris's.

"Well, that is fortunate." Kris interrupted the staring contest and drew their eyes to her. "I'm still waiting to hear back from the scouts I sent out. We are fairly certain that the last of the Crooked went up the mountain towards the snowline. The first batch of scouts I sent out yesterday returned this morning with news of mutilated animals and signs of a makeshift camp, but they reported no actual sightings of the Crooked."

"What about the group you sent to the old mine?" Koda's question drew a look from the other three hunters, but Kris just smiled and answered him without hesitation.

"Nothing. They didn't delve deep into the old mine complex, but there were no tracks at the entrance and no trail leading up to it. Unless there is another war party hiding near the old mine without going into it, then we know the last of them are up the mountain. The trail and the mutilated animals we found leads towards the Windwalker's Retreat like we had guessed, but we haven't got confirmation that was their goal or if they went deeper into the mountains."

"Headwoman!" another of the hunters protested, a woman with avian features and the feather-hair that Koda remembered from a few of those who had gone with him to the first combat site. "That location is secret."

"Oh hush, Gina," Kris sighed at the woman, rolling her eyes before looking pointedly back at Koda with a mysterious smile. "Koda would not divulge our secrets. And regardless of that, someone has to have told them about it since the Crooked appear to be heading in that direction."

"We should start moving that way then," Koda suggested, glancing at Sienna to check on her and getting a nod of agreement.

"Why are you letting this stranger give orders, Headwoman?" Apparently, Kris's reprimand wasn't enough to silence Gina. She was now glaring at Koda intensely.

"Because, Gina," Kris said quietly, glaring at the woman wholeheartedly now, "were you not listening? Have you just ignored the talk throughout the village in the last day? Koda came here and helped us defend our homes. Not satisfied with that, he raced off ahead of our hunters to save the villagers captured by the Crooked and slew a champion in the process. Then, not even taking a full day's rest, he set off to purge more of their taint from our vale. In the process, he secured one of our treasured historical sites, Last Fang Cave, with only Sienna as backup."

"To be fair, Sienna did a lot both times. She was right there beside me for the fighting, and Sienna killed the sorcerer that was trying to defile Last Fang Cave," Koda cut in, shooting the wolf woman a smile as she rolled her eyes at him.

"And Koda is forgetting to mention that he slew a *second* champion at the cave, as well as more than a dozen other Crooked while my count was only four or five from this encounter," Sienna protested.

"One of which was that sorcerer, though," Koda reminded her.

"That was after—"

"Ah, no. You killed it, you get the glory." Interrupting Sienna's protest, Koda held up a hand before turning back to Kris. "Sorry about that. You know Sienna. She doesn't want to take credit for her hard work, even if she got injured doing it... What?" Koda trailed off when he realized the three hunters were staring at him dumbfounded, while glancing towards Sienna every so often.

"A sorcerer?" Even Kris looked startled at this, staring directly at Sienna. Apparently, his defeating another champion wasn't any surprise to her, but she also knew his status as Thera's champion, too.

"Yup, all by herself. Chopped their head right off with that spear there," Koda spoke before Sienna could find her words, grinning broadly while the wolf woman shot him a dirty look. "Take the compliment, Sienna," he added a moment later in a quieter tone, and she sighed.

Turning back to the trio of hunters who were looking impressed now, as if they were seeing Sienna in a whole new light, Koda crossed his arms over his chest.

"Any other questions?" Kris asked acidly, turning to grump at the trio once more.

"No, Headwoman!" the three chorused.

Chapter Nineteen

They talked for another hour, making plans and trying to decide what the best approach would be.

With the lack of response from the scouts that they had sent up to Windwalker's Retreat, there was some hesitation about what to do next. Koda pushed to head out immediately, but Kris had rejected the idea. She had a force of around forty people willing to fight, but they couldn't leave the village entirely unguarded. People needed to secure their homes and prepare those who would stay behind.

"Kris, how about Koda and I scout ahead of the group? I don't know about the rest of you, but we are tired of having these monsters in our vale. I want to get a full night's sleep and not have to worry about some bent monster weaseling its way in down the chimney," Sienna suggested, eying Koda while he thought.

"Are you sure, Sienna?" Kris turned a slightly concerned look toward the wolf-eared huntress.

"Yes. I would rather push to the finish on this hunt than stretch it out and let some of them slip through the net.

Twice now we've found them either in the midst of some kind of depraved ritual or preparing for one. If they are doing something similar, we need to know and be ready to interrupt it." Sienna shot several glances at Koda as she spoke, gauging his reaction to her suggestion.

Koda was watching her with a thoughtful look in his eyes, arms crossed over his chest, and the sharp claws on his gauntlet were tapping away on his bare left arm, leaving tiny dents in his skin but not actually piercing it.

"That is basically my concern," Koda said when the others all looked at him. "I don't know much about magic personally, but I know that whatever they were doing, it wasn't good. And I have a duty to get rid of the threats to the village."

"Duty?" murmured Gina, her head tilting in confusion while her feather-hair fluffed slightly.

"Koda promised me that he would do everything he could to help us. He takes those promises seriously," Sienna said quickly, hoping to divert their attention away from the momentary slip of the tongue.

"And I am very glad for his offer of support," added Kris, shifting to lean heavier on her walking stick. "With how things are going lately, we will need the extra support."

"Not to mention, when we were down at the cave before, Sienna mentioned something about another village being nearby? If the Crooked hit them as well, then they might need help. We can't even risk going to check on them until after we have the area secured here." A series of nods met Koda's statement as everyone in their little group agreed with his summation.

"Ultimately, are you sure that this is a good idea? Heading out now won't let you reach the supposed site before nightfall. Would it not be better to sleep in a bed and start out in the morning?" Kris tried one last time to sway Koda, but he shook his head.

"The more information we can gather before we clash, the better. If Sienna and I at least keep moving, we can make a good start and hopefully meet up with your scouts. That will let us begin planning while the rest of you catch up. There is enough evidence to show they are heading in that direction to get us moving in pursuit."

The discussion continued for another few minutes, hashing out plans and who would accompany Sienna and Koda. One thing that Kris was firm on was that the two of them would not be going alone, given the mischief they'd gotten into unsupervised already.

Sienna led the way back to the building they had slept in for Koda's first night here, intent on refreshing her supplies from the stores there while Kris sent the trio of hunters off to gather a small group to accompany Koda and Sienna as a secondary scouting team and advance guard.

"Thanks for having my back there," Koda said, leaning against the rail of the bunk beds while Sienna rummaged through a chest and pulled out fresh bandages.

"You had a good point. The others are just... well, scared isn't quite the right way to phrase it. I think a lot of us are still stunned about what happened, and since we saved those people that the Crooked took in their raid, a lot of folks want to pretend that the problem is solved and not think about it." Sienna shot him a small smile, her ears twitching happily while her tail whipped back and forth before digging back into the cabinet.

"What makes people so afraid of the Crooked? I mean, beyond the obvious," Koda said with a wave of his hand, grimacing as he tried to find the right way to describe the disturbing appearances of the Crooked.

"The Crooked are bogeymen for a lot of people. Ours especially." Sienna glanced over her shoulder to check, but there were no others in the simple log building of the hunter's hall right now. "Kris would tell us stories about them. Of how the Crooked came into being. How it was mostly their work that drove Thera from her throne and our people from our homes in the ancient past."

Koda blinked in surprise, staring down at Sienna for several long moments as she continued to work silently, her wagging tail slowly stilling.

"What makes them so terrifying? The ones we've encountered, except for the champions, haven't been that bad. Other than being visually disturbing," Koda asked after a long pause to think.

"It's because of *what* they are," Sienna said with a sigh, flipping the top of her pack down and buckling it into place. Koda helped her get the pack settled without stressing her injured arm, and they headed back out into the street towards the central fountain to wait. "If the stories are to be believed—and after what we've seen, I believe them—then the Crooked used to be just normal people. Long ago, they made a deal with a dark power, and that dark power twisted them into what they are. Corrupted them to the core of their beings. They are called the Crooked because everything about them is crooked. Their bodies, their hearts, and their souls."

"That is very dark," Koda muttered, reaching out instinctively to help steady Sienna when she stumbled on a rough spot in the cobbled road.

"They are legends," Sienna said with a shrug, smiling up at him while steadying herself using the haft of her spear. "But legends have roots in reality, and after seeing them, well..."

"Those roots are a little easier to see?" Koda suggested, clearing his throat and looking away abruptly as Sienna's eyes tried to capture him once more.

Sienna's ears wilted when Koda looked away so quickly but recovered when she no doubt spotted the faint blush on his cheeks.

Biting her lip, she shifted to lean into him while they walked. Not enough to throw him off balance, but enough that their arms or hips would bump into each other on occasion.

"Yes, exactly. And it makes me worry about what else the legends have right about them. The Crooked have many forms, and all of them are twisted facsimiles of normal people. We know that they use foul rituals to change captives into more of their own. That alone is enough to give us a reason to fight them. There are enough monsters in the world without having to imagine your neighbors or family being turned into more."

Emerging from the side road into the center of the village, the two of them settled against the wall of the inn to wait for the others that would be coming. To be accurate, Koda leaned against the wall. Sienna ended up leaning back against him, pinning his left arm and side to the wall once she slipped her pack off to set on the ground by their feet.

"Comfortable?" Koda teased, glancing down at Sienna while her pointed ears flicked. He could see the faint hints of a blush on Sienna's cheeks, but she refused to look up at him.

"Yes," she replied shortly, not moving from her spot.

Her tail continued to bounce slowly against his thigh, the mass of fluff stirring just from being in proximity to him. He could't help himself, and let his fingers play over the base of her tail gently, stroking over the soft fur. Sienna shivered in response, biting her lip to suppress a moan but not moving away from him.

They remained like that for several minutes, enjoying the quiet bustle of the village and greeting villagers as they went past. Sienna could see that the citizens of Silverstone–he had found out earlier that the village was named after the vale–had not grown complacent. Everywhere she looked, people went about their day armed, even if it was just a cudgel or a knife on their belt.

"Really need to see about getting actual guards for the village," Koda muttered, his mind clearly whirling back along his previous thought processes regarding what sort of construction he might be able to set into place to help secure the village. "I need to know more about what sort of threats are in the area, though. That'll determine what kind of defenses are priorities."

Sienna listened to Koda mutter quietly for several moments while turning over the conversation she'd had with Thera the previous night. She remembered the moment that the goddess had turned away from her and chastised someone just out of her sight for spying. Someone that she *knew* was Koda, even before the goddess had said his name.

How much did he overhear? Sienna wondered silently. She shifted carefully to not disturb Koda as he continued to ponder and mutter to himself. The feeling of his hand lightly stroking over her tail as it wagged behind her was pleasant, wonderful even. *Would it be too fast? I've already seen his commitment to us, and Thera is right that we can't lose him.*

Emotions swelled in Sienna's chest. Joy at speaking to a goddess that she had always hoped was listening to them. Fear of losing that hope now that she had it. Desire to share that hope with others. While Koda might not see it, she could see the wariness that the normally jovial villagers viewed the world around them with, and it tore at her heart.

"Koda?" His name slipped from her lips before Sienna could stop herself.

Koda paused in his thoughts and glanced down to meet her gaze, his eyebrows rising questioningly.

"Did you... hear what I spoke with the Pack Lady about last night?" Koda blinked slowly once, not looking away from her. Sienna worried that he wasn't going to answer her at first, but after a moment that dragged on for far too long, he did speak.

"I heard part of it. About not wanting to lose my bloodline again." Sienna's blush deepened, but Koda either didn't notice or didn't care as he had lost himself in her eyes. "I remember you offering to help her, and I appreciate that greatly."

Sienna's heart paused in her chest. He already knew? But before she could panic and say something, Koda continued.

"Having someone like you to look out for me, to watch my back, it's really reassuring to know that you want to help keep me safe."

"I-I... that is... I m-mean," Sienna began to stutter, the hope in her heart fluttering and nearly going out before Koda interrupted her.

"The rest we can worry about as we get to know each other, Sienna." His arm slipped from its previous position to wrap around Sienna's hips from behind, pulling her back against him gently so that she was snuggled into his side and shoulder. Her tail began to bounce again, gradually picking up speed as her ears perked up.

"Then..."

"It might be fast, but I really like you, Sienna. Of all the people I've met so far, you are the one who comes to mind first when I think of my promise to Thera to protect her people," Koda said quietly, leaning in to bump the tip of his nose against hers.

Sienna squeaked in surprise, blinking rapidly before her eyes crossed to look at the tip of her nose, then the tip of Koda's while a fierce blush raged across her cheeks.

"Oh, would you two kiss already!?" a familiar voice called from nearby, causing both to jump in surprise.

Looking up, Sienna felt her embarrassment flare even higher when she spotted the grinning face of Netta, the hawk beastfolk that had come with them on their raid at the standing stones. Behind her were another five hunters from a mixture of beastfolk races, and all of them were grinning.

"Well, if the spectators insist?" Koda said with a grin before grunting in pain when Sienna elbowed him in the chest. The blow got a round of laughter from the hunters.

"Guess not, lover boy. Come on, you two, let's get on the trail since you want to push so hard to finish this fight," Netta snickered, gesturing for them to follow her as she turned to lead the group of hunters out of the village.

Chapter Twenty

THE ADVANCED TEAM RESTED SOME WAYS UP THE mountain, still within the tree line. By unanimous decision, they kept a cold camp, not wanting to risk a fire and help any Crooked looking to spot them. All throughout the day, even within hours of leaving the village, they'd been seeing signs of the monstrous creatures passing. No one wanted to be attacked in the night.

Sienna and Koda were told to rest first since they'd had to split watches the previous night. Koda hadn't argued with Netta about that. He'd put on a strong front, but the fight, half night of sleep, and the fast march back to the village earlier that day had worn him out.

It was only a slight surprise to Koda when Sienna laid her bedroll out next to his, muttering something about staying close to share warmth before curling up to sleep.

Koda woke up twice in the night, once when Sienna wiggled under his blankets to snuggle into his side, and then again near dawn when she slipped out once more to return to her bedroll.

He'd dreamed of chasing Sienna through the trees, following the patter of her feet, flashes of movement, as well as her flicking tail. The dream was odd, though, because he wasn't the only one chasing her. He was joined by a large shadow with long brown hair that also laughed along with him, helping to herd the nimble wolf beastfolk into his arms. The last image he had was of flashing yellow eyes and a lusty smile as he caught Sienna, her giggling and flailing to escape matching up so well with her careful wiggling to free herself and get back to her own bedroll.

Based on the glances and smiles from Netta and a few of the other hunters, Sienna hadn't been nearly as sneaky as she might have thought in her night expedition, but she didn't rise to her friend's gentle teasing.

Throughout the rest of the morning, eating the simple breakfast of cold bread, cheese, and smoked meat, Sienna stuck close to him.

She stayed by his side while he packed up his bedroll and while they walked to the stream nearby to refill their waterskins.

When Koda settled onto a rock to eat, Sienna plumped down next to the rock and leaned into it, ending up with her back pressed to both it and him. She didn't look back when Koda froze mid-bite and looked down at her, instead just sitting there primly while she nibbled on a strip of meat while facing away from him.

Gently, he felt her tail bump against his boot while it wagged behind her.

The desire to be close to him persisted throughout the morning, with Sienna marching next to him on his right. She kept herself by his side, but not so much that she got in his way.

Partway through the morning, he considered asking Sienna about it. Something had changed recently. Then he remembered their conversation the previous day and the gentle scent of her as she curled up against his side in the night.

Lucky son of a bitch you are, he thought with a mental laugh. *Not even here for three days, and you don't even have to question whether a girl is interested in you. You better not go waffling back and forth on the 'does she, doesn't she' side of things either. Pretty sure I know what she and Thera were talking about with the whole 'preserving my bloodline' talk in the dream. If she wasn't interested, then she'd have said something or just kept her distance.*

While they walked through the thinning trees, the air became slowly cooler as the game trails they followed wound around the edge of the tall mountain that loomed over the vale. And as he walked, Koda turned over the events of the last few days in his mind and thought about the future.

When she'd brought him here, Thera had promised him a home, somewhere to belong. She'd promised him a family as well. Hell, one of the first things she'd offered as an incentive to him was women, after all. Koda couldn't help but smirk at that.

How many men would have willingly dived through the portal at that idea? he thought while navigating around an old fallen tree. Sienna kept close behind him before reclaiming her spot to his right, spear still slung over her shoulder. *Not that I'm far behind them. I kind of committed to this whole thing with little thought, just purely on the idea of not being alone anymore.*

Glancing sidelong at Sienna, he caught her profile as she studied the ridge ahead of them, and her blue-green eyes glinted like polished crystal. Determination etched her features while the wind tossed her short red hair, gently stirring the fluff that hung around her pointed ears. She looked like a fierce warrior, straight out of a historic painting in her leather outfit, hunter's cloak, and with her spear over one shoulder.

Those pointed ears flicked suddenly, and the moment shattered.

Sienna glanced to her side at him and blushed when she caught him staring. Rather than glance away like she had caught him doing something wrong, Koda just smiled at her and gave her a nod before he turned his gaze to the front once more.

I need to find out what sort of social expectations they have here, Koda resolved to himself. While some might think it early to be considering things like love and a relationship, he'd learned firsthand just how dangerous this world was. *If Sienna is interested in me, I need to see if there are any ceremonies that her people follow. If this is going to be something between us, I'm not going to just have my fun and leave her in the dust. I can't do that to her. No, I refuse to do that to her.*

Koda felt something shift in his chest and harden, settling right next to the determination to make good on the opportunity Thera had presented in bringing him here. The possessive, protective feeling that had haunted his soul after Sienna got hurt curled up and went to sleep again.

Feeling something bump against the back of his totemic gauntlet, he glanced down to see Sienna's left hand as it slowly swung away from bumping into him.

Shifting as he walked, and being mindful of the blades on his fingertips, Koda caught Sienna's left hand in his right, squeezing it gently. When Sienna's gaze jumped to their joined hands and then up to his face, Koda smiled at her. Tentatively, Sienna smiled back.

Just behind her, he caught sight of the red-black mass of her tail picking up speed as the light swaying of the appendage from her walk turned into a full-on wag.

They encountered more and more signs of the Crooked's passing. Strange marks carved into trees, small animals turned into bizarre territory markers, the ashes of old fires, and twice they found meadows trampled by a large group in passing. These last ones got the most study from the group of hunters. The group would pause to inspect them and use the time to take a break from their forced march.

It was also the only time that Sienna went farther than a few feet from him.

The redheaded wolf woman would confer with the other hunters, counting tracks and trying to get an estimate on how many of the Crooked there were in the valley still, based on the camp size and arrangement. But the naturally chaotic layouts of the camp made doing so hard.

The only things that they could confirm was the presence of at least one Crooked champion because of the larger and deeper footprints that kept to one section of the camp, and the fact that there had to be at least another sixty or more Crooked with it.

Koda did what he could to learn from the hunters, studying the grass and undergrowth where they pointed when discussing the camps, but all he saw was a mess in the grass, piled refuse, and old fires. It honestly reminded him of when he'd find the remains of a frat party kegger up in the mountains, just minus the scattered beer cans and food wrappers.

It was while inspecting the remains of the second campsite that the other group of scouts found them.

Purely because he was keeping watch while the hunters conversed, Koda spotted the movement in the trees, and he opened his mouth to say something.

Before he could speak, Sienna's ears popped up, having heard the sound of movement. She whirled to lift her weapon, only to relax when she recognized the trio of hunters emerging from the trees at a steady jog.

Koda didn't know any of the three, but clearly the other hunters did as the two groups merged, and questions were thrown back and forth rapidly.

"Did you find them?"

"How many are there?"

"Did they stop at the Retreat like the headwoman thinks?"

"People!" Sienna's terse bark quieted the storm of questions, and everyone looked to her curiously.

Koda slipped in to stand at her back, content to listen and let Sienna handle this. He got a few curious looks from the new group, but he guessed that either Kris had told them about him or they had heard about the initial fight at the standing stones because none of them questioned his presence there.

"Report what you've seen," Sienna said once the talking quieted enough, her ears flicking in irritation while her tail puffed slightly.

Koda laid his left hand on her back, just above her tail. The contact seemingly reassured her, and a bit of the tension left Sienna's posture while the group circled up to listen.

The leader of the trio, a pinch-faced man with gray-wolf features, was the one who spoke first.

"As expected, the Crooked have camped within the Wind-walker's Retreat. We weren't able to get too close as they have plenty of guards stationed around the entrance, but we heard the sound of picks on stone. Enough that it sounds similar to late-spring hail." The wolf-man squatted and began using a stick to draw in some of the disturbed dirt of the meadow where the passage of feet had pounded the grass away. "We watched the site and gathered what information we could. But with the walls so high, it is difficult to get a good view unless we go all the way around and up the mountain."

The drawing in the dirt showed a small valley, almost like a volcanic caldera, that had high, sloped walls wrapping around either side of it. The hunter marked two spots on the outer wall with X's.

"There are two entrances to the Retreat. Both had guards, around ten or so Crooked between the two," he was saying before one of the other hunters interrupted him.

"If you can even call what they are doing guarding. They just sort of stood around and blocked the entrance, either painting on the walls with blood or arguing with each other. I swear a troll would be more aware than they are." The speaker was an older female with the features of a spotted hunting cat to her ears and tail, clutching a bow in her off-hand while her tail lashed in anger.

"Be glad that they aren't trolls. I guarantee they'd have done even more damage to the village than a few messed-up buildings and scorched roofs," Netta said acidly, her feathers fluffing up before she turned her attention back to the first man. "What else can you tell us?"

The wolf beastfolk took a moment to consider his map before drawing another long line out to wrap around one side of the little valley.

"We didn't see any signs of them along the goat track that goes to the high meadows. Which is a pity. If they went up and harassed the steelhorn herds, then that might make our jobs a little easier."

"Steelhorn?" Koda asked quietly, directing his question to Sienna as the group of hunters studied the map.

"Natives to the high mountains. They are a breed of mountain sheep that are rather ornery," Netta actually hopped in to answer the question before Sienna could. "They aren't any more durable than regular sheep, but they don't eat just grass. They also look for and consume iron ore during their ranging months. That ore hardens their horns and hooves to the point that they can fight off most predators. Only mountain trolls, stonecracker leopards, and the occasional lucky wolf will bring one down. We cull the herds when we can, but we have to be careful not to over-harvest them. Steelhorn ewes only birth one lamb a year."

Sienna nodded in agreement with her friend before glancing back at Koda, the question obvious in her eyes.

Do we keep going or head back?

"I want to see the Retreat myself," Koda said quietly, hoping to keep his words to just him and Sienna. "We already came out here with the intent of scouting it out more and trying to plan an attack. No reason to head back already. If we send these three back, they can meet up with Kris and fill her in."

"Yes, that's what I was thinking," Sienna muttered, the swish of her tail picking up as she stole glances up at Koda's face, a small smile on her lips. "If we are fortunate, we might be able to pick off a couple of their hunting parties while we wait and get a better count on their number. Otherwise, we can keep watch to ensure none of them wander too far or break off. It'll give our small team a chance to settle in as well."

Koda nodded in agreement, and Sienna turned back to the drawing once more to explain the plan.

"That really makes for one heck of a secure camp," Koda mumbled as he peeked through the branches of the tree he had climbed to look up the slope.

Before they had separated, the trio of returning hunters had advised them of several trees on the slope that had enough cover to give them observation perches. It was in those trees now that their party was concealed.

It had taken another few hours to get the rest of the way up the slope, and now Koda was studying the walls of Wind-walker's Retreat through a simple telescope that he'd borrowed from Sienna as the sun began to dip behind the mountains.

"There's a reason that a wendigo used the valley as a den in ages past," Sienna gently ribbed him back. She was a few branches higher than him, having made use of her lighter bodyweight to get a slightly higher view in the thinner branches. "Pass me that thing."

Silently, Koda handed it up to her while thinking over what he'd seen.

Farther up the slope, a nearly sheer cliff wall rose like the beginnings of a mesa. The vertical rock wall was easily sixty feet tall, with only the barest of chinks and cracks to provide grips or a means to climb it. Lichen studded the gray stone in smears of yellow, green, and white, giving the cliffside a mottled look.

A steep mess of scree and loose rocks fronted the rock face as well, ensuring that anyone approaching along the rough path to the cliff was in plain sight. He couldn't tell from down here, but it looked like the sheer cliff wrapped around before merging into a longer set of cliffs, giving the back of the nook a solid rear defense as well.

The only thing dividing the sheer wall was a pair of slim cracks in the stone. One only reached up about eight feet and was barely wide enough that Koda thought he could squeeze into it. The other traveled the entire length of the cliff face to the top and stood wide enough that two grown men could walk side-by-side through it.

The Crooked guards crouching in front of both meant that no one would be sneaking up on this camp, though.

Unlike the first camp in its shallow valley, there were more than a few Crooked standing watch, though Koda agreed with the huntress from earlier that it was a distracted one.

He had watched as three of the bent humanoids tossed rocks into a small circle scratched on the stone floor of the ravine, grunting at each other and trading small objects back and forth. He wasn't sure if they were playing dice or some kind of marbles game as the stones they threw did not have regular shapes. Four more Crooked leaned against the wall, wandered back and forth, or napped.

At the smaller crack, two more guards were painting the walls with obscene signs using the blood from the corpse of some kind of small rodent.

Distantly, a faint curl of smoke rose above the cliff, and Koda could hear the quiet *clink* of metal on stone and the rumble of voices shouting.

"Ugh, I wish we could see how many there were in there. It would help figure this out," Sienna grumbled above him.

"How steep are the walls of the Retreat?" Koda asked, watching that twist of smoke rising over the cliff in thought.

"Steep. If it wasn't for the cracks in the walls, the only way in or out would be by air. It's why they called it 'Windwalker's Retreat' after all. The wendigo that nested there was the only creature who could get in or out for a long time. Why?"

"Was thinking that if we could get around to see it from above, we could wreak quite a bit of havoc up there. Throwing stuff down into the ravine and the like."

Sienna was quiet for a moment, thinking as she tapped on the leather-wrapped brass barrel of the little telescope.

"We might be able to creep around if we go down and then up a different trail. We'd have to go over the scree and up the game trail if we didn't want to lose hours, though. If we go at night and move extremely carefully, then it might work to get a view without going around. Whoever did it would have to have excellent night vision to avoid being spotted." Sienna made another quiet humming noise as she thought before letting out a quiet laugh.

"What's up?" Koda asked, glancing up at Sienna. She was sitting with both legs draped over a branch and leaning back against the trunk of the tree, a sharp smile creasing her pretty mouth while her tail slowly brushed against her leg.

"Well, you had such good luck setting fire to their camp before. Why not repeat that feat, but this time with a bit more style?"

The grin that grew on Koda's face mirrored Sienna's for savagery as the two shared a long look.

Chapter Twenty-One

SIENNA AND KODA HAD RUSHED TO DESCEND THE TREE before sending the quickest runner of the hunters back down the mountain with orders to get back to the village and try to catch Kris before the headwoman left. They would need as much pitch and lamp oil as the village could spare.

While they waited for the rest of the force to arrive, Koda scouted around the area and found a few fallen logs and branches that would work for his part of Sienna's plan.

With the help of two of the hunters, he set about preparing them while Sienna spent the evening scouting out the approach that she thought might succeed in circumventing the guards while staying out of sight.

"You sure this is going to do what you think it will?" Netta asked while they worked, being careful to keep the noise of their blades as low as possible.

"It's not meant for foot troops, more for cavalry, but it'll work. If we could dig some tiger pits or lay actual traps, that would be even better, but we will use what we have," Koda countered. "We'd have to draw them out of the ravine to get those to work, and that will be counter to the plan."

He had given up using his belt knife after a few minutes and was instead using the claws of his gauntlet to flay the bark off the log. The sharpness and durability of the bone talons attached to his totemic gauntlet still astonished him at times.

It shouldn't be that surprising, Thera made this thing for me. I just wish I could take it off for a while. I'm always worried about clawing up my face in my sleep. Koda thought, using the claw on his thumb to smooth a knot out before he began notching the log. *This would be so much easier if I could just shape the wood like it was clay or something... but this is still pretty awesome.*

"But how do you know they will work? Were you part of the army before you came to our village?" Netta asked, her feather-hair flexing slightly.

The motion caught Koda's attention. He looked up to check on her, but the part-hawk woman had her eyes on her work.

"I know a lot about historic battles and tactics. You could say I studied them," Koda said after a moment of watching her.

Can't really tell them about the Discovery Channel, after all. That ancient weapons montage was great for when I was too tired to think after work. I might actually be able to build something like a trebuchet if I had the time to experiment. And the right tools... Koda thought with a stifled smirk and got back to work.

"What's your intent with Sienna?" Netta asked after another moment. The hawk-woman grunted when the other hunter who was helping them elbowed her. "What? It's a legitimate question. I worry about her."

"Worry about her after the fight. You don't need to be stirring up shit when none of us know if we'll still be here next week," chastised the other woman, a bear beastfolk who Koda didn't have a name for yet.

Netta grumbled and got back to her work, though she didn't stop shooting the occasional glance at Koda.

"What my plans for Sienna are will depend on what she wants to do. And that is something that I don't want to pressure her on while we have distractions," Koda replied a moment later. He knew that he didn't need to answer Netta's question after the other hunter had chastised her, but he could respect her concern for a friend.

The quiet *snick* of parting wood continued for several more moments before Netta broke the silence again.

"She's not one to trust quickly. The fact she's so attached to you is surprising. I worried at first you'd cast some kind of compulsion on her."

"Nope. Not unless you consider telling her outright that she's beautiful to be a compulsion," Koda countered with a snort.

"Have you actually done that?" Netta asked, glancing up occasionally as she took up the next branch and began sharpening one end of it.

"Not yet. Like she said"—Koda nodded to the bear woman— "we don't need to deal with distractions right now. Honestly, I've just been treating Sienna with respect and appreciation. She's a great person, and I'm glad to know her. I want to make sure we all survive this mess, then I'll worry about raining compliments on her. She knows she's special to me."

A soft sensation of something brushing against Koda's back and over his left shoulder made him jump. He glanced to his left and ended up with his face buried in red-black fluff that patted against his cheek a few times before slipping away.

Glancing to his right when he felt something press into his side on the downed log he sat on, he found Sienna settling there with a blush obvious on her face and her ears laid to either side in embarrassment.

"I swear, Netta. You were doing that just to make me look stupid," Sienna growled at her friend, the expression one of irritation mixed with amusement.

Despite her embarrassment, Sienna still leaned into Koda's arm with her tail whipping back and forth behind them to pat lightly into his lower back. Clearly, she'd heard what they talked about and appreciated what Koda had said.

Netta didn't have to trick me into saying that, but whatever, he thought with a small grin.

"Nope. Well, not entirely. I was partially curious and partially wanting to embarrass you. If I made him uncomfortable, it was a bonus. But he took it like a champ," Netta shot back, her reserved and judgmental look gone to be replaced with a broad smile, her feathered hair fluffing and smoothing in satisfaction.

"Was... Uh... Did you mean..." Sienna stuttered, clearly trying to force a question out while darting glances sidelong at Koda. Her ears flicked up and then laid flat again.

"Yes, I meant it all." Koda's words stilled her anxious ears. A moment later, they perked up, and her tail began stirring faster. "You know this already, Sienna. Why would you question it?" She didn't answer, only shrugged.

Pausing at what he was doing, Koda threw an arm around Sienna's shoulders and pulled her into a side-hug that was strong enough to make her squeak in surprise. The redhead nuzzled her head into his shoulder, the tips of her ears tickling his face and chin.

"Aww, so cute," opined Netta, getting another smack from the older woman on her other side.

Following Sienna in the near pitch darkness was difficult for Koda but not impossible.

Of the small group of hunters that remained behind to keep watch on the camp, there was only one other besides Sienna who had good enough night sight to attempt the trip around to finish surveying the Windwalker's Retreat from above. Koda had volunteered to go because he didn't want Sienna to be very far away from him. While his night sight wasn't anything impressive, he could see relatively well in the low light. The other hunter with them was a cat beastfolk named Hannah who had black fur like Kris, the headwoman.

They had initially planned to wait for the reinforcements from the village to arrive so they could send individuals with more applicable skills. However, the opportunity arose during the night when clouds appeared over the mountain.

So the three had prepared and gotten into place to take the opportunity when the moon slipped behind the clouds and the night darkened further.

Glancing up the slope of broken rock, Koda squinted at the bright point of light some hundred yards from them where the Crooked on guard had a torch in one hand. The guard was waving it about and making shapes with it until one of the others smacked it, making the monster-man drop the torch for a brief moment before a fight broke out.

"Go," murmured Hannah from right behind him, urging them to hurry along and take advantage of the distraction.

Sienna picked up speed, disturbing only a few rocks amongst the boulders as she went. The hunter's cloak wrapped around her lithe form gave her outline a distorted shape that made it hard to spot her, but Koda did his best while Hannah whispered directions if he wandered too far off the route.

They made it to the goat track that wound around in front of the entrance to the Windwalker's Retreat before the argument and fight between the Crooked guards died off.

Koda saw Sienna go still, leaning into the rock next to her and letting her cloak fall into an irregular shape like the boulder she was leaning against. So he did his best to mimic the feat.

They'd talked this out, and they had agreed that the most dangerous part of the attempt to sneak past the guards was the section of trail they were on right now. It was the closest to the light, and the area was the most open. Thankfully, their cloaks would help them blend in with the loose scree and bare earth as long as they didn't make any large movements.

After a few seconds, Koda felt a single light pat on his back from Hannah, the prearranged signal to move, so he repeated it by patting Sienna's back. They'd agreed to creep along like this, with Hannah signaling when to move because her night sight was the strongest.

His aim must have been off, because Sienna twitched as he patted her ass. But she didn't whirl on him or yelp. Instead, there was a slight delay before she began creeping forward, and that was enough for Koda to realize what he'd done.

Grimacing, he promised himself that he would apologize as soon as it was safe to do so.

They eased forward another ten steps before Sienna went still again, holding for a good dozen breaths until the signal from Hannah came again. This repeated for the next half an hour as they slowly crept up the trail, using large rocks to block themselves from the view of the watchers.

Twice, Koda heard a quiet grunt from Hannah as she lobbed a rock to distract the guards before receiving a trio of pats, which was the signal for a quick move. Koda knew she had to be careful doing that as the click of stone shifting pulled all the watchers, even those with their dice game, into motion to investigate. They always had to wait longer after she did it, but it was the only way to get past the sections that were the most exposed.

Finally, they made it around a large boulder on the upper edge of the slope, and Sienna slumped against it, flipping her hood back to take a breath of air and fan at her face with one hand.

"Good lord, that was tense," she murmured barely above a whisper.

"You two did great." Hannah popped her head around Koda to shoot a smile at Sienna. "Never would have thought you could improve that much with your stealth, Sienna."

"Oh, it's easy. Just have to threaten me with grotesque punishments and torture at the hands of monsters," Sienna snarked back at the part-cat woman, rolling her eyes.

"I'll have to remember that when I train the next batch of young hunters."

"Don't you dare, Hannah. You were enough of a terror when you taught me, and you were still fresh back then."

"Should we keep moving? The night is only so long, and we will have to sneak back down." Koda's words cut through the two women's playful bickering, and they both nodded.

The trio still paused there for several minutes to catch their breath and rest. While the short trip hadn't covered much ground, standing tense and ready put a hell of a strain on the body.

They had to continue up the steep goat track before too long, though, not wanting to waste the opportunity. The trail eventually evened out, and the slope curled around to another set of sheer cliffs. This one was only about fifteen feet high. The goat track wound further up into the hills, but they departed it now that they had reached the right spot.

This time, it was Hannah who led the way, nimbly scaling the stone face while Sienna and Koda stood guard. Once she reached the top, the cat beastfolk uncoiled a rope from around her waist and secured it to help the other two make their way up.

Sienna had to coach Koda how to use the rope to ascend. Once he had the technique of clamping the rope between his feet while reaching up with his hands, Koda's boosted strength came into play, and he was able to shimmy up quickly.

Reaching the top, Koda immediately dropped down into a low crouch and peered around.

The quiet *chink* of iron on stone had been a constant chorus throughout the day and most of the night, but up until this point, it had sounded a lot like distant crickets or some rather hoarse cicadas. But up on the cliff edge like this, there wasn't nearly as much to block the noise now.

The cliff itself was about twenty feet across where he stood, with another, taller cliff face rising to his left. Even crouched like he was, Koda could see the ring of the cliff as it cruised out into a flattened half-circle, only broken by the largest of the entrances.

The darkness of the night wasn't nearly as thick up here. The light of fires down in the little gully that made up the Windwalker's Retreat burned bright enough to make what was happening below *very* easy to see despite the thick layer of smoky haze that hung over the whole place.

Below them, the Crooked had another of their haphazard camps laid out over the front half of the ravine. The large, multi-sided tent that Koda was beginning to associate with the presence of a champion sat towards the back of the little ravine, separated from the regular tents by a strip of bare earth .

To one side, tucked up against the cliff in a slight depression where it would be somewhat protected from rain, was the source of the clinking and tinking noises.

A dozen Crooked wielded iron picks as they chipped away at the cliff and the floor of the ravine. From the scars on the stone and the piles of rock that lay about, it was obvious they had been hard at work for some time, though their progress was not great.

"What are they doing?" Hannah asked in a low tone, peering over the edge on his left as Sienna settled in on his right.

The three of them laid out on their bellies and peeked over the edge to survey the camp, doing their utmost to keep their profiles low while they watched. Koda had to fight the urge to jump when Sienna finally got her revenge for him patting her ass earlier by squeezing his, but just shot her a questioning look, getting a smirk in response.

"They are looking for something," Sienna murmured, shifting to the side slightly so that she pressed into Koda's right arm with her left.

The insistence of the wolf-woman to always be in contact with him was more than a little endearing to him, so Koda leaned into it as well while they observed. There was something that just felt so *right* about having her there against him.

The Crooked continued to labor through the hours, chipping away with their picks until a lump of stone would pull free. Then they'd stop and inspect that stone before tossing it aside onto a pile against the wall.

Over the entire operation presided another Crooked in robes with a hood. The hooded one would occasionally bark something in their twisted tongue at the workers or club a laborer with a bent bit of wood that it was leaning on as a staff.

The trio observed the workers in silence for the better part of an hour, studying the camp for any weaknesses that they could observe. In that time, two of the Crooked workers collapsed.

When one would fall over, the robed Crooked would first berate and strike them with its staff, before ordering two others to drag the exhausted worker aside. Two of the workers would leave with their comrade in tow and return with another to take the unconscious worker's place a short while later.

"Are they trying to make a burrow?" Sienna asked after a large chunk of rock fell away to the excitement of the workers.

"Maybe? But if they did, wouldn't it make more sense to do it somewhere else that was easier to dig?" Koda suggested, watching as the laborers fell on the large rock and hammered it to pieces before slumping in dejection and sweeping the fragments away before returning to their work.

They stayed to observe for several more hours, getting a rough count of the forces. The entire time, Koda watched for any sign of a champion, wondering if the robed Crooked was the owner of the tent. But the robed one never moved far from its vigil, watching over those digging into the stone and administering punishment.

As the night waned and the clouds began to clear on the horizon in preparation for the dawn, Hannah hurried them back down the cliff, wanting to take advantage of the clouded moon to get them past the guards again. They'd watched a guard change head through the splits in the cliff an hour before, and now was a good time to head back as the guards would have settled in and started getting complacent.

Chapter Twenty-Two

Two groups of Crooked hunters emerged from the ravine the next morning. One group headed up into the mountains, following the goat track, while the other headed down the mountain towards the village. Neither group was large, only five Crooked, two with bows and three with spears.

There was a bit of a debate about whether to take them out. In the end, they all agreed that it was too dangerous to risk the group heading down the mountain finding some evidence of the watchers or their camp. There was also a risk that the hunters not returning might alert the camp, but they expected Kris and her other hunters to arrive sometime that day. The last thing that they needed was this small group of Crooked to see Kris's group coming and race back to warn their people.

Given that the hunters in the group had spent most of their lives combing this mountain for game, it wasn't hard for them to sneak up on the interlopers and take them by surprise.

A quintet of arrows eliminated the two Crooked with bows, while Sienna, Koda, and the other two hunters took the other three out by surging out of cover and rapidly striking them down in melee.

The corpses were dragged off the trail, and the blood was disguised quickly, with one of the locals leading the way to a nearby ravine where they dumped the corpses to conceal them.

"Should it bother me that these things don't freak me out as much as they used to?" Netta asked as she tipped the body of a male Crooked whose hands only had three large fingers arrayed like a bird's toes into the ravine.

"We've been lucky so far," Sienna muttered, keeping a wary eye on the trees and back up the slope as the others used dirt and leaves to scrub blood from their hands. "We've managed to take them by surprise and even things out. What would it have been like if this entire group raided our village, rather than splitting up like they did?"

Grim silence descended on the group of hunters as they all thought about that. Even Koda took a moment to envision what it would have been like if hundreds of Crooked had attacked the village, rather than the few score that did.

"Come on, we need to finish preparations before the others get there. The longer we let this fester, the more complicated it's going to be to dig out the infection," Koda said after letting the reality of the situation sink in.

We got lucky with the last fight, but I doubt that is going to continue, he thought as they wound back through the woods to their camp, taking a different route and making efforts to break their trail to prevent it being tracked. *Even if we had an even number of fighters, I just know we are going to lose people.*

Unconsciously, his eyes went to Sienna where she walked next to him, her pointed ears bouncing slightly with the uneven ground they crossed.

The bandage on her arm was fresh. They'd changed it just that morning, but so was the wound underneath. The salve they had put on it before had kept the wound from going foul, but he knew that it still pained her to wield that broad-bladed spear of hers at times.

Sienna must have felt his gaze on her because she glanced to one side, meeting Koda's eyes with her crystalline orbs. The familiar feeling of falling into them ensued, and Koda couldn't look away until Sienna blinked.

"No."

The quiet statement from his lupine companion startled Koda.

"What?" he asked, his forehead wrinkling in confusion.

"I said no, Koda. I'm not staying out of this fight." Sienna's voice was firm as she turned to look forward once more, releasing him from the depths of her blue-green eyes.

Koda blinked a few times himself, staring at Sienna's profile for a long moment. He followed the line of her graceful brows to her slightly upturned nose, then back down to the soft pillows of her lips and around to her slim neck.

Gods, she's gorgeous. The thought wandered through his mind as casually as a cloud across an open sky.

"Did you hear me?" Sienna's question snapped him out of his distraction again.

Coughing, Koda gripped his wandering mind and forced it back on track, remembering what she had said earlier.

"I wouldn't—"

"Don't lie," Sienna interrupted. "I may have only known you for a few days, Koda. But I've spent that time studying you. I know what was on your mind while you were looking at my injury."

"Sienna, I am allowed to worry about people. I worry about everyone who is going to be fighting in the coming battle," Koda said slowly, trying to find the best way to explain it.

She snorted doubtfully, glancing sidelong at him. Koda made sure to not lose himself in her eyes by focusing on that slightly upturned nose.

"I worry about everyone," he continued assertively, leaning closer to her. "But I worry most about you. Not because of your injury, but because I care about you."

Sienna's cheeks darkened to crimson as Koda spoke, her ears perking up while her tail began to whip behind her.

"But you—"

This time it was Koda's turn to interrupt her, "Wouldn't ask you to not join in the fight for your home. I'd just ask you to be careful, so I don't lose you."

The blush got darker on Sienna's cheeks, and a low, almost canine, whine came from her throat as her tail thrashed faster behind her.

Glancing around quickly, Sienna confirmed that the other hunters were moving at the front of the group before pausing. Koda naturally came to a stop with her. He opened his mouth to ask her what she was doing, but Sienna grabbed the front of his shirt and hauled him forward to slam her lips into his in a fierce kiss.

Not willing to argue with the lovely woman in his arms, Koda wrapped his arms around her and held Sienna as she folded into him, her tail whipping furiously as their lips met, and his heart swelled with love.

Kris arrived late in the afternoon, with barely a few hours left before the sun would disappear behind the horizon. With her, she'd brought nearly forty of the villagers. Most of them wore the leathers and forest colors of hunters, but a little over a dozen had the look of miners and laborers who had chosen to fight to protect what was theirs. The weapons they carried were a motley assortment of old swords, boar spears, woodsmen's axes, and bows. The bows were the things that had been maintained the best, with the hunters having loaned out any extras they had to arm as many folks as possible.

That the headwoman had come along with the fighters was surprising, but she reassured the group that she wouldn't be getting into the thick of things. She was here to lend her assistance differently. Apparently, she knew the basics of some shamanic magic that would help protect the fighters, limit the number of injuries, and heal what she could.

The messenger had gotten back to them in time for Kris to grab the supplies they had asked for. While she'd been able to bring several clay jugs of lamp oil, the pitch had been harder to get as there had been a demand for it in the reconstruction of the village after the damage from the Crooked's first attack. She'd brought along a small jar of it, as Sienna's message had just been for however much the village could spare.

"It'll still work. We just have to change the proportions," Sienna had said to that revelation, and they had set to planning.

The lead up would be the most challenging part as they had to get everyone into position before it went off. Part of the plan required a group to sneak around to the upper edge of the cliff that overlooked the Windwalker's Retreat.

One hunter, an older man with the pointed ears of a fox, said that he was familiar with another trail that would take them down and around to the high meadows, but it would be several hours and well after dark before they made it around.

"I hate to ask it of you all, when you hurried the whole day through to get here," Koda said, glancing amongst those present for the planning session.

It was currently him, Sienna, Kris, and a half-dozen of the fighters. Apparently, on the way up to meet with Koda, they had elected leaders and formed squads to make organizing things easier, and that was who had been meeting. The others were all either resting or putting the finishing touches on Koda's ideas that would go with what Sienna had come up with.

"Us mountain folk are hearty. I've pulled longer shifts in the mines while we were clearing out rubble to find more ore," chuckled a thick man with shoulders that resembled two boulders and had the floppy ears and horns of a bull.

The bull-man had introduced himself as Hans earlier, and while Koda could feel the strength in the man's grip, Hans hadn't tried to crush his hand. Oddly, he just insisted on being called 'Hans' and refused to give his family name.

"Hans is right. You talked before about making this final push to clear out our valley. Trust that we will give it our all," Kris interjected as well. The black-striped cat beastfolk sat on a stump nearby, leaning forward onto her knobbly walking stick with a small smile creasing her wrinkled features.

"I do trust you all. Never doubt that. I just had to be sure. I don't want anyone to be less than prepared, is all." Koda's response got a round of nods from everyone before he continued. "So, we need to send some of our best shots around to get into position. We risked sneaking under their noses last night, but that was purely because we had clouds covering the moon. I don't want to gamble on that happening again tonight."

"Then we need to hurry if we are going to get into position using the other route," interjected the fox-featured man. "As it is, with the two exits to the ravine, you are going to need most of the folks comfortable being up close down here. I'll take the best dozen of our archers around. Along with Sienna's little surprises."

"I'm still not sure I'm okay with this," Kris protested for the third or fourth time.

"Given where they are, what they are doing, and the tree line? You don't have to worry too much about it getting out of control," Sienna tried to reassure the older woman.

"It's the 'too much' in your statement that makes me worry." The older woman sighed, shaking her head. "But we must endure. Corruption has come to our doors once more, and we must cut it out at the root before it takes what little we have left."

The pained determination in the old woman's voice stiffened everyone's back, even Koda's. Plans were finalized, and signals were determined before the fox beastfolk left with his group in tow, taking with him most of the jugs of lamp oil and the rest of the pitch, as well as the arrows that the others had prepared during the meeting.

Everyone else who would be hitting the last bastion of the Crooked from the front settled in to wait and rest. All but the two in charge of watching the camp tried to catch what sleep they could in the cool afternoon. They would have to be patient until the other half of their force was in position.

Koda couldn't sleep. The anxiety of what was to come was playing havoc with his nerves. He couldn't pace to work it off, so he just sat on a log and used the claws of his totemic gauntlet to continue to carve out several more stakes for the barricades they had prepared.

"We are lucky that they are so complacent," Kris muttered as the aged feline beastfolk settled onto the log next to him.

"Agreed. I just didn't want to say it out loud and jinx us," Koda replied, looking up to check over the group of villagers resting. His eyes lingered on Sienna, where she chatted quietly with Netta while the hawk beastfolk continued to tie bits of cloth to the shafts of arrows.

"At this point? What will happen is out of our control." Kris's words as she spoke were filled with the calm acceptance of a long life of weathering chance encounters. "We just have to do the best that we can with what we have. Speaking of, I have something for you, Champion."

Koda started when she used the title for him, glancing up from the wrist-thick branch he was flaying with as much difficulty as if it was a hotdog.

At some point while she was sitting there, Kris had produced an ancient wooden box bound with thin strips of metal tarnished so dark they looked black. It was roughly the size of a deck of playing cards but about twice as thick. She offered the box to him with both hands, her aged eyes watching him intently.

"Thank you," Koda said after a moment, accepting the box and scrutinizing it. A simple latch held it closed, and he glanced up at Kris questioningly while toying with it.

"I didn't give that to you for you to just sit there and play with it," she said with a quiet laugh.

Koda did as instructed, opening the small box as the ancient hinges squeaked in protest. Soft cloth, like silk, lined the interior of the box and was a deep blue in color.

Lying in the middle of the box, its chain coiled along one side, was a silver pendant in the shape of a claw, somewhere between a bear's and a large cat's. Despite the age of the box, the silver of the pendant gleamed like it was newly made. Thin symbols danced in carvings, centered on a symbol of a fist holding an axe at the base of the claw.

Koda felt the totemic gauntlet twitch, the spasm nearly sending the bone claws on it slapping into the box, but he caught himself in time and held it with his left hand to study it, clenching his right to keep it still while Kris explained, the older woman not having noticed the gauntlet's attempt to attack the talisman.

"That is an artifact from before the fall. A necklace handed down in my family from one of the last of the priesthood. It is said that it bears the blessings of both Thera and her sworn sister, Chandra Wildheart. I remember stories that my grand-dame told me about the champions of old that carried them. The goddesses cared so much for each other that they would gift these treasures back and forth to ensure their chosen were as protected and powerful as possible. The stories say that, even during the Fall, Chandra took in many of our people who fled our homeland. She opened her world, the Howling Sanctuary, to the beastfolk so that Thera could do battle with the ancient threat without distraction. And it is said that Chandra still weeps for the death of her sister."

The trembling in Koda's right fist stopped, the gauntlet quieting as Kris continued her story.

"When the fight turned against the Pack Lady and Chandra believed that her sister had fallen in battle, Chandra stepped between worlds and risked herself. She did this to destroy the great gates that lead between the Moonlit Realm, our ancient homeland, and the Howling Sanctuary. With that act, she believed she guaranteed the survival of her sister's people. But she nearly doomed us." Kris let out a long sigh, staring into the blue sky overhead. Koda felt his gauntlet twitch again and did his best to hold it still.

Clearly, there is more to this story, he thought. *Thera, calm down. I'm sure she had a good reason. And you survived despite it all.* He tried to direct the thoughts into the gauntlet, to his patron, but wasn't sure if they made it as there was no response. So instead, he asked Kris.

"Did no one ever reach out to Chandra? If she cared so much for Thera, why not ask her for help? Unless this"—he gestured around them with the hand still holding the pendant in its box—"is the Howling Sanctuary?"

Kris let out a low laugh, shaking her head wryly as she let her gaze fall from the sky back to Koda.

"No, this world is Eassemund. When Chandra destroyed the gate, our forebears had to fight their way to an alternative exit. No one knows for sure exactly why our people chose to settle here rather than seek refuge in the Howling Sanctuary, but I believe it was to allow the Pack Lady time to recover. Even if she presented herself to Chandra, without her priesthood, there would be no way to recover."

"But that's changed," Koda spoke half to Kris and half to his gauntlet, expecting that Thera could hear through it. "I'm here now, and she's recovering."

Kris nodded sagely, a small smile on her lips. "Indeed, and that is why I return this token to you now. It was given by the last of the champions to my ancestor for safekeeping so that the bond between the sisters was not lost. That champion went into battle to give our ancestors time to escape through the portal to Eassemund and was never seen again. And now, with a champion returned at last, it just felt right for it to join a champion in battle again. I'd have given it to you sooner, but to be honest, I had forgotten about it until after you'd left the village to come up here."

Koda studied the necklace once more before lifting his right hand up to lightly trace the clawed tips of his gauntlet against the metal. He wanted to know if Thera was okay with this, given the gauntlet's earlier reaction to just the sight of it. The claws twitched slightly, spasming in indecision before calming, and he carefully extracted the necklace from the box.

The chain was long—long enough that it would easily tuck safely out of sight in his shirt. Against his skin, the metal felt cool as Koda slid the chain over his head, tugging his hair free of the chain and slipping the claw out of sight. As it settled into place, he felt something. A frisson of energy traveled over his skin. A moment later, his mind and senses sharpened abruptly.

Sister... the single, mournful word echoed through his mind in Thera's voice.

Koda felt a deep sadness roll over him before something tugged it back, putting it away for now. But he could feel that distant longing echoing down his connection with the deity he worked for.

Once again, his resolve rose up and encapsulated that longing, making a silent promise to reconnect the two if it was within his power.

Chapter Twenty-Three

KODA WOKE WHEN SIENNA DID, WHICH WASN'T REALLY surprising given the fact that she was curled up against his side.

He'd been trying to nap earlier to be ready for when the fighting started, but it hadn't been going too well. Even after exhausting himself in the wake of his conversation with Kris, he just couldn't find enough peace to sleep. Every time his eyes closed, his mind drifted back over the conversation he'd observed between Sienna and Thera, and he wondered at the yellow-eyed woman who he'd seen lying between them and the interest he'd seen in her eyes.

Sienna had noticed Koda's struggles and came over to sit with him. With her gentle weight tucked against his side, Koda drifted right off with only a brief image of that yellow-eyed woman smiling happily from the shadows. So when Sienna stirred again, it brought him right out of sleep into full wakefulness.

Night had descended in the brief time since Koda had lain down. Now, the moon was high overhead and sending threads of silvery light through the trees. Netta crouched nearby, on the side where Sienna lay, her hand slowly retracting from having shaken her friend awake.

"It's time. The group who went around just signaled they were in place," Netta whispered, the excitement in her eyes warring with fear and anxiety.

Koda could understand that as his own stomach knotted. This was the most they'd planned and prepped for an attack as the last two encounters had started before they were entirely ready. They would be the ones choosing the time to engage, but that also meant that they'd had more time to worry over what might go wrong.

"Got it," Sienna murmured, stretching slightly and getting a few pops from her ankles and shoulders. "Come on, Koda, let's get this done."

Koda was about to respond when Sienna sat up and leaned over to loom over him before pressing a soft kiss to his lips. Koda wasn't sure in the much lower light, but he thought he saw a small blush on her fair cheeks. Then Sienna was leaning back before he could confirm. He did see the shit-eating grin on Netta's face as she watched them, the hawk beastfolk clearly excited for her friend.

"Ahem. How long do we have?" Sienna asked, rolling to get to her feet.

The motion had the unfortunate effect of clubbing Koda in the face with the fluffy mass of her tail, though it didn't do much damage besides make him sneeze and fill his lungs with the scent of her, making Koda's heart race.

"Not long." Netta's amusement faded at being reminded of the battle to come. "Since we can't really communicate with the advanced team, we have to be the ones to pop it off. That's what will signal them to join in. As you both know."

"I just hope they wait long enough to let the Crooked congregate before starting up." Koda's voice was still raspy with sleep, but after the kiss from Sienna, he was wide awake.

"They will. I'm not a fan of using this tactic more than we have to. We do what we must, right?" Sienna's nose wrinkled cutely as she said this, and Koda nodded in agreement.

"Let's get ready then."

It only took them a minute to prepare. Koda didn't have any armor to put on or weapons to prepare, so he helped Sienna get her gear settled.

We are going to need to look into armor, Koda thought as he held her spear while Sienna got her bow strung and settled over her shoulder. *They've survived this long on being fast and elusive, as a hunter should. But I have a feeling that things are only going to get more dangerous from here on out.*

When everyone was ready, their group of around thirty combatants staged near the edge of the trees. The sentries gave their report on what had been observed. The Crooked hunters from the upper meadow had returned, dragging two of their number and transporting a dead sheep slung on a pole. As far as they knew, all the remaining Crooked were within the Windwalker's Retreat. No alert had been raised for the missing group, yet.

Koda went back over the plan one last time to make sure no one had questions. There were none, but Koda could see that the group was nervous. A glance towards Kris got a bob of the head from the headwoman. Koda considered for a long moment before nodding his agreement. He'd held this secret long enough, and if these people were going to risk death, they deserved to know.

It's going to get out, and I might as well use this to help encourage them. If it helps even one survive, then it's worth it. Besides, if I cannot trust Thera's people, and by extension my people, then who can I trust?

"Listen, before we go into this. I want you all to know something," Koda said slowly. The other hunters clumped around him, various eyes narrowing or heads tilting in confusion. Koda hesitated for just a moment before he felt Sienna's hand slip into his left and give it a reassuring squeeze. Taking a deep breath, he continued. "You all know that I basically showed up out of nowhere the other day, right?" More nods. "What actually happened is that I was brought here, from somewhere very far away. Where I came from is not important, but what is important is *who* brought me here."

Koda paused again, glancing amongst the collected group of hunters. He had most of their attention now. Even the scouts who were keeping watch on the Crooked camp had their heads tilted to hear, even if their eyes were aimed away.

No way they are going to expect this. Hell I barely believe it, and I lived it. Thera, I hope this works to encourage them... Koda thought wryly and just tore the bandage off.

"I was brought here by someone you all have heard of. She has many titles, but the first of them is the Queen of Beasts."

As one, every member of the fighting force twitched.

Those looking at Koda had wide eyes, and those looking away turned to stare at him, not moving any more than absolutely necessary to get eyes on him. He had everyone's attention now.

A tension rose in the air as the group digested that thought, and Koda knew that they were considering if this was somehow a threat. From what Sienna and Kris had told him, the village had been guarding the secret of Thera's survival for centuries. So great was their conviction to this task that, in all that time, no word had leaked out about her final refuge while the goddess attempted to regain her strength.

"It's true." Sienna was the one to break that tense silence. All eyes shifted to her, and Sienna stood strong in front of the suspicious gazes of those she would consider being family. Koda felt a burst of pride swell in his chest as he watched the elegant huntress square her shoulders and stare back at her fellows. "I have *seen* the Pack Lady. She grows in strength once more. Koda is her champion, born of the bloodlines of old. The Pack Lady stretched her hands out to the cosmos, seeking a fragment of hope to send to us in our time of need, and she found him waiting for her."

Murmuring grew amongst the hunters as people's expressions began to change. Some remained suspicious, others took on a look of hope to replace the resignation of battle, and some wore savage grins of pride. One voice broke out above the others, the stern voice of Hans cutting through the murmurs.

"Headwoman, is this true?"

Hans had been watching the group intently and had noticed that Kris didn't react when the information was revealed to them. A simple miner he might be, but the bull beastfolk was clearly not stupid. He'd likely learned to watch for small signs, clues that might be the only warning of an impending collapse, and this wary observation had probably saved his life in the past.

Kris nodded as eyes fell to her, the graying cat beastfolk smiling tiredly as she did so.

"Yes. I have not witnessed the return of our Lady. But, just as you all do, I know Sienna. She would not lie to us. And the champion has shown us with his actions that he is here to help. He speaks true. The Beast Queen, Thera, is returning to us!"

Koda hadn't expected it, but the old woman's voice took on a strident tone as she spoke, the very air rippling with energy as she intoned her declaration. He swore that he could feel a faint echo like the distant two-tone screech of a cougar far up the mountain, adding weight to her words.

The war party reacted immediately. Doubts faded, worries vanished, and determination took the place of hesitation. Eyes hardened and backs straightened all around the group. As one, they turned their gazes to Koda.

Doing his best to not quail at the weight of their combined eyes, he returned their intense looks with a nod.

"The Queen of Beasts is returning to this land, but she needs help. She needs all of your help," Koda said slowly at first, feeling out their reactions. When he saw people beginning to nod, he committed and let the words flow from his heart. "For the entire history of this village, you have kept the secret of her survival. That is something to be proud of. Now, though, that secret has teeth and needs to be fed. As her champion, I can claim sites of power that will allow for the Pack Lady to grow in strength once more. Sites of power like the standing stones or Last Fang Cave."

He paused, tracing his eyes over the faces of those standing before him. While his words had not whipped them into a religious fervor, Koda was no orator and had no illusions of becoming one, so he didn't expect that. What he did know was that with a bucket of determination and the right tools, one could move mountains. And before him stood almost thirty men and women with the tools. Now, he just needed to fill their buckets with determination.

"Sites of power like the Windwalker's Retreat. The Crooked not only threaten the safety of your homes, the bodies of your family, and the sanctity of your minds. They threaten the return of your lady. A mother who desperately wants to return to her people, her children." As he spoke, Koda could see in his mind's eye the hopeful face of Thera as she spoke of saving her people.

Sienna stepped up beside him, her lips twisting into a snarl of determination as she slammed the butt of her spear into the soil beneath her feet with a solid *thump*.

"And it falls to us, the children of the Beast Queen, to do this! Let us wipe this stain from our land and throw wide the door to welcome our mother home!"

Koda felt something lurch in his chest. An energy surged within the totemic gauntlet on his right hand. He followed the instinct that welled within him and held his hand out, palm up, with claws pointed to the sky. The tips of his claws glinted as if the moonlight was collecting on their bladed tips.

Guided again by knowledge he knew was coming from Thera, Koda brought his left hand around and pricked the pad of his thumb on the middle finger claw.

When he drew his hand away, a delicate bead of red blood glistened on that claw. Between seconds, the light of the moon sank into it. That reflected silver light engulfed the tiny red sphere entirely. The bead then ran from the tip of the claw to pool in his palm, swelling until his leather-clad palm was full of the silvery-red liquid.

Distantly, Koda swore that he heard a joyous howl on the wind, followed by a proud ursine roar, then a woman's high, joyous laughter. The sounds brought tears to the corners of his eyes as his heart swelled again, knowing that Thera approved of his words and the words of her people. She wanted them to succeed. *Needed* them to succeed.

"Come and anoint yourself with the blood of our champion," Kris spoke up again.

Her voice, normally reedy and high with age, instead creaked with the sort of confident power that ancient trees held when they defied centuries of wind and rain. In this moment, age did not weaken her. Instead, it hardened her resolve and gave her words an unshakable confidence.

The gathered hunters and miners had the presence of mind not to cheer. Instead, they began to stomp their approval in a low, thudding beat as they formed a line. Sienna was the head of the line, bowing her head in front of him.

He knew what he needed to do without hesitation, again supplied from within his very being by the goddess that stood at his back.

Koda dipped his index and middle finger into the small pool of mixed blood and moonlight in his palm and quickly sketched the shape of a bared claw onto Sienna's forehead. A symbol that he wore in silver around his neck and weighed against his skin. The mixture shone for a moment in the moonlight easing through the trees before fading into Sienna's skin, leaving nothing behind.

They hit the Crooked guards like a rock-slide.

There were eight Crooked split between the two clefts in the stone that led to the Windwalker's Retreat. Six on the larger entrance and two on the smaller to one side. The night was calm, and the moon flew high to illuminate the world, but the Crooked were foolish enough that they stood close to their fires, and this stole their night sight.

The guards never saw the arrows that took their lives.

A humming of bowstrings was the only warning that they got, and only two of the eight guards looked up and tried to identify the sound. That meant that the arrows aimed for their heads took them in the throat instead. They fell gurgling to the ground and thrashed until death took them. That one volley eliminated all of the watchers.

Koda and the miners were moving as soon as the arrows flew. They carried the things Koda and the others had been working on the entirety of the last day, racing over the broken earth and disturbed stone towards the two ravine entrances.

Their movement and the flight of arrows had been the signal for the hunters up on the ridgeline.

Sparks flew and caught in bunched cloth, glowing dully there for a moment before flaring to brilliant flames. Moments later, the hunters on the ridge threw jugs of lamp oil off the lip of the ravine, trailing flaming wicks of soaked cloth, and into the midst of the Crooked camp.

There were distant crashes as the jars burst, and then screams followed as they ignited tents and flesh alike. The fire spread along with the oil as the first blows of the battle were joined.

It had initially been a concern for Koda that the lamp oil wouldn't burn once the jars broke open as then it wouldn't have an easy wick to hold the flame, back when Sienna had suggested using the jars as improvised bombs. The thought had been good, but lamp oil was actually a lot more stable than most thought.

Thankfully, one of the older miners had spent time amongst the army. He had come up with the suggestion to pour off some of the oil and stuff dry grass into the jug as well, giving the oil a natural wick to cling to and something the initial flaming wick could light. This would make the oil clump more, but it could still soak into any cloth it came into contact with.

They'd poured the extra oil into a few spare empty water-skins. That would be used to douse the cloth and pitch wrapped heads of the arrows that he knew the hunters above would be firing into the camp as well, ensuring the fire spread as much as possible, and if the wicks didn't light the payload of oil, then the arrows would serve as secondary wicks to help the flames spread.

"Get them in place!" Koda roared, the need for silence and stealth long gone as they hurried up the slope of shifting rock, hefting the bound, sharpened logs overhead as they ran. The miners cheered in agreement and hurried to do as ordered.

They'd spent the last day creating something that Koda had called a Cheval de frise. This was a series of young trees tied together with their tips sharpened. They leaned against each other, forming a slightly larger than ninety-degree angle between logs with the sharp points at roughly chest height. At least, that was how they would normally be built.

Koda had insisted that they make the barriers so the points were about stomach height for this fight. He remembered seeing the original form being used to impede cavalry charges, but these would serve to constrain the Crooked as they came through the narrow passage of rock. The fighters from the vale didn't need to stop a mounted charge, just direct the flow and make the Crooked regret trying to cross.

The miners set the first barrier directly in front of the smaller crack, at a thirty-degree angle to the wall to force those racing to exit off to one side and leave them silhouetted against the cliff wall. The other three were brought to the larger exit to the Retreat, with two set up perpendicular to the cliff and narrowing together at their end while the third locked in parallel to the cliff at the narrow end of the first two. The formation would force the Crooked into a large T shape and allow for both archers and hunters with spears to deal with them while the sharpened barricades kept the enemy at bay. Those without pole weapons would guard the barricades to stop any who made it close.

Koda led the group towards the larger entrance, bearing most of the weight of his half of the defensive fortification, while those on his team worked to just keep it straight. The log walls weren't terribly long, barely six feet each, but they would help keep his people safe, and that made getting them into place essential.

As soon as he got into position, Koda kicked the body of a still-dying Crooked man out of the way and slammed the barricade down, using the weight of the logs and his own prodigious strength to seat the sharpened feet of the barricade in the earth. A moment later there was another crash nearby as the barricade opposite him hit the ground at Hans' direction.

Already, the shouts, screams, and bellows of the Crooked inside the burning camp were rising. The amount of fire on the other side of the cliff face was now throwing bright light through the crack and partially illuminating the barricades. Koda could hear the whistle of arrows and the crackling of fire, as well as the indistinct roars of the Crooked commanders while they tried to rally their troops.

As he did not have a long weapon, Koda fell back to the top of the T formation, allowing those with boar spears or other pole-arms to stand ready to strike down their enemies as they arrived, fleeing the fire.

The first Crooked to emerge from the crack wore the form of a man, but his head and legs were attached to his torso backwards. The bizarre monster had to walk in reverse just to see where he was going. His arms flailed oddly while he pushed through the crack, reaching with extended joints to pat at smoking parts of his clothing before he paused in surprise at what waited for him.

Hans's two-handed mattock stove in the monstrous creature's chest before the bull man yanked his weapon back, sending the body to the ground and further cluttering the footing.

Koda briefly wished they'd had time to build wood or stone caltrops to scatter in the open space, but then the first surge of Crooked raced out of the slit, clothes burning and screaming in surprise.

The hunters fell on them with ferocious determination. Spears thrust, arrows flew, and the enemy who tried to climb over the barricades were met with picks, hammers, and axes.

Their attack only caught the first wave of Crooked by surprise, though.

The second wave had weapons ready and improvised shields, pushing farther into the barricades as several focused on hacking at the ropes holding the waist-high logs together. They were driven back, with a few being knocked so far that they impaled themselves on the spikes on the other side of the divide. This wasn't a good thing, though, as the Crooked simply pressed on that spot harder, using the bodies of their comrades, dead or alive, to protect them from the spikes.

A scream of pain came from one miner, the stout woman falling back with blood trailing from her side. The Crooked who had stabbed her cackled with glee, waiving around what looked like a pitchfork but with two sets of tines on it that shone dully in the moonlight. A moment later, that cackle cut off as an arrow snapped his head to the side.

"Bastards," Sienna snarled, drawing another arrow back on her string.

She stood just to Koda's right and slightly back, her spear leaning against the Cheval de frise that made the top of the T while she picked shots with her shortbow. The others with bows were grouped to one side, sending shots at targets they could, but the scrum was rapidly dissolving into the kind of melee that would risk hitting their allies if they were not careful.

Koda was glad to have her solidly by his side, the ember of affection in his chest glowing brighter just having her close.

I will protect her. I will protect all of them, he thought with determination as he turned to signal the four villagers who had volunteered to evacuate wounded from the fight.

Farther behind him and to the left, Kris wove her staff through the air while chanting, gesturing towards the wounded woman. Koda couldn't see what happened, but her cries of pain tapered off after a moment, so he knew that the old headwoman must have been using that bit of shamanic magic she had as she promised. Koda desperately wanted to watch and learn more because it was *magic,* but he needed to focus on the fight.

Koda waited, ready to move forward when something went sideways, even as the bodies of the Crooked began to pile up at the entrance to the chasm. He knew that something was going to go wrong. It couldn't be this easy. It never was after all, and he had to be ready to react when he saw it.

You actually have back-up this time, Koda reminded himself, clicking the claws on his right hand together while he waited. So far, none of the Crooked had made it to the exits of the T where he waited. *There isn't a guarantee that something will go wrong. But now that you've thought that, you've tempted—*

A roar of fury echoed from inside the Retreat, making the air reverberate like a struck drum. The press of Crooked grew thicker as those already in the crack redoubled their attempts to press through, and a second miner went down with a slash to his arm. But that wasn't what Koda focused on.

Within the wide crack, an enormous form was barreling forward.

Those of the Crooked that could pressed themselves to the sides of the crack, trying to get out of its way. However, the large form trampled right over top of two of them, leaving groaning and broken wrecks behind as the howling Crooked champion emerged from the cliff face, moonlight shining off its twisted form.

Chapter Twenty-Four

"MEAT! MEAT! SLASH AND BEAT! CROOKED KILL, AND Crooked eat!" shrieked the champion, its thunderous voice making the air reverberate as it swung its weapon through the air and clove into the right-hand barricade in a storm of splinters.

"That's our signal!" Koda shouted, ducking around the edge of the barricade and charging into the fray.

As he approached, the Crooked champion lashed out with one elephantine foot and kicked at part of the barricade.

The ropes of the barricade, already beginning to slacken from losing tension in the middle after being cut, snapped, and several of the pointed logs went flying. This left a gap in the barricade that the Crooked champion began to push through, waving its weapon overhead.

The Crooked champion was like many of the others Koda had run into over the last few days. Twisted and gnarled, its left arm hung swollen at its side and looked as if someone had grafted a giant's arm onto a regular body. But unlike the others, this one's legs were also swollen and ended in broad, almost rounded, flat feet. The weight of its arm had it hunched slightly to one side, but Koda was sure that if it could stand tall, the Crooked would have loomed almost seven feet.

On the other side of the wrecked barricade, the miners were falling back at the creature's broad swings, trying their best to evade hacking blows from a greatsword that bent close to the crossguard like some kind of massive, rusty kukri.

One miner, a stout wolf beastfolk that Koda hadn't gotten a name for, didn't move fast enough, and the massive sword tore him in half in a spray of blood. The Crooked who had evaded getting trampled by the champion cheered at the sight of death and surged forward.

Koda, with Sienna only a half-step behind him, crashed into the champion like a runaway truck. Koda went low, ducking under the still-outstretched arm of the champion and around its front. His claws lashed out, cleaving through the knotted flesh under its arm, across its chest, and then up to slash over its face as Koda went past.

Sienna slid to a stop a few feet back and, with a delicate twist of her waist and a soft grunt that was lost amongst the clamor of battle, slammed the broad-bladed head of her spear into the creature's side with all the force of her charge.

The Crooked champion's roar of exultation turned to a screech of pain and anger. As Koda was the one directly in front of it, the beast pursued him even as Sienna wrenched her spear from its side to keep from being yanked around as the distorted man turned and raised its bent sword over its head to bring it down on Koda.

Koda waited. He could hear the other Crooked approaching from behind him as they were not exactly subtle about their movements right now, cackling in their garbled language and stomping over the loose stone.

He'd used a champion's disregard of its fellows against them in the past, and he would do so again. On the other side of their foe, he could see Sienna resetting herself to drive her spear forward, but the swaying gait of the champion threw her aim off.

The sword, its bent length bathed in blood that glimmered in the combination of moonlight and reflected flames, descended in an arc towards Koda.

He waited the half of a moment needed to ensure that the champion had committed before throwing himself forward, back towards the creature's left side, the side on which the weapon descended. This time he sliced with his claws at the champion's wrist, catching it and digging deep even as he lunged by.

The world slowed all around him, seconds marching on like minutes and gave Koda the time to aim precisely and dodge deftly. His claws struck out like a flash of lightning. Tendons parted and blood flew, and the champion lost his grip on the heavy iron weapon.

Greatswords were not meant as throwing weapons. They weren't even meant to be wielded one-handed like the brute had been. Raw strength and size allowed one to ignore some rules, though, but the throw wasn't intentional, so it didn't hit squarely.

However, force and size had a power all their own.

Sparks flew as the heavy weapon crashed into the Crooked that had been trying to sneak up on Koda from behind. The bent blade caught it in the hip and cut deep before the impact itself threw the Crooked into its fellows, and they crashed down into a pile.

Bleeding from several wounds, the Crooked champion slapped out at Koda with its much larger left hand, missing him barely as it turned and took Sienna's spear in its forearm, rather than its side. Another scream of pain followed as Sienna used her weapon's purchase in the thick limb to lever it out of the way, which gave Koda an opportunity to make the kill.

The Crooked champion had one leg bent and the other straight as it came around, clearly looking to kick at them as it tried to yank its bleeding left arm away from whatever had hurt it.

Koda changed directions and turned to plant his right boot on that bent leg. He used it as a platform to propel himself upwards high enough to drive his clawed fingers, locked in a knife-hand position, into the champion's throat.

For the entire fight, Koda felt like the world was operating like a clicking camera shutter. One moment he was in one spot, seeing the beast before him, and then he was lunging forward, then he was behind it as the creature whirled in slow motion. This time, the camera shutter captured the disjointed mouth of the creature, drooping to one side like its face was melting and bearing multiple rows of teeth as it dropped open in shock, its beady eyes widening in surprise.

And then, a blow struck his left side from the creature's much smaller right arm. In his precarious midair position, Koda was knocked flying away as the champion flailed about itself while blood gushed down its front.

Koda braced himself to impact the hard ground, but instead of landing on the unforgiving stone, it was Sienna who caught him. The wolf-eared woman valiantly tried to slow his fall, but Koda's weight was too much for her, and they both tumbled to the ground in a heap.

"You okay, Koda?" Sienna panted from under him. Her hair was askew from its normal short-cut mop, and a bit of blood speckled her face, but the disheveled look was so very attractive on her.

"Yeah, you?" Koda replied, stuffing his attraction down.

Once this is all done and it's safe, he promised himself as the two of them untangled from each other.

"Fine. Better than Piers at least." Koda guessed that this Piers had to have been the miner who had been hit by the champion as Sienna helped him sit up.

"We need to reinforce the gap. This was only going to work if we kept them from breaking out." Koda's statement got a nod from Sienna, and the two of them finally managed to get to their feet.

The Crooked champion lay gurgling nearby, eyes still moving and body flailing weakly, but the cut throat was a death sentence. Not wanting to let the creature suffer, despite its actions, Koda quickly snatched up one of the broken pieces of log and brought it down on the champion's head with a crunch, ending its life.

These claws you gave me are not exactly merciful, but then again, you don't strike me as big on mercy for these creatures, do you, Thera? Koda thought while Sienna retrieved her spear, and the two of them rushed to join the impromptu battle line forming where the barricade had been smashed.

From deep within his psyche, in the place that the urges and guidance for how to use the totemic gauntlet as a weapon came from, Koda felt approval, agreement, and pride welling up. It was clear that Thera agreed with his summation.

With a part of the barricade destroyed, the Crooked could push through without injury and force the miners back.

Koda and Sienna fell on them quickly, and the next minute was a frenzy of blood, screams, and evading blows.

The downside of using the barricades meant that the space to confront the enemy was much more constrained, but they did their job of helping to keep the enemy from flooding out in an ever-increasing number.

Koda feinted, slapping weapons out of hands and laying debilitating slashes over Crooked warriors. Sienna wove around him like a dancer, chopping with the broad blade of her spear, thrusting with the tip to force back an enemy while Koda savaged one who was down or slapping with the flat of the blade to deflect attacks from her partner.

While Sienna watched his back, Koda covered her openings. Twice he sank claws into the body of a Crooked and hefted it up to act as a shield from an arrow coming at them from deeper in the crevasse, and he worked to keep himself between the enemy and Sienna so that she could strike at the opportune moment and not worry about encirclement.

The triumph of the two of them over the champion and the fury with which they tore into the ranks of the Crooked renewed the motivation of the Silverstone Vale fighters. Koda could distantly hear Hans bellowing as he laid about with his two-handed mattock, the massive mining tool slick with gore. Two other hunters, wielding boar spears, held back attackers while others dragged a third of their number away from the fight to be treated for an injury.

Movement by the smaller crack told Koda that the enemy was trying to circle them, and the fight was continuing there, too. The barricade shifted as several Crooked threw themselves onto it. The barricade began to tip away as the feet had not been properly seated in the earth, the weight of the enemy upsetting.

"Shit," Koda swore, and Sienna turned to check in the direction he was looking.

"I've got it. You hold them here!" Sienna called, bounding away as the fighters at that barricade caught the wooden construction from behind and tried to heave it back into position, even as the Crooked that had impaled themselves on the wood snapped at them with ragged teeth. She was away in a flash of movement. and the red-black, trailing flag of her tail whipping behind her, before Koda could say a thing or protest.

Sienna raced over the broken ground with intense focus, arriving just as the Crooked began to win the shoving war.

Her spear flashed, rising and falling like a splitting axe as she took heads from shoulders and struck mortal blows on the side of the Crooked. As the bodies began to pile up, it made it harder for those behind them to force their way past, and the number of Crooked pushing through the crack began to taper off quickly.

Koda ducked low to dodge a horizontal swipe of a sword, trying not to stumble on the accumulated bodies of the fallen. He snatched up a bent spear from the fingers of a corpse. Imitating Sienna's twisting thrust that he'd seen before, he slammed the spear into the Crooked's gut before kicking it in the hip, sending it flying backwards to foul its friend's footing.

A deep bellow from the other side of the stone wall was almost drowned out by another *whoosh* of flames catching, and Koda couldn't help the savage grin that marked his face.

The archers above had followed his direction and waited for the Crooked to clump up before throwing the next round of jars. He knew that just on the other side of the crack that led to the Crooked's secure camp, there was a mass of the monstrous humanoids flailing about while covered in burning oil. In fact, he could see the growing glow as some fought to escape the fires by diving in amongst their fellows pushing to the fight.

"Hold them back!" Koda roared, snatching up another piece of the broken barricade to lay about himself with his left hand while slapping and slashing with his clawed right hand, leading the charge to push the Crooked back behind the barricades.

Another bellow and a chorus of surprised yells from behind tried to draw his attention away from the fight, but Koda had forced his way too deep into the enemy battle line. He couldn't risk turning to look and just had to hope that it would be okay.

His weapons rose and fell, slashed and beat. The bodies piled up around him. Koda tried not to think about the fact that every time his peripheral vision turned in their direction, there seemed to be fewer and fewer of the warriors on his side standing by the barricades or pushing with him into the enemy lines.

On his other side, Hans blew like a bellows as he slammed the flat chisel-head of his mattock down to crush one of the Crooked before spinning it to drive the pick end into another's chest. He could see the bull beastfolk beginning to flag as the battle raged on. Blood dripped from a number of small cuts on his arms and chest, but he persevered.

A flight of arrows descended from above to cut into the ranks of the Crooked and finally gave Koda the breathing room to step back and reassess the situation.

The intact barricade had shifted slightly. Most of the spiked wooden ends bore a sick harvest of dead Crooked on their tips.

A third of his fighters were either missing or dead, he couldn't tell which. But the number of Crooked forcing their way down the corridor had dwindled to a trickle as fire burned on the far end of the cleft that served as their gateway.

He took all of this in with a glance, but the fight raging by the smaller entrance was what drew his attention the most.

The barricade had been knocked askew, but the small group of fighters did battle to keep it in place. Sienna had relieved enough pressure that they could at least properly sink the Cheval de frise into the ground, but it wasn't at nearly as sharp an angle to the cliff wall as it had once been. The reason for that was obvious as Sienna feinted and danced around the scorched form of another Crooked champion.

This one reminded Koda of the first he had fought, only days before, but it felt like weeks. Both of its arms bore thick muscles, while its legs were short and stubby. It wielded a club that looked more like it had uprooted a tree and driven iron spikes through it, and Sienna was leading the creature away from the barricade as she lashed, stabbed, ducked, and dodged.

As Koda watched, preparing himself to race to his partner's rescue, another brace of arrows raced down to join others speckling the creature's hide. Loosing another roar of frustration, the champion whirled to confront what it thought was an additional threat.

This presented an opening that Sienna was more than willing to take.

She skipped forward nimbly, lunging upwards with her gore-slicked spear. This drove the broad head of the weapon into the champion's knotted back, right at the base of its neck.

Like a puppet with its strings cut, the champion slumped boneless to the ground. Her blow had gone right through its spine.

Sienna had to react quickly to get her spear free before the creature's weight tore it from her hands. She did not hesitate, sidestepping to chop the blade against the back of its neck and sending the bowling ball-shaped head rolling across the ground.

A ragged cheer came from the group defending the smaller cleft, and Sienna spun with a grin on her face to look towards Koda, checking on him.

Their eyes locked from across the distance, her sparkling blue-green orbs once more engulfed Koda and drew him into their depths. Though the spell broke rapidly as her joyous smile at winning her fight against a champion turned into a twisted look of surprise and fear.

Koda did not need her cry or the pointing finger she raised to know that something had changed.

He whirled towards the larger entrance in time to see that the flow of Crooked soldiers had petered out entirely.

Instead, the form of a third champion had replaced it, slowly emerging from the wide cleft. But this one was far different from the others, and Koda could not fight it when first, a thrill of fear ran through him, then one of anticipation at the challenge he knew was striding his way.

Chapter Twenty-Five

The Crooked champion was broad-chested and heavily muscled like its fellows had been. But while every Crooked he had faced up to this point had distorted and twisted bodies, this one remained proportional. It was just that she had a few extra proportions to go with the others.

Arms as thick as Koda's thighs danced and wove with an extra pair of elbows on each side, each nearly seven feet long and wielding a pair of thick-bladed swords that were clearly cared for and properly forged for once. Legs like the trunks of old trees kept a steady and measured gait as the champion walked forward, while eyes the color of old blood watched from under a thick mop of pitch-black hair. Wide hips made her stalking walk more of a sashay than a thunderous march, and a full chest gave her a bizarre allure as she stood silhouetted from behind by the fire and outlined from above by the moonlight.

What startled him the most wasn't her femininity, though. There had been dozens of female Crooked amongst those he'd fought in the last few days. They'd all been just as vicious as the men had been, and he'd had to get past any hangups about fighting women quickly.

No, it was the fact that, while the other Crooked had only worn clothing, even the other champions and the spellcasters, this Crooked wore real armor.

A chain shirt was belted tight at her waist, hugging that full chest tightly, with sleeves running down to her elbow to protect her arms. Heavy hide pants protected her legs, along with steel-shod boots.

Over the top of the armor she wore a tabard with the symbol of the Crooked on it—one he'd seen on flags before. A bent-tined pitchfork crossed over a warped arming sword.

"You." The Crooked woman twisted at the waist almost elegantly, her too-long right arm flicking like a snake to point directly at Koda. "You are the reason that our dealings in this valley have not been as simple as expected. I can smell the power of one of the Divines on you. If I drag you back to the masters, they will be pleased to forge you into something useful. And until then, I can enjoy you."

Koda abruptly revised his estimations of what was creepiest about the female champion. It wasn't her many-jointed arms, or the fact she was wearing armor.

It was the fact she spoke clearly and without the burbling or rhyming that had embodied every other Crooked that he'd heard. Her voice almost sounded elegant.

Her many-jointed limbs, swaying like a set of scorpion tails, abruptly lashed the air and struck at something Koda could not see. The shattered shafts of several arrows clattered against the ground a moment later.

"Do not interrupt me," the Crooked woman hissed, glaring over her shoulder up at the top of the cliff. "I will get to the rest of you. Be patient. I can only break one toy at a time."

"I've got this," Koda called when he spotted the shapes of more Crooked pushing their way through the rent in the cliff, clearly coming to reinforce the woman. "Keep them from getting out here!"

The Crooked champion opened her mouth to say something, but Koda was already moving. Skittering to one side, he snatched up one of the sharpened logs that had been part of the barricade and threw it at the bizarre woman. Her swords lashed the air, and the log splintered, bits of broken wood flying in all directions.

"You have spirit. That will be amusing for the time you spend in my bed before I give you to the Masters. It will be fascinating to see how they bend and remake you," the Crooked woman hissed and lunged for him.

Over the last few days, Koda had been growing used to the increased strength and speed that came with being a champion. He had to focus to ensure that he didn't accidentally crush someone's hand or outdistance someone walking with him.

It was only during a fight that he'd been able to let go and allow both instinct and the power granted to him by Thera's gift to carry him through. It was only the fact that he'd let go of his restraints that Koda could dodge the attacks as they raced in at him.

The twin swords of the Crooked champion whipped through the air in front of him, lashing like striking snakes as the extra elbows in the woman's arms bent at impossible angles to bring them whirling around. Koda batted one aside with his totemic gauntlet, the effort of deflecting the blow jarring his arm, while turning so the other slashed past him to slam into the rocky earth. Chips of stone exploded from the impact site, sending a pattering of stones flying into his legs.

"Koda!" Sienna's cry made his heart lurch, and Koda lunged forward towards the Crooked champion, slashing furiously to keep it distracted. The last thing he wanted was for her to turn and engage Sienna.

"Stay back! Help the others at the barricade," Koda screamed, rolling aside as the woman kicked out with one thick leg in a blow he was sure would have shattered his arm if it had connected.

Koda used the opportunity to slash at the exposed leg as he dodged, claws raking over the thick leather and barely parting it but not drawing any blood. He dodged away, drawing the champion into following him onto the open, rocky hillside away from the others.

"Such a confident little man," hissed the woman, the elegance giving way to annoyance. "Let us see how confident you are when I remove a few of your limbs. It will keep you from running off until we finish what we came for here."

His instincts screamed, and Koda rolled backwards over the broken rocks. He felt a few cut into his back, but like the fragments hitting his legs earlier, he couldn't spare a thought for minor injuries right now. The other champion's blows whipped through the air where he had crouched a moment later, clearly aiming to relieve him of an arm or leg.

"Why did you wait so long to come out of your little hole? Did you have something against the other two champions? Wanted to wait till I bumped them off before you acted?" Koda spat, scooping up an oval stone twice the size of an apple and hurtling it at the woman, forcing her to dodge to one side.

"They were lesser than I, so why should I concern myself for them? They could not master their power, and so it broke them, leaving only brutes behind. I am the warleader of this band, and all in it serve my whims."

The woman's voice took on a religious fervor as she lunged forward, thrusting with one bizarre arm while the other coiled back in a fleshy facsimile of a spring-loaded boxing glove that ended in a sword rather than a padded fist.

Trusting in Thera's gift, Koda met her lunge with a swipe of his gauntleted right arm, deflecting the blow to just outside of his shoulder. He felt the blade of his opponent's sword scrape over the bone and stone inlay on the back of the gauntlet, dull sparks being struck from the sword at the impact.

Using the woman's thrusting momentum and his own counter-charge to power it, Koda lashed out with his left fist, burying it in the woman's gut.

Pain shot through Koda's hand, followed by stars racing across his vision. The blow hadn't done nearly as much as he had hoped, blunted as it was by the chain armor the woman wore.

Koda felt himself crash to the ground a moment later, rolling several times over the broken stone as his mind tried to catch up with all that had happened. The Crooked woman had returned the punch with her coiled arm, using the hilt of her sword to add weight to the blow. That had sent him flying over the ground like a thrown frisbee.

Knowing that she wouldn't give him long to recover, Koda let the roll carry him over onto his hands and knees before shoving himself upright with both legs, his head still clearing. It was fortunate that he chose to keep moving as the

Crooked woman's follow-up blow missed rather than taking his leg off at the knee.

They clashed several more times, with Koda accumulating even more bruises and a shallow slash on his thigh. In return, he only managed to open up a cut on the back of the woman's right forearm. A cut shallow enough that it only leaked black blood.

As they skirmished, Koda could catch glimpses of the fight at the barricades. The Crooked had rallied again with their champion's presence, and they were pressing hard at the villagers. Sienna was doing her best to keep the enemy back. The walking wounded that Kris had patched up had returned to the fight as well, their bandages making them stand out amongst the others.

"Remarkably determined, you are. Why do you struggle so much? This world is bending already. Why fight it?" The woman's sultry voice was almost conversational as she flicked out with one sword, the tip whistling just over Koda's head as he deflected it, scooping up another rock from the ground in his left hand. "Do you have something to fight for? To struggle for? Do you think you are protecting someone? A mother? Father? Siblings?"

The woman's eyes, which contained no iris or sclera—they were just orbs the color of old blood—narrowed slightly as she drew her weapons back, laying one sword on her shoulder while she studied the thin rivulet of blood that still clung to the other.

"Maybe a lover?" The intensity in the Crooked woman's voice sent a chill down Koda's spine, and when he locked gazes with her over the blade of her sword, he felt like her eyes were expanding to devour him, a sickening mirror to how Sienna's crystalline orbs would draw him in. He fought it, though, pulling his gaze away to settle it on her chin.

"I am right, aren't I? Good, having something to lose will make breaking you easier. These villagers would be good for nothing but fodder, but they will serve. The Masters originally planned to give me the strength of the wendigo, but binding its essence to you instead will be acceptable. If you survive the process."

Koda's mind flashed back to the ritual that he'd interrupted, when the robed spellcaster was imbuing something into that Crooked using the bloodied mother bear as an altar.

Had they been trying to make another champion then? To draw in the spirit of the ancient bear? Is that why they came here and targeted the sites of power? To draw on them to make more of their champions? The thought rang true in his mind. It felt *right*. Which meant that what they were digging for in the rock had to be some remnants of the wendigo that had once called that hollow home.

What did Kris say? The land reclaimed its remains long ago? What does that actually mean?

Koda's thinking was interrupted when the Crooked champion feinted another lunge at him, forcing him to step back to get away from her. On instinct, Koda threw the stone he'd been holding in his left hand. But the woman hadn't been fooled by his feint earlier, deflecting the rock with a slap of one of her swords.

"I wonder, who is it that you fight for? Is she here?"

The Crooked champion's head tilted to one side, her neck bending far further than it should so that her head dropped below the level of her shoulder. Previously, her arms had made it hard to appreciate the fullness of her form, but the eerie way her neck bent double sent the disturbing straight into a level that Koda normally only saw in late-night horror movies.

Without meaning to, his eyes darted over her shoulder, seeking reassurance and sanity with a glimpse of Sienna.

He realized his mistake a moment later when the woman began to laugh, her voice growing deeper and more savage by the second.

"Ahh, I should have guessed. I'm done playing with you now, though. I think the time to begin the taming in earnest begins."

With that statement, the Crooked champion whirled, leaping with the grace of a wolf spider back up the hill of broken stone that they had been using as a battlefield towards the barricades. The barricades where Sienna and the other villagers were desperately fighting to keep the Crooked back.

"No!" Koda roared in dismay and fury. He hadn't expected her to outright flee from him, and he scrambled furiously to catch up.

The Crooked champion continued to laugh, the noise going from one of joy to dark glee as it echoed over the clash of weapons and screams of the dead and dying. It was the only warning Sienna got, but she was able to turn in time to present her weapon to the enemy.

A defiant figure with her red-black hair whirling around her head and the shadow of her fluffy tail and ears stark against the fire burning behind her.

It took three attacks to bring her down.

The first blow slapped out, deflecting the thrusting blade of Sienna's spear to one side. The second blow, a cross-body chop, separated the spearhead from the shaft. And the third was a thunderous kick from the Crooked champion that sent

Sienna flying into the darkness to crash into the cliff wall, where she slumped motionless.

That encounter took less than two seconds, and then it was over. Koda still had another ten yards to clear before he could intervene.

A weight settled on Koda's chest, suffocating him with fear. Fear for Sienna, fear for them all, fear that he had failed Thera, and this was the beginning of the end. Had he been too rash, wanting to assault this place in a rush? Had he doomed them all with his unreasonable confidence gained from a few easy fights?

"There, your purpose lies broken. If you are a good boy and submit before I have to remove limbs, I'll keep her to entertain the soldiers, and you can make use of her, too," the Crooked champion sneered, not looking back at Koda. The flickering light of the distant fire in her camp threw savage shadows over her triumphant, perfect face.

The fear crystallized into fury. The weight on Koda's chest burned away in a flash of heat that was so intense, he felt as if his skin burned.

She endangers your mate, your family, your den, and any sort of future you might have. She is a threat! END THE THREAT! a voice roared in his mind, from far deeper within his psyche than even where the fluttering presence of Thera dwelt.

Koda had tapped into the primal side of himself in his fights before. Where anger met instinct and forged itself into the will to survive against all odds. Now, that drive to survive was cast aside as a new drive welled up.

Righteous rage merged with the protective instincts that had been hovering around the edges of his mind whenever he beheld Sienna. Together, they forged themselves into defiant wrath.

He'd felt a ghost of this sensation in the Last Fang Cave, and it drove him to a height of power and instinct.

Back then, the brief surge had turned the fight in his favor. The moment had felt like riding a charging horse, one possessed with its own determination to break through an enemy line. It had driven him to greater power and tapped into bestial instincts to defend Sienna.

This, however, was like riding an avalanche—one that he didn't care if it crushed him as long as he could drag down his enemy, too.

The roar that erupted from Koda's mouth reverberated off the mountainside like the boom of thunder accompanying a stroke of lightning touching down within arm's reach.

Deep within his chest, Koda felt power flow up and out as ancient memories buried deep within his unconscious mind burst free of the shackles of time and distance.

He felt as if a hundred wrathful ghosts, from a thousand past lives, wrapped around him to guide him to one purpose: to protect those under his care.

And distantly, Koda felt something else rise up and roar with him. A sound that echoed through every part of his being as if someone had tapped his very soul with a tuning fork as he felt everything around him coalesce into focus. Along with it came another voice, not the same primal and vengeful one that demanded he end the threat to his mate. This one was a gentle, feminine voice that reminded him of Thera but spoke in a deeper tone. With it came the intense, hooded gaze of yellow eyes from beneath a mass of brown hair.

Like this, Champion. Let me show you the strength to cleave the valley's from the mountains so you may protect your mate. She has the kind of spirit that you will need!

The righteous fury of a protector filling his limbs, Koda launched into a flying leap that carried him like he'd been shot from a cannon. Directly into the Crooked champion.

Around his left arm, an arm that was bloody and bruised from having to parry attacks and catch himself on sharp rocks without protection, the ghostly form of a second gauntlet formed. Great claws sheathed his fingers, and shaggy fur lined his limb, rather than smooth leather of his other gauntlet.

The roar had frozen the fighters, save the champion. Those who were looking in the right direction swore that the silhouette of an enormous bear encased Koda as he flew, its mouth wide open as it joined in his bellowing challenge with claws like scimitars reaching in from either side of him, closing off any avenue of escape for the Crooked champion before him.

Light raced through the black stones and coiled over the bones lining his totemic gauntlet, a light that was echoed by the necklace he wore, glinting from under his tattered and bloody shirt.

The champion, to her credit, was only stunned for a bare moment before she spun on one heel as fast as a thought. She brought her crossed swords up to receive his charge, snarling in defiance.

Koda struck those crossed swords dead center, driving his clawed fingertips into the metal where they met.

Metal screeched in protest as he bore her to the ground, the weight of his charge slamming her flat despite her much greater size. There was a sharp *ping* of breaking metal, and then the momentum carried him over top of her and into a roll.

Skidding to a stop and sending rocks in all directions, Koda was already scrambling forward, moving on all fours as he had before at the Last Fang Cave. He propelled himself with much more force and speed than such a pose should have allowed for a human man.

The Crooked champion was already rolling over, intent on rising to her feet, when Koda struck her again from the side.

His first charge had snapped one of her swords, the weight of the hit and the angle of it breaking one blade against the other.

Koda's second tackle knocked her other blade flying from a broken hand as he slammed her to the ground once more, pinning her face-down on the rocky earth with the weight of an angry mountain.

The world around him went red as Koda slashed at the pinned champion with both sets of claws. Fresh strength continued to flow into his limbs as he struck out, devoting everything he had to finishing this fight. Physical and spiritual weapons tore into the enemy, for that was all that she was to him at the moment.

A threat to those under his protection.

Metal links parted, and rings of chainmail flew, unable to resist the greatly increased strength of the man turned to incarnate fury. Enemy blood spattered against stone, and bones shattered. Through it all, that deep, ursine roar continued to echo off the mountainside.

The threat struggled against him, but Koda refused to relent even as he felt blows strike him and something pierce his side. Blows that grew weaker by the second before dropping away finally.

Enough, Daughter. You have aided my champion. The gentle voice of Thera bubbled up from the dark places within Koda's mind. *You mean well, but you will only harm yourself more if you overstretch.*

There was a deep, familiar-sounding grumble that reminded Koda of the visions he'd had. Of Thera with the bear spirit at her side. Of the dream of chasing the tall woman through the trees while she laughed joyously. When that familiar-sounding voice had guided him to strike with the wrath of his ancestors to bring down the one who had hurt Sienna.

Sienna!

The veil of rage faded, and with it the single-minded rage that his blood-memories brought up from the ancient past.

Koda threw himself off the bloody mess that had once been his enemy, scrambling across the broken stone towards where he'd seen Sienna land earlier. She was sitting upright, still clutching the broken haft of her spear. But, as he approached, her eyes fluttered open.

"Koda?" The words were weak, but he saw her chest rise and fall as the wolf beastfolk took a breath, then blinked those beautiful, crystalline orbs that she tried to focus on him. Those orbs that drew him in, saw the wounds and fear his heart bore at the thought of losing her, and softly healed them without effort.

"Shh, it's okay, Sienna. I got her. You are safe now, love."

Koda didn't even realize what he'd said until Sienna blinked several times, her face twisting in a mixture of confusion and amusement.

"Love?" she asked, raising one eyebrow up at him while a smile crossed her lips.

Chapter Twenty-Six

KODA HADN'T REALIZED IT, BUT WITH HIS RESOUNDING defeat of the woman, the spirit of the Crooked force had broken, and they fled back into the Windwalker's Retreat.

By the time he'd stammered out an explanation to Sienna and gotten both of them to their feet, the fight was over, save for those on the cliff above.

He learned later that the hunters on their vantage point had continued to pick off any Crooked that moved within the still-burning camp. Apparently, the threat of death from above and burning was less terrifying to the twisted remnants of the enemy force than facing the one who had literally torn their warleader limb from limb in a rage.

Never mind that Koda had a cracked rib and a dagger wound in his side from the champion's last attempts to protect herself. All they saw was the blood, and all they heard was the fury as their champion was bested.

When it became obvious that the Crooked within the camp were either dead, dying, or unwilling to escape, the remaining members of the Silverstone Vale war band dragged what remained of the barricades over and used them to block off the entrances while they waited for the fires to burn out.

In that time, they tended to their wounded and the fallen.

Koda refused to waste Kris's time with his injuries, insisting that she had more critical cases to tend to. Which was true, but the only reason that no one countermanded him was purely because too many people were unwilling to argue with someone so heavily caked in blood that was not his own.

Only Sienna was willing to approach him for the time being, and she wasn't in much of a condition to argue with Koda either. The kick that had sent her flying had cracked one of her ribs, and she had bruises all up and down her back that made moving difficult.

Despite her injuries, Sienna ordered Koda to remove the shredded remains of his shirt and set aside his cloak so she could look him over while the few uninjured fighters stood guard over the rest.

"You are an idiot, you know that, right?" Sienna muttered while she carefully washed the stab wound in his side with a delicate touch. There was no anger in her tone, just the sort of bone-deep exhaustion that Koda could feel in himself as well. This didn't stop the slow wag of her tail, though the motion looked stiff compared to the appendage's normally animated dances.

"I'll be your idiot if you'll have me," Koda said, his voice catching from the pain as Sienna's hand tensed against his wound. "Sorry if that is forward, but I figured that after earlier..."

"Fine then, my idiot," Sienna said quietly, her tail moving just a bit faster now. "You need to be more careful and actually *think*. I know I saw you pick up the discarded weapons of the other Crooked during the fight with the other champion. Why not do the same with the warleader? Why did you throw yourself on her like a mother bear defending her cubs?"

Koda shrugged, blushing slightly. He didn't want to admit that he'd been freaked out too much to think tactically during the early parts of the fight, or that his anger that she'd gotten hurt had gotten away from him so much.

The last thing I want is for her to feel like I'm upset with her, Koda thought, wincing again as Sienna prodded at his wound with the wet cloth. *I am responsible for my own actions and reactions. The fact that one of them got her hurt is my fault.* He was also doing his best to not react to her tacit agreement of a relationship with the statement, though Koda was unsure of how successful that attempt was based on the wry smile that Sienna was wearing.

"I was focused," he said after a long moment of silence, and he got a snort of amusement from Sienna in response.

"Sure you were," Sienna drawled, wincing when she shifted and pain shot through her.

"Anything I can do to help you?" Koda asked automatically, reaching out to rest his left hand on her thigh. Lifting that limb any higher hurt, and Sienna barked at him the first time he did it that he would tear his wound open.

"Nothing right now. I've injured my ribs in the past. All that we can do is wrap them and wait for now. I am not going to ask Kris to waste her magic on me when people are dying," Sienna said quietly, glancing over to the area where the headwoman continued to work.

The fight had not been without losses. Nearly every one of the Silverstone Vale natives had taken an injury of some kind. Many were simple cuts or bruises. A few had actual wounds or broken bones. But, of the forty or so of their fighters, five lay dead to one side. Another ten were seriously injured and either resting or being tended to by Kris and her assistants.

The aged cat beastfolk moved quickly from person to person, her staff weaving in a steady rhythm and cool light working to keep as many of her people as stable as possible.

While Koda watched, several of the lightly injured were already heading over to help tend to those they could.

"Thank you, Koda."

Sienna's words were quiet in his ear. As he turned to look at her, Koda felt something soft bump into his lips as Sienna's face covered his.

Their lips touched gently, far more so than their last kiss. Their previous encounter had been fierce, as both had sought comfort in the other before the battle. This one was sweet, two hearts connecting in the ashes of fear and battle to bring forth hope.

Koda wanted to deepen the kiss, to do so very much more to express his growing affection and lust to Sienna. He knew that it was far too soon to be in love with this glorious woman who was pressing into him. A woman he'd fought for, bled for, and killed for. But there was no other name than love that he could put to the surging emotion that welled up in his heart right now.

For now, though, he was content to enjoy the feeling of her lips and the gentle pressure of her body on his.

Once his wound had been cleaned out and bandaged, Koda had dozed off with Sienna in his arms, only intending to close his eyes for a moment. He woke suddenly when Kris prodded him with her staff while healing his injury.

When he protested that she should use her power on someone more injured, she actually smacked him in the shoulder with the rounded head of the staff and chastised him that his health was too important to risk.

Under Kris's watchful gaze, he'd helped bind Sienna's ribs to ensure they would heal naturally and helped her drink a pain-relieving tea that the headwoman had been passing around.

With that, the treatment of their injuries was complete. Koda and Sienna joined the rotating watch and stood by the barricades, with Sienna not straying far from Koda's side at any time.

They didn't have to say it aloud, but both were silently glad that they were not part of the group on the cliff above as the faint scent of burning flesh still snuck through the crack in the cliffs.

When the sun finally graced the horizon, the hunters who had been stationed above came back down the narrow goat track to let them know the fires had finally gone out. After discussing it with them and Kris, Koda decided to wait for a few more hours to let the stone cool before they went in to make sure this was finished.

Koda had a feeling that he was going to find another of the disturbing altars of the Crooked in the camp, and even if he didn't find one, he still needed to claim this site for Thera. While they waited, those able to help but too keyed up to sleep worked together to fashion stretchers to bring the wounded and fallen back to the village. They piled the dead Crooked up against the cliff to be dealt with later.

When the time came, Koda led a small party into the main rent in the surrounding cliff. The group was made up of him, Sienna, a tired Kris, a bandaged and grumpy Hans, and the older fox beastfolk that had led the flanking group of hunters whom Koda learned was named Todd Westeye. The others amongst the group of fighters followed in a ragged line, but the group of five led the way into the charred husk of the camp.

The fires had burned hot, but not so hot that it had left the camp as nothing more than a greasy smudge. He could faintly feel the heat of the fire still underfoot, but the rock underfoot wasn't so hot that it melted the rubber soles of his boots.

All around them, the dead lay scattered. It was hard to count how many Crooked had been in the camp, but there had to have been at least a hundred. Koda hadn't bothered to count the enemy dead out on the hillside, but there had to be at least half that many scattered around. Some bodies had escaped the fire, huddling over in the area that they had been hacking away at with the pickaxes. These were marked with arrows and as dead as the others.

Koda was actually somewhat grateful for the fire at this point; the scent of burned cloth, wood, and flesh was mixing enough that his sinuses had decided to close shop and go on strike.

"Should be over that way," Todd said abruptly, the word breaking through the somber air around them, and the other four heads turned in the direction the older fox was pointing, which was towards the back of the camp but one side of the scorched remains of the large tent, tucked up under the rocks. "I saw the robed bastard running that way and made sure to get him myself."

Without a comment, the group turned and started in the indicated direction, circling around between the burned camp and the dug-out area. Koda kicked a partially burned pickaxe to one side as he went, the head coming free of the scorched shaft to clatter loudly over the stone. The noise made the others jump in surprise before Sienna laughed in relief.

"I don't know what I was expecting," the wolf-eared woman muttered. "I know what sort of damage fire can do, and I did suggest burning them out."

"Seeing the devastation is still something different to just thinking of it, child," Kris replied somberly. "It's been almost three decades since the last bad fire broke out in the village. May it be many more before another occurs."

"Aye," chorused Hans and Todd, with Koda and Sienna just nodding.

They spotted the body of the robed Crooked sprawled in the shadow of the cliff side a moment later. Half a dozen arrows protruded from the thin corpse, but Todd still drew one more from his quiver and sent it into the still form before anyone could react.

The corpse didn't react, other than to shift slightly from the impact of the arrow.

"Was that necessary?" Sienna demanded, the sudden movement of the hunter having made her jump and reach for her dagger. She'd recovered the head of her spear but had not had time to attach it to a new shaft.

"The bastard shot lightning at me after the first arrow and kept trying to crawl after the third. Arrows five and six were to make sure. This one was because I don't trust these shits to stay dead," grumbled Todd, though the old fox looked sheepish at his own paranoia now.

"It's fine. Better to be safe than someone getting hurt," Koda said gently while skirting around the body. He made sure to hook the fallen staff away from the hands of the corpse, just in case.

They proceeded to the bowl of nightmares that was tucked back in the hollow of the wall, just out of sight and safe from the weather in a natural nook in the wall.

Like the other two he'd encountered, the altar that the Crooked had set up was a brass dish the size of a cooking wok. It balanced on a stand made of twisted and gnarled bones that seemed to melt and merge at random to provide a place where a fire could be laid underneath the dish.

Inside was a small bundle of something that had once been living, but Koda didn't look at it too closely. Instead, he did the same to this altar as he had the first two.

Piercing his left thumb with one sharp claw, Koda smeared the red liquid on each of the sharp bone talons before striking out at the profane object in front of him. The claws of his totemic gauntlet slashed through the metallic dish like it was made of fog, just as it had the other two.

A flicker of black fire danced over the decorations on his gauntlet before racing out the claws, turning a bloody red as it consumed the altar in a flash of light before a pulse of force shot out from the point of impact.

Koda had prepared this time and braced himself, so the pulse only made his clothing stir as a result. He'd warned the others in advance, so the four with him were ready as well, the ripple barely stirring their clothes. The others who followed at a distance to observe out of curiosity were not as prepared, and several stumbled at the pulse, and it knocked one woman off her feet.

As it had before, the distant sound of an animal calling out echoed through the air.

It had been a wolf's howl for the first altar Koda had destroyed, and a bear's bellow for the second. The third started out as a gurgling screech like a tea-kettle full of pond-scum trying to boil. That sound rapidly resolved into the triumphant bugle of an elk, though with a distinctly predatory trill to it. Almost as if the elk bugled through a mouth full of sharp teeth.

As the red fire burned out, the tanned hide of an elk appeared in the hollow instead, a stone bowl settling into place on top of it.

"That's that, then," Koda said with a tired sigh. He felt even more exhausted than usual from this fight, possibly because he'd been constantly on the move for the last few days and could finally take a breath to rest.

"Koda!" Sienna's shout of surprise had him whirling with his totemic gauntlet raised to fight, as more shouts of surprise echoed from the others in the little hollow.

As the elk's bugle faded away into the evening air, the ghostly form of a long-limbed creature rose up from beneath the scarred stones to Koda's right. The creature was bone thin and hollow-eyed, with arms that hung to its knees and a back bent forward as if it had been a man of great age, an image dismissed by the rest of its appearance.

Dense gray fur covered its body up to its head, which had been replaced with the skull of an elk, though it had the interlocking fangs of a predator in the place of the normal, flat teeth of a herbivore. A massive, spreading rack of antlers protruded from the top of its ghostly head. Antlers that made a quiet rattling noise as it shook its head back and forth like the tines rubbed against each other without moving somehow.

The creature hovered just off the ground, its legs ending in scorched nubs a few inches above where ankles should have been on a human.

"Wendigo," gasped Todd as more of the hunters gasped and scrambled to ready weapons.

The ghostly apparition turned to look first at Todd and then Koda with bottomless, empty sockets in its skull-head. It shook its head once, as if to deny the hunter's statement, before looking towards the charred remains of the Crooked camp.

Koda blinked, and then the creature was gone, already zipping forward as if it was a small bird carried on an afternoon breeze. The apparition skated over the ground without touching it. Wherever the spirit of the wendigo passed, the bodies of the Crooked faded away, and the stone lay scoured clean of any marks of fire.

All that was left behind were the tattered remains of the Crooked forces' tents, and what few supplies survived the fire.

"Be at peace, my children. The wendigo serves me now, and cleanses its once-home of our enemies' taint."

Koda jumped again, whirling towards the nook that contained the altar once more. This time he was smiling when he beheld the ghostly figure of Thera as she strode out of the stone behind the altar, her fur skirt whirling about her hips while a striped tail flicked behind her back. She looked nearly solid to him, and Koda felt a knot in his chest unclench at that sight.

There was a sudden rustle of movement from behind him, and Koda glanced back to see that everyone, save Sienna and himself, had dropped to a knee, bowing their heads towards the goddess. He glanced back at Thera with a quirked eyebrow. She rolled her eyes slightly before shrugging as if to say, *what can you do?*

"Please, rise, my children. I wish to see your faces after being away from this world for so long," Thera called, her polished silver eyes glinting as she surveyed her people. Even as she did so, those who had not entered the retreat began to trickle in, first curiosity and then awe painting their faces.

Slowly, starting with Kris and Hans, those attending rose to their feet and peered up at the goddess. The same fires of hope that Koda had kindled in their eyes the previous day were now burning fresh in faces marked with fire, blood, exhaustion, and triumph.

"I cannot stay with you long, but I commend you all for the loyalty that you have shown me. Your families have remained true to your faith and protected me in my weakened state," Thera declared as her tail flicked behind her back, disappearing from view. Meanwhile, a smattering of feathers flowed out of her hair to fluff out slowly as she spoke.

"As my champion has told you before, I am returning to you all. Every day that passes, I gain more strength. As such, our people will grow once more. I have no way to give voice to the proper gratitude that I owe you all for your loyalties over the centuries, but I will do all I can to see our people flourish. This opportunity to bless you all has come to me because of my champion and the labors of his companion."

Thera extended her hands towards Koda and Sienna. Koda rolled his eyes at her, making sure none of the villagers could see him do it. He knew that Thera was clearly posturing with her first appearance before her faithful to further reinforce her position as a goddess, so he couldn't begrudge her that. It must have felt good to speak to those she called her children again.

Sienna just blushed furiously, clearly taken aback to be thanked by her goddess so publicly.

"For now, though, trust in your headwoman. Trust in each other. And trust in my champion, Koda Aegisclaw. For the greatest wrath of my champions shall rise up in defense of another."

When Thera spoke his name and gave him the title, Koda felt something pulse inside his chest. No, that wasn't right. Something *on top of* his chest pulsed as he felt the pendant he wore throb with purpose and energy.

The goddess turned towards him, the feathers in her hair melting away, and a massive, ghostly set of fox ears replaced them, the features of different beastfolk flowing over her as usual, changing from moment to moment.

The ghost of the wendigo skated past again, bugling its bizarre cry of joy before diving into the earth beneath the altar and vanishing from view.

"Aegisclaw, I will speak to you soon in depth. But for now, thank you for your work here. Silverstone Vale is now secure because of your work. The Ivory Spear tribe owes its improved fate to you."

With a smile and a nod, the goddess faded from sight. This left Koda and Sienna standing in front of the new altar to Thera, with the entirety of the hunting party now staring at them in awe.

Chapter Twenty-Seven

IT TOOK A GOOD HALF-HOUR FOR THE QUESTIONS TO stop flowing and for the others to stop treating Koda like he had somehow just pulled their goddess out of his pocket. While he had—sort-of—caused her to appear, it had been far grander than just pulling her out covered in lint.

The wendigo spirit had removed all signs of the fire and the bodies from the Retreat, even the ones piled outside of the walls of the tiny valley. That was an immense relief for everyone involved as that meant that they did not have to hang around to burn the bodies this time. Instead, they could simply proceed directly back to the village with the wounded.

Several of the miners still took the time to salvage what would be useful from within the remains of the camp. Apparently, every bit of metal, whether it be hinges, tool heads, or even the crudely forged swords of the Crooked, could be put to good use.

All the items were collected and piled into several packs to carry back. From what Koda heard, they'd be either melted down, reforged, or just repurposed in the recovery efforts.

Anything of value, like coins or jewelry, was split between the ones who found them and the headwoman, whom Koda assumed was collecting that share to help with rebuilding the village and other expenses.

Seeing their goddess manifest before them gave all the villagers fresh energy, and they finished scavenging the camp within an hour.

Anything that they would not be taking with them was piled outside the walls of the Windwalker's Retreat and covered with the loose stone of the mountainside to allow nature to reclaim it. Things like the scraps of tent, spare clothes, or damaged chests mostly ended up in the pile.

The march back down the mountain to the village was much easier than the one up had been. The victorious fighters made very good time, with those able to hold the weight rotating through stretcher duty to transport those who could not walk or the bodies of their fallen allies.

Koda put his goddess-improved strength to use by carrying heaviest bundles of metallic tools and scavenged weapons, bearing the burden of two full packs himself to allow the other fighters more rest.

Though they did not talk much, Sienna remained at his side for the entire trip. The two stole soft and heated glances at each other, believing themselves to be subtle.

They were not. Much to the amusement of those that caught them, but none called the two out on it.

When the group finally neared the village, the sun was teasing the horizon.

Kris sent one of the youngest hunters ahead to alert those who remained behind of their return. When the war party left the trees on the edge of the village, it was to the sight of their families waiting for them with open arms and broad smiles on their faces for the survivors, or tears for the fallen.

They were engulfed in that swirling mass of welcome, with many a clasped forearm or hugged neck for all. Even Koda got a royal welcome from several of the villagers—mostly younger women, he noticed wryly.

"Everyone!" The boom of Hans's voice broke the rumble of conversation as the unruly mob of people continued to ramble and block the streets into the village. "Everyone! We understand you are happy to see us, but there are far better places to celebrate than the edge of Farmer Oslo's orchard! The headwoman bids you all to move this to the main square. I'm sure Banno would happily provide better drinks than the evening dew on the trees!"

A roar of approval rose from the group and, as one, the mob turned and dragged the returning fighters deeper into the village.

Hands relieved Koda of his pack and steered him into a chair at a table that appeared magically in the square just outside the door of the inn. A wooden tankard full of something that smelled of apples and spices landed in front of him, while a platter of roast meat and steaming potatoes joined it a moment later.

All over the square, more tables were being set out, with everything from footstools to barrel ends being used when the chairs ran out.

"Eat, Sir Koda. Banno sends it with his thanks for your work in protecting the village," chirped a smiling young woman in a low-cut top and full skirt with the ears and tail of a feline beastfolk. The server whirled away before he could say anything in protest or even thank her.

"Seems you are getting popular, Aegisclaw," Sienna teased, settling into the chair next to him with a groan and draping her tail over her lap.

"Oh, don't you start with using that name, too," Koda protested even as his stomach growled, demanding food. It had been hours since the hard bread they'd eaten for breakfast, and the hike down the mountain had been without breaks as all of them wanted to make it home to sleep in actual beds.

"Why not? I happen to like it. Your claws have risen in my defense multiple times after all." Sienna paused in her finger-combing of her bushy tail to steal a bit of potato off his plate.

Koda gave a put-upon sigh as if it was such an imposition to have a title of honor. Honestly, it was somewhat embarrassing as he could hear the other fighters talking about his title, the fight, and all manner of things.

The tables continued to fill up, and more serving girls whirled out of the tavern with drinks and plates of food. He did note that none of the servers seemed to expect payment for the food and drink, though he noted Kris handing off a pouch to an older woman who watched from the door to the inn, dressed far more conservatively than the young serving maids.

The village came to life as he ate. It gratified Koda to see that the worried and fearful looks that he had witnessed only days before were gone, instead replaced with bright smiles, hopeful eyes, and cheerful voices.

In the time it took for him to devour the first plate of food in front of him, Koda heard at least three different renditions of his fight with the Crooked warleader, each one even more exaggerated than the last. Sienna would poke fun at him when she heard a particularly ridiculous line, still stealing food from his plate without a care.

Even the wounded were getting in on the party. Those unable to walk had been set up on cots amongst the revelers so that they wouldn't be excluded and were regaling anyone who stopped by with stories of the fight. The dead had been placed in a location of honor as well, at the other end of the square where their spirits could observe the festivities and for those who wished to have a quiet word with the fallen.

There were several times while he ate that Koda caught sight of people sitting close together and speaking in whispers. The first time he dismissed it as just a friendly conversation, maybe even mourning, but the sight became more common and spread through the revelry quickly as eyes stared in wonder at him and Sienna.

"Is it just me or are they talking about us?" Koda asked Sienna in a low tone, pushing away his plate when he could eat no more. The other seats at the table were empty at the moment. Different people would swing by to talk to the two of them, but never for very long. Hans had just wandered off saying he needed to check on some of his men with a knowing smile at the two of them.

Sienna smirked out of the corner of her mouth at him, toying with a bit of potato on the end of her knife before she answered.

"They are likely hearing the details of your conjuration of our goddess," Sienna whispered, her eyes glittering with amusement at the flush that crossed Koda's cheeks. "And before you ask why it is being done in whispers. Well, some habits are hard to break. It is not time for Thera's name to resound from the mountaintops yet. You still have a lot of work left to do before it is safe for her faithful to come out of hiding. But our people are invigorated with her appearance."

Koda thought that over as he sipped at his drink, enjoying the flavor of the spiced cider while the party continued to whirl full-swing around him.

Behind him on the steps of the tavern, the whine of a bow being drawn over a fiddle's strings brought a ripple of silence over the crowd that was quickly followed by a raucous cheer. Koda turned to see what was happening.

"Right, you louts! Clear up a spot for dancing!" roared a bone-thin man bearing a pair of goat horns on his head just before he started sawing away on his fiddle as clapping rose up from the crowd.

A great scraping of wood on stone preceded a rush of movement. Tables and seats were shifted, with several villagers scampered into the growing darkness to return with instruments of their own as the goat beastfolk strode through the crowd to leap up on the edge of the fountain in the middle of the square.

Within moments, couples were dancing in pairs while larger groups went through circle-dances that looked to have more points for being energetic than organized.

Netta was the next to join them at their table, the hawk beastfolk dodging through the crowd with a bowl in one hand and a mug in the other. She still bore the smears of smoke in some spots, but she'd taken enough time to wash the blood from her hands and face before joining the party, something that made Koda feel even more grubby as he hadn't had the chance to. Every time he tried to get up, someone else stopped by to speak to him.

"How are you two guests of honor holding up?" Netta asked, taking a deep drink from her mug and sighing in relief.

"Guests of honor?" Koda asked in confusion, glancing around for whoever Netta might be talking about.

His expression made Sienna laugh outright, a bright and clear sound that tickled his heart and brought a smile to his face.

"Your humility is a credit to you, if it's honest. And you are an ass if not," snarked Netta around a mouthful of steaming potatoes. "Sienna, tell him."

It took Sienna a minute to master her giggles before she could, being set off once more by Koda's expectant expression.

"Whenever the village celebrates, whoever are considered the guests of honor sit at this table. It started out as Banno's grandfather wanting them close to make sure their food was hot and their drinks never ran out, but it became a tradition over the years. It's why people don't hang around for too long, so everyone can come by to talk to us."

Koda was about to respond when a trio of young women oozed out of the crowd wearing even more daring tops than the serving girls had. They forced their way onto the bench with Netta, nearly knocking the hawk beastfolk over in their enthusiasm.

"Good eve, Sir Aegisclaw!" two of them said in unison, while the third just batted her lashes at him, tugging on her bodice to reveal even more pale, curved flesh.

"Good eve, ladies," Koda replied politely. He was surprised when his simple statement produced blushes and giggles from all three girls.

As they seemed too preoccupied with blushing and nudging each other to respond, Koda took the time to study the three newcomers.

He couldn't help but compare them to Sienna at his side. While the huntress was lithe with the muscle of someone who spent her time outdoors, her skin kissed by the sun, these three all had the delicate softness of women who spent their time indoors.

Soft hands were folded on the table in front of them, and pale skin glimmered in the lamplight. All three had full figures, within a cup-size of each other, and generous hips. Koda felt he could get an excellent judge of that as the upper edge of their tops barely covered their nipples. In fact, he saw the upper crescent of pink on one of them that hinted she was nearly ready to burst free of her top.

"So, what are your plans for the night, Sir Aegisclaw?" the one on the end asked, the pointed shells of her feline ears fixed on him, while the stripy, orange length of her tail flicked back and forth behind her, and she toyed with a strand of her dark hair, wrapping it around one finger.

Her two friends, a pair of deer beastfolk he guessed based on their floppy ears and the white specks that decorated the appendages, hung on his response with wide eyes.

Koda took a moment to think about if he had any plans. His mind wasn't running very quickly because of the alcohol in his system and his full stomach after the previous several long days.

He was about to respond when a fluffy mass whacked him in the chest before dropping down into his lap. Sienna's tail bounced once before settling as Koda set his hand on top of it.

"Koda will be taking his leave of the festivities soon," Sienna said, her voice tight as she glared at the trio, who returned her glare with equal measure.

"Are you sure about that, Sir Aegisclaw?" purred one of the deer beastfolk, tugging on the upper hem of her top and exposing the rose-colored peak of one breast to his eyes with a wink. "All three of us would like to spend a bit of time to... *know* our savior better." Her two companions nodded rapidly in agreement, and Sienna let out a huff of irritation.

Of course, Netta said nothing. Only watching with a smirk while she ate.

"I'm sorry, ladies, but Sienna is right. It's been far too long since I had a chance to properly wash, and I am exhausted. I wouldn't be proper company for very long." Koda did his best to let them down gently.

While their obvious offers intrigued him, he didn't feel that same raw attraction as he did for Sienna to these three that so blatantly offered themselves to him, at least if his interpretations of their words were accurate.

Without thinking, Koda's hands settled onto his lap and began combing his fingers through the fluff of Sienna's tail. The eyes of the trio dropped to his lap before turning to narrow at Sienna. Then the tense moment passed, and the feline of the trio spoke again.

"Well, if you change your mind, come and find us, Sir Aegisclaw. We will happily entertain you *all night*." She put such emphasis on the last part of her statement that Koda was somewhat surprised that some hadn't dripped off to land on the table between them.

The trio rose, and they shot Sienna another round of dirty looks before disappearing into the milling crowd that was surrounding the dancing space.

"Nicely done, Sienna," Netta chuckled. "You two should slip away now if that's what you planned. The dancing will distract people for a good bit."

"It wouldn't be rude to leave early? You just said we were the guests of honor," Koda asked. He didn't really want to stay. The exhaustion tugging at his body made him desperately want to just curl up somewhere, preferably in a spot with enough space to have Sienna tucked against him again.

"Nope. Guests of honor get to do what they want, and no one will begrudge you from wanting rest after the last few days," Netta replied with a grin, making shooing motions with her hands.

Koda traded looks with a blushing Sienna, who nodded. Regretfully, he released her tail, the softness so at odds for her trim and athletic body, and offered her a hand to her feet. Sienna accepted, blushing faintly, and then tugged him towards the edge of the inn where they could get out of the square without being witnessed.

Out of the corner of his eye, Koda caught it when Netta shot Sienna a broad wink and a thumbs-up, making the wolf-beastfolk blush even more furiously.

They walked until the rumble of the party was a distant noise, moving around the edge of the celebration before angling towards the hunter's hall, comfortable silence settling between them once more.

"Koda?" Sienna asked after a minute of silence, still holding the hand that he had offered to her earlier.

"Yes, Sienna?"

"I've been meaning to ask you... has Thera..." Her voice dropped low as she spoke the goddess's name, and Sienna cast a quick look around. "Has Thera told you of her plans?"

"To protect all of you and see your people flourish, I would think that'd be obvious after her statement earlier today," Koda answered.

Sienna stopped with a huff and turned to look up at him, irritation dancing in her eyes along with the reflection of moonlight. With her free hand, she gestured at herself.

"I mean about me."

"What about you?" Koda blinked down at her in confusion. He knew that Thera had spoken with her about something. He'd observed part of it, though the details were hard to recall.

Sienna sighed through her nose, muttering under her breath to herself.

"She's right. Kind of dumb, but in a cute way. Lucky for that..." she grumbled before locking eyes with him.

"Koda, I know you overheard that conversation I had with her in my dreams. We talked about it a bit. We've danced around it for days. This morning you said you loved me."

Koda felt his heart seize in his chest, and he stared down at Sienna, his gut knotting. Had he overstepped something?

Sienna saw the concern in his eyes and shook her head, dispelling the worry with a small smile. She seemed to take a moment to gather herself before she spoke next.

"She's right, I'm going to just have to say it out loud, my idiot." She said the word 'idiot' with deep affection, shifting to press herself against Koda's chest while looking up at him. "Koda Aegisclaw, you've been on my mind since that first day you came to help us. My goddess asked me to bond with you before so that our people would not lose your line again. But I'm asking you to bond with me because I love you, idiot. Will you finally make me your mate?"

Koda didn't answer her with words, as words could not convey the joy he felt welling in his heart at the blatant confirmation of Sienna's love for him. Instead, he wrapped both his arms around her, cradling the lithe wolf-woman in his arms and claimed her lips in a wordless 'yes'.

Chapter 28

<3 <3 <3

Sᴵᴇɴɴᴀ ᴄʜᴀɴɢᴇᴅ ᴡʜᴀᴛ ᴅɪʀᴇᴄᴛɪᴏɴ sʜᴇ ᴡᴀs ʟᴇᴀᴅɪɴɢ Koda. Instead, she towed him towards the edge of the village. They passed the hunter's hall and kept right on going.

Koda wanted to ask her where they were headed, but the smoky looks that Sienna continued to aim his way would consistently scramble his brain. So instead, he just followed after her, eyes fixed on the bouncing bundle of red-black fluff that was her tail.

They emerged at the village edge, and Sienna confidently led them into the trees along a narrow, well-traveled path that wound its way leisurely through the darkness.

As soon as they were away from the edge of the village, the light level dropped precipitously. The full moon overhead was the only source of light, and it struggled to penetrate the interlocking branches. The flickering movement of Sienna's tail, along with her tugging hand, was what allowed Koda to follow after her.

After only a few minutes of walking, they emerged from the trees into a scene that looked like it came right out of a storybook.

In the center of a clearing in the trees sat a pool of water surrounded by ancient gray boulders on three sides. A thin shore of pebbles made up its near side. The moon rode high overhead and reflected its glory in the dancing silver specks on the surface of the water. A thin stream bubbled out of one side and flowed away into the trees. The water was so clear that Koda could see all the way to the sandy bottom.

A shush of cloth on skin drew his attention away from the sight of wild nature in front of him and instead to the natural beauty to his left. He hadn't noticed when Sienna released his hand, being too caught up in the allure of what he was seeing. But now, as she quickly pulled off her shirt then turned to drape it over a low boulder with a conspicuously flat top, Koda was staring for a whole new reason.

A button was flipped on both sides of her pants and Sienna gave a sinuous roll of her hips, peeling the close-fitting garment down and revealing her firm ass. Her lightly tanned skin shone in the moonlight like a fresh peach.

The fluffy mass of her tail protruded from the base of her spine, and it swished back and forth tentatively while she carefully stacked her clothes. The dancing bundle of fur always managed to hide the view of her treasure from behind, but that was a problem that was rapidly alleviated when Sienna turned to look towards him with a nervous smile.

Koda had spent the last few days in nearly constant contact with Sienna. The wolf beastfolk woman had been shy, aggressive, fearless, and timid all in equal measures and different times, but in the moment right then, she looked absolutely adorable as she posed in the moonlight for him.

Her bare, full breasts swelled out from her chest, pert hand-fuls topped with rose-colored nipples that were hardening in the gentle breeze even now. A delicate wisp of curly hair decorated her womanhood, trimmed and neat. While the light of the moon was enough to see her by, it didn't overly highlight the lithe muscles of the athletic woman before him.

Sienna looked soft, vulnerable, and absolutely precious to him in that moment.

While he hadn't been a monk before, Koda had only had the opportunity for one or two fumbling interludes with women before work actively devoured all his time and energy. He'd then spent almost all his time trying to get to a financially stable position before he could work to find himself a part-ner. He'd always thought that the stability and ability to provide for others were going to be key to being able to attract a life partner.

I don't know if that's what Sienna wants right now, but gods, I hope so, Koda thought as he drank in the sight of her before him.

The wagging of her tail picked up when Sienna realized she had captivated Koda, a small smile stealing across her lips. Striding forward, her hips swinging ever so slightly as she moved, Sienna came to a stop in front of Koda.

They were of a height, with Koda only topping her by an inch, so their mouths connected in another kiss without effort.

Sienna knotted her hands in Koda's shirt, pulling him down into the kiss even as her soft breasts pillowed into his chest.

On autopilot, Koda's hands settled onto her bare hips, drawing a short, sharp intake of breath from his fiery-haired lover. A breath that she stole directly from Koda's lungs as their lips refused to part.

While they kissed, Koda let his hands slowly begin to wander, running up and down Sienna's sides. Satisfied that he would not try to escape, Sienna began to unbutton his shirt before attacking his belt. All the while, Koda could hear the quiet swish of her tail as it danced merrily behind the woman.

Sienna pulled back from the kiss to yank his shirt off, before immediately diving into his arms once more, her whole body shivering at the sensation of Koda's nails running over her skin before dancing up her ribs to caress the undersides of her breasts. They then slid around her back to run down along Sienna's spine before one settled on her bottom to give it a light squeeze, while the other began to rub the base of her tail.

This drew a moan of desire from the redheaded huntress, and she gave Koda's pants a sharp jerk before they fell with a clatter to the stones. Sienna pulled back from the kiss, her eyes wide and pupils dilated with desire.

"Koda, go wash really quickly? I want to start making good on repaying some of the debt we all owe you, but we both smell of the fight." The begging tone in Sienna's voice sent a thrill down his spine. "I'll put your clothes up and join you in a minute."

"Sure."

The one-word answer to Sienna's entreaty sent her tail wagging even more furiously, and a smile blossomed on her sweet face, lit from above by the moonlight. She quickly knelt to help remove his boots and then tug his pants off, leaving Koda as bare to the world as she was.

He nearly jumped out of his skin when she planted a single kiss on the top of his thigh, barely inches from his hardening member.

"I'll see you in a minute," Sienna muttered to his cock, her voice thick with desire.

And then she was away, up and moving while carefully folding his clothing to drape it over the stone. Koda watched her full bottom bounce in time with the swaying of her tail. He had to fight the urge to slide up behind her when Sienna bent forward over the stone to lay his things out, her tail flicking just enough to one side to expose the wet treasure that lay beneath it for a bare moment.

Swallowing hard, Koda turned away and quickly stepped into the spring. The water was chilly to the touch, but given how hot Sienna had made him with just that one action a moment ago, he wasn't fazed by the temperature in the slightest.

The bottom of the spring was sandy, and he could feel a faint tickling on the soles of his feet as the water rose from beneath the ground. It had a strangely effervescent feeling to it that didn't distract him from his desire for longer than a second.

Remembering Sienna's entreaties to wash so that she could reward him, Koda scooped water up and quickly scrubbed off, making sure to wash the sweat from his intimate places in hopes that this would go the way he was expecting. As he didn't have any soap, he used a bit of sand to help loosen the dried blood.

A splash from behind him drew his attention that way, and he couldn't help the lusty smile that stole across his lips as Sienna waded into the water after him.

Between the glow of the moon on her hair and the rippling sparkles that the celestial body cast over the tiny droplets of water left behind as she rinsed herself, Sienna looked like some kind of goddess descended to earth.

Her pointed ears flicked and rotated slightly on top of her head, not quite camouflaged in her short mess of hair. They seemed to track every sound in the trees—and many that Koda wasn't even aware of—until her ears adjusted. But they always turned back to him as if her intense focus on him was all that mattered in the moment.

The water only came up to his knees. Koda turned to stare at Sienna, just devouring her with his eyes as she approached him. She stopped only inches away, looking up at him with affection blazing in her crystalline blue-green eyes. Eyes that quickly captured Koda as was becoming their habit.

Sienna leaned forward, and Koda felt two hard points dig into his chest for just a moment before they were engulfed in warm softness as the rest of her breasts squished against his chest.

Koda didn't need any urging to meet her lips this time, his hands sliding over the top of her hips to palm her firm bottom and pull her against him.

She let out a quiet groan of desire into the kiss, her hands coming to rest on his chest lightly while she leaned into his embrace. Sienna was the one to break their lip-lock eventually, but she did not stop kissing him entirely.

The wolf-eared woman danced kisses down across Koda's jaw, up to his ear, and then back down his neck. Twice he felt her nip at his throat, but a heated dart of her tongue quickly soothed those sharp points only seconds later.

Koda continued to smooth his hands over her firm bottom, palming and then kneading the muscled flesh there. Sienna moaned hotly in his ear as he leaned forward enough to slip one hand between her thighs from behind, lightly teasing her entrance.

"Not yet," Sienna panted hotly. "I want to please you first, Koda Aegisclaw. Champion to my goddess and savior of my people." She pulled back just enough that their eyes could meet, and Koda was about to protest the titles when he saw the amusement twinkling in Sienna's eyes. "My idiot," she whispered huskily.

Koda had never heard the insult spoken with such desire and endearment, and he felt a thrill run up his spine. A thrill that was repeated as Sienna leaned in to press another kiss to his collarbone before she began to kiss her way down his chest.

As Sienna's kisses crossed to his hip while her firm hands gripped his hard erection and began to stroke it slowly, Koda ran his hands over her hair and shoulders, caressing her cheeks lovingly.

Sienna settled to her knees in front of him, the water lapping around her waist just below her breasts. Idly, she scooped up a handful of water and poured it over her chest. Koda was sure that he saw her nipples harden even further in response to the cool caress of the liquid before he was distracted by her lips kissing across the crease of his thigh. Sienna hummed happily, nuzzling one soft cheek against the side of his member before kissing up its length.

Pleasure shot through Koda's body as Sienna's pillowy lips wrapped around the head of his shaft. She just held herself there, the head of his shaft trapped between her lips, and waited. It took Koda a couple of seconds to get his brain in gear, and he looked down to check on her. When their eyes met, Koda felt like he was falling into those blue-green orbs once more.

Settling her hands on his hips, Sienna began to bob her head slowly, never looking away from Koda or breaking their eye contact as she bobbed her head back and forth, stroking his shaft ever so delicately with the softness of her mouth. Koda felt the occasional hard point surrounded by softness pressing into his leg as she moved and her breasts brushed against him, but that was nothing compared to the electric pleasure running from his member as Sienna tickled the underside with her tongue lightly.

Her movements were imprecise and hesitant at first as Sienna clearly worked to seek out what would bring him the maximum amount of pleasure. She was a quick study, though, and it wasn't long before she was bobbing her head back and forth in long and slow strokes while humming quietly, pausing at the top of each stroke to run her tongue over his head before engulfing him once more.

Still, Koda could not look away even as Sienna's eyes grew hooded. One hand fell away from his hips to cup and stroke her breast before vanishing beneath the water to dive between her legs.

The only thing that threw Sienna off her rhythm was when Koda decided that he needed to repay her somehow, and that he needed to touch her more.

His hands settled in her thick hair, stroking and rubbing at the furry shells of her ears and gently guiding her to maximize her movements. Sienna twitched when his hands met her ears, her eyes going cloudy with desire before her head bobbed once, hard, and she gagged on his shaft. The hot pleasure of her throat gripping around him made Koda weak in the knees, and he nearly fell over, his hips pumping a few times on instinct.

"Don't hold back," Sienna pulled her mouth off him to say. "I want to taste the seed of a champion before I give myself to you. Even if Thera hadn't asked me to be your mate, I'd have done so willingly after everything you've done for all of us."

"As my huntress wishes." Koda's voice was husky with desire. He knew it wouldn't take much to send him over the edge. This entire encounter was far too much stimulation for his affection-starved mind and heart for that.

Shifting his hands on her head, Koda continued to tickle and stroke Sienna's ears, drawing moan after moan from her even while he aided her bobbing strokes with a gentle bounce of his hips.

He didn't force her down on his shaft again, but Sienna had seen how much her gagging on him had aroused Koda. So every few thrusts, she would press her face into his crotch and swallow against the head of his shaft. It wasn't true deep-throating, but it was close enough that it sparked Koda's desires even more. Sienna made sure to lavish attention on the rest of his shaft with her hands and tongue while she took him as deep as she could.

His climax came with little warning.

Sienna had just started to pull back from him, drool running down her chin as her sucking had been getting messier and messier by the second, when Koda felt his balls tense up, and he grunted in warning. The smooth rhythm from earlier devolved, and a wicked grin twisted Sienna's lips. She shifted to receive what she knew was coming.

Koda made it three more strokes, gently fucking her mouth with all the control he could muster before pulling back until only the head of his shaft was lodged between her lips. He came hard, filling her mouth with his seed as his muscles trembled with the effort of keeping him upright.

Sienna let out a muffled squeal as his hot seed painted the inside of her mouth, the hand between her thighs busy while her other had dropped off his hip to cup her breast and lightly tug at her nipple.

He thrust twice as he drained himself into her, seeking just a bit more pleasure to prolong the climax. The second of his thrusts bounced against the back of Sienna's throat and drew another quiet gag from her. A sound that sent another ripple of pleasure up Koda's spine.

Then he was finished. Koda felt like the strength in his body suddenly rushed out of him as if he was a bucket with a dozen holes in it. Sienna pulled herself off him with a quiet *pop* of wet lips on skin and smiled up at Koda.

The entire time, they'd never broken eye contact as Koda was lost in those orbs again. She freed him a moment later by closing her eyes and making a production of swallowing down his seed in a long gulp, the hand on her breast rising to caress her throat sensually.

Through the clear water, Koda could see the hand still nestled amongst the curls between her legs was busily working away. That view, combined with the happy hum of his love as she opened her eyes to smile up at him, sent new strength racing through his body.

The erection, which had only started to even think about softening, thickened as blood rushed back to duty. Sienna *eeped* quietly when the throbbing appendage nearly bopped her on the nose as Koda shifted.

"I want you." Koda's voice was a husky growl, and Sienna shivered in desire.

"Then have me. I'm yours," she replied in a submissive voice.

Koda bent forward, and using his enhanced strength, he scooped Sienna up out of the water. She squealed in surprise, giggling happily as he cradled her to his chest and sloshed over to one of the large boulders by the side of the pool.

Sienna ran her fingers up and down his back as she ground herself against him, the heat of her sex blooming against his stomach.

"Don't be gentle, Koda. I am a woman of the wild. Take me as such," Sienna whispered into his ear as he pressed her to the rock. "Mount me like a beast and claim me as yours, Champion Aegisclaw. My idiot, Koda."

"Your ribs?" Koda asked, worrying about her injury, but Sienna just ground into him, nipping at his neck.

"Don't hurt right now. Right now, all I want is you. I'll tell you if that changes, but take me now, my wild champion."

Growling deep in his throat, Koda leaned forward to nip and bite at her throat, each contact of his teeth there making Sienna whimper in desire.

When he leaned back to survey her beautiful body laid out like a meal in front of him, Sienna posed, cupping her breasts with both hands and squeezing them like she was offering them to him as she sprawled out on the ancient gray stone. Her legs splayed out lewdly, offering him the cradle of her thighs without reservation. The image of a goddess descended returned to his mind, and he grinned lustily down at her, his long black hair swirling about him like a shroud.

"You want to be taken like a beast?" Koda rasped, running his hands over her hips and slipping one between her legs to cup the wet heat there.

"Yes," moaned Sienna.

Her mind was clouded with lust, but she understood his question. With a bit of help from Koda, she rolled over and slid down to stand in the water once more, bending to press herself flat on the boulder and arching her back to expose her soaked flower to him. Her tail danced like a fluffy banner, no longer attempting to hide her arousal as she shook her hips to tempt and glanced over her shoulder.

Sienna looked like she was about to say something, her mouth opening to speak, but Koda did not hesitate. He pushed forward with his hips and felt the head of his shaft catch in her womanhood for a bare moment before sinking into that gripping, wet heat.

Instead of a lewd invitation, Sienna's mouth opened in a shivering moan that sent a ripple of desire up Koda's back as she thrust back into him, her tail stiffening in pleasure.

Their hips met with a quiet *plap* a moment later as he bottomed out in his wolfish lover. Koda relaxed there for just a moment, savoring the gripping, soaked sensation of Sienna's insides. He leaned forward, careful not to bend her tail, and pressed a kiss to the back of one of her ears.

"Mine," he growled into that fuzzy shell. Sienna's entire body tensed, her sex clamping down on him like she'd never let him go.

"Never going to leave you," Sienna whimpered, nuzzling into the side of his head and laying a light kiss on his cheek. "Take me, Koda?" she begged.

So he did.

Sienna had asked before to be mounted and taken like a beast, and while he started out slow to let her adjust, Koda picked up speed without hesitation until their hips slapped together, and water splashed all around them in a dance of desire as old as time itself.

As their bodies crashed together, Koda could not hold back growls of his own as his fingers sank into Sienna's hips while he pounded her from behind.

Each blow sent delicious ripples through her lithe body. The fluffy banner of her tail flicked back and forth as she howled her own pleasure to the moon. Koda knew, deep in his heart, that she was loud enough that anyone in the village might hear them.

But he didn't care.

He laid kisses and bites across Sienna's shoulders. Each time his teeth sunk into her muscled shoulder or neck, he could feel her body tense up around him.

Koda felt her orgasm twice during their furious, animalistic fucking, each time heralded by a splash of her hot love juices against his thighs.

"Breed me, Koda," Sienna panted as he continued to fuck her towards the peak of her third orgasm. "Fill me with your cum, and make me yours. I want no other!"

With a request like that, Koda couldn't help but comply.

He made it another dozen furious thrusts, each one producing a lewd clapping of his hips against Sienna's bottom, and then Koda reached his climax again.

Gripping Sienna's hips tightly, he hauled her back against him and buried himself as deep as possible inside her before painting her insides with his seed.

Sienna's moan transitioned into a howl as the hot sensation of him filling her up touched off her third climax. She arched her back like a bow, turning to bury her face in his neck.

On instinct, Koda let go of her hip with his right hand and brought that up to cup Sienna's neck. Her howl cut off abruptly in a whine of desire, and he felt her tense again in another miniature orgasm at the possessive grip he had on her.

They trembled together as their climaxes wound down, Sienna's whining pants sounding like sweet music to Koda's ears as she pressed kisses into his throat and jaw.

"Again, my love? Take me again?" Sienna begged sweetly once she could speak once more, thrusting with her hips back towards him while squeezing with her sex, both her hands clinging to his forearm.

"Always," Koda rasped, gently squeezing her throat with his right hand while sliding his left around to tease her clit, eliciting another sharp moan of desire from his lover.

Chapter Twenty-Nine

THE SUN ON HIS FACE WAS WHAT STARTED THE PROCESS of waking up, but what finished it was when something soft began tickling his nose. Flapping his hand at it, Koda thought it might have been a bit of stray hair before the same soft object smacked him in the face again, this time with a bit more force.

"Lover, it's time to get up and greet the day. I know you put a lot of effort into pleasing me last night, but even the hero of the village isn't going to get to sleep in too late," Sienna's sweet voice laughed from above.

Koda blinked his eyes open, and all he could currently see was the gently wafting tip of a fluffy red-black tail as it came to smack him lightly on the nose again.

"Ack, why are you beating me, Sienna? Are you regretting—"

"No! Never think that I regret my choice to mate with you, Koda."

Sienna's face immediately replaced her tail as she turned and bent to kiss him lightly on the lips. This also treated him

Sienna *eep*'d quietly, a blush scampering across her cheeks, and she made as if to cover herself before mastering herself and arching her back again to present herself to him, though the blush did not fade.

"Sorry, didn't mean to stare," Koda mumbled, dragging his eyes away from her assets and back up to her face.

"I don't mind, my mate," Sienna stuttered, her blush darkening for a moment. "I... it will just take a bit of time to get used to, is all. It's just, I'm not normally this forward."

"You were certainly forward last night," Koda teased gently, settling onto his hip while looking around, trying to figure out where his clothes had ended up after their evening romp in the spring.

348

"That was overdue," Sienna stated firmly. "I'd resolved to give myself to you the other day, but it took far longer than I had wanted to find the opportunity."

"Days, eh?" Koda's gaze returned to Sienna with a confident smile. Her bright eyes promptly ensnared him, his idea trailing away into silence as she smiled softly at him.

"Yes. Ever since you saved me out by Last Fang Cave, I had resolved to reward you. When I spent that vision talking to Thera, she gave me guidance as well, and I do not regret the choice I made."

"Fair, no regrets here either," Koda drawled as he fell into those crystalline orbs.

They sat like that for several more minutes, just staring in comfort at each other: Koda completely naked, and Sienna wearing only her pants. It was distant calls from the direction of the village that finally broke the two of them out of their combined distraction.

"Let me have a look at your side," Sienna said abruptly, glancing over her shoulder. "We should have washed out our injuries in the spring, but I think our other activities had us too distracted."

"Not denying that. You are quite distracting. You know that, right?" Koda teased, shifting to begin unwrapping the cloth that covered his chest and held the compression bandage over his stab wound. "I wasn't too rough with you, was I? I'll admit I wasn't thinking too clearly towards the end there."

"No, I feel fine, actually." Sienna stretched slowly. She'd removed the strapping for her ribs to wash the night before and quickly peeled off the bandage on her arm that had covered her slash wounds.

Both of them said nothing for several long moments as they inspected their injuries before turning to meet each other's eyes, then dropping their gazes to the other's injury.

"Healed?" Koda was the one to break that silence.

"It appears so..." Sienna drawled, bending to poke at the spot, just below Koda's ribs, where the other champion's dagger had driven into before. A spot that had been red, swollen, and leaking blood before she had wrapped it to come down the mountain. Now it was just a small knot of scar tissue.

The same was true of her arm. Where it had borne the slash wound of the Crooked's blade before, there was nothing more than a hair-thin scar. Testing her ribs, Sienna was confident that she would have no trouble from them either, the cracked ribs having healed.

"That... How?" Koda asked eloquently. Sienna just shrugged.

"The goddess looks after her champion, and I guess me, too?" Sienna asked in confusion. "We should get dressed and go check on the others. See if anyone else received miraculous healing."

The two of them worked to get dressed. Koda helped Sienna into her top, though she didn't need it. He just wanted the excuse to caress her bare skin some more, and Sienna was happy to enjoy his touch. She returned the gesture, helping him into his pants with a few well-placed kisses that both reminded him of their previous night while simultaneously making it harder for him to actually *get* dressed.

It was as she was helping Koda to get his shirt on without his totemic gauntlet tearing the sleeves that she paused, staring at the weapon on his arm thoughtfully.

"What is it?" Koda asked, following her gaze to the tool.

"Did you take that off last night?" Sienna asked quietly, tilting her head the other way and making her ears flop over adorably.

"No, I don't—" Koda abruptly cut off, staring down at the leather, bone, and stone weapon on his arm. He knew what she was asking.

When they'd tasted each other in the spring, Koda hadn't even thought about it, but he didn't remember having the weight of his gauntlet then. He just remembered the soft feeling of Sienna's skin on his hands.

Both of his hands.

"Something else to ask Thera about," Koda sighed, shaking his head and focusing on dressing once more. Sienna just nodded silently and helped him.

Returning to the village, the two of them were met with knowing smiles and winks from several of the villagers who were up and moving about. Koda and Sienna bore up under their playful teasing with only a few blushes. Neither was willing to go far from the other, though. They walked hand in hand proudly down the street.

While the sun was sitting firmly in the range of mid-morning, there was still evidence of the party that had gone on last night.

The market at the center of the village had yet to open for business again. Instead, it still bore the liberal scattering of detritus from the previous night's celebration, both in the form of unconscious villagers and strewn foodstuffs. Those that were up and about moved carefully around the unconscious forms of their fellow villagers, focusing on picking up what they could. A few spouses stood over their unconscious partners, shaking their heads with wry amusement or prodding the still-drunk celebrants to wakefulness.

"Koda!" The call caught Koda by surprise from one side, and he turned to see Kris's smiling face poking out of the window of her house to one side of the square.

"Ah, Headwoman. What can I do for you?" Koda asked, diverting his and Sienna's path slightly so that they angled towards the older woman.

"Well, if you are offering, I do have something that you could do for the village as a favor." The older woman gestured for them to come up to the window, glancing from side to side as she did so, clearly hesitant to just speak up where casual listeners might overhear.

When the two of them arrived by the open window, the headwoman leaned on the sill and smiled up at them. Despite the fact that Koda remembered seeing Kris the evening before on the battlefield, giving as good as she got with her knobbly staff when needed and working to heal the injured, she was still as energetic as if she'd had spent a week relaxing.

Confirming that no one was lingering nearby, the headwoman bent close to whisper to Koda and Sienna.

"I would like to request that you consecrate the meeting hall as holy ground to Thera. While we cannot have a temple in her name at this time, I would dearly love to again be able to worship the Pack Lady, and I know many that would as well."

Koda was about to decline, stating that he had no idea how,

when he felt a brief pulse from the gauntlet, and the knowledge of how to sanctify a location raced through his mind.

"Sure, I'd be happy to," he said after a moment of thought.

Kris's grin grew even wider at that statement, and she clapped her hands joyfully.

"Oh, thank you, Champion. I know that many of our people already know of your status, but this will help cement the fact in the minds of those who were not there to witness our lady's appearance at the Windwalker's Retreat." Kris scampered away from the window, a rhythmic series of thumps from her cane through the window heralding her arrival at the front door of her house. She quickly led the way across to the extensive building on the other side of the tavern.

The ceremony to consecrate the building as a holy site to Thera was extremely simple.

Koda used the claws of his totemic gauntlet to prick his left thumb. When blood oozed from the injury, he smeared it in a curving slash on the lintel of each doorway and window on the inside. When he completed the last one, he tapped the claws of his gauntlet to the bloody mark and felt a surge of heat well up from inside him. The same black fire that had destroyed the Crooked altars before raced from the bone reinforcements on the gauntlet to dance over the claws. As it passed from his fingertips, the fire turned red once more.

As one, all the blood marks flared with red fire, and Koda felt something in the air shift. He could feel Thera's gaze on him and the approval that flowed from her for his actions.

"There, all done," Koda said with a sigh, glancing over at the headwoman.

The cat beastfolk grinned again, doing a surprisingly dexterous little jig in the middle of the simple wooden floor of the meeting hall. "Beast Queen be praised! Our people's faith is vindicated, and we can look to a bright future once more!" Kris cheered, a look of joy and peace filling her old eyes, and her wrinkles lightening.

Sienna smiled as she watched the older woman celebrate, trading loving glances with Koda for a moment, leaning into him.

Sienna's motion was not lost on Kris as the older woman came to a stop, her eyes twinkling with amusement as she stared at them.

"Well then. This is not unexpected, but do I have another reason to celebrate?" the headwoman asked pointedly, looking at their joined hands and Sienna leaning into Koda.

Sienna saved Koda from a stumbling explanation, simply blurting out, "Yes, Headwoman. Last night, I offered myself to our champion as a mate, and he accepted me."

Koda half expected the old woman to glare at him in response to Sienna's statement, but Kris's grin only grew wider.

"Excellent! I was hoping as much, based on the noises we heard. Oh, don't worry about it, Sienna." The old woman laughed when Sienna's blush grew deeper. "You weren't the only one celebrating the return of safety to the village last night. More than a few of our more... vigorous citizens also joined in on that celebration. With good reason as well! But I didn't ask just to make you blush, child."

"Could have fooled me," mumbled Sienna, her ears folding back while her tail hung limp behind her.

"It was just an added benefit," Kris jabbed with a smile. "No, I asked because I have a gift I have prepared for our champion here. And now it is a gift for you, too, my dear!"

"What is that?" Koda asked, releasing Sienna's hand so that he could wrap an arm around her shoulders and pull her tight to him.

"A house, of course!"

Chapter Thirty

THE PREVIOUS NIGHT, IT HADN'T REALLY OCCURRED TO Koda what the full implication of taking Sienna as his 'mate' would be.

Apparently, in the eyes of the village, they were now basically married. It meant that Sienna would be moving out of the hunters' hall, which was only for unwed hunters, and into whatever home he had claimed as his.

Kris had apparently taken it upon herself to have one of the unoccupied homes in the village freshened up for them. A gift as thanks for both Koda's work rooting out the Crooked and both of them successfully defeating several enemy champions.

Sienna had perked up immediately when Kris had told her which one they were being given. She'd then blessed Koda with a deep kiss, not even caring that Kris was standing right there, and raced off to collect her things so they could move in immediately.

Still kind of stunned by the entire series of events, Koda just followed Kris in a daze as she led him to the new home. A home that was just for Sienna and him.

"I know that it is a bit forward of me to just arrange for a house for you, but I highly doubt that you would really have that much of a problem with it. Especially so that you and Sienna have a place to call your own," Kris was saying as they threaded through the buildings. "Unless Thera had plans for you to leave on a mission, but even then, I think having somewhere to call your own would be good for both you and Sienna. It is calming to the mind to know that wherever you end up going, you will always have a home to return to."

"It's something I appreciate. Do not doubt that, Head-woman," Koda answered without hesitation. "I intend to do my best to look after Sienna and provide for her. You giving us a house will go a long way to making that easier to handle."

He expected his statement to get an approving nod or a smile from Kris, not the wholehearted laughter the older woman produced.

"Provide for Sienna? Aegisclaw, I am glad she was not around to hear you say that. Your Sienna is not some shrinking violet who needs someone to provide for her. She is an accomplished huntress and more than capable of caring for herself."

"That's not what I had meant to imply," protested Koda. "I just wanted to reassure you that I would look out for her and make sure she had all she could need." He didn't say out loud that he wasn't quite sure how he'd do that, but he resolved to make it happen, regardless.

"Sienna is not the kind of person to sit about and wait for such things to be done for her. She is far more likely to go out and earn the things she desires for herself. You are a team now, so rely on her," the headwoman chastised with the air of a grandmother playfully scolding her favorite grandchild.

"Yes, Headwoman," Koda responded with a small smile.

With a satisfied nod, knowing he had received her message, Kris stopped in front of a rather large stone and wood building. The entire first floor had walls made of stacked stones mortared into place, while the second floor was solidly built of a mixture of wood and stone. Windows broke up the exterior every so often, currently open to take advantage of the breeze, but each had solidly built shutters to block them off for the winter. A steeply slanted roof of slate tiles sat atop the construction, ready to provide solid protection from rain and snow.

Koda couldn't help but appreciate the sturdy look of the building. It had a settled feel to it as if the building had been there for some time. Not so long that it was beginning to decay, but long enough that it had gone through the initial settling that all houses did and came out stronger for it.

"This is gorgeous..." Koda breathed as he looked up at the building.

Kris just smirked, giving the young man a chance to take it all in.

It took Koda several minutes to be ready to get moving again, and when he did, there were many questions ricocheting through his head. He took a deep breath and organized his thoughts before asking the first one.

"Don't get me wrong, I am not at all unhappy. But I do have to question how it is that you can just *give* away a house this nice?"

Kris glanced up at the building before sighing gustily through her nose. She leaned on her staff heavily before answering.

"The village had this building built a decade ago when the baron informed us that they would be sending a representative to oversee the village. They would have taken over my position as headwoman and been a mayor instead. To be ready for them, we had to build them a home that was worthy of a kingdom noble so they could live in comfort while helping bring our village up to speed amongst the rest of the kingdom. The missive said that the new mayor would be bringing guards as well, to resume the city watch."

"Said? I take it that something happened?" Koda stepped sideways so that the shade from the building kept the sun from his eyes.

"Yes. Exactly so," Kris sighed. "The kingdom official never arrived. We waited patiently for some time after their anticipated arrival date, but they never came. When I sent a message to the local baron, the return missive I received advised that the baron had re-tasked the representative with a higher-priority mission, but he would find someone to take up the posting as soon as he was able."

"And that was a decade ago?" Koda's irritation spiked when Kris nodded. "So you had this building prepared for them, and they never showed up? That's just ridiculous."

"It was." Kris looked back up at the building with a small smile, though. "The villagers all contributed to building this in hopes of making a good impression. So I hope that it makes you happy, Koda. The kingdom may have abandoned us out here on the frontier, but you and our Lady have not."

A warmth grew in Koda's chest, and he nodded firmly to the

smiling elder in front of him. "It certainly does, Headwoman."

"Why don't you head inside and have a look around? Sienna will be along shortly, but I'm sure you'll be able to get a feel for the place in the time you have. Maybe put some thought into things you'd like to do in the different rooms?" The headwoman gave Koda another broad grin and waggled her eyebrows at him, making the younger man blush.

Cackling to herself, Kris handed off a heavy iron key for the door before heading back down the road, muttering something about needing to check on her patients.

Shaking his head as he stared after the headwoman, Koda just couldn't help the laugh that bubbled up in his throat. After all the trouble of the last few days, the close brushes with death, and the number of people he'd had to kill, a few dirty jokes from an old woman just felt like par for the course right now.

Glancing between the key in his hand and the building in front of him, Koda shrugged and stepped up onto the porch. Fitting the key into the lock on the door, he gave it a turn and heard the tumblers clunk heavily before he pushed open the door.

The first floor sprawled out almost the entire footprint of the building as an open space, likely for dining or socializing, Koda guessed. He could see a door along the wall that also held an enormous stone fireplace which he guessed probably led to the kitchen. That way the kitchen fires could share the chimney. On his right was a pair of doors that, when he opened them to peek inside, led into a meeting room and an office, respectively. The floor in the building was all carefully sanded wood planks stained a dark brown. The interior walls were also made of wood. Straight ahead of him was a set of stairs that led up to the second floor, which he guessed held the bedrooms.

"I think we'll be pretty comfortable here," Koda muttered, standing in the middle of the open space. There were a handful of pillars that supported the second floor scattered about, but they were all solid and had decorations made up of elaborate carvings of animals hunting and playing.

"I'm glad." The words came from behind him, only inches away, but Koda felt no threat from the speaker. In fact, he only felt amusement and affection as he turned and beheld Thera standing there.

The black-haired goddess smiled at him shyly, her arms behind her back while her hip cocked to one side, and her head tilted the other way. Silver eyes glimmered under her slender brows while the sleek fur of her wrap top and open-fronted skirt shimmered and reflected the light.

This time—unlike when she had appeared after he destroyed a Crooked altar—Thera did not have the ghosts of the animal features as ears or tails of shifting smoke either. But as always, the bouncing curls of Thera's lustrous mass of hair made him a bit envious, but Koda swallowed that to smile at the goddess who had given him this opportunity.

"Hello, Thera. I was wondering if I'd see you again in the flesh." Koda bowed his head slightly to her in respect, getting a snicker out of the goddess.

"So irreverent. You are my champion, Koda Aegisclaw. You should show proper deference to your goddess," Thera teased, literal sparks dancing from her silver eyes to send glimmers through her hair and highlighting the faint spot pattern hidden within her curls.

"I have a feeling that you would have chosen someone

different from me if you really wanted subservience," Koda said in return.

"I suppose that is fair. Your first act in my name that didn't require blood being shed was when you and your fair mate consecrated that spring last night." The lascivious wink from the goddess left him with no illusions to what she meant. "It's why you two healed so quickly. Any who bath in the spring will heal more rapidly now, especially if they are my faithful."

Koda just nodded, unable to speak at the moment, partially due to his embarrassment regarding the fact the goddess was intimately aware of his sex life.

"I wanted to ask you something about this, actually." He held up the totemic gauntlet wrapped around his right hand.

"Good, because I had something I needed to tell you about that, too," Thera said with a grin. She prowled around him in a slow circle, the motion full of unconscious grace and lithe agility, telegraphing her status as a predator for all to see.

"You go first then, my lady," Koda said with a somewhat mocking bow towards the goddess.

"You have pleased me with how much you have accomplished in my name in such a short time, Koda Aegisclaw," Thera began in a formal tone, coming to a stop just off to his right. "During your battle with the Crooked warleader, you were able to draw on the strength of the beast spirits to empower your blows. My reward to you is confirming that power." Thera leaned in, her silver eyes sending another small shower of sparks into the air as she brushed her lips lightly against his left cheek.

Koda felt a rush of power race out from that point of contact. It made his teeth rattle like branches in a strong wind before diving down his throat, curling around his heart, and then slithering through to his left arm.

A moment later, Koda felt an abrupt constriction against his skin on his left arm starting at his elbow, then rolling down to the tips of his fingers. Looking down at that arm, the sight of a mirrored version of his gauntlet greeted him. The same style of bone reinforcement along the back of the leather glove, interspersed with polished chips of stone that ran into an armored glove, whose fingertips ended in sharp claws that were viciously effective in combat.

"Thank you. This will go a long way towards ensuring I can protect Sienna," Koda said while gently tapping the claws on both hands together.

"You are welcome, Champion Aegisclaw. I have even more rewards waiting for you as you claim more places of power for me in the coming days. Rewards, I am sure you will enjoy. Now, you did it last night unconsciously, but you can actually hide the gauntlets away."

"Oh, that was what I was about to ask," Koda sighed in relief, getting a surprising giggle out of the serious goddess.

"Yes, just focus on the gauntlets and the thought of not needing them, of mentally 'sheathing' your claws," Thera explained with a small smile.

Koda did as instructed, closing his eyes to focus and trying to put himself in the mindset of being relaxed, at ease, and not needing to fight. The loss of the pressure on his hands, something he'd grown familiar with over the last few days, was his first indication that it worked.

Opening his eyes, Koda smiled to see his bare fists in front of him. Without needing prompting from Thera, he focused, and the gauntlets sprang into existence, fading in around his hands like they were ghosts taking a physical form.

He looked up to thank Thera when the patter of running feet on the porch preceded Sienna bursting into the room with a pack on her back, an armload of clothes, and her bow and quiver in one big bundle.

"Koda, I've got all my stuff here. Where are—" Sienna cut off abruptly as she spotted the 'guest' in their new house. "Pack Lady!"

"Shh," Thera warned her with a conspiratorial wink. "I am here to speak to both of you, actually, but not the whole village. I brought you a gift as well as your mate."

Sienna flushed fiercely at being called Koda's mate, but her tail immediately began whipping up a storm. She glanced around, looking for somewhere to set her things, and frowned a moment later.

"It's so barren in here... I'll have to talk to the carpenter and get furniture arranged." She said the last part with such determination that Koda couldn't help but smile, feeling proud of his partner's focus.

"Here, give that to me," Koda said gently, holding out his hands to accept the bundle from Sienna. She turned it over willingly, after blinking in surprise at his gauntlet-free hands.

"You figured out how?"

"Thera told me," Koda admitted.

He carried Sienna's things over and set them at the foot of the stairs. He could take them up later when they figured out where the bedrooms were. If there wasn't a bed in here yet, well, they had slept on the hard ground before. Having a home by itself was a great start to a strong future.

"Sienna." The single word from Thera immediately dragged Sienna's attention back to her. "I wanted to let you know that, as Champion Aegisclaw's bonded mate, I have rewarded you with access to the magic of the land itself. It will take some practice for you to get the hang of it, but your headwoman can set your feet on the path."

While he'd known her, if she wasn't asleep, Sienna was always in motion or doing something. So when she went dead still at Thera's statement, Koda stared at her in surprise.

"Magic? Me?" Sienna stuttered a moment later, her eyes round in surprise and wonder.

"Yes, my child. If you are to stand at my Champion's side as a proper mate should, then you will need to have powers of your own beyond your skill with a weapon," Thera replied with an indulgent smile.

"Thank you, Pack Lady." Sienna finally shook off her paralysis and bowed deeply to the goddess, her tail whirling behind her in excitement. "I promise to use the power responsibly and never make you regret your choice in giving it to me."

"See, this is how you properly express gratitude to a goddess," Thera teased Koda with a broad smile. He rolled his eyes at her and pretended to sigh mightily, getting a giggle from the goddess.

"Oh, I wanted to let you know—call it an incentive if you will—that after you claim two more sites of power, I will be able to send the first of my daughters to your side," Thera said with a broad smile, gesturing like she was giving them a great gift.

"Daughter?" Sienna was the first to speak, looking up from her bow and blinking owlishly at the goddess.

"Yes, she will come to assist Koda with my plans for the future to ensure our goals are met," Thera answered simply, and Sienna nodded thoughtfully.

Again, before Koda could speak, Sienna jumped in.

"Will she be able to speak to me, too? I would like to converse with such a being if possible, and it would make things easier..." Sienna said, letting the thought trail off wistfully.

"Of course. My daughter will be able to take on a full form similar to yours, as well as her spiritual war-form," Thera answered dismissively, waving one slender hand as if to waft off the question. "If she could not, then it would be nigh impossible to achieve her secondary task."

"What secondary task?" Koda asked quickly to get in ahead of Sienna, who had already opened her mouth.

Thera glanced at him and then at Sienna with a meaningful smile. When Koda turned his attention to his canine lover, Sienna's blush grew even deeper before she took a deep breath and locked eyes with him.

Immediately, Koda felt himself falling into those hypnotic, crystalline orbs, but her next words shook him out of his distraction.

"Koda, you said once that you wanted a home and a family more than anything else. Well, we have a home here, and I will endeavor to make sure that you have that family." Sienna's hand settled lightly over her stomach, and Koda suddenly felt short of breath. "I will make sure your family is large and full of love, too, Koda Aegisclaw," Sienna said, her voice overflowing with emotion.

"And I cannot accept the risk that I took once before," Thera interjected gently. "I will ensure that your line spreads and is shared amongst many women. We cannot allow your bloodline to be lost once more."

Koda opened his mouth to ask about that, his brow furrowing in concern, when a thump from the upstairs drew his attention with a snap.

Chapter Thirty-One

"WHAT WAS THAT?" SIENNA WAS THE FIRST TO SPEAK, and her words drew Koda's eyes to his mate. He couldn't help the small smile at seeing his fierce wolf mate with her hand on her dagger.

Need to get her spearhead re-mounted, he thought before darting his gaze back to the ceiling when the floorboards creaked again. He felt the familiar weight of his gauntlets form around his hands once more, and he carefully flexed them in readiness for trouble.

"Don't worry, you two. That is just Arthene." Thera's words didn't provide as much relief to Koda as she might have hoped because he just glanced at her with a questioning look.

"Oh? Is she feeling up to being around already?" Sienna asked, her stance relaxing and hand dropping away from her belt knife.

"Who the hell is Arthene?" Koda demanded, not letting his guard down as the quiet creaks of the boards shifting continued across the upstairs floor and headed towards the stairs.

"My daughter. Well, I call her that, but she is not directly the fruit of my loins, as a goddess does not bear children like that," Thera explained, her voice amused. She tossed her head lightly, sending a shimmer through her black curls before glancing towards the stairs. "Come on down, Arthene. You are not doing a very good job at being subtle right now, sweetheart."

The quiet creaking of boards became a steadier thump of footsteps before they led to the stairs and began to descend.

"It's fine, Koda," Sienna said gently, coming up to grip his right arm above his elbow where the gauntlet stopped. "Arthene is not a threat to us. You trust Thera, right?"

Koda grimaced but nodded, allowing his focus to lessen and to mentally 'sheathe' his claws, which caused them to fade out.

"It's smart to be wary of the unknown!" a deeper feminine voice with a bit of a country burr to it echoed down the stairs as the speaker strode into sight.

She was tall, easily over six feet in height, with the broad shoulders and muscled body of a fighter. A thick mane of brown hair fell behind her shoulders like a cape, falling to her waist. Her hair had the wild look of someone who had just rolled out of bed and couldn't be bothered to brush it out but still managed to look sexy despite that. Her upper body was entirely bare save for a broad chest-wrap of brown-furred hide that restrained a bountiful bosom that fought the covering.

A bare stomach with defined abs led into flared hips that supported a wrap-skirt similar to what Thera wore, but rather than the shorter version the goddess wore, Arthene's skirt fell to her knees in the back while soaring up to expose the muscled expanse of her inner thigh before crossing over at mid-thigh. The skirt was also made of the same thick-furred leather as her chest wrap and was supported by a broad belt with a silver buckle in the shape of a bear's paw.

Koda followed those muscular legs down to find a pair of bare feet leading her down the stairs. Reaching the bottom, Koda's eyes darted back up to the top, to a pair of familiar yellow eyes.

"Well?" Arthene asked when she reached the bottom of the stairs, spreading her arms wide with a smile that was equal parts amused and amorous as she studied Koda intently.

"You..." Koda muttered, not looking away from those intense yellow eyes. While they did not draw him in and drown him like Sienna's blue-green orbs, they still held him with a predator's focus.

"Me," Arthene said with a smirk, settling her large hands on her hips and cocking one to the side. "I have to say, you are even more handsome in person than in your dreams. Thank you for keeping him safe so far, packmate. We are going to have our work cut out for us in that department." The second half she directed at Sienna, her eyes slipping to stare at the wolf beastfolk.

Koda glanced to one side to check on Sienna but found her smiling up at the newcomer as well. He felt the slight slap of her tail wagging against his thighs and let out a slow breath.

"I appreciate any help I can get to keep our mate safe," Sienna said earnestly, squeezing Koda's arm where her hands still rested.

" 'Our mate?' " Koda asked pointedly, his words drawing all three women's eyes to him. "Don't I get a say in this?"

"Of course you do, my mate," Arthene laughed, not moving from her spot at the foot of the stairs. "I would never dream of forcing myself upon you. When you are ready, I will happily accept you into my bed. I owe you my life, my sanity, and my very being already. They are yours to claim whenever you wish them." The words were spoken with such earnest conviction that Koda felt his anger, which had been slowly building at the idea of having a choice taken away from him, abruptly drain out of him like a balloon with a hole in it.

"Koda," Thera's voice drew his attention to where the goddess stood to his left, "I promised you everything your heart desires to get you to come through to help us. You said that all you wanted was a family and a place to belong." Thera held her hands out wide as if to encompass both the house they stood inside and the women standing near him. "Here are both, and I will continue to shower gifts on you as I am able."

"You don't have to give me—" Koda began to protest, but he was cut of by Arthene when the tall woman spoke up, striding across the room to stand in front of him.

"Thera isn't giving me to you. Banish that thought from your head, my mate," Arthene rumbled, the smile still firmly fixed to her lips. "I would have given myself to you for your actions to save my spirit regardless. Add in the fact that you are giving her a chance to return, and with that a chance for all of us to return? The spirits of all the beasts who dwell in earth and sky will flock to join you for even attempting it." Her grin grew even wider as she paused, staring down at Koda by nearly a full head of height, her hands settling into the familiar pose on her hips. "I'm just at the front of the line, and I am *very* happy with what I am seeing."

The Lost Bloodline Book 1

"What makes you so sure you'll be happy? You don't even know me," Koda protested, not moving away from the big woman even as Sienna leaned comfortably into his side. Thera remained quiet, observing their interaction.

Arthene shrugged, a motion that sent her chest swaying and sent a shimmering ripple through her wild mane of hair. She continued to stare down at Koda, her yellow eyes unblinking.

"I will know you. That will come with time. But I have observed you since the day you purged the Crooked from that cave. When you tapped into your ancestors' fury and the primal core of your being to protect your future-mate?" Arthene let out a deep, throaty rumble of approval. "I am Arthene Deepclaw. Arthene the Wrathful. Den-Mother. I am the primal bear spirit, and in that moment, I saw a heart that can move *mountains*."

Koda remained silent, just looking up at the tall woman in front of him. He couldn't kid himself that he wasn't attracted to her. She tickled every part of his subconscious, even the faint crush he'd had on *She-Hulk* as a kid.

But you have Sienna, a part of his mind protested. *Is she not enough?*

Glancing to his right, Koda was surprised to see Sienna biting her bottom lip, a faint blush on her cheeks as she stared at the brown-haired woman standing in front of them both. He could see the hint of attraction in her eyes, and the way she held onto his arm was not possessive. She didn't feel threatened by the woman in front of him. She was attracted to her, too.

Arthene continuing her statement drew Koda's attention back to her.

"You impressed me, Koda Aegisclaw. I thought my Lady's protectors had all died out, but here you are. A son of an era past, hundreds of years distant from those heroes, but their blood still burns hot in your veins." Arthene leaned down so that their noses were only inches part, the motion giving Koda an impressive view down the front of her top, but he refused to take his eyes from hers. The smirk that sauntered across Arthene's full lips told him she knew and found it amusing.

"And then you did it again. You drew on your primal heart and called upon your ancestors once more. I was interested in you before and would have given myself for that act alone. But when you shook the mountain in defense of your future-mate? You, with only the barest of blessings from my Lady? As weak as the least of her champions were in the last war?"

Arthene let the moment drift into silence, still refusing to blink. Koda did not look away. He wasn't trapped in her eyes like with Sienna, but his heart told him to let her finish. They paused for a long handful of seconds, continuing to exchange stares before Arthene finished.

"I saw a man who would do more than move a mountain. I saw a man who could tear them out by the root and beat any who stood in his way to death with it."

Arthene's words were a bare whisper, but Koda felt something brush against his very soul in that moment. It didn't feel like the boiling rage he remembered from the battle with the Crooked warleader, or even the wrath of a challenged protector. It felt calm, loving even. The gentle touch of truth, affection, and respect. Of *knowing,* deep within his soul, that Arthene spoke concepts into being even as she watched him.

Leaning forward ever so slightly, the distance between them was minuscule at this point, Arthene bumped her forehead into his affectionately, her soft mass of hair falling forward to brush against his cheek and enshroud them in shadows. In that darkness, Arthene's yellow eyes glowed faintly, never once looking away from him.

"You are worthy, Koda Aegisclaw. You and your mates will achieve the impossible, I just know it. And I'm going to be right there with you." The words were spoken at barely a whisper, but they echoed inside Koda's head like it was a bell being struck repeatedly.

Then, Arthene leaned back away from him, and the moment was broken. She flipped her messy mane of hair back over her shoulders with a negligent toss before looking towards Sienna with a broad smile and winking. The slight intake of breath from his wolf-eared lover made his heart race, and Koda just couldn't help a chuckle that boiled up from his throat.

"Koda?" Thera's questioning voice drew his attention to her again.

The goddess stood with her arms crossed under her own generous bust, a small smile on her lips and one thin brow arched. The smile showed just the barest hint of her sharp, predatory teeth—a subtle reminder of the ferocious nature of the goddess standing in front of him.

"I'm fine, Thera," he said, only slightly surprised that it was true. The worries that had been boiling up in him, the anxiety over the impressive woman who had just stomped into his life and declared that she would become his mate as well, and the lingering fears left over from his past life all faded into the background. They weren't gone, as he would have to work through them in time, but their voices did not scream so loudly in his mind anymore.

"Good. I leave Arthene in your care." Thera let her arms fall to her sides once more, and she strode forward to stand just to Koda's left.

Her movement meant he was surrounded on three sides by buxom women. Koda felt a brief spike of anxiety as there weren't very many 'safe' places to look right now given how much pale, curved flesh was on display, but he stuffed it down when he saw the smirk on Arthene's lips and heard the amusement in Thera's when she continued.

"While my daughter should be resting more to recover from her past injuries, she shares your drive to get things done." Arthene snorted at Thera's declaration but did not try and counter the goddess. "She is weaker than I would have liked. But, as you can see, Arthene has already chosen to incarnate herself into a physical form. So I trust you both to look after her."

"I'll be the one looking after them, my Lady," Arthene protested, frowning playfully at the goddess. Koda noted that, despite the fact that Thera called the woman in front of him 'daughter,' Arthene referred to her with a respectful title.

Something to ask about later, Koda thought, resting his left hand on top of Sienna's where they met over his right biceps. His wolf-eared lover had been quiet for a bit, and she glanced up at him with bright eyes, a small smile turning up her lips. In those eyes, he saw acceptance and love glowing before she leaned in to nuzzle her face into his shoulder contentedly.

"Regardless of who does what, there is still more yet to do." Thera's words dumped a chill down Koda's spine, and he snapped around to look at her.

The regret was obvious in Thera's eyes, and she nodded sadly. Koda ground his teeth for a moment before sighing again and squaring his shoulders.

"Okay, then what is left? We wiped out the camps in the vale. The threat is gone."

"Gone from the vale itself, but not from its borders," Thera said, with Arthene nodding along with the goddess. "Crooked are not native to this world, so they had to have traveled by portal to get here. Which means that there is likely a camp outside of the vale housing the portal. In order to fully secure this place, you will need to end the threat presented by that portal. You have time, but it would be best not to put it off for too long. The longer the portal remains open, the more Crooked can come through to terrorize the countryside."

"Right, killing the flies in the house won't do anything if we leave the damn window open," Koda growled.

He didn't need to look at Sienna to know she was nodding in agreement with him. It was the same with Arthene. He'd known the big woman for minutes, but he could just *feel* the warmth of her eager smile from where she stood in front of him.

Chapter Thirty-Two

"I GUESS WE HAVE ONE LAST MISSION TO GO ON BEFORE we get to relax for a while," Koda grunted, glaring down at the floor in front of him. He blinked in surprise when a hand landed on top of his head, gently smoothing back his hair.

"Don't worry about it, Aegisclaw. With me to help out, we can knock this out in no time," Arthene said with a small grin as she petted him.

Koda wanted to grumble at being treated as a child like this, but there was something extremely soothing about feeling Arthene's clawed fingers scraping against his scalp. The soft sensation of her fingers running through his hair, punctuated by the thin threads of sensation from her claws, made for a luxurious scalp massage that ensured he had a hard time focusing enough to feel grumpy.

"She's right, Koda," Sienna said from her spot on his right shoulder, rubbing her cheek back and forth on him while she squeezed his arm with her hands. "We handled the Crooked warleader, sorcerers, and champions. With proper planning, we can handle this camp around the portal."

"While I am happy in your confidence, please be careful," Thera cautioned. The raven-haired goddess had settled in on Koda's left, barely inches away from him. In fact, she was close enough that Koda swore he could feel the warmth radiating off the woman as she leaned in. "Portals are hard enough to establish that they will be working hard to protect it, especially if they are bringing more forces through. If this was just a small raiding party, then your odds are far better than if it was a sizable army. You will need to strike quickly and without warning to overwhelm the guards so that they cannot just bring troops to defend it from the other side."

"So, we scout it ahead of time," Arthene said with a shrug, not shifting her hand off of Koda's head and continuing to play with his hair distractingly. "If it's something we can handle—and based on the groups that Aegisclaw and his mate dealt with before I expect it will be—then we attack. If not, then we will figure out something else. Worst-case scenario, I can bait off a good number of the guards while the others attack from a blind spot. Let humans and dwarves fight in lines and armies. I am a beast, and I will hunt my prey in the most efficient manner I know how."

"Well said, my daughter." Thera gave Arthene a smile. "But you can still take the rest of the day to recover. I would recommend bringing at least a dozen warriors from the village if the headwoman can spare them. It will make travel a bit slower, but having reinforcements will be beneficial."

"Mostly archers," Koda grunted, trying to blink his way free of Arthene's affections. The incarnated spirit paused in her gentle petting and leaned a bit closer.

"What was that, Aegisclaw?"

"Mostly archers," Koda repeated, able to focus more since the stimulation had paused. "Sienna and I make for strong front-line combatants, and if I am going to hazard a guess, you are pretty dangerous up close too, Deepclaw."

Arthene chuckled low in her chest, her clawed fingertips going back to stirring Koda's hair and scritching at his scalp again.

Good lord, if head scratches feel this good, I'm gonna make sure to spoil the hell out of Sienna later. And maybe Arthene, too, if this all works out how they want, Koda thought as he relaxed again.

"Call me Arthene, Aegisclaw. I expect to be sharing your bed as a mate soon enough, so no need for formality."

"Then you should call him Koda as well," interjected Sienna.

Koda cracked an eye to look towards his beastfolk lover and was gratified to see the smile still firmly parked on Sienna's lips.

"Fair point," Arthene rumbled with a laugh. "I am already inserting myself into his life, though, and did not want to impose further."

"Nonsense. Right, Koda?" He grunted in agreement with Sienna's statement, nodding just enough that it conveyed his meaning without dislodging Arthene's hand. "And you should call me Sienna as well. If we are to be family, then we should be close," Sienna said firmly, her hands on his biceps squeezing gently. Koda could hear the swish of her tail's happy wagging, so he just squeezed back.

"All right then, Sienna. I look forward to spending quite a bit of time with you and our Koda." Arthene's voice was rich with happiness as she said this, and again, he swore he could feel the warmth of the large woman's smile.

"Now, the Pack Lady has set us a task," Sienna said with a cute little huff of determination through her nose. "Well, several but one that is pressing. If we are going to complete the others she has for us, then we need to truly secure the vale and ensure that the threats to it are ended."

"Well said, Sienna," Thera said gently, but before she could continue, Arthene had to add her two cents.

"After all, it's hard to carry cubs when you have to go racing off to battle!" laughed the curly-haired giant.

That statement was the one that finally pierced the distracting fugue that was surrounding Koda's mind, and he sputtered briefly, blinking away his distractions and staring up at her in surprise. Arthene shifted her hand around to cup his cheek from the right, stroking his cheek with a thumb while she smirked down at him.

"She is right..." Sienna was the one to speak next, and Koda tilted his head to look down at her in surprise. The wolf beastfolk was blushing furiously, biting her bottom lip to suppress a smile while her tail danced merrily back and forth behind her. "We promised you a family, after all, so we need to make sure this is a safe place to bring them into the world."

Koda's heart lurched in his chest, and he shifted his right arm to pull it free of Sienna's grip. She let him go willingly, only to be drawn into his side and a loving kiss that got smiles from the two supernatural women in the room.

"Aww, they are so sweet together," crooned Arthene.

"And you will be just as sweet when you are with him," teased Thera in return.

"I can only hope," was Arthene's reply, though the longing in her tone tugged on Koda's heart as well.

When he finished his kiss with Sienna, he turned to look up at the big woman with her sparkling eyes and messy mass of curls. He wouldn't deny that she was attractive to him, in a wild and primal sort of way. Power, grace, and feminine allure rippled off her body as she stared down at him, and Koda swore that he could see the sparks of affection or even love glowing in her yellow eyes.

Not even here a week, and I've got a mate in Sienna and someone else queuing up to join the family. It's like I'm living in one of those harem anime plots that Walker used to talk about during lunch on the job sites, Koda thought with a grin. *I'll be damned if I end up as clueless as those protagonists if I do. These two deserve someone to love and care for them, not someone who gets lost in a pity party. I need to trust them to say what they want and come to me when they have problems so we can work on them together. What was it that the one guy said? 'Communicate, communicate, communicate, and when in doubt, communicate.'*

"You'll get your turn, Arthene. Just keep in mind that I've only been in this world for a few days, so I might need a bit to adjust." Koda's words made the large woman's face light up with another smile, and she leaned in to rub her forehead in his hair lightly, still cupping his cheek with her right hand before leaning back and finally letting her hand fall away.

Koda did his best to not protest the end of his head scratches, but from the amused twinkle in Arthene's eyes, she would dole them out again for him.

"Anyway, back to the serious point. I know that the Pack Lady is the one who helped engineer this all"—Sienna gestured between herself, Koda, and Arthene from her spot tucked under Koda's arm—"but she did have a serious point about the portal. I remember her saying that it was taxing on her to maintain a form like this, so we should cover what she needs to tell us before that becomes too much of a burden for her."

"Yes, while I appreciate watching my children bond and love on each other, I don't need to wear a form to do that," Thera said with a wink, getting a groan from Arthene.

"Yes, my lady. Now they know that you spy on them. That was just the thing to admit to," Arthene grumbled, getting a set of looks from Koda and Sienna.

"Well, I hadn't quite made that connection yet, but now I know," Koda said dryly. Arthene's put-upon expression morphed to a smirk, and she winked down at him, clearly conveying that was the point of her actions.

"Regardless," huffed Thera, a small frown of annoyance on her full lips, "you will need to head out again no later than tomorrow. With the securing of the sites of power within the vale, my power continues to grow. Any more you can discover will only help further."

"And they'll help me, too, though to a lesser degree," Arthene added, settling back on her heels and crossing her arms under her full chest. "More strength means I'll be able to better protect both of you and the rest of our family. But we do need to be careful. We can't just go racing off across the countryside claiming sites of power. For one, another deity might have dominion over them, and for everyone we take, that is another opportunity for the greater powers to figure out what is happening and come to stop us."

"That is something else I don't quite understand," Koda interjected. "You've mentioned that you lost a lot of your power and followers fleeing a catastrophe. Why didn't anyone help you? I know there are other deities. I learned that when I heard about Chandra." Koda's left hand unconsciously went to stroke the silver medallion that hung beneath his shirt.

Arthene grimaced, glancing towards Thera, who was also frowning before she responded.

"I'll explain it to you later, to save my Lady the time? It's not that you are trying to hide anything from you, but I'm already aware of it, and there's no need to waste her energy," Arthene offered with an earnest look. Koda thought for a moment and then nodded. He could accept that.

"To your point, though, it would be bad if the others found me in this form. There is a reason my faithful kept my survival secret this long. So we must build our strength in secret for now," Thera added, getting another nod from Koda.

"So the order of operations is: eliminate the Crooked portal and camp, consecrate any sites of power we find, keep your secret, and make babies so as to spread out this bloodline that I have which is integral to regaining your strength?"

"Not in that order, necessarily," Thera replied, a smile coming back to her full lips. "But yes, that is about the level of it. I also want you to protect your mates and yourself as a matter of priority. I know you have a penchant for throwing yourself into danger to protect others, Koda, but I can't lose you."

"I know, I'm the last of the—" Koda started to say, but Thera cut him off with a sharp gesture.

"No, not just for that. I can't..." Thera grimaced, letting her statement trail off as she fought to find the right words.

"We will do our best to keep each other safe, my Lady," Arthene interjected. "We need to speak to the headwoman, though, as she will need to give permission for us to take some fighters with us. I'm sure she will agree when we explain our reasons, but it is only polite to actually ask."

Thera seized on the distraction hard enough that Koda and Sienna did not miss the relief on her face at not having to finish her previous statement.

"Yes, of course. I will summon her back here. I should have thought to make myself known earlier while she was here, but there is nothing to be done about it now." Thera made a quick gesture, and the faint outline of a small cat formed in her palm. Another gesture and the ghostly figure of the animal hopped down and raced away, vanishing through the wall as if it wasn't there.

"I'm concerned about the fighters from earlier," Sienna murmured, staring after the cat. "Everyone was so exhausted from the fight up on the mountain, and they are all likely still recovering from the party last night. Is anyone going to be physically able to come help us?"

Koda considered her words, remembering the glimpses he'd caught of the different members of their little fighting group the night before. Netta had been reserved, just enjoying the food and conversation. He'd seen Hans dancing rather energetically with a female cow beastfolk, but only for a short while. He didn't remember seeing Hannah either, the cat beastfolk having separated from the group and vanishing as soon as the party started.

"Hard to say," Koda said after he finished thinking. "Some might be coherent, but I would still feel bad calling them back into action already. And nearly everyone got injured in some way." He grimaced again, remembering the covered bodies of the fallen in the square as well.

"You two are forgetting your newly blessed spring," interjected Arthene with a grin. Sienna blushed in response to the big woman's words, remembering exactly *what* they had done to 'consecrate' the spring, as Thera had said earlier. "Just let your headwoman know of its powers, and she can start having people rotate through it. In fact, I think I might have pulled a muscle earlier." Arthene made a show of rubbing at her shoulder and grimacing before letting her sparkling eyes fall on to Koda, and that grimace turned into a smirk. "Think you could help me wash my back to relieve the pain?"

Koda blinked up at the big woman for a moment before his brain connected over her teasing statement.

Really? Well... I did resolve not to be one of those idiot harem protagonists... Koda thought for a moment before smirking back at her and giving Arthene a wink.

"Sure, I'd be happy to help. But with all that hair you have, I'd need a hand to make sure a dirty girl like you is fully cleaned up. Wanna lend a hand, Sienna?" he said, turning the tease towards his wolf-eared lover. Arthene's grin deepened, and they both turned their attention to Sienna, who was blushing brightly and gnawing on her bottom lip while she nodded quickly in agreement.

"Such a cute one!" Arthene sighed happily, plopping her hand on top of Sienna's head this time and stroking her hair as well. Sienna swayed against Koda, going boneless at the sensation of her ears getting rubbed. Koda held back his amused laughter while steadying his redheaded partner, returning the favor from earlier for her.

Arthene's teasing of Sienna was interrupted a moment later by a rapid patter of footsteps on the stairs before the front door flew open as Kris rushed in. The old cat beastfolk was panting for breath, but her eyes were wide with excitement, and they only grew wider when she spotted the four who were standing before her.

Chapter Thirty-Three

Kris was awed to find out who the large woman standing next to Koda was, and with the extra weight of Thera being the one to ask her to spare a few fighters from the tribe, Kris readily agreed. Especially when Thera revealed the blessing on the spring near the village and what it would do.

Koda was just grateful that Thera didn't go into details about *how* the spring got to be blessed. He knew that Kris would figure it out eventually. The old cat beastfolk was clever enough to do so when she wasn't distracted, but he hoped that she wouldn't make the connection until after they had left.

Sienna remained quiet and tucked into Koda's shoulder, listening quietly while they talked.

"So, tomorrow morning, I'll see that we have a dozen warriors to go with you on this. I'm sure that there will be plenty of volunteers from amongst those who fought beside you on the mountain," Kris said at last, leaning heavily on her cane while she nodded. "I will need to get moving to inform them and get people rotating through the spring. The twelve volunteers will get first use of the spring to restore themselves."

"Good." Thera smiled at the headwoman, getting a tentative smile back. "I appreciate you doing all that you can to support my champion. Unfortunately, I can't stay longer, but as you have a temple consecrated, I will hear you should you need to speak to me. I must go now."

"Of course, Pack Lady. Thank you again for sending your champion to us," Kris said with another bow.

"Koda came to you of his own free will. I simply opened the door and asked him to step through," Thera said with a gentle smile before her form faded away as if made of smoke and a wind had just come along to spread it out.

"Finally," Arthene said with a sigh of relief. "My Lady is a good person, but I can't help but feel tense around her most of the time." The big woman had stepped around to stand on Koda's left and just behind him while the goddess and the headwoman talked. Now she leaned forward, planting an arm on Koda's shoulder for support and ran a hand through her hair, which didn't snag despite the mess that her hair looked to be.

"I should go as well," Kris said stiffly. Koda could tell that the irreverent actions of Arthene surprised the older woman, but Kris clearly didn't want to comment because of the woman's own divine origins. "There is much to do to get things organized." She glanced around the bare room once more and frowned before looking at Sienna. "You should speak with the carpenter about furnishing your home. They can get a start on that while you two..." She paused for a moment and glanced at Arthene before continuing. "You *three* are gone. The village will shoulder the cost of furnishings."

"That's not necessary," Koda interjected. He was about to protest further when the older beastfolk woman glared at him.

"Yes, it is necessary, Aegisclaw. Our village owes you and your ladies much, and that debt will continue to grow. But more to the point, I put aside a portion of the coin that we acquired from the Crooked during our attack to help pay for this because I had a feeling you'd argue."

"Accept the gift, Koda," Arthene murmured into his ear from her spot draped over his shoulder. "It's good to be independent, but it is rude to turn away gifts from the grateful."

"She's right, my mate." Sienna pulled back slightly to look up at him. "I'll talk with Kris about it so we can get the bulk of the house furnished. Until things settle down and I can start bringing in money hunting again, this is our best bet."

"Fine..." Koda sighed. "I should know better than to argue with the women in my life."

"You would be a wiser man for knowing that," Kris said with a wicked smile that smoothed out the wrinkles on her aged face. "Trust in your mates to know what is best for your home."

Koda grimaced slightly at the statement of 'mates,' but that was because he was still getting used to the idea himself. Arthene had introduced herself as his mate when Kris had come in to talk to them.

"Headwoman, do you know what kind of budget we have to work with?" Sienna's question was simple enough, but it sent a brief chill down Koda's spine.

Shopping for furniture with Sienna hadn't been nearly as bad as he'd expected. She'd spoken with the carpenter, who turned out to be the bull beastfolk that Hans had been dancing with the night before, and asked her to come have a look at the house. The woman had come and done measurements for the different rooms, discussing wood types and stain colors with Sienna for a bit before leaving.

Koda had honestly forgotten that this word didn't have something like a furniture warehouse or an IKEA where he could just go pick the furniture up already made. The woman had been polite and friendly the entire time, only occasionally glancing at the looming form of Arthene as the large woman followed them from room to room.

When the carpenter finished making her measurements, she finally introduced herself to Koda as Lily Trunkbender before promising to get to work on the furniture as soon as she could before taking her leave.

It had all fallen within the budget that Kris had given Sienna, with a bit more to actually stock the pantry from the general store. They agreed that it would be better to wait until they would be spending more time in the house to actually do that.

With that finished, Sienna set to work getting her spearhead mounted on a fresh shaft so she would be ready to leave in the morning. Arthene lent her a hand, using the large claws on her fingertips to help shape the wood down and drill the holes for the pins that would hold the head in place.

"Arthene?" Koda asked while he watched the two women work from the deep back porch of his new house. Sienna and Arthene were sitting on the steps in the afternoon sun while they worked, and he just leaned back against the building to relax. So when Arthene looked up at him, they were actually at a more even height than they had been before.

"Yes, Koda?" Arthene asked with a serene smile that lit up her face while she held the spear shaft steady for Sienna to slather on the pitch, which would help hold the head in place.

"I wanted to ask you something, but I didn't want it to come across as rude. So I've been hesitating, but I figured I might as well just ask outright and get a straight answer. You don't seem like the kind of person to get offended by someone being straightforward."

"That is an accurate guess. I'd much rather you just say something outright than beat around the bush. Unless it's my bush you are beating around." Arthene gave him a smirking wink, and Koda rolled his eyes. Arthene had been quiet most of the day but wouldn't hesitate to make a bawdy joke on him.

"You said before you were a primal bear spirit, which has me confused as to what you are exactly?" Koda asked, hoping that she wouldn't take his question as rude as it sounded to him. Arthene laid his fears to rest a moment later when she snorted out a giggle.

"I'm sorry. I shouldn't laugh at you for that, Koda. But your face..." Arthene bit her lip for a moment before mastering herself enough to elaborate. "Yes, I am of the bear clan. But you misstate my rank. I'm not *a* primal bear spirit. I am *the* primal bear spirit. I was nothing more than a concept, wild and free, until my Lady rose to power. When she did, she elevated many of us primal spirits to full intelligence, and in return, we gifted her with a portion of our power and blessed her people to carry our features."

"But you don't—" Koda began to protest.

"Have animal features?" Arthene grinned and wiggled her fingers at him to show off the sharp claws that protruded from her fingers where nails would be. "Admittedly, my people have lost some of my features, but I have all of them. Most of the beastfolk nowadays have grown away from their primal roots so only have the ears and tails, or sometimes the teeth of their people. And what cute features they are."

Arthene leaned forward and reached to tickle the tips of Sienna's pointed red-brown ears where they protruded from the top of her head. This resulted in a playful swat from his wolf-featured lover before she went back to forcing the spearhead onto the shaft.

"So you have the same kind of ears and a tail?" Koda asked, his curiosity piqued.

"Is that a request for permission to go rummaging in my pants to look for a tail? You know you don't even have to ask, my future-mate," purred Arthene, grinning at him wickedly.

"Arthene, can you? Yes, just like that," Sienna interjected, and Arthene reached forward to grip the metal base of the spear where it wrapped around the tip of the shaft and pulled back firmly to seat it for Sienna. The wolf beastfolk was quick to slip the metal pins in, getting them set into place so that they would let the pitch harden. "Thank you for that. I was worried about how I'd get it firmly seated enough to get the pins in place without cutting myself."

"Any time, my dear. Once it has set up, we need to head over to the blacksmith to have them rivet it properly. Can't have you losing your weapon during a fight due to a little negligence," Arthene said with a smile, letting Sienna take the spear from her to set aside before turning back to Koda, who had waited patiently for her attention to return before he continued his conversation with her.

"If you are offering, I might go fishing about. But it was more to do with what it means to be a primal spirit," Koda said back, half-teasing to get used to the idea of the big woman becoming his lover and half-serious about his question.

Arthene nodded, leaning back against the log post that supported the porch overhang. This allowed the afternoon sun to highlight her form quite well, adding a golden gleam to her sun-kissed flesh and deepening the shadows of her bodice as well. She draped one arm over her upright knee while the other leg sprawled out into the small backyard of the house, and she thought for a moment in silence.

"The best way to explain it would be... well, I am not sure." Arthene let out a bark of laughter at that. "I wish you had asked while my Lady was here. She would have likely been better able to explain it. How do you explain what it means to just *exist,* after all?"

Koda just shrugged and waited. Sienna finished settling her spear against the porch support and trotted over to plop down against the wall next to Koda, leaning into him with casual abandon and letting out a contented sigh.

"Just do your best, Arthene. I'm not expecting an exhaustive answer. I've met bear beastfolk, and you are noticeably different from them," Koda suggested and got a nod from the larger woman that sent her messy hair bouncing.

"As a primal spirit, I am both more than and similar to the beastfolk that I share a form with," Arthene began to explain, drawing the claw of her index finger over the wooden deck and carving a small curl of wood up with it. "My natural form is that of a great bear, but I do not normally have a physical body. I can choose to incarnate myself at the cost of some of my spiritual powers. This gives me the ability to affect the world around me, but also, I risk harm to myself by doing so." She brushed away the curl of wood and looked up at Koda through the fringe of her hair with those piercing yellow eyes.

"Why did you choose to do that? Can you go back?"

"I chose to because I wanted to help my savior in return. As to going back, sure." Arthene shrugged in such a way that it sent her full bosom jostling distractingly, and when Koda dragged his eyes back up from it, she was smirking at him. "My mortal form just needs to die in order to release my spiritual form once more. Until then, I am bound to the mortal coil. My physical body will live, age, and eventually die as well, if combat doesn't claim me."

"Why didn't you just go back to Thera when you died before? Why was your spirit at risk in the Last Fang Cave?" Sienna interjected, and Koda could feel the slight tickle against his cheek of her ears flicking back and forth inquisitively.

"That is partially due to how weak my Lady was at the time. She barely had the energy to support herself, and since we primal spirits had bound ourselves to her, returning to her would have put an extra strain on what little energy she did have. So I waited and slept in my cave," Arthene said with a shrug.

"And if Thera had faded away?" Koda asked with concern. Arthene's response was not reassuring as she grimaced and shrugged.

"I don't know. But either I would have continued to slumber until I faded away or I would have lost myself immediately when she did."

"Are there other primal spirits?" Concern filled Koda's voice as he asked, and Arthene's grimace transformed into a smirk.

"Why? Looking to add more of my kind to your growing harem already?" She wiggled her eyebrows at him suggestively, and Koda rolled his eyes at her.

"If there are others like you, vulnerable in the world, then we need to look out for them. I don't want the Crooked to get the opportunity to twist them like they tried with you." Koda's statement sobered the large woman, and she nodded, though the glance she shot him next overflowed with affection and respect.

"We will do just that. I would prefer that none of my kin lost themselves, but this world is harsh and dangerous. I will do my best to look after you and our family, to blaze the trail to our better future."

Since they didn't have a bed yet to sleep in, Koda and Sienna set their bedrolls up in the main room of their new house. Arthene didn't mind, though she insisted on sleeping next to the two of them, playfully offering herself as a pillow for them both.

With a glance at Sienna, who was giving him puppy-dog eyes, Koda caved to the women once more.

They ended up sleeping in a pile. Sienna was in his arms with her face buried in his stomach, while Arthene sprawled above them, and they used her muscled stomach as a pillow. Koda woke up with one of Arthene's hands on his ass while Sienna had stuffed both her hands down the front of his pants while he slept.

He'd learned that morning three things about Arthene that he had missed the previous night when they got ready for bed. One, she did have bear features beyond her claws: a pair of rounded ears hid inside her messy mane, and a stubby tail protruded from the small of her back. Two, the bear woman slept in the nude as a matter of habit. Three, she had been teasing him about having a 'bush' to beat around previously.

Meeting up with the other warriors from the vale, Koda was glad to see a host of familiar faces. Netta, Hans, Todd, and Hannah were leading the group, while the other eight present were people from the previous fight with the Crooked.

They all met up in the square before heading out of the village at a quick hike. While they walked, Koda talked with Todd as the older hunter was the most knowledgeable about the vale and its surroundings. He confirmed that all of them were feeling good in the wake of making use of the enchanted spring during the previous day.

On Todd's recommendation, they would march for the Last Fang Cave and camp there before heading down into the plains through the pass.

"It'll give the best view of the surroundings, and you said before you saw tracks when you and Sienna made your little heroic stand at the cave," Todd suggested. The gruff fox beastfolk eyed Koda for a moment before glancing at Arthene, who was walking beside Hans and trying to talk the bull beastfolk into an arm-wrestling match. "Who is that, anyway?"

Koda followed his gaze to Arthene and debated his answer for a moment mentally. Eventually, he just shrugged and answered as honestly as he was willing. The old fox had been with them when Thera appeared, but he didn't want to spill any of Arthene's secrets, as that should be her right to choose who knew the specifics.

"She's a future mate of mine. She came to spend time with me and Sienna, as well as help out with the village's problems." Koda didn't elaborate further, but from the meaningful glance that Todd shot him, the fox got the underlying information. Todd knew that Thera had sent him here, so if Arthene had come here because of him, the big woman had to be somehow connected to Thera as well.

Todd gave him an understanding nod before peeling off to speak to the other fighters with them. From the way the conversation would lead to darting glances in Koda's direction and then to Arthene, he was pretty sure that Todd was spreading the word to the others.

I have to hope that these people keep up the habit of secrets from the outsiders, Koda thought with a grimace. Arthene hadn't had a chance to fill him in on all the subjects Thera had promised, but he knew it would come... eventually. The biggest worry was the need for secrecy, after all.

They reached Last Fang Cave without a problem. Koda was gratified to discover that the pyres he'd built to deal with the dead Crooked had burned out without leaving behind too much damage to the clearing. Arthene spent more than a little time glaring at the charred stains on the clearing in front of the old cave, wandering over the ground and kicking at the piles of charcoal and the scorched earth itself while the others set up camp on a clear spot closer to the road.

Koda left her to her venting as he had already checked on her once and heard the big woman muttering depreciative comments about the Crooked who had stained her old den with their presence.

Instead, he helped Sienna set up the small camp the three of them would be using. Some of the hunters had brought tents with them, while others were content to sleep out under the stars. Sienna had recommended they do that as well. The season was warm enough that they wouldn't need the cover of a tent, and it would save having to carry the weight of the tent.

Sienna was digging out a shallow bowl of earth with her hands to make the firepit when Arthene returned with an absolutely massive femur over her shoulder that she set on the ground with a solid *thump*. Her approach had been so silent that, in spite of her size, it startled both Koda and Sienna until she had announced herself by dropping the bone.

"Koda, I need your help with this," the bear woman said, gesturing at the ancient bone. "Your claws are sharper than mine. Can you help trim down one end for me? I need to narrow this side down to make a grip." She pointed at the end with the knob of bone that would have met the hip socket when the bone was originally encased in flesh.

"Sure?" Koda said in confusion, staring at the large bone. It was easily six feet long, and the narrowest part was as thick as his wrist. "Did you—"

"Take my bone back from the cave? Yeah, it's mine, after all." Arthene shrugged with a grin. "I feel like it's poetic justice to fashion myself a weapon to fight the Crooked out of my own remains. That bone is harder than iron, so it's going to be a bitch to shape, but your blessed claws should be able to help it along."

Koda considered her words for a long moment in silence, looking between the ancient bone and the bear woman's smiling face in surprise. While he thought that over,

Arthene turned a confused look towards Sienna where she kneeled by the firepit.

"Dear Sienna, why are you doing that with your hands? I know my Lady granted you magic. Didn't she tell you?"

Now Sienna was staring at the big woman in surprise as well, clearly having forgotten that, too.

Chapter Thirty-Four

"You weren't kidding..." Koda punctuated his statement with a grunt of effort as he carved a sliver of bone off the head of the femur, being careful to not damage the ball joint on the end.

He wanted to leave it there to help Arthene keep her grip on the crude weapon. Each small sliver took quite a bit of effort to remove, and he gently set each fragment aside as they were all sharp.

Snuggled up against the tree line of the clearing, their little camp gave them a clear view but still provided shelter from any rain that might blow in overnight.

"Fighting is one of the few things I don't kid about," Arthene replied with a smirk, sitting next to Koda and holding the bone steady for him while he dragged his thumb claw along the grip to narrow it more. "Thank you for this, Koda. I could have used it before, but these alterations will let me get a better grip."

"Wouldn't doing this weaken the bone, though?" Sienna sat on the other side of Koda with her back to a tree, alternating between watching him and inspecting her arrows to see if any needed sharpening.

"If this was a regular bone, then yes. But since it's *my* bone, I can infuse it with spiritual energy, and that allows me to strengthen it just like I did when it was inside my body," Arthene said in a matter-of-fact tone that made Koda grimace.

"Still weird to me that you are so chill with the idea of using a piece of your own body as a weapon."

"Don't forget, my future-mate, I'm not a normal woman. I am an incarnate spirit." Arthene patted her generous chest with one large hand, making the restrained orbs jiggle and dance as she jostled them in her furred chest-wrap. "This body I wear right now is the sixth or seventh one that I have created for myself. I've seen millennia pass and known the lives of millions of those who share my form."

Arthene's words landed between them with the weight of an anvil crashing to the floor, and Koda finished carving up the strip of bone to look up at Arthene. Her yellow eyes gleamed in the late afternoon sunlight while she stared down at the end of the femur she held. He didn't know what to say, so he was glad when Sienna was the one to speak up.

"How do you do it? I don't think I'd be able to keep myself sane with that many memories." The redheaded wolf woman was staring at the small whetstone she'd been using to sharpen the arrows she found in need of it.

"By living in the moment. I still treasure my memories and past lives, don't ever think otherwise. But my past is just that, my treasure. And it is a treasure none can take from me." Arthene's smile bloomed once more as she snuck a glance towards Sienna. "Not even the gods can defy time. So, good or bad, the past is safe from interference. I live in the moment so that when each moment drifts into my treasured past, it will be worth as much joy as I can draw from it. When I slept in my cave, before our mate found me, I dreamed of my past and visited my hoard. But now I have a chance to add to it once more, so I will seize that with all the strength I can."

The concern over Arthene's great age and experience, something that Koda had only just now noticed as it began to fade, settled once more in his chest and relaxed.

She has a point. Treasure the past, love the present, and look to the future. It's simple and straightforward. Something I'm learning more and more is a very Arthene outlook, Koda thought, returning to his work and carefully carving up another sliver of bone.

"Ho, you three! How goes it?" Hans' voice broke through the gathering night, and Koda glanced up to see the large, horned man approaching.

Hans had his mattock over one shoulder, and poking over the same shoulder was the rounded corner of a wooden shield banded in iron where it hung over his back on a leather strap. Netta and Hannah were with him, while the other warriors of the tribe continued to putter around their fires while Todd was ordering several men to sentry duty.

"Good, come have a seat, Hans. Ladies." Koda gestured with his right hand to the small fire.

Arthene had rolled over several fallen logs to act as backrests earlier—something that had confused Koda as she resolutely plonked herself down next to him, rather than using one of the logs as a seat.

"Don't mind if I do! Been wanting to ask you more about our new friend here," Hans said with a laugh that welled up deep in his broad chest. The heavily muscled bull man let the girls select where they wanted to sit before claiming a log for himself. Netta settled herself on the ground next to Sienna, giving her friend a smile, while Hannah perched on the nearest log to his wolf-eared lover.

"Ask away, friend Hans," Arthene interjected with a grin, shifting herself slightly so she could look at him while still steadying the bone that Koda was carving on. "I haven't had much of a chance to dig into my mates' lives yet. So I appreciate any juicy tidbits you can give."

"Mates?" Hans's eyes widened in surprise, and he glanced towards Koda and Sienna questioningly. Sienna was blushing fiercely under the pointed looks from Netta and Hannah but nodded in agreement. Koda just shrugged as he was rapidly giving up on trying to keep Arthene from just bluntly pointing things like that out.

"Oh yes. I'm determined to join Koda's family, and that means I get Sienna as a bonus, after all." The bear woman's grin turned decidedly wolfish as she shot Sienna a wink, making the smaller woman's blush intensify for a moment before Sienna forced her back straight and coughed.

"Just remember, it's *Koda's* family. His word is the last one in the decision of who joins it," Sienna reminded Arthene firmly. The bear woman barked out another laugh and nodded.

"Don't you worry, dear Sienna. I would never forget that. I'm just doing my best to ensure I'm part of his decision is all!" Arthene shifted to wrap one arm around Koda and yank him into her, mushing the side of his head into her full breast in the process and nearly knocking him over.

Hans stared at them for several more seconds before a surprised chuckle bubbled up from him, and the bull beastfolk just started shaking his head.

"I can't help but envy you, Aegisclaw. Not only did you draw the affections of our best and smartest huntress, but your other woman is clearly smitten with you. What's your secret? Share with your buddy Hans. Don't be stingy now!"

"Animal magnetism?" Koda mumbled around the faceful of tit-flesh and furred garment as Arthene hadn't released him.

"I don't think what he has can be taught," Netta laughed, the feathers of her hair flexing slightly in amusement as she nudged Sienna. "Right? Just something about the man that snatches your attention, after all?"

"I'm rather partial to how glorious his hair is," interjected Hannah with a smirk. "Such long and straight hair, and so dark!"

"Nothing I can do about my hair," grumbled Hans, clearly interpreting their words as suggestions. He reached up to try to smooth out his mop of brown hair between his long horns, floppy ears flicking in annoyance.

"I don't think you'd look as good as Koda does with his long hair," Arthene said candidly, finally releasing Koda from her pseudo-headlock and taking a moment to run her clawed fingertips through the mentioned hair to straighten the long falls of black once more. Koda wanted to protest her rough handling of him, but the return of the head scratches was just too pleasant for him.

"Agreed. Not to mention, I bet you'd get annoyed with it being so long while you worked in the mine and then cutting it with a knife again," snickered Sienna, clearly eager to deflect the embarrassing revelations away from herself.

"I did that one time, just ONE time," grumbled Hans, his put-upon expression getting a laugh from the three girls native to the village. Arthene just smirked and tossed her hair, making the shaggy mane bounce behind her. It still looked like she'd just rolled out of bed, and Koda couldn't help but wonder if he'd even be able to brush it out with a steel-toothed comb.

My luck, it'll break the bristles right off. I wonder if Arthene even wants it combed or if she likes the 'fresh from bed' look? Koda thought idly, studying the large woman. Arthene must have felt his eyes on her because she turned to shoot a questioning look his way, which quickly melted into an alluring smile with a teasing wink tossed in for good measure as she clearly guessed what he was thinking.

Leaning in close, Arthene whispered low enough so that only he would hear it.

"I like it messy... both my bed and my hair afterwards."

"Such a dirty girl," Koda mumbled in return. A sudden wet warmth on his cheek surprised him, and he shot a sidelong glance to see Arthene leaning back from him with a smirk, her lips still pursed from the kiss she'd left on the side of his face.

"So sweet of you to remember. Don't forget, I want both you and Sienna's help to ensure every *inch* of me is nice and clean when we get a chance."

Koda didn't really have a counter to her statement as he'd been the one to suggest double-teaming Arthene in the spring with Sienna, so he just shrugged.

Double-teaming in more ways than one, I think, Koda thought as he snuck a glance towards Sienna who was still blushing but more faintly now. He could see the shadow drifting behind her of her tail wiggling happily, and she was smiling at him, so he knew that she was okay with this.

Sitting beside Arthene, Koda couldn't really back up his statement about her being a dirty girl in more than just her mind. The big woman's scent lingered, and even with his human nose being less than stellar, Koda had learned to recognize the smell that was uniquely Arthene.

While Sienna had a faint scent of pine and green buds of growth to her, the wild bear woman had the smell of warm berries in the sun lingering around her. A smell that encouraged Koda to just sprawl out and take a nap to enjoy it.

"So, I'm sorry if this is intrusive, but I am curious what brought you to the vale... Arthene, was it?" Hannah asked when the laughter at both Hans and Koda's expressions had faded some.

"This fellow right here." Arthene dipped her head in Koda's direction. "I'd been planning to come along to support him, but he impressed me so much that I decided to move up my schedule. Didn't want to fall too far behind."

This time, Koda ducked and successfully dodged the arm that had been reaching to pull him into her side, shooting Arthene a serious look as he sat back up. His part-glare was met with a pouty expression that was remarkably adorable on the larger woman.

"If you want me to actually finish this"—Koda tapped the end of the femur in his lap with the tips of his claws—"then you are going to have to stop distracting me by trying to stuff my head into your tits."

"But it's fuuuun!" whined Arthene, getting another round of giggles from the girls.

"Arthene." Sienna's interjection got the big woman's attention, and she broke eye contact with Koda to look towards the wolf beastfolk. "If you let him finish, then you can use both hands to reward him for helping you." The pout on Arthene's face immediately blossomed into a grin once more, and she settled back to let Koda finish.

"I thought you were on my side," grumbled Koda towards his wolfish mate.

"I am, Koda. Trying to get you more of those head scratches you enjoyed so much yesterday," Sienna replied with a grin, her tail stirring even faster behind her.

"And if Arthene gets a few more handfuls in the process?" Koda protested, clearly having forgotten the other three sharing their fire at the moment.

"Why in the world would you complain about that?" Hans was quick to butt in and remind Koda of what he'd forgotten.

"Yeah, Koda? Why would you complain about that?" parroted Arthene, her pout back in place once more.

"While I enjoy poking fun at our savior as much as the next woman, maybe we should ease up a bit?" Hannah suggested, her slender black tail flicking behind her as she watched the byplay with a neutral expression. "After all, we don't want to drive him off, do we?"

"Fair, sorry about that, Aegisclaw," grunted the chastised Hans.

"You can all call me Koda," the man in question said. "We've fought side-by-side after all. No need for formality." Hans looked like he wanted to protest, but Hannah wasn't going to let the conversation be sidetracked again and immediately pressed forward with another question.

"What are you two working on, anyway?" The cat beastfolk nodded towards the bone that shared both Koda and Arthene's laps.

"Weapon for me. While I'm still good with these"—Arthene tapped her claws against the knobby head of the bone club— "I prefer to have a bit more range, and this should let me apply some actual force. Besides, it's not like the previous owner needs it or cares."

Koda had spent long enough around Arthene in the last day to recognize the forced-nonchalant tone she was using, and he snuck a glance at her to see that she was looking towards the cave on the ridge above them with a slightly wistful expression.

Hannah followed the other woman's gaze and made a quiet yowling noise in her throat when she made the connection.

"You took one of the bones from the cave?!"

"Sure, why not? They are just bones, after all," Arthene answered with a shrug. "Like I said, their previous owner isn't using them anymore. They aren't serving a purpose, just lying in that cave. They've slept long enough. It's time to take them on an adventure to see how the world has changed since the last time they walked about."

Hannah continued to gape at the big woman in surprise, while Hans and Netta shared a glance before shrugging. Neither of them looked comfortable with the idea of Arthene having taken a bone from what they viewed as a sacred burial ground, but after some thought, they accepted it, given that Koda was shaping the bone into a weapon. Netta actually spoke up to that effect a moment later.

"She does have a point. The old legends said the guardian who lived there liked to wander the mountains on patrol. Besides, if there was a problem with it, do you think Koda would be helping her?"

Hannah scowled but nodded, clearly finding the entire thing more than a bit disturbing, though. So, Koda decided to speak up and try to reassure her some more.

"I can guarantee that the former owner of this thing would be quite happy to serve once more. I think she'd be lonely remaining in that cold cave, given how long she's laid resting there."

Koda's words did their job, and while Hannah was clearly still not *happy* about the situation, she was accepting of it as they diverted the conversation to other subjects as the sun continued to set.

After another half-hour of carving, Arthene declared his work done and set to smoothing the handle-part down more with her claws. While they could not pull up slivers of bone like Koda's claws could, they did compress the bone and polish it well before Arthene wrapped a leather strap she'd gotten from Sienna around the grip.

Hans was the first to head off to bed, declaring that he could always use more sleep before a long hike. Hannah and Netta both rose to leave a few minutes later as Todd had stopped by to tell them they had the last shift of sentry duty at dawn.

No sooner had the two of them stood up than Arthene suggested they also get to bed before beginning to strip her top off without a care in the world.

The bear woman ignored the protests from the other three girls, tossing her clothes beside the pile of bedrolls before grabbing Koda and dragging him towards the bedding as well.

"Come on, my future-mate. I don't like sleeping alone, and you can help keep me warm," Arthene teased, burrowing into the laid-out bedrolls and pulling Koda to her chest, assuming the big-spoon position and holding him like a teddy-bear.

"Arthene, I'm still fully dressed!" Koda protested verbally, though he didn't struggle as much physically. With his goddess-enhanced strength, he was fairly certain he could break free of her grip without problem, but Koda didn't want to risk hurting the affectionate woman.

Not fazed in the slightest by his token protests, Arthene glanced over her shoulder towards where Sienna was standing next to the other two with her mouth open in surprise at Arthene just stripping so bluntly.

"Sienna? Come, be a dear and help our mate out of his clothes so he can get some sleep?" There was a double helping of innuendo in Arthene's tone as she suggested it, and Koda glanced over in time to see Sienna's tail, which had been hanging limply in surprise before, immediately began whipping back and forth in excitement.

"And that's our cue to leave. Come on, Hannah," Netta said firmly, grabbing the cat woman's arm to drag her off. Hannah only took a light tugging to get moving. "Don't be too loud, you three!" Netta called over her shoulder.

"Too loud? No such thing," Arthene playfully grumbled as Sienna scampered over, setting her weapons near the pile of bedding and quickly peeling herself out of her clothes. "There's our gorgeous mate. You have such a good eye for things, Koda," Arthene purred as Sienna stripped to her underwear—just a set of panties around her hips as she wasn't wearing a chest-band—and wriggled into the bedding to join them.

"I'm not—" Koda began to protest, only to be cut off by a gentle squeezing hug from behind that pressed him into Arthene's full and warm chest.

"It's fine, future-mate. I said before that you can come to me at any time, and I will accept you. But I won't rush you," Arthene breathed into his ear. "Please, just let me feel your warmth against my skin, though? You were not wrong when you mentioned how cold my cave was..."

The longing in Arthene's voice defeated the last of Koda's protestations, and he let Sienna peel his clothes off before snuggling her back into his chest while wrapping his arms around her waist.

As he drifted off to sleep there in the pile of blankets, Koda couldn't help but find it amusing that they were stacked together like spoons in a drawer, with him being sandwiched between a big and a little spoon at the same time.

Chapter Thirty-Five

KODA SLEPT. HE KNEW THAT HE WAS ASLEEP BECAUSE of the weightless feeling that engulfed his limbs. There was no other way to describe the sensation at the moment besides comforting. It felt like he lay suspended inside a roll of velvet.

"Koda?" the deep, rumbling voice that echoed from the darkness behind him drew his attention, but he couldn't find traction to turn to look at it. He didn't need to, though, as a pair of familiar arms wrapped around his waist from behind and pulled him against a firm torso. His head settled onto two pillowy masses that parted to sandwich his head slightly.

Arthene? Koda thought, unable to find the controls for his lips to be able to speak.

"Yes, it's me. Don't worry, future-mate. I'm not going to take advantage of you here," Arthene purred reassuringly into his ear, squeezing him against her. The velvet-soft sensations of the void were fading now along his back as the expanse of warm skin pressed into him.

What is this?

"This is my spirit-den, the place my soul dwelt in while I slept, though it doesn't have a form at the moment. I spent a good amount of the power that supported my spirit-den to incarnate myself. This pocket of eternity is still mine, though." The possessiveness in her tone was reassuring to Koda, and he continued to relax into her soft touch and enjoy the sensation of being wrapped up in his new partner's arms.

The only thing that would make this better would be if Sienna was here, too, Koda thought wryly.

"I could only bring you here, future-mate," Arthene said sadly. "I wanted to bring our little wolf in as well, but my strength is low. I could do so with you because of our bond." Arthene's arms shifted from around his waist to wrap over top of his arms, her longer limbs matching up almost perfectly with his and drawing his arms up to cross over his chest.

I understand, Koda thought slowly. His mind was still confused and full of fluffy clouds, but he didn't feel threatened here. This felt like the most wonderful bed of all time, and he just wanted to curl up and sleep with his lovers in his arms in this place of safety and serenity.

"I'm glad that dwelling within my spirit feels so safe to you. But before I send you back to rest, I should tell you something."

What is it? Koda asked, fighting off the grasping hands of sleep now. Someone needed him, and while Arthene was someone he'd known for barely a day, he already felt a connection to the brash and energetic woman.

Arthene's chest rumbled with a hum of approval, and she

squeezed him tighter for a moment before relaxing but not releasing him.

"Well, there are two things. As I grow stronger, I can draw you and your mates in here with me while we sleep. That will allow them to rest and recover more and have a host of other pleasant effects." Arthene's breath across the back of his neck sent a thrill down Koda's spine, and he fought down the urge to imagine what the other 'pleasant effects' she was implying were. "Also, it occurred to me while I slept and considered that while I reassured you I would wait until you are ready to consummate our bond and become full mates, I didn't explain something."

Communicate, communicate, communicate, Koda thought playfully, getting a small snort of laughter.

"Yes. Well, to that point. If my affections truly bother you, whether it be my desire to touch, snuggle, or tease, please tell me so I know to stop? I'm not the most observant sort, and my long sleep has left me out of touch with the more emotional part of courting a mate."

I will, Arthene. Nothing you've done so far has really bothered me for more than a moment. It's just who you are.

"Good, now back to rest, future-mate." The soft feeling of lips against the back of his neck punctuated Arthene's statement, and Koda felt his consciousness spiraling away as the softness of sleep wrapped him up once more.

———

"Smoke!"

The cry brought everyone's attention to focus forward as the group had been navigating down the slope of the pass. Koda was in the middle of the group with Arthene right behind him and Sienna walking ahead of him. Todd and Netta were leading, having the best eyes of the tribe's hunters, while the rest trailed behind their small group in a rambling group.

Since Netta was pointing, it was easy to follow the line of her arm to the distant smudge of gray on the horizon. The obvious ribbon of the road wound in that direction, so Koda guessed that it had to be coming from the distant town.

A rush of worried murmurs rose from the others before Hans's deep voice cut across them all.

"We all expected that Amberpost would be pressured, but their town is far larger than our village. Also, they have a garrison of guards there. We have to trust in the garrison to hold until we can get there."

"And the best way we can help them right now is cutting off that portal to prevent further reinforcements," Koda tacked on. Eyes that had been turning towards Hans now snapped to him. He could see Arthene's confident smile and nod out of the corner of his eye, so he continued. "Our numbers are too small to turn a toe-to-toe fight, but if we can hit them in an ambush? That is where we can make our smaller numbers count. But we have to secure our own flank before we try to turn the enemy's. Focus on the portal and that camp because it threatens our home and the other settlement." He gestured with one hand toward the distant curl of smoke.

Koda didn't want to mention the fact that, if they were already able to see smoke from this distance, then the town itself might have already fallen to the Crooked. The thought that there might be people that were being dragged off even now hurt Koda's heart, but there was only so much that he could get done at a time.

One foot in front of the other, and handle the task in front of you before you start worrying about the fourth or fifth on the list, he reminded himself, repeating the mantra that had gotten him through so many long days on the construction site.

Murmurs passed along the line of marching fighters, but Netta and Todd shared a nod before beginning to lead the way along the rough road once more. Slowly, the group picked up their march once more, though Koda felt like there was a higher level of urgency to it.

"You are getting better at that," Sienna whispered to him with a small smile, her fluffy red-black tail stirring slowly behind her as she let her steps slow enough to fall in at his left with her spear couched on her right shoulder.

"Our mate will lead armies one day, you just watch!" Arthene enthused, slipping up on his right side.

The big woman had her improvised bone club slung over her right shoulder, idly holding it there with the handle tucked into her elbow while her hand hung down in front of her. The bleached-white bone gleamed in the afternoon light, and Koda swore that he saw the beginnings of something being drawn on the shaft and the knob at the end of the massive femur, but he couldn't quite make it out yet.

When he'd woken up that morning, he'd found himself tucked against Arthene's side, using her biceps for a pillow with Sienna tucked into him, her face buried into his chest. Arthene had been lightly running her clawed fingertips over the shaft of the bone club, not digging into it but following a pattern he hadn't been able to see with his sleep-addled mind that morning. Now, though, the sun gleamed oddly in certain spots along the bone, and it made him wonder until Sienna spoke his name and pulled him out of his distraction.

"Armies? While I don't doubt Koda, I would prefer that to be sometime in the future. He's been racing nonstop since he got here. I know I'd like a few slow days to just relax and enjoy having a mate..."

There was a wistfulness in Sienna's tone that tugged at Koda's heart. He reached out instinctively, wrapping his left arm around her waist and pulling her hip to bump lightly into his.

"Love you, Sienna. Slow or fast days. They are all good ones with my mate beside me," Koda said quietly, holding her eyes when she glanced his way. A coloring of Sienna's cheeks came, followed by a loving smile and a blown kiss.

"You two are just so adorable. I can't wait to see him try that with me!" Arthene said with a laugh.

Koda turned towards the much taller woman and quirked an eyebrow.

"Oh, I wouldn't try the same thing with you, Arthene. You are far too wild-natured for that to work on you. Getting hold of your hair and pulling you down to my level for a kiss when you aren't expecting it?"

Koda's statement clearly surprised Arthene as her eyes went wide, and she just stared at him with her pale cheeks reddening slightly while her breathing picked up.

"Koda, if you are done flirting with your two beauties, can I steal you for a second?" Netta's voice cut in before Arthene could find the words to react to Koda's statement.

"Sure thing, Netta. Don't want my favorite feathered hunter to feel left out. Did you want some flirting, too?" Koda replied automatically, turning to grin at the hawk beastfolk woman.

Netta had turned and was walking backwards while Todd kept them on the trail of the Crooked war party that had come up the mountain. This allowed him to meet her eyes, and when he offered to flirt with her, she just rolled her eyes and beckoned for him to get over there.

"You don't have nearly enough meat on your bones yet to interest me, Aegisclaw. Also, I don't like to share, so not gonna happen. You'll just have to keep appreciating my fine, feathered fanny from a distance," Netta huffed with a smirk, turning to pat her leather-clad bottom with one hand.

"Oh, you actually have feathers there? I'm even more interested," Koda joked, getting a snort of laughter from Todd when Netta sent him an offended look while he picked up speed to walk with the two hunters in the lead. "Seriously, though, what did you need, Netta? Any problems."

"None yet," Todd grunted in answer, his eyes not leaving the hard-packed road. "The Crooked left a trail like a herd of cows racing through a pasture. It's not hard to follow."

Koda squinted at the hard-packed dirt, and all he saw were the faint tracks of wagon-wheels and the occasional boot-print in the dirt. Nothing that really stood out to him. Shrugging, he mentally relegated this to why he had asked for trackers to come with them and waited for Netta to explain as the slope of their walking finally reached the flatlands of the plains, and they continued along the road, looking for where the Crooked came onto it.

"So, Todd and I were talking about where the portal camp might be, trying to figure out if there was something that we could use to orient on in the plains besides the mountains behind us." Netta hooked her thumb over her shoulder before waving it towards the empty lands around them. "As long as we can keep a landmark, it's hard to get lost out here. But there are all sorts of nooks, crannies, valleys, and washouts that aren't obvious until you are right on top of them."

"Which is why we are following the road till we can hook their trail. It's likely a week or more old at this point, but with that many bodies traveling at once? It should still lead us directly to their camp," Todd said while looking up from the trail to scan the horizon. Koda noticed his eyes lingered on the distant smudge of smoke, but Todd turned back to the road a moment later.

"Yes, exactly. And I was thinking about what else is in the area. Resources we can tap into like water sources, natural cover for camps, the small copses of trees that would provide firewood. That kind of thing," Netta said, reclaiming the lead in the conversation once more. "There's a natural spring nearby, maybe an hour off the road, that I was thinking might be good to visit. There are a number of different local legends about it, but I heard about it from a few of the plains tribe hunters that I met a year ago when we came across them near the vale. We traded supplies, stories, and medicine with them, and in thanks for the medicine, they told me about this watering hole."

Koda hummed thoughtfully, following the line of thinking that he could see Netta was chasing. A secret spring with legends around it had the ring of a site of power.

"I think that sounds like a good idea." Arthene had increased her pace as well, moving with surprising grace and silence for someone so large. Sienna was right behind her and nodding along, clearly thinking the same thing. "If the location is only known to the tribes that wander the plains, the odds that it's held by one of the other powers are small. Any extra power he can gather will be helpful for dealing with the portal camp."

Netta nodded sharply in agreement before elbowing Todd lightly.

"Told you he'd go for it."

"I never said he wouldn't. I just suggested that it might not be the most efficient use of our time. Every hour we spend not pursuing the destruction of that gateway, the more Crooked pour through to taint the land," Todd grumbled, the older fox beastfolk slapping halfheartedly at Netta's elbow when she tried to get him again.

"There is a balance, though. More strength means it will make the challenge easier. We can't hesitate to take opportunities," Koda interjected, agreeing partially with Todd's worries but also wanting to claim the site as well. His memories of the night before, the physical conversations with Arthene, and the one within his dreams, too, further pushed him to find more of those sites of power to restore both her and Thera.

"Well, we have a bit before we need to go off the road to get there. We can make the call when we either pass the offshoot or see where the Crooked found the road."

They continued to talk for another hour while they marched, Todd and Netta pointing out the tracks they were following and Koda doing his best to learn what he could. Arthene and Sienna fell back behind him to hold a quiet conversation between themselves for now, though Koda could feel their eyes on his back as they kept watch over him in turns.

Netta was just pointing out a section of torn cloth on the side of the road, the distorted patterns showing it as having come from a Crooked soldier, when Arthene gave a short, sharp whistle that made all of them jump.

"Hey! I think I see where the Crooked came onto the road ahead. The path is pounded out in the long grass," the big woman called as she hurried to catch up to the three in the lead.

"How? You aren't that much taller than us," Todd demanded, annoyance showing on the fox-man's face that he was being shown up in his hunting skills.

"Well, first of all, a little bit can go a long way. But mostly because of that dust cloud over there," Arthene replied sharply, tossing her head off to the south of the road. Glancing that way, Koda squinted to try to see what Arthene was talking about.

On either side of the road, the grass grew long and wove back and forth in the wind. Green-brown stalks danced and swayed against the sharp contrast of the blue sky, with the constant wind from the south being the only thing that kept the traveling warriors from baking in the pounding light of the brilliant sun overhead.

At first, he took it for a gauzy cloud in the distance, but the cloud moved differently from the distant white puffs that cruised in the blue expanse overhead, slowly growing in size.

"Shit," Todd swore, clearly coming to the same conclusion as he spotted the haze. "I'd seen that, but I didn't make the connection that it could be a dust cloud until now. Either we have a storm coming in, or that's more troops moving. And knowing our luck..."

"It's Crooked," Koda said as a certainty settled into his gut, "headed towards the road and likely the village."

Chapter Thirty-Six

"OFF THE ROAD, NOW!" SIENNA BARKED, MOVING without hesitation to start directing the tribe's warriors to either side of the trampled area where the Crooked had passed previously.

"What?" Arthene's head snapped to the wolf woman in confusion before turning to look at Koda as if he would countermand Sienna's orders.

"She's right. We need to get off the road and out of sight," Koda immediately agreed, nodding for Arthene to join them as the fighters melted into the tall grass and found spots where they could observe.

"What about the group that is coming? Are you just going to let them pass?" Disbelief was thick in Arthene's voice, and she initially refused to be budged, even when Koda hooked his arm in hers and his goddess-improved strength came into play.

"No, of course not. But I'm also not going to throw lives away when I have no idea what is coming. We attack from ambush, and we ensure none of them escape to threaten our

425

home." Koda's response was clipped and stern. He didn't know where the doubt in Arthene's tone had come from, but he didn't like it.

Grimacing, the big woman nodded once.

"Sorry, Koda. I jumped to a conclusion that I shouldn't have," Arthene said as he led her onto the trampled and churned path the raiders had traveled until they were the farthest group from the road, before pulling her off it. Sienna joined them a moment later, the hood of her cloak pulled up, and the mottled green and brown cloth helping her to blend in with the plant life.

"What?" Sienna shot the big woman a confused look, and Arthene's grimace just got deeper.

"I thought that Koda wanted us to hide from whatever is coming. You both attacked my old cave without hesitation, and you hit the group squatting at the Windwalker's Retreat from the front..." Arthene let the sentence trail off, and Koda understood now what she was meaning.

"You forget that we ambushed a patrol before hitting the Retreat, and we attacked the Retreat by surprise. Like I said, I'm not going to throw lives away. We need to use every advantage we can get," Koda reminded her.

Since the three of them were crouching in the grass, Koda could reach high enough to dig into the mess of Arthene's hair, finding one of the rounded bear ears she'd shown them the previous night and giving her a good scratch behind it. The owner of said ear let out a happy groan, leaning into the touch.

"Speaking of advantages," Sienna muttered, still glancing between Koda and Arthene warily and clearly annoyed with the larger woman's doubt, "any tips on how to use this earth magic I'm supposed to have?"

426

Seeing an opportunity to make amends, Arthene nodded eagerly and began describing several things to Sienna. They sounded like nonsense to Koda at first, something about reaching into yourself and finding the core of one's being, then pushing outwards with that to 'enforce her will' on reality.

Sienna, on the other hand, listened raptly to the directions and began nodding quickly. When she held one hand out over the grassy earth to her side, Koda was astonished to see the earth part abruptly, forming a trench that was as wide as her palm, three inches deep, and maybe a foot long.

"Perfectly done, sweet Sienna!" Arthene cheered, glancing up towards the oncoming cloud of dust. Koda followed her gaze and could make out the distant shapes of people moving several hills over, clearly following the trampled path and moving quickly.

From what he could see in the distance, the people in question were moving up and down rapidly, bouncing rather emphatically. A collection of banners waved overhead, though they were too distant still to see more than the flapping outlines.

While Arthene coached Sienna on what to do next, he did his best to sneak back through the grass to where the other tribal warriors were waiting.

"Netta?" Koda hissed, not wanting to shout in case it carried over the grasslands. The hawk-featured beastfolk melted out of the tall grass on the other side of the road, tilting her head at him curiously, not verbalizing her question, but it was clear in her eyes. "Are they Crooked?"

Understanding dawned in Netta's eyes, and she nodded furiously, holding up her left hand and flashing him three sets of five and one set of three fingers.

Koda swore under his breath.

Eighteen is far too even a fight, and from how fast they are moving, they look like they are mounted. Let's just hope Sienna can cook up something to even the odds, he thought before nodding to Sienna.

"Sienna is going to start this off. We need to make sure none of them get away. Pass it along!"

Netta nodded and shot him a thumbs-up before ducking back into the grass.

"I think most of us heard you, Aegisclaw. You fight like a demon, but you really need to work on your woodcraft," Todd's sardonic voice whispered between the tall grasses right behind him, and Koda smothered the urge to yelp. He turned quickly but couldn't spot the fox beastfolk hunter.

"That's why I have all of you, Todd. Get ready, and make sure everyone knows what the plan is."

"What is going on? You just said Sienna is going to start us off, and I don't know about you, but the numbers have me nervous." This time Todd's voice came from his right, barely audible over the rustling grass, and Koda stomped on the urge to whirl in that direction. He had a feeling the older hunter was messing with him.

"I don't know yet either. I just know Arthene is coaching her. So expect something violent."

"Hmph, got it."

Message delivered, Koda did his best to keep low and behind the tufty grass as he made his way back to his lover and potential future lover.

Still so weird to think of her like that, Koda thought with a smirk. *But Arthene has made her interest known. I have a* feeling that, if we had the time last night, she might have tried to drag both Sienna and me into something more intimate than just snuggling. Gotta love it when a woman is honest and doesn't beat around the bush. Thoughts of bush beating and the lewd comments that Arthene had made in that vein distracted Koda enough that he almost tripped over Sienna.

"Where's Arthene?" Koda asked, lying down next to his wolfish love while she had both hands pressed into the ground.

Sienna didn't respond, but Arthene did. A hand nearly large enough to cover his face poked out of the grass beside him and gently gripped his right hand, before following it up to his shoulder and then down to palm his butt while a muffled giggle emanated from a thick bundle of grass.

"Don't distract your clever mate, Koda." Arthene's voice was equally muffled, but he could hear her. "She is preparing a surprise for the fools charging us. She even gave me a bit of cover, too."

"That's not going to get in the way, is it?" Koda asked, quirking his eyebrow at the thick greenery that was wrapping around the much larger bear woman. Now that he knew where to look, he could see the rough hummock of earth and grass that concealed Arthene, as well as a narrow slit that she could see out of in the front, and the small hole she'd poked to stick her arm through to grope him.

His only answer was another pinch to his butt before Arthene pulled her hand back out of sight.

The Crooked that Koda had encountered so far seemed to take the concept of disturbing to a personal and extreme level. Except for the warleader he'd fought only days before, every single one of their forms was twisted or misshapen in some way. Between extra limbs, hands, or facial features, bent bodies, malformed bones, or gnarled flesh, no single Crooked ever really looked exactly the same. Even their champions and the handful of spellcasters he'd run into had something just not right about them.

It turns out that not only are the individuals twisted but their animals are, too, Koda thought with distaste as the group of cavalry descended the closest hill and began to close with the concealed ambush.

The numbers Netta had given him were accurate. There were three distinct groups of six approaching, riding in irregular clumps. Each group of six had a banner with the familiar symbol of the Crooked flying on it: a bent sword crossed with a twisted pitchfork. The riders were all dressed in better-maintained outfits to what Koda had been used to seeing with the regular foot soldiers of the Crooked. Each wore a tabard of the same mildewed-looking cloth over top of leather armor that was roughly cut before being boiled to harden it and set with metal plates. Two of the groups carried spears, while the last group carried pole-axes as they galloped over the already torn grass towards the road.

But the horses were something else entirely.

Each Crooked he'd encountered, even the odd champions, looked like someone had started with an uncooked human as the basis, then applied radiation until 'done.' The horses that these monsters pretending to be men and women were riding, though, looked like the cooking process had stopped partway through.

The animals moved on four legs, which was already more regular than most of the Crooked he'd encountered, but whether those legs ended in hooves, clawed paws, or human-looking feet varied from animal to animal. Their hides were mottled gray and mud-brown like a sickly appaloosa pattern that left them appearing diseased. The animal's heads were also far too wide for horses, easily being twice as wide as they should be, but they were still the same long, equine shape, bearing mouths full of sharp teeth.

This is going to suck, Koda thought, flexing the mental muscles to 'extend' his claws, causing the gauntlets to form around his arms. *I really need to get some actual armor figured out. Heck, Thera gave me another gauntlet. Maybe she can give me some armor as a reward for the next few sites I claim?*

Before Koda could follow that line of thought any further, the front pair of groups discovered Sienna's surprises while moving far too fast to react.

Three horses on the left group and two on the right abruptly pitched forward with a bandsaw-screech of surprise when one or both of their forelegs found concealed potholes scattered in their way. A sickening storm of cracking noises followed this as the bones gave way under the abrupt pressure caused by suddenly finding themselves trapped in the ground. This was further compounded by the riders just behind them, not being able to react in time and riding right over top of the other horses.

Riders flew through the air, squealing like overstressed septic pumps. The only group that wasn't entangled in the pileup caused by the potholes was the six pole-axe wielders at the back of the group, who could slow in time.

"Come on. Come on, you fuckers. Turn this way," Koda heard Arthene muttering from within her earthy burrow.

As if thinking the same thing, a trio of arrows zipped over Koda's head, picking off two of the spear-wielders who had stayed mounted and were trying to work their mounts free of the chaos and injuring a third. The six still mounted shouted something that Koda couldn't hear over the shrieks of pain from animals and riders, but he saw the leader of the group— so designated because he carried the standard for his squad —pointing in the direction the arrows came.

That group of six spurred their horses into a juddering trot around the pileup as more arrows raced into the fray, picking off riders or knocking them off their mounts wherever possible, ensuring that the chaos continued.

As the six finally got far enough around the chaos to get a straight shot to where Koda knew Todd and part of their group was hiding, Arthene sprung her part of the trap.

The riders had just managed to get up to an appreciable speed when the big woman pushed herself up and out of her prone position, scattering dirt, grass, and stones in all directions. Her mane of messy curls still held sprigs of grass and twigs in it, leaving her looking like some vengeful spirit of the earth. Koda had just a moment to wince again while thinking of the trouble that would come from trying to clean such a mess before the big woman lashed out with her bone club at the nearest of the mounts.

To their credit, the riders didn't hesitate, lowering pole-axes to angle their charge towards Arthene, but they did not take into account the raw power the incarnate spirit possessed.

Arthene's blow came in across her body, from left to right, powered both by the bunching strength in her shoulders and the torque of her hips as she threw her weight behind it. Her target, the mount of the lead rider, had extended its head forward, mouth open wide to take a bite of the woman even as its rider thrust forward with the bent-hafted halberd it carried.

The end of Arthene's club caught the twisted horse in the side of its head, and there was a *crunch-splat* noise that reminded Koda of the sound an egg made when it was thrown against a wall as the horse-monster's head exploded in a shower of gore and bone fragments. The blow continued, snapping out to tag the nose of another of the mounts, shattering that too and sending the animal's head to one side, causing it to twist and fall, throwing its rider like a screaming missile through the air.

Arthene's left hand caught the halberd just below its crude iron head, and with a grunt, she snapped the blade off before twisting her wrist and ramming it into the rider's gut even as she let her blow spin her to the side, allowing the dead body of the horse-monster to plow into the grass at her rear.

All of this happened in a matter of a few heartbeats, and then Koda was locked into his own fight.

Given the much shorter range in his claws, he focused on dodging the longer weapons and landing maiming blows on riders and mounts. Hamstrings and guts were slashed, saddle-straps torn, faces raked, and riders disarmed. He caught sight of Sienna moving through a spinning series of stabs and lunges with her spear, covering Arthene's back and ensuring those the big woman unhorsed stayed down.

The ambush, from start to finish, took less than three minutes. It only took that long because of the twisted pile of bodies that the first two squads had become in the pileup.

Even Arthene didn't want to get close as the injured horse-monsters began taking their rage out on anything near them, whether it be their own rider or another of their kind. It was only after the other threats were taken care of that Koda's team took a few of the long-hafted weapons that survived the crash and began using them to put down the injured they could reach, while the archers made sure to pick off any that still had a weapon or reach to strike back.

"Thera's tits, what a rush!" Arthene barked with a laugh. The big woman looked even more wild, with blood dripping from her claws and the knobby end of her club, as well as speckling her face, and with long grass still poking up in her hair. The thigh-bone club showed not a single scratch from the battle, the only marks being the liquid variety from her many victims.

"I would prefer to avoid that kind of rush for a while, given the choice," Sienna panted, shaking her head and wiping the blood from her spear. "Especially because I hate the damn clean up. What the hell are we going to do with all these corpses?"

Chapter Thirty-Seven

"AYE, THAT WILL CAUSE A PROBLEM." HANS GAVE ONE of the limp bodies of the Crooked a kick before slinging his bloody mattock up to rest on his shoulder. "We can't burn this lot. The smoke will attract the attention of anyone for miles.

"Well, we can't just leave them here! Anything that scavenges from the bodies will get sick and spread that disease even farther," growled Todd, carefully yanking an arrow from one of the dead and inspecting the tip before wiping it clean on the grass and sticking it back into his quiver.

Arthene completely ignored the two men arguing and was instead pulling great tufts of grass from the ground to wipe first her face and then her weapon clean. The dirtied grass was tossed onto the pile of corpses when she finished with it, and then she'd take another handful to try to clean herself.

"You are just making it worse, Arthene," Sienna huffed, her ears laying back in annoyance. "Come here and let me see to what you got on your face."

Either the bear woman didn't notice Sienna's irritation or she didn't give it any weight. She grabbed another handful of grass and went back to scrubbing the bits of blood and viscera from the head of her bone club while walking over and taking a knee so Sienna could reach her face with the wet cloth.

Koda just dragged his claws through the stirred earth to remove the grime from them before mentally 'sheathing' them and allowing the gauntlets to fade away. This left his forearms clean and allowed him to get out a bit of cloth and his waterskin to wipe the blood from his face while he watched as Sienna fussed over the larger woman.

Amusing that Sienna didn't bloody anything besides her blade. She's got just as much range as Arthene does on her weapon. Then again, Arthene was a bit more... emphatic in her strikes. A club is far messier than a spear after all, Koda thought with a wry smirk.

The entertainment he felt faded and was replaced by a clenching sensation in his gut, and he grimaced.

Am I a monster for finding that amusing rather than horrifying? I've killed... so many things in the last few days. And in rather gruesome ways, too. How can I be okay with it?

A hand in his hair drew Koda out of his introspection, and he looked up to meet the sparkling blue-green orbs of Sienna as she bent close, her forehead wrinkling cutely while her pointed wolf ears twitched. She'd snuck up on him while he'd stared at the ground and been lost in the memories of the battles. Now, he was drowning in the delicate pools of her eyes, and they were a far more welcoming place to lose himself.

"You don't need to fear, future-mate." Arthene's rumbling words came from just behind Sienna.

Koda couldn't look away from Sienna as the oceans of her eyes had him firmly in her grasp, but he could see the large form of his newest partner as she crouched behind Sienna. A pair of thick arms reached around both of them, and they were dragged into Arthene's large bosom, with Sienna letting out an *eep* of surprise and turning away to glare up at Arthene, and thus setting him free of those crystalline pools.

"Why would he be afraid?" Sienna asked before Koda could find his voice. This might have been because Arthene's arm had dragged him headfirst into her cleavage, and while he could hear, he wasn't able to talk around the mouthful of boob.

"Our mate is from a place far away from this. He has been thrust into something that you have had your entire life to come to terms with, and he worries about losing himself," Arthene explained, her normally booming voice a bare whisper while she spoke just for their ears as she loosened her grip on the two. "He forgets at times that he isn't alone. Give him a kiss, sweet Sienna? I would do it, but our mate's heart isn't open to me yet, though it's getting there."

Since he was no longer drowning in Sienna's gaze and could move his head now, Koda looked up at the wild-haired woman to find Arthene smiling affectionately down at him, approval showing in her eyes. Her primal beauty struck him, so similar to Sienna, yet so very different from his wolfish lover. The arm around his shoulders squeezed him gently and then a hand took his chin.

Koda didn't fight Sienna's grip as she turned him to face her, and as such, he was rewarded with the sweet sensation of her soft lips on his. His left arm automatically went around Sienna's waist. His right tried to do the same but instead snaked around Arthene's hips as the big woman still held the two of them close.

That rising panic over his theoretical lost humanity had begun to fade when Sienna had first gotten his attention. The hug from Arthene had lowered it further, and then the kiss from Sienna had stuffed that fear down into a dark place, locked the door, and sashayed off with the key. The gentle brush of something soft against the underside of both his arms reminded him that the two women he was holding were anything but human, but Koda found that he didn't care.

I love Sienna. That's all that matters there. And Arthene is slowly but surely pounding down any reservations I have about her joining us, too. The thought chased itself around the inside of Koda's skull, and again, he found not a single dreg of fear at the thought. He knew, deep in his heart, that he could trust Sienna, and he was coming to trust Arthene as well.

> *It's not like the fact I've only known her for a day or so is anything telling. I fell fast and hard for Sienna, and I find myself doing the same for Arthene. If Thera changed me somehow to make this happen, I suppose I should be happy. Far better to open my heart to love than fill it with fear and anger.*

"There he is," Arthene murmured into his hair, the big woman having been alternating between nuzzling the tops of his and Sienna's heads. "Our mate is back to himself again. Good job, sweet Sienna."

"Of course, Arthene. My mate needed me," Sienna said with conviction when their lips parted, a shy smile on her lips.

"Love you. Thank you. Both of you," Koda said quietly, squeezing both of their waists with an arm each.

Sienna hummed happily and nuzzled into his neck, while Arthene let out a low, happy growl and buried her face into Koda's hair again.

The three of them shared an affectionate embrace for another minute or two before duty called them back to reality. There was still a great deal left to do, even with the day drawing to a close, and they still had to deal with the bodies of their enemies.

"Did anyone get injured?" Koda asked once he'd peeled himself free of the two women.

"No, thank the Pack Lady for that," sighed Hannah, the cat beastfolk looking up from the saddlebag she was rifling through. "These riders weren't equipped for a long patrol. I think they were either intended to reinforce the raiding group up in the vale or to head towards Amberpost."

"What tells you that?"

"No tents or camping gear. They'd have had to sleep under their cloaks for shelter. And no cooking gear, just dried rations. Even then, they didn't have much of those." Hannah wiped her hands on the grass and stood. "Any idea of what we are going to do with the bodies? You seem to have a knack for coming up with ideas outside the normal line of thinking."

"Why not have Sienna bury them?" Again, it was Arthene who interjected a suggestion, having collected her bone club after releasing her hold on Koda and Sienna and then coming over to stand behind the pair. For someone her size, she could move with unnerving silence.

"That will taint the ground, or so I'm told." Koda sighed, leaning his head back to look up at the taller woman behind him. Out of the corner of his eye, he saw Todd nodding in agreement with this.

"That's easy enough to fix," Arthene said offhandedly, and Koda blinked in confusion.

"It is?"

"Yup."

"You aren't going to just tell me, are you?" Koda quirked an eyebrow up at her, and Arthene's smirk deepened into a broad smile. But she didn't speak.

Sighing, he turned fully to look up at the large woman and crossed his arms over his chest for a moment before speaking in a tone of faux reverence that was even stranger given his irreverent posture.

"Oh mighty Arthene, Den Mother. Arthene the Wrathful. Please bestow upon this supplicant your infinite wisdom so that he may implement it and see wrongs righted and salvation delivered to the needy."

Koda could tell that many of the tribal warriors were staring at him in a mixture of surprise and horror as he stared up at the incarnate spirit who had literally turned a monster's torso into paste with a single swing less than an hour ago.

The two of them exchanged bland stares for several long seconds before Arthene smirked and rolled her eyes.

"You really need to work on the sucking up, though I suppose you might have other skills that balance it out. I'd have to ask Sienna about that, wouldn't I?" Arthene bobbed her eyebrows suggestively, and Koda snorted. "It's simple, Aegisclaw. You just have to bless the land where they are

440

buried. That will prevent the taint from spreading and allow the land to reclaim them."

Koda blinked up at her, his annoyance fading into surprise. He opened his mouth to ask how he would go about blessing the land when the knowledge flooded into his mind, and he grimaced.

"Of course, more bleeding for me. Yay..."

"You'll be fine, future-mate. It will only require a bit to water the earth and lay the runes. Then that will handle the problem," Arthene encouraged, stepping close to ruffle Koda's hair gently.

"Fine. Let's get the bodies piled together and collect anything that we can use. Sienna? You think you can bury them all?"

The thoughtful nod from his wolfish mate was enough for Koda, and he squared his shoulders to begin the gruesome work.

Chapter Thirty-Eight

It was actually harder for Koda to sanctify the area than it was for Sienna to open the earth up.

She did it slowly, keeping careful watch over the hole as it widened and then deepened, taking the dead down into the embrace of the earth before sealing the hole up once more. Another gesture sent the grass surging over the small mound.

It took her only a couple of minutes to do, and Arthene proudly proclaimed that Sienna's speed with earth magic would only increase with time and practice. The bear beast-folk didn't need to elaborate on the idea that they all expected more combat in the days to come, which would naturally lead to more opportunities for Sienna to practice, especially under duress.

For Koda, though, the process was decidedly easy but far less pleasant. Much like when he sanctified the building for the headwoman, it required him to bleed at certain spots around the circle. The bleeding wasn't hard, given the sharpness of his totemic gauntlet's claws. It was the actual act of cutting himself that was the problem, coupled with the fact that everyone was watching.

It also wasn't as simple as just dripping blood, either. Koda had to draw the same claw symbol he'd used on the meeting house on several rocks before making a series of gestures. Which was made more difficult by the spectators and their fascinated gazes.

When he finished with the little ritual, Koda felt energy rush out of him in a torrent like he was a balloon with a large hole in it.

Swaying on his feet, Koda fought to keep upright as his vision swam for a moment before stabilizing. Arthene and Sienna both reached out to steady him until he got his balance back. Before Koda could thank either of them, a thick blue-gray mist blasted upward from the ground.

The fog blew outwards, shredding in the wind and the sunlight before it made it more than a foot off the ground, but it took a good ten seconds before the billow abated, and then Koda could see through it to the ground once more.

"There you go, all done," Arthene said with a grin, slapping Koda on the back firmly. "Blessed ground has cleansed the taint, and now the earth will see some use of their bodies. You did good work, future-mate. If it was up to me, I'd reward you for it tonight."

"Lucky bastard..." Koda heard Hans mutter from behind them.

"How? It's not like he doesn't earn it?" Hannah replied, also in a whisper that was just loud enough to be heard.

"I'd do just about anything to earn a shot at a woman like that," Hans hissed back. Koda heard a quiet snicker from Arthene and knew that the big woman could hear the byplay between the two. "Hey, Arthene. I have an honest question for you."

"What is it, Hans? Before you ask: no, I'm quite happy with Koda here. Anticipation is its own spice, after all," Arthene replied, turning with a grin to the bull beastfolk.

"Not what I wanted to ask. I know better than to try to get between Aegisclaw and something." Hans was smiling as he stepped closer. "To be honest, I was wondering if you had any sisters? Not meaning this as any sort of insult to Sienna, but a woman like you is something that any man would offer the moon to have a chance at. So if there was even a small opportunity—"

Arthene cut him off with a raised hand, the smile on her face softening the denial as she spoke.

"Yes, I do have sisters. But no, none of them are available currently. Last I heard, each of them has their eye on someone already."

She finished the statement by shooting Koda a look that sent a thrill down his spine.

That is going to be trouble... Koda thought before glancing towards Sienna, only to see his wolfish mate grinning as well, her fluffy red-black tail whipping back and forth happily. *Hard to be worried about it, though. I'll just have to take things as they come.*

With the problem of the bodies resolved, the group trooped along the beaten track the Crooked had made until Netta signaled for them to step off it. The hawk-featured beastfolk then led them roughly half a mile farther into the hills until stopping near a small ravine that was heavily overgrown. So much so that Koda would have likely ignored it as just a small washout or gully if he'd been hiking, but Netta pointed out a pattern in the earth made by stones set into the turf that she said marked the location as the correct one.

"The tribes that wander the plain move between several camps over the course of the year with their hunters, chasing the different herds that live out here. They may have the bulk of their tribe living in remote areas for most of the year, but the hunters know the best places to camp or pursue game." The explanation she gave reminded Koda of some of his history classes that talked about how the different plains tribes of Native Americans would follow herds across the great flatlands that made up most of the United States back home.

Kind of wish I'd paid more attention in those history classes, but then again, they never really talked much about how *things were done. Just that they happened. Makes me wish I'd gotten into the boy scouts growing up.* Koda shook off his introspection as Netta led the way down into the gully, pushing past the thick patches of sage that blocked vision by using her bow to bend the stems back.

The gully itself wasn't horribly deep—maybe ten or fifteen feet at the bottom. The narrow path they followed down was one of three ways into the little gully, and the brush that covered the edges of the low cliff walls helped block it from sight. In the middle of one wall, a natural spring bubbled up from the stone to form a pool that was only about five feet across but very deep before it flowed across the tiny valley and vanished into another break in the stone, returning to the earth after it divided the space in half. The ground was a mixture of plush grass and gravel near the waterway, making it relatively easy to cross and would ensure that setting camp here was easy enough.

"I would never have thought to look in here. Hell, my kind of luck I'd have tried to push through the thick brush and *fallen in!*" Arthene laughed as she strode across the clearing to stare down into the pool of water. She bent low, sniffing the air above the water as the other hunters entered the clearing, a gesture that made sure more than a few of the males amongst them stopped and stared as the brief leather kilt that the big woman was wearing rode up to expose more of her muscled thighs without crossing the line of decency.

"Arthene!" Sienna had spotted the group of staring eyes and hurried over to the woman as she continued to bend over further. Koda silently thanked Sienna before turning to the others with a stern look on his face in an effort to make it appear like he hadn't also been staring.

"Well, this will make a suitable spot to camp, but we will need to set a rotating watch on one of the hills above just in case the Crooked are sending out another of those mounted groups."

Todd nodded, his pinched face thoughtful as he considered who would be best to assign for such a job. Hans was just grinning, though, and gave Koda an exaggerated wink paired with what passed for a subtle thumbs-up from the bull man. Koda grinned back at him. He'd only known Hans for a short time in comparison to Sienna, but the horned man was rapidly becoming someone who Koda felt he could trust.

"Two-person watches should do it. We can rotate a few folks through. I'm just glad that it's normally pretty warm out here; otherwise, the watchers would freeze sitting out in the wind tonight," Todd said as the rest of their group threaded through the narrow pass and began to spread out and inspect the clearing.

Nodding in agreement, Koda rolled his head on his shoulders and began loosening the straps on his pack.

"Well, let's get settled in and get comfy. It's getting late enough it would be better to camp here than possibly stumble onto the Crooked camp in the night. And I know everyone is tired after the fight."

That statement got a round of agreement from the other fighters, and they quickly made the secluded little valley into a comfortable camp. Bedrolls were laid out, but tents remained stowed as they wanted to be able to move quickly if they needed to. A small fire was built using the driest of wood they could find in the small clumps of bushes along with the supply that they had brought with them from up in the hills.

Koda hadn't thought about it when loading up, but all the hunters who had worked the plains before on hunting trips knew to bring their own firewood with them as wood was very scarce out in the waving expanses of grass unless one kept to the handful of rivers that crossed the great plains.

Arthene and Sienna finished their inspection of the spring, with Arthene declaring that it was a site of power, purely from the fact that the spring welled up from *very* deep within the earth. It brought the blessings of the land up for those who walked the surface, and its water carried a very faint hint of power that even a normal person could make use of.

"It likely feeds into one of the rivers farther out in the plains by traveling through the ground or another underground channel. For now, though, this is a safe place to drink from and wash—as long as you do that last part farther down the stream. But you should wait to claim it, my future-mate," Arthene counseled as she gave her report while everyone ate the communal stew that had been thrown together on the one fire they had laid. The dry wood put out very little smoke, so everyone sat around it to enjoy the warmth and relax after the long day of hiking down out of the mountains and the scramble of the fight.

"Why wait?" Hannah asked, her thin feline tail flicking behind her in curiosity as she picked through her bowl of stew with a two-tined fork. "I would think that you'd want him to do it immediately, so that more power could return to our Lady?"

Arthene didn't answer immediately, upending her bowl of stew to get the last of it before setting the dish to one side. One large hand caught Sienna, who had just gotten her bowl of food and was looking for a spot to sit near the big woman. Arthene tugged Sienna to sit on the ground and lean back into her chest.

"Here, sweet Sienna. You can lean on me to eat," Arthene said, the amusement thick in her tone as she pulled Sienna into position between her legs. The wolf beastfolk let out a rather cute little yelp of surprise before twisting to glare petulantly up at Arthene.

"You could have just asked, you know?"

"I could have," Arthene replied, her grin growing wider before wrapping one arm around Sienna's waist to secure her there. "But you might have said no. This way avoids that, and I get to enjoy having someone cuddled up with me." Sienna looked like she wanted to protest at first until Arthene bent to whisper something into one of the pointed ears protruding from Sienna's hair that made her relax and nod.

"I could never get away with that." Hans sighed, stirring his spoon through the bowl of stew he had. The horned man sat on the other side of the fire, his mattock leaning against his thigh so it was close at hand if he needed it. "I'm sure I'd get smacked if I did."

"Depends on who you try it on, Hans," Arthene said, looking up from where she was carefully smoothing her fingers through Sienna's short red-black curls like she was combing them while leaning back on her other arm. Since Sienna wasn't trying to escape, she'd unwrapped the arm around the wolf-woman's waist. "If you have a lady that you like already, and she likes you back? She might appreciate a bit more assertive approach. If you were to try something like that on Netta? I think she might stab you."

"No might about it," Netta replied airily. "Anyone who grabs me without warning can expect to get stabbed first and questioned later."

"Back to what I was asking, though?" Hannah huffed, her small, black, cat ears flicking in annoyance. "Why wait? I remember the Lady saying that power flowed into her from these places. It's why we took the time to come here."

"While my future-mate is powerful and nearly inex-haustible, he did spend quite a bit of his spiritual energy sanctifying the Crooked we slew before. He could probably claim this spring with its deep roots, but he'd likely pass right out afterwards. And I would prefer he not be entirely limp when we settle in for bed." Arthene's innuendo was thick enough to cut with a knife and made Hannah blush. Koda just rolled his eyes though and collected Arthene's bowl from the ground.

"I appreciate it as well," Koda said as he walked the dinner plates along with his own empty dishes over to the stream to wash them. "I'd rather be awake because I'm not sure I could trust either of you not to get up to some mischief in the night."

"You can always trust me to get up to mischief, especially in the night." Arthene's grin was wide and confident, and she patted the ground next to her. "Come sit by me, future-mate. You are welcome to use me as a pillow as well."

"If it wasn't for her size, I'd say you might have to fight Sienna for that right," Netta hedged, leaning forward to peer at her friend. "It looks like she fell asleep with her food half-eaten."

"Then let her sleep. I know we all need rest," Koda said as he returned from the stream and tucked their bowls into his pack.

He glanced back towards Arthene, who patted the ground next to her left hip assertively with another smirk. A thought crossed Koda's mind, and he decided to run with it. Arthene sat near the cliff wall, but there was enough space behind her that someone could squeeze past if they needed.

She did say that some women like an assertive approach. I swore I wouldn't be one of those idiots, Koda thought to himself and gripped his confidence tightly.

A glance confirmed Sienna was asleep, so he gently took her bowl and set it to one side before grabbing a blanket from the bedrolls he had already laid out.

"That was thoughtful of you," Arthene murmured, the lewd grin on her face shifting to a simply affectionate one as she continued to smooth Sienna's hair. "Our sweet Sienna pushed herself hard today, working that magic for you. It is good to see you look after her as well."

"Of course," Koda said simply. When Arthene tried to hook him with her free hand to pull him down next to her, he slipped away from her grasp and ignored her pout. Instead, he slid behind her and settled down at her back.

"What are you doing?" Arthene asked in confusion as Koda

pulled her back into his chest, in a larger mirror of Sienna tucked into her front.

"Looking after my mates, both current and future," Koda said simply, and he began smoothing his fingers through Arthene's thick mass of curls, gently tugging out the bits of grass stuck in it and helping sort the wild mass out some.

Arthene looked like she wanted to protest at first, but when he started mirroring her actions with Sienna totally, she leaned into him with a happy sigh.

I imagine for someone her size, it's not often she gets to be the little spoon, Koda thought with a grin. He caught a flash of movement over Arthene's shoulder and looked up to see both Hans and Netta now shooting him thumbs-up and grins, while Hannah and a few of the other hunters watched on in amusement.

Chapter Thirty-Nine

THE NIGHT SLIPPED BY WITHOUT A PROBLEM. KODA ended up pinned beneath the sleeping Arthene and Sienna for the entire night, a smirking Todd telling him that the three of them were excused from watch duty. Koda was also pretty sure that the grinning fox-man just didn't want to deal with trying to wake up Arthene, as the big woman was clearly sleeping soundly, and no one wanted to be the one to startle her awake.

Having a woman sleeping against him wasn't something that Koda was going to complain about, though, and Arthene's mess of hair was warm enough that it served the purpose of a blanket as well. He had just drifted off, holding her while she held Sienna as he watched the thousands of twinkling points of distant stars far above them.

When the sky began to shift from the dark purple of the deep night into the lightening blue, the camp stirring was quick to wake Koda again.

At least parts of him.

While serving as a pillow for Arthene had been pleasant and warm for the night, as soon as Koda moved, he discovered the flaw to that plan.

Every one of his limbs had fallen asleep, so pins and needles raced up and down his body like the marching of thousands of ants. And as Arthene was taking her sweet time to wake up, Koda was left to just sit and wait as the big woman mumbled and rubbed at her eyes while still holding Sienna to her chest like she was some kind of stuffed animal.

The wolf woman in question wasn't much better, having apparently slept very hard and was now struggling to wake up. It wasn't until Arthene began to sleepily play with one of Sienna's ears that the smaller woman woke with a start.

"Koda?" The worry in Sienna's voice faded when he grunted her name from behind Arthene. He could only see the tips of those ears over the shoulder of the larger woman leaning on him, so when Sienna peeked over Arthene's shoulder to stare at him, it was a rather adorable sight. "Arthene, you need to budge up so he can move. Koda, are you okay? Did you sleep like that?"

"Yes, and also yes," Koda grunted. "And I was comfortable until I actually woke up and tried to move."

Sienna's confused expression melted into one of concern and understanding as she realized what he meant. From there, Sienna was quick to herd Arthene off him and set to rubbing his numb limbs—something that Arthene was happy to join in once she realized it was an excuse to fondle Koda.

"Lucky bastard," Hans laughed as he bent to blow into the fire to re-light it and get the morning meal cooked while the sun continued to slowly lighten the sky.

"I remind myself that every time I see them," Koda shot back at the bull man, doing his best to not smirk when Arthene's smile grew even brighter.

Every move he made that indicated he was accepting the spirit woman's affections and place beside him seemed to further endear him to her. And her honest happiness at even the smallest of affections made Koda want to lavish more and more on Arthene. The fact that Sienna was also joining in on making the other woman feel welcome was doing wonders for calming his concerns about jealousy and the like.

Breakfast was a hearty oat mash studded with bits of dried meat that had been re-hydrated during cooking. Koda found himself wishing for something as simple as eggs, but carrying that kind of foodstuff with them while hiking was just asking for trouble.

Small things that you miss, right? he thought in amusement while sandwiched between the two women vying for his affection. Arthene sat to his left, this time taking up the position of backrest and insisting he lean back into her while he ate. Sienna was tucked into his side while she ate, too. *I need to figure out other things I can do to make sure these two never question my affection. Thera, you better know what you are doing by sticking me with Arthene as a mate. I'm going to be very upset if this causes any problems with Sienna. Both women deserve devotion, and I don't want either to ever lack.*

A brief pulse of warmth from within him made Koda think that the goddess might have heard him, the soothing feeling that followed further reinforcing that thought.

Reassured, he focused on his breakfast and what they hoped to achieve today.

While the others packed up camp, Koda set to work sanctifying the site of power and claiming the spring for Thera. Since there wasn't already an altar here—he'd carefully checked to make sure before starting as he didn't want to piss off any natives that had claimed the area for their gods— he could claim the location with just a few drops of blood.

The pulse of power released was simultaneously calmer and more ferocious at the same time. The pulse was calmer in that it didn't try to knock Koda off his feet and onto his ass as it passed by. In fact, it barely stirred the grasses or the surface of the spring in its passing. But a point deep within the spring, where the water bubbled forth from the stone, began to glow. It was faint at first, a dim green-brown light that looked like a glowing dot seen at a great distance. That dot grew in size rapidly until the pulse of energy rocketed out of the fissure and slammed into Koda.

Claiming the spring had taken some energy from him— something Koda hadn't honestly noticed all that much before as he'd always been tired in the wake of a fight. But when that pulse of energy hit him, Koda felt like he'd just touched a live wire. A wire that was trying to pour its energy into him, but the power itself was incompatible. That lack of compatibility was hurting him.

"Send it to Thera, Koda!" Arthene barked. "Grasp it with your totem and send it to her. There was far more here than we expected!"

Koda did as Arthene directed, snapping up his gauntlet-clad right hand to block the stream of energy that was burning into his chest. The second the gauntlet contacted the river of light, the burning stopped, and Koda saw the chips of polished stone worked into the gauntlet begin to glitter and glow from within as they accepted the river of power.

Distantly, he heard the screech of a hawk in flight and a woman's excited yelp that he imagined was Thera getting the surge of energy.

Energy... She said Arthene hadn't waited long enough to finish recovering. Is there a way to split this? Koda thought, and the knowledge came to him immediately, the sound of Thera's voice filling his ears as she spoke within his mind like she stood right behind him.

Hold your other gauntlet out to her and will it to be so. My daughter will need the strength in the days to come to protect her mates, so I do not begrudge her a share of this unexpected bounty. I could use this power to strengthen you more, but returning her to full strength will do that as well.

The fact that splitting the energy like this would lessen some of his own power didn't even bother him. Koda would rather empower both women with him to ensure they were as strong as possible, so he didn't hesitate.

Doing as Thera directed, Koda allowed the left gauntlet to form as his claws unsheathed themselves from the spiritual place he stored the weapons. Arthene was standing close to him on his left. She watched raptly as his gauntlets consumed the bolt of energy. So he simply laid the palm of his left hand over her muscled stomach and willed the energy to divide.

A burning pain raced across his chest like a raw sunburn forming in seconds, and Koda saw a ribbon of light surge out of the rear of his right gauntlet, spiraling up his arm and across his chest before sinking into the left. That same green-brown light erupted from the palm of his left hand and sunk immediately into Arthene's belly. The bear woman grunted in surprise, her expressive yellow eyes flashing from a bright sunflower color into burnished gold as she accepted the power into herself.

Koda caught this shift as he glanced over to check on her, and he also caught the faint silhouette of an absolutely massive bear forming around Arthene, towering well over the large woman. The claw-studded paws looked oddly familiar to him as well, but between having to focus on redirecting the pulse of energy and the pain that it crossing his skin was causing, Koda couldn't think straight.

As suddenly as the bolt of energy had emerged from within the wellspring, it faded out once more. The burning sensation across his skin also faded away into just a faint tingling, though the memory remained.

"That was unexpected," Koda muttered, shaking out both his arms and staring down into the gently rippling water of the spring. "I wonder if that was because it's been undisturbed for so long?"

The answer to his question was not forthcoming as Koda's moment of introspection was abruptly interrupted by being snatched off his feet by Arthene and yanked back into another hug that would have seen him buried headfirst in her ample cleavage if he'd been facing that way.

"Thank you, my mate!" Arthene crowed happily. "That was so thoughtful of you to share that with me! Because of that, I am even stronger now! Our foes will stand absolutely *no* chance against us in the days to come!"

"You... are... welcome... Arthene," Koda grunted out as the affectionate woman shook him back and forth in her enthusiasm. The vigor of her thanks was making it hard to focus, and when she spun in a circle with joy, it got even worse.

As they turned, Koda caught sight of the stares from the other hunters and the amused smirk on Sienna's face as she finished packing up their unused bedrolls. The wolf-eared woman was the only one not stunned into staring.

"I will be sure to show you proper appreciation soon for how thoughtful that was, my mate," Arthene crooned, continuing through another half-spin before setting him back on his feet. "I can show off for you now as well. Any hesitation or concerns I had about dealing with this portal are now far distant from us."

"What was that?" The numb question came from Netta, who was blinking owlishly at the two of them, her mouth hanging open and her pack dangling from one hand as she had been about to strap it on.

"Nothing!" Arthene crowed, her excitement still riding high. "I was sent here to help my mate excel, and he has further enhanced that ability now with his kindness in sharing this blessing. Come! We should be on our way. I need to burn off some of the energy here so that I don't break my mate's hips later when I thank him properly."

Arthene had set him down and immediately bounded over to scoop her club off the ground before storming towards the path that led back up and out of the ravine camp. Most of the other hunters continued to stare at her as she left, but Hans and Netta were both looking at Koda now. Hans was grinning and giving him an encouraging wink, while Netta looked slightly concerned for him.

"Well then, looks like you have a date to keep with our mighty one, my Koda. Shall we?" Sienna's droll statement shook the others out of their staring, and everyone scrambled to get moving and catch up with Arthene before she got too far away.

Koda couldn't help but think about how Arthene had switched so readily from calling him her 'future mate' to just 'mate' now.

I guess that means she's done waiting? Or maybe that she's sure of it now?

Chapter Forty

Chasing after Arthene wasn't nearly as hard as Koda had expected. The large bear woman didn't rush, but she was inexorable. It only took about ten minutes for the others, along with Koda and Sienna, to catch up with her and form up around the larger woman.

Arthene led the way back towards the track the previous army of Crooked had left behind and then turned to head deeper into the flatlands without hesitation.

Along the way, the hunters checked the trail to discern if another group had passed in the night. Those who had been stuck with watch duty had said that they had observed no passing groups, but they would rather be sure as the night had been dark with the moon less than full. Like this, hours passed as they persistently followed the trail back for several hours as the sun climbed towards the midpoint in the sky.

"I'm just saying, I don't like that we have been singled out and get to avoid having to stand watch," Koda was saying to Sienna while he eyed Todd. The fox beastfolk was about fifty feet ahead of the group, hurrying up a rise in the ground while scanning the disturbed plant life at his feet.

"It's not that we are being singled out," Sienna said gently from her spot at his side. While Arthene was stomping ever forward, muttering to herself under her breath while still maintaining a manic and focused smile on her face, Sienna stayed right there at his side. "Everyone acknowledges that you and Arthene are the fulcrum that our success in this will sway on."

"You are right there, too," Koda grumbled, and Sienna spared him an indulgent smile, the noonday sun glinting off her red-black hair.

"Yes, but *I* did not bring down a Crooked warleader in single combat, Champion Aegisclaw. And anyone who looks at her can tell that Arthene is far more than she appears, and I mean that beyond how good her bottom looks in those leathers."

Sienna's tone drew his gaze, and he caught her blushing again while glancing towards Arthene's bottom as it bounced while the bear woman mounted the hillside at a steady march just ahead of them. Koda considered her words and shrugged. He couldn't really deny Sienna's statement. Arthene was attractive, and he had absolutely zero reason to argue that idea.

"Fair, but I don't understand how that translates to not sitting watch," Koda sighed. "I don't want to be seen as being better than everyone else or more important."

"But you are, my idiot mate." Sienna tore her gaze away from Arthene's rather distracting derrière and instead turned her smile towards him. "You represent the sole contact our people have with our goddess, with our progenitor. Someone that we all view as a loving parent and one who gave everything they had to protect our people in an impossible situation. A mantle that you seem determined to take up yourself as well to protect our people. I can only hope that our children will follow tightly in your footsteps."

Sienna's mention of children made Koda stumble, and she giggled at the look he shot her. It was obvious she was going to tease him some more, but a hiss of warning and sudden movement ahead of the group drew both of their attention like a lightning rod draws electricity.

By the time they both turned in that direction, Todd was already on the ground, waving one hand behind himself to urge the others down. Arthene was crouched and hurrying up to the fox man's side, her club held out low to her right.

The rest of the clan warriors pulled in close, and they all crept to the crest of the hill to see what it was that Todd had spotted.

When Koda and Sienna, leading the group, arrived beside the other two, Koda heard Todd talking in a low whisper to Arthene.

"Just over the crest of the hill is a low valley like the one we camped in. Someone has cleared the brush away from the whole thing. I caught sight of a stone ring projecting up into the air that was glowing, and there is nothing I know of in the plains that does that naturally."

"Then it is just as well you did not hesitate to take cover." The excitement was thick in Arthene's voice, and Koda could see her hand clenching and unclenching on the haft of her bone club. "This is likely their camp, and what you spotted is most obviously their portal."

"Are you sure, Arthene?" Sienna whispered as she crawled up between Koda and her, the pointed ears on top of her head flicking slightly. "Not that I am doubting you, mind."

"No, questioning is good. It's how cubs learn after all." Arthene turned a glowing smile on the smaller woman, and Sienna blushed, clearly happy with the praise. Though, from how her tail was only flicking slightly, he guessed she wasn't sure how to react to the reminder of just how ancient Arthene was.

Timeless is a better expression, Koda thought as he eyed the wild-haired bear woman. *She may have seen centuries pass by like we would watch a cloud cross the sky, but they don't seem to weigh on her. I have a feeling that the only thing that has changed over the centuries is that she's gotten better about not getting caught when up to mischief.*

As if drawn by his thoughts, Arthene's eyes lifted to meet his, and those gleaming yellow orbs twinkled with amusement and a hint of what he was beginning to think was arousal as well.

Shaking himself to push those thoughts away for now, Koda turned and crawled towards the top of the hill, mirroring Todd as the other man parted some of the tall plants and peered through to study what lay beyond.

The rolling hills covered in grass had been relatively ubiquitous for the last day. The only thing that would change throughout their travel was the shape of the hills and what type of grass or plains bush grew on them. They'd passed over two dry streambeds as well, where short trees clustered along the banks, but other than the one oasis they had passed by, Koda had seen no water at all.

Below him was another of the narrow valleys, just like Todd had described to them, but this one had a different feel to it. While the one they had camped in felt like it had been gradually washed out by the movement of the spring, this had the oblong look of an old lakebed that had long since dried up, with the sloped bank being a lot gentler than the cliffs at their previous campsite.

All the brush and familiar grass that had clad the hills was gone from the area, cut back or just pounded flat by the passage of feet. A shanty town of tents had sprung up on one side of the large cleared space, with the same disjointed organization that he had observed of other Crooked camps.

Unlike those other camps, though, Koda could see that the Crooked were actually patrolling around the perimeter in a somewhat-regular fashion. There was also a rough paddock made of gnarled wood and hairy ropes that held a half-dozen of the bizarre horses they had encountered the previous day, and three more were being ridden in a long and lazy patrol around the cleared space that the camp occupied.

"I count three of the larger tents," muttered Todd, and Koda nodded in agreement.

The tents he had come to associate with the presence of champions were clumped toward the inside of the camp, where the bizarre stone structure rose from the blasted soil.

The stone structure that Arthene had labeled as the Crooked's portal looked like someone had tried to build a stone doorway, but they had someone with only one eye and a severe case of the shakes do it without any measuring tools. The two posts were of different heights, which set the crudely carved lintel at an angle. Struts of wood and long bars of steel had been hammered or wound into place to support the entire rickety construction.

"That whole thing looks like it's just one good shove from being knocked over," Koda muttered.

"Looks are deceiving, my mate."

Arthene's statement from right beside his right ear made him jump, but that just resulted in him pressing up into her chest as the big woman had somehow managed to sneak up on him and now nearly lay on top of him.

"Elaborate?" Koda asked, doing his best to not growl out the statement while he worked to get his pounding heart to calm once more.

"Look between the posts." Arthene's warm breath tickled his ear, and the wild scent of the big woman enveloped him with the smell of sun-warmed fruit and the aroma of clean sweat that he was rapidly beginning to associate with her. "The portal that is active within them helps to support the entire structure."

Koda did as he was directed by Arthene. As the interior of the door sat at an angle to him, he had to squint, so it only revealed a sliver of what lay between the two upright posts. It took a moment for him to make it out, but the air between the two had a faint shimmer, and it showed a scene of barren rock on the far side where grass and hills should lie instead.

"So, how do we interrupt it? Can Sienna upset the foundation with her magic?" The question got a huff of amusement from Arthene, and he heard her take a breath in to answer him when something stirred near the portal.

They both paused, watching as a disjointed figure walked into sight wearing a long and flapping garment about it and began waving its hands over its head. A moment later, the portal flared with a sickly brown-blue light, like water tainted with a swirl of fresh mud, and tiny figures began to issue forth from the portal.

"Ah, they are bringing more troops through," Arthene growled as she settled down half on top of him and half on the ground, having inserted herself between Koda and

Sienna. The wolf-eared woman gave up space without complaining, gazing at the growing crowd around the portal as more and more troops issued forth.

Koda wanted to protest having Arthene on top of him, but the soft sensation of her breasts pressing into the back of his neck was actually grounding him and helping prevent the panic that he knew would be welling up as the enemy numbers continued to swell.

"The question is, are they heading for the village or to Amberpost?" Netta asked from his other side, and Koda grunted in agreement that he wanted to know, too.

Thankfully, the answer was revealed only minutes later when the swarm of foot troops formed up into a messy mob and began marching towards the far side of the camp. Koda scanned quickly and spotted the other beaten trail that angled away toward the distant threads of smoke they had seen before.

"Okay, if Amberpost is still holding, we need to prevent reinforcements from getting to them, but we need to shut that portal down so we don't have even more reinforcements coming."

Koda's firm statement got a growl of agreement from the others. A growl that rattled his very bones as Arthene joined in because of her pressing into him. A growl that he realized a moment later he was echoing as well, the anger that had faded back into his subconscious over the last few days flaring up higher in his mind as they prepared to lay waste to their enemies.

Chapter Forty-One

"THIS IS GOING TO BE DIFFICULT." THE FIRST WORDS TO counter the plan actually came from Sienna, of all people. But they weren't an outright denial, instead highlighting a potential problem, and that was something Koda could appreciate and work with.

"We never thought that it would be easy. We've got plenty of potential now. Just need to make sure we hit them from an unexpected angle," Koda countered as the group huddled up.

They'd watched as the newly arrived force hurried out into the grasslands and vanished from sight. Then the tribe's warriors had pulled back to plan while Netta remained on watch to ensure that the Crooked in the camp didn't somehow wise up to what was coming for them.

"I'm still not sure how we, with fifteen fighters, will overcome a group that is easily five or six times that." Hans had a determined scowl on his face despite the concerns he voiced, and Koda reached over to pat the bull man on one thick shoulder reassuringly.

"Realistically, we've been overcoming numerical issues every time we encounter the Crooked. I'm just glad they don't have more of those cavalry. I did not fancy having to deal with more of those again. Especially since not all of us have the pleasure of reach."

"Sounds like a personal problem," Hannah huffed playfully, her feline tail flicking in amusement behind her as she fingered her bowstring.

"Never said it wasn't, but I have my ways. Something we are going to need for the future is to figure out something for the rest of our fighters. Hans, I know you and your fellow miners were willing to help before, but you don't have military training, do you?"

"No, it's why I use my mattock in a fight. I know how to wield it with precision from digging out seams of ore, and enough power can make up the difference. I wouldn't mind learning to defend myself since things are getting rather rough around our little village. But I'm not light enough on my feet to really learn from the hunters. I plan to see if the men who spent time in the baron's army will train me later."

Koda nodded in understanding before looking over the rest of the group.

"Hans' point is right on the money. We've gotten by with luck and surprise, which has given us the experience we need to get by for now. But training will need to be something we consider. I'm not willing to lose any of you to something a little sweat would have protected you from. Even you hunters. I want you to start practicing with something in a closer range than just your bows."

"Spears are a straightforward choice, and we have enough of them," Sienna interjected when Koda paused. "It's easy enough to pick up the basics as well. I'm sure the blacksmith will forge some other options as well if we can give him time."

"Do you really think that we are going to need it?" This time the question came from Todd, but several others echoed it with nods and questioning looks.

"I don't want it to be"—Koda sighed—"but since I've come here, I've spent more time chasing Crooked and planning fights than I have spent sleeping. And not once have we had any kind of assistance from the people who collect taxes to actually look after you. Yes, I am expecting trouble to continue, and I have the sneaking suspicion that we are going to have to fend for ourselves rather than actually get the support you are due."

He let that sink in, watching the grimaces and resigned nods from the others. It was clear that they understood his point of view on this. It would be far better to be prepared than not, and if all being prepared cost was some extra work and a few more blisters, then it would be done.

"Now, back to the plan. I know you said that Amberpost had guards and could hold out, but that was easily another sixty or more troops headed their way." Koda didn't need to continue the statement as Hannah was already answering the question.

"No matter how good they are, the town guard for Amberpost is probably less than a hundred people. They'll have armor and proper weapons, unless their town council has been playing fast and loose with their funds. I remember the headwoman grumbling about how we were to report major issues to the Amberpost guard, back when they stripped our garrison, and how she was just thankful we'd never had a problem."

"Okay, so we need to try to head that group off, if possible. It took us a good day's travel to get here from the road, but we were slowed with that fight and looking for the spring. How long do you think we have?" Koda let his gaze pass over the other fighters, who considered the question.

"I think we have around two days," Todd answered, finishing his mental calculations first. "They are heading out at midday, which means they'll need to camp. Also, they are going overland and at an angle. Which means they won't be able to march quickly, not with their numbers."

"And do you think we'll be able to catch up to them?"

"Definitely." Arthene's decisive statement pulled attention to her.

The big woman had settled onto her knees to keep under cover and had been inspecting her bone club while listening to the conversation going back and forth between them all. The fight the previous day had left faint stains in the carved lines that Arthene had been tracing onto the head of her club, but the pattern to them was still unrecognizable.

Even now, Arthene was running the clawed tips of her fingers through those grooves, scraping them slightly deeper with each pass, though the faint stains remained to outline the carvings. Koda wanted to ask about them, but now was not the time for such curiosity. While he was stuffing that question into the back of his mind, Arthene elaborated more on why she was so confident.

"I doubt it will take us more than an hour to handle the camp. We should give them a few hours to get distance, to minimize the chance they come back this way to try to help if they notice. Then we hit them hard. We can have Sienna lay some more traps and then drag them into a killing zone before wiping them out."

Confused expressions were exchanged as the other fighters parsed what she had just said, but it was Sienna who broached the big question.

"What about the portal?"

"Oh, that is easy. You, Koda, and I will take care of it and as many of their champions as we can before dragging the rest of their fighters into the trap."

The eyes of the other fighters had bounced from Arthene to Sienna when she spoke, then back to Arthene in her answer. Now they dropped onto Koda, and he could feel the physical weight of their questioning gazes, demanding to know what it was that made Arthene so sure of her plan.

As Koda had no idea what the big woman's plan was, he started working backwards from the end state to try to figure it out.

"Sienna, if you are up to it, then traps would be good. Maybe some hides for our fighters to ambush from. I'd like to get them as they are coming up the other side of the hill. That will give us the height advantage. Maybe some low walls disguised as part of the hilltop to slow or stop a charge, and loosening the soil to send them sliding back down the hill? That'll give the archers somewhere to fire from as well."

"But the portal?" Sienna insisted, looking between Koda and Arthene. "If I do that much, I don't know if I can bring down the portal. Working with soil and plant life is easy enough so far, but rock fights me a lot harder. Part of what exhausted me so much yesterday was having to shift and shape the rocks to bring that many bodies under the earth."

"Oh, the portal I can deal with. I just need you two along with me in case something goes wrong." Arthene's smirk was widening even more as she climbed to her feet and planted the knobby head of her bone club into the ground. "Plus, I need one of you to carry this thing for me."

"Why would we need to do that?" Sienna asked, her forehead wrinkling in confusion.

"Because. I want to show off for you two. For you, sweet Sienna, so that you know you can trust our mate's safety to me. And for Koda to thank him for being so generous to me earlier. I promised you I would show you why your selfless choice was a good one."

Arthene didn't give them a chance to ask about the how and why again. Her bright yellow eyes flashed, and the wind that had been stirring her mountain of curly brown hair picked up. That cape of hair began to flap and sway faster and faster as Arthene leaned forward, hunching her shoulders as she did so.

The pose was intimidating enough to begin with, but when Arthene smiled, it revealed lengthening teeth that came to sharp points.

And all of that was before Arthene began to grow in size.

Chapter Forty-Two

"If you drop me, I am revoking my approval to you joining the family, Arthene!" Sienna's voice was high and thready with fear as she clung to Koda's back tightly.

"Oh, it's not that bad," Koda laughed, craning his neck to look over his shoulder at his wolfish mate.

Sienna twisted just enough to glare up at him, her eyes glittering with a mixture of anger and fear through the wind-blown mess that her short red-black hair had become. Both sharp points of her wolfish ears were laid back tight to her skull, and the arm she had around his waist was like a band of iron, clutching tightly to him.

"You shut your mouth, Koda Aegisclaw! Or you are sleeping on the *porch* when we get back to the village!"

Her response drew another laugh from Koda, but he turned back to focus on what lay ahead of them.

"All right, Arthene. Time to show off some!"

The response from the bear woman was a deep, earth-shattering bellow as her lumbering trot broke into a charge. The motion sent both him and Sienna bouncing on her broad back, drawing another squeal of fear out of Sienna, and she buried her face in his back once more.

Roughly half an hour ago, the three of them had circled around to come at the enemy camp from the far side. Their intent was to charge through, cause as much chaos and damage as possible, and then lead the way into the trap that Sienna had spent the last two hours preparing. They had learned that, as long as she took things slow, it was a lot easier for the newly minted mage to make changes to the environment.

Koda ran his mind over the dugouts and hides that Sienna had created in the hills, as well as the various pit traps and their locations to make sure he remembered them all as Arthene's charge led them up and over the hilltop and down into the camp.

Whooping at the top of his lungs, Koda waved the length of Arthene's bone club over his head as the trio drew eyes from all over the camp. To be fair, though, those eyes were all dragged to Arthene specifically, rather than to him and Sienna. But he couldn't fault the Crooked for that.

It was not often you saw a prehistoric titan descend with the fury of a rock slide.

When Arthene had started to change in front of their very eyes, Koda had been surprised and then excited as he realized their odds of success had increased vastly. The others with him had sworn in surprise, and more than a few had readied weapons until a reassuring hand had stopped them.

Arthene had taken on her full bear form, and just like her beastfolk form, she was mighty.

Another bellow tore out of the massive dire bear that Koda

and Sienna perched on as she lumbered into that rolling, ungainly run that bears were capable of.

Arthene plowed directly into the row of ramshackle tents, sending canvas, wood, metal, and bodies flying as she simply pounded over top of them like they were nothing more than a pile of leaves.

Koda had been initially concerned with this plan, just charging through the enemy, given how he'd used a headlong charge to bring down a larger foe before. But Arthene had told him it would be fine as it would take more than a base stick to pierce her hide like this.

Hahaha! Yes, petty Crooked! Wrath and ruin has come for you! Arthene's voice echoed in Koda's mind, a little bit of madness seeping into her normally deep, rich tone, but Koda couldn't really fault her. He was laughing too from his perch nearly eight feet off the ground.

Koda had decided that calling something a 'dire' breed of animal had been diluted in modern media. It didn't really give full gravitas to the sheer *size* of the creature in question when confronted with a real member of the species, and that was something he was still trying to grasp in relation to Arthene.

She'd stood handily over six feet tall when in her beastfolk form, but now the tall perch that Koda and Sienna sat upon was even higher than that. It felt like he was riding an elephant covered in coarse brown fur into battle, and nothing could stop the over twenty-foot-long hurricane of claws, teeth, and pounding paws as it charged.

The echoes of Arthene's bellow began to fall away, and Koda could only hear ringing in his ears now as a result. Ringing and distant screams of fear and anger.

A paw the size of a car door slammed down on top of one Crooked warrior who lunged forward with a spear. The weapon struck the pad of the paw and shattered without penetrating before the blow smashed the Crooked flat onto the ground.

Koda swung down with the bone club he was carrying, the weapon somewhat awkward to use, but like his claws, he felt something guiding him in the motion. His blow clipped the head of another Crooked who had been lifting a bent greatsword over its head to strike down at Arthene's side and caved in the monster's skull.

"Sienna! Come on, you can do this, trust in Arthene!" Koda called as he let the weight of the heavy club carry it forward and then up over his head before bringing it down on the opposite side onto another of the lumbering Crooked who was attempting to defend the camp.

He felt more than heard Sienna growling in annoyance, but she released the death grip around his waist now that Arthene had slowed from her bouncing charge into a lumbering rampage, and she began using her spear to strike at anyone within range.

My mates, it looks like the cavalry are trying to mount up. Do we push for the portal or deal with them? Arthene's voice in both of their heads was deepening in the bloodlust, but again, Koda did not fear her. The love that he heard in her words when she said 'mates' reassured him that Arthene had a firm grip on herself right now.

"Yes, stop them!" Koda called, and Arthene responded immediately.

Turning, Arthene swept one big paw in front of her to clear the way before lumbering into a jog that plowed through anything in its path with the same level of cheerful irreverence that Koda imagined a bulldozer would have when confronted with a town made of balsa wood.

Ahead of him, Koda could see a small swarm of the Crooked working to corral the vicious mounts that they preferred. The twisted horse-like abominations were not making their jobs easy though, biting or slashing at the Crooked who dared enter their pens.

"Sienna!" Koda called. He didn't have to say more as his beautiful wolfish mate thrust forward with her spear towards the corral. The already churned earth inside the rough barrier immediately bubbled and turned to a thick soup that sucked at feet. The Crooked within the corral suddenly could not dodge as easily, and the vicious mounts fell on them with gleeful enthusiasm, tearing off great hunks of their supposed allies and devouring them.

A bellow of anger—Koda could barely bring himself to call such a noise a true bellow after hearing Arthene roar—came from their right, and he turned to spot one of the Crooked champions emerging from a nearby circular tent.

The creature was distorted like its fellows, but unlike the previous champions he'd run into, this one was more or less properly proportioned except for its right arm being easily twice as large as his left and clutching a massive hammer made of gnarled and pitted iron.

Let him come! Arthene sang in his mind, not deviating from her pointed charge towards the paddock. *He won't reach us before I get there. Sweet Sienna, firm up the ground when I arrive. I don't want to get stuck and throw you two off.*

"That's the plan!" Sienna shrieked, snatching hold of the back of Koda's jacket when Arthene's lumbering nearly bounced her free as she stomped down on several Crooked who were trying to swarm the bear's left side as one.

Just before they arrived, Sienna reversed the gesture with her spear, and the ground inside the paddock abruptly solidified.

The Crooked who had been trying to escape the mounts squealed in surprise when they were suddenly locked calf-deep in packed earth.

Meanwhile, the horse-monsters shrilled even louder as the sudden change caught several by surprise, and their shifting weights on suddenly stuck feet broke legs with gruesome crackling noises.

Arthene slammed her way through the rough wall of the paddock and rolled right over top of the entire group without a care in the world. Koda's ride became briefly rougher as she did so, and he slung one arm around his back to help secure Sienna. And then they were past the group.

The scent of blood, death, and the innate *wrongness* of the Crooked was filling his lungs, and Koda shook his head like he could shake away the smell as Arthene began to curve back towards the portal.

The champion with the hammer was now most of the way to them, and Koda could see the frothing madness in the monster's eyes as he squared up directly in front of Arthene.

The hammer came up before arcing down towards Arthene's head like a comet as her charge carried her into range.

The comet was not fast enough.

Sienna, who had been focusing on her magic this whole time, had seen the champion prepare to strike out at the woman, who was rapidly becoming a friend to both her and her mate. Koda had only a brief moment to wish he'd had a bit more range when Sienna acted for him.

Her spear was already in flight as the hammer came up, and as it started to come down, that broad, iron blade slammed home into the champion's chest just below its throat. The blow held so much force that it knocked the champion backwards and sent his hammer spiraling away in another direction.

A wild bout of laughter crackled through Koda's mind as Arthene made her approval known. She hadn't even tried to avoid the champion's blow, and Koda wasn't sure if that was because she'd trusted them to handle it or if she wasn't really worried. Her head was so large that she would have made some dinosaurs jealous of her bite radius, and Koda had no idea how strong her skull was. He was just grateful they wouldn't have to find out.

Leaning over as they plowed past the dead, Koda snatched the shaft of Sienna's spear and yanked it free. The wolf woman was quick to reclaim her weapon from him and resume fighting as the Crooked of the camp all let out yells of fury and scrambled headlong after them.

That looks like it has whipped them up. Good! Now to the portal and then our trap!

Arthene suited actions to her mental words and charged through the camp once more. It was only a bare hundred feet to the ramshackle structure that held the portal. Koda could see the spindly, robe-wearing figure of a Crooked spellcaster standing near the portal, hands waving as he did something.

"Nope! Now it's my turn. Arthene, deal with the portal. Sienna, help her. I'll deal with that one!" Koda snapped as they neared.

Arthene grunted, and Sienna growled—sounds that he assumed meant they agreed with him because neither protested when he threw himself off the back of the charging dire bear and into a roll.

Koda had already donned his gauntlets, the leather and bone constructs flowing into place as soon as Arthene charged down the hill earlier. As he had in the past, Koda felt instincts welling up from deep within his psyche to guide his motions.

Coming up and out of the roll less than ten feet from the spellcaster, Koda had the bone club in his right hand while his left dug into the ground, and he bounded forward. Again, he spared only half a moment to think about how such a leap was more canine than humanoid in motion, but somehow, it felt natural to him.

A bolt of lightning the color of mucus snaked over his head, striking at where he would have been if he had moved like a human should. Rather than ozone, Koda could smell a sulfurous stink of bad eggs instead. He heard a gurgling shriek behind him and couldn't help the smirk when he realized the sorcerer had instead struck one of its fellow Crooked.

Koda hit the ground at the end of his first leap with three out of four limbs, propelling himself even faster and to one side as he lashed out with the bone club at knee height.

The Crooked was not fast enough to evade or even do more than stumble slightly before the blow caught it across both legs. The result was both gruesome and comical as the creature pitched forward with a shriek of pain, legs literally folding over the weapon though they bent the wrong way, and it slammed headfirst into the ground.

Not hesitating, Koda let the weight of the club spin him around in place, slamming the knobby head of his borrowed weapon into the cowled skull of the Crooked spellcaster before it could do more than flop about on the ground. The crunch that followed was all that Koda needed to know that his attack was successful.

Turning, he raced after Arthene, who was nearly upon the stone portal structure now.

From behind and on the ground, Koda felt the comparison to an elephant was even more apt for Arthene. She was absolutely enormous, and she showed the sheer power of that much mass moving with determination a moment later when she reached the portal.

From a distance, the portal had looked bizarre in its construction. Up close, it was even stranger. The stones that made up either post had rough shapes, hewn by hand into crude prisms that balanced a third stone lintel overhead. The twisted timbers and rough metal stakes helped prop the whole thing up, making it look like something a third grader might build in their parent's garden with whatever they could get their hands on, though the obscene runes carved into the stone and wood were something that only could have come from a nightmare.

That nightmare image was furthered by exactly what lay beyond the portal. Blasted stone, twisted trees, and another, larger, camp of Crooked that Koda could see was stirring as more enemies raced about.

Distantly, he saw what he had first mistaken for a hill the color of a fish's belly shudder and begin to rise as it turned towards the portal as forces rallied to try to cross over and defend the camp.

Despite the shoddy construction, though, the portal weathered Arthene's charge with surprising strength. The massive bear barreled into the shortest of the two posts, cracking wood and bending the metal supports as she shoulder-tackled the stone. The pillar refused to budge at first, but the nearly foot-long claws on Arthene's paw scored deeply into the stone as she snarled and lashed out at it, disrupting several of the runes.

Sienna still perched on Arthene's back, and as Koda watched, the taller of the two stones shifted slightly. Because the Crooked had set the whole thing on the bare earth, he could see that Sienna was driving the dirt away beneath the massive stone, revealing its shallowly buried base. This caused the entire structure to lurch as the massive weight of the stone joined Arthene in attempting to upset the entire construction.

The rippling magic that existed between the two stones flickered, revealing a brief glimpse of the plains on the far side before snapping back into place. The lumbering, grotesque creature was closer now, and Koda spotted several of the Crooked champions charging towards the portal on distended limbs.

"You got this, girls!" Koda called as he finally caught up to them. "Push!"

Rather than climbing up to safety on Arthene's back, Koda ducked between her paws and planted his shoulder into the stone, right between the large, raking marks her massive claws had left. This allowed him to add his own goddess-enhanced strength to their attempts to upset the rock construction.

A moment later, a shriek of discordant noise and a shockwave of discharged energy slammed into Koda, and abruptly, the resistance to his strength faded away as they sent the rock careening backwards to slam into the bare earth.

Glancing to one side, he took in all that he needed to know in a moment. The portal was closed, the other stones falling to the earth. Before he could speak, Arthene's jaws settled around him, and she picked him up with the delicacy of a mother cat collecting her young before tossing him up over her shoulder to land on her broad back.

Hold on! Now we need to get back to the ambush! The laughter in Arthene's mental voice gave him new strength, and Koda scrambled over her broad back to settle in behind Sienna as their 'mount' rumbled into a run, the screeching horde of Crooked in close pursuit.

Actually luring the Crooked into the ambush was surprisingly easy.

Koda had observed in the past that bringing down a champion usually had one of two effects on the regular foot soldiers. Either it demoralized them to the point they would all scatter or it enraged them to suicidal levels. It was impossible to tell which it would be until the act was completed, though.

Thankfully, the reaction to the champion going down, as well as the sorcerer, had been the rage one, and the Crooked blindly pursued them across the intervening plains into the section they had prepared. As soon as they were far enough along and enemies began falling into the concealed pits,

Arthene wheeled about, and their allies struck from concealment.

The sole remaining champion had been extorting her soldiers to revenge, to capture the enemies so they could be twisted in punishment for shutting their route home down. Hannah's arrow in her throat silenced the four-legged woman, but it was Hans' mattock to her skull that ended the creature's life as it continued to fight even with the arrow in its neck.

Using the concealed strong points to attack from, the hunters sent arrow after arrow into the enemy ranks, while the handful of those with only melee weapons joined the line that Arthene, Koda, and Sienna made to lock down the enemy's charge.

It was a brutal and bloody fight, but it only took them around ten minutes of frantic fighting to bring down the last of the enemy. It took another hour to bandage injuries, sort through the dead, end those who still clung to life, and tip the whole lot into the pit traps.

From there, Sienna and Koda repeated their actions from the previous day and sealed the dead Crooked away beneath consecrated earth. The billows of gray smoke signaling the purging of the corruption from the bodies came regularly and quickly enough that no one lost their focus since they still made people jump in surprise.

Koda was just grateful that they'd manage to escape the entire encounter with only injuries this time. The deaths from the previous battle up on the mountain still haunted him. He knew deep down that they wouldn't always be able to get everyone through fights, but he resolved again to not spend lives callously.

Returning to the camp, they discovered it was entirely empty of living. Only the hammered remains of the dead and the detritus of the camp remained behind.

At Arthene's suggestion, they dragged the mauled remains of those who had been killed during their rampage through the camp to the paddock and then used that as one last mass grave. The tents, equipment, and everything else they would leave behind for now.

No one complained about leaving that all behind. Those with energy rifled through a few tents for valuables, with the three tents that had held the champions being the only ones with anything of value worth taking as one had a chest full of tarnished coins.

Koda made sure that anything written was collected, and after confirming none of it would be useful, he burned the lot of it in one of the Crooked campfires. When asked about why he was so insistent on that, he admitted that the books bound in human skin were giving him the creeps, and he didn't believe anything valuable would be inside.

With that done, the group gave the now-deserted camp one last look over. Arthene had reverted back to her regular form to help with the sifting of valuables and moving of bodies, and the bear woman was the only one of the group who seemed to be unaffected by post-battle exhaustion.

"We should get moving. If we can get a few hours of travel before we camp, then it'll be easier to catch up with the other group before they reach Amberpost." Todd's statement made sense, and everyone agreed with it, but it was also not something that anyone wanted to acknowledge at the moment, either.

Arthene, though, had something that would help.

"I saw something as we were circling the camp. There is a river that runs in that direction. If we move quickly, everyone can get a wash in before we camp. I don't know about you lot, but I would prefer to get the blood of the Crooked off me again."

That got everyone moving in quick order, and the big woman led the way out of the camp, following the trail that angled towards Amberpost rather than the one they had come in on.

Her promises proved true in mere minutes when they crested one of the low hills that surrounded the former Crooked camp and spotted a winding ribbon maybe a mile distant over the plains.

The pounded trail the Crooked left behind wove towards it before angling sharply away towards the distant tendrils of smoke that marked where they knew Amberpost was.

"Okay folks," Koda called as they hurried down the slope. "Keep your eyes open for any signs of the Crooked and wash quickly. We can't spend *too* long dipping our toes, but it'll help refresh so we can cover as much ground as possible. We've eliminated the big—and final—threat to the village. Now we need to help our neighbors handle their problems so it doesn't become *our* problem."

"I dunno about 'dipping toes,' Aegisclaw," Hans called from where he walked to Koda's right. "More than just my delicate feet need washing. Right now, I'm swimming in ball sou—"

An elbow to the gut cut the bull man off, coming from one of the other miners who had taken up arms, but everyone laughed at his coarse words, even the women in the group.

"Dip whatever you want in the stream, but we can't take too long is what I'm meaning." Koda did his best to sound stern, but when a large arm wrapped around him from behind and hauled him backwards and off the ground to pin him to a well-muscled side, he learned how hard it was to maintain dignity while one dangled.

"You all can take as long as you like. *I* know that I have plans for Aegisclaw that will take at least an hour now that I've burned off some of that... enthusiasm from earlier. Sweet Sienna?" Arthene rumbled, grinning down at her trapped prize where Koda was pinned to her side, his feet barely brushing the ground as she continued to march resolutely towards the river.

"As long as you don't go breaking any hips," giggled the wolf woman, her eyes dancing in amusement as well.

"Oh, I plan to be thanking you, too, my dear." Arthene's blunt statement and waggling eyebrows dismissed the amusement from Sienna's face and replaced it with a fierce blush. "And yes, of course you have a say in this, my mate," Arthene said, directing a grin down at Koda now, her yellow eyes flaring with arousal. "But are you honestly going to tell me no?"

Koda sighed, feigning disappointment before letting that fall away too and smirking up at Arthene. This blunt and earnest woman had made her goals clear from the moment they had met, and he realized that he loved her for that and more.

"Fine, you got me there. Arthene Deepclaw, you've managed to bludgeon your way into my heart. Hopefully, you are gentler in bed."

The smile that she gave him was even more excited now, and Arthene's stride grew as she hurried ahead of the group, a laughing Sienna following after her.

As far as new lives go? This isn't so bad, Koda thought with a grin as his current mate, and the one who would shortly become one, hurried ahead of their laughing warband to find a secluded spot by the river.

"Don't take too long, you three! We still have ground to cover!" shouted Netta teasingly. The laughter that followed her words relieving after the tense battle they had just completed, and the one they all knew was to come.

Chapter 43

<3 <3 <3

ARTHENE DIDN'T RELEASE KODA UNTIL THE THREE OF them made it to the wide river and into a secluded set of trees that would shelter them from view. Even then, she only set him on the ground long enough to undo the clasps that held her top and skirt together, dropping both to the ground before turning to start working at Koda's clothes.

"Easy there, my mate," Koda said, catching Arthene's large hands as they started yanking at his pants like she intended to simply tear his belt off.

Slowing her attack on his clothes, Arthene's large yellow eyes snapped up to his, and a small smile crossed her lips.

"Call me that again?" she asked, her voice deep and husky with desire.

"My. Mate," Koda enunciated both words without looking away, and he saw a shiver of desire flash through the large woman. She broke their staring contest a moment later, letting her eyes fall closed as she straightened, taking a slow breath in like she was savoring the words.

Koda seized the moment to study Arthene's bare body. She'd slept naked beside him multiple times, not being shy about her charms or desires. That openness had endeared her to Koda, and he couldn't help but return it as he appreciated the large woman's body.

Arthene was powerful. That much was obvious from the firm muscles that covered her body, but that strength did not conceal her femininity, either. Her curves were full, with a generous bust large enough that Koda had already gotten lost in it once. Hard pink nipples capped those luscious mounds, standing tall and demanding attention that he would be happy to give.

Thick thighs sprouted from a muscled bottom, and Koda couldn't help but wonder if this world had watermelons or something similar. Seeing Arthene crush one with her thighs would be arousing as hell. He couldn't wait to see those legs shake as he gave Arthene what they both wanted. And at the junction of those thighs was the thick mess of curls that decorated her womanhood, without blocking it from view, just as wild as the rest of the fierce woman in front of him. Koda swore he could see the tip of her clitoris peeking out of her sweet pussy. He desperately wanted to step forward and begin to devour the feast set in front of him, just as he had Sienna only a few nights before.

The fact that Sienna was as interested in the other woman as he was made the lust that had been burning in Koda's chest ever since Arthene had made her proposal easier to simply accept and go with.

Thinking of his wolfish lover, Koda came back from his moment of appreciation of Arthene's lush body to realize that Sienna had also seized the opportunity of distraction as his belt came loose, falling to his feet and taking his underwear with them to leave him exposed to the air.

"She's gorgeous, isn't she, my mate?" Sienna breathed in Koda's ear as she pressed into his back, her arms wrapping around him to begin tugging his shirt up and over his head while her own full bust rubbed over his back.

"You both are," Koda said automatically, not taking his eyes off Arthene but leaning over to nuzzle into the side of Sienna's face, where it rested on his shoulder.

Arthene didn't open her eyes, but her smile grew wider, and she stretched her arms over her head, arching her back to press her full breasts out in his direction. A shift and a wiggle sent the soft mounds bouncing only inches from his face. Seeing no reason to resist, Koda leaned forward, intent on wrapping his lips around one of those hard nipples so close to him when Arthene turned away.

The motion nearly clubbed Koda in the face with the breast he was targeting, but it missed him by inches. Instead, the close passage of bare flesh wafted the scent of Arthene over him again: warm summer berries laying out in the sun—a scent so close to fresh pie that it made his mouth water. A condition that became real as Arthene completed her turn and presented her backside to him.

Another wiggle and shake sent the full hemispheres of her muscled ass jiggling tantalizingly, while the fluffy stub of her tail bounced excitedly from its spot just above them.

Her mane of wild hair obscured most of her muscled back, but Arthene pulled the mass over one shoulder to bare herself to him, and Koda was treated to the sight of her broad, powerful back, full bottom, muscled thighs, and the delicious curve of her full breasts as they ballooned out to either side of her torso, too large to remain hidden by her body. And tucked between those sweet thighs was her delicate slit, lips swollen and wet with desire.

493

"Do you want me, Aegisclaw?" Arthene's voice was a low rumble filled with lust and the promise of carnal delight that sent a thrill up his spine. "To take someone who is nigh on a goddess in her own right? To mate with a being who has seen the passage of centuries? To please a creature from an entirely different realm of existence? To mark one such as I with your scent, your touch, and your seed?"

Koda didn't answer verbally as Sienna finished pulling his shirt off with a quiet whimper of desire all her own. Instead, he stepped forward and wrapped his arms around Arthene from behind, cupping her full breasts with both hands as he ground his cock into her ass.

Arthene moaned, a deep and guttural sound of desire as he pressed into her. The large woman ground her ass into his crotch as she leaned back to lay her head on his shoulder. While Arthene was taller than him by several inches, she didn't tower over him to where it made things awkward. In fact, her increased height made some things even easier, actually.

After savoring the feeling of her muscled ass cheeks clenching at the underside of his cock for a moment, Koda pulled back to let it fall down between her thighs and then thrust forward once more. With their differences in height, it allowed the top of his shaft to brush up against her soaking wet lower lips, pulling another loud moan from the large woman.

"Is this what you want?" Arthene asked, her hands coming up to lay over his and press his fingers into her bounteous curves. "To just rut with me here in the middle of a clearing? Where the world could be watching?"

"You are a wild creature, Arthene. One with the world and nature, so why shouldn't the world see it?" Koda growled in her ear, sending another shiver through the big woman while he slowly pumped his hips, stroking his shaft against her vagina.

Out of the corner of his eye, Koda caught sight of Sienna scampering around the two of them, naked as the day she was born and grinning while her tail whipped up a storm.

"I think it's only fair, Koda," Sienna breathed as she came to a stop in front of Arthene, her wide blue-green eyes taking in the sight of them both while her hands caressed up her tummy to cup her own breasts. "You claimed me beneath an open sky. Why not make it a tradition?"

"All creatures should run free beneath the open sky," Koda murmured into Arthene's ear, nipping at her neck lightly while mirroring the promise that Thera had made to him when he first came here.

A full-body shudder ran through the big woman, and she moaned low in her throat. The wet heat of her sex pressed to his cock got even wetter, and Arthene's thick thighs clenched tight on him, but the lubricant she'd been leaking made her thighs too slick to prevent the slow thrusting.

"Yes..." Arthene hissed, her eyes narrowing to slits as she studied Sienna's form as well. "Join us, sweet Sienna? You will always be welcome in my bed when our mate is with me."

Sienna needed no further urging, stepping forward to press herself to Arthene's front. The height of the two was such that Arthene's full tits rested on top of Sienna's when they pressed close like this, which meant that Sienna was ideally positioned to caress them while Arthene returned the favor.

Since Sienna had the big woman's chest handled, Koda allowed his right hand to slip up Arthene's front to settle over her thick neck. Something on an instinctual level told him that this was right, and from the rapid inhalation from

Arthene as he gripped her neck lightly, and the fluttering of her pussy lips against the top of his cock, she approved.

"If you join us, Arthene, there is no going back," Koda growled in her ear, squeezing gently with the hand on her neck. Arthene let out a happy mewling noise, turning slightly to press her lips against the side of his face. "You will be family and belong to us just as we will belong to you. Do not betray the family."

"Never." Arthene's fervent answer got a possessive growl from Koda, and he used the grip on her neck and his thumb on her cheek to direct her so that their lips met in a kiss. Koda's blood thundered in his ears as he held this mighty woman in his arms, pinned between himself and his mate. He wanted Arthene, on a level so deep that it was spiritual.

And nothing stands in the way of you taking her. Accepting her. She will belong to you as surely as Sienna does, and she will never betray either of you, a voice said deep within his psyche. He wasn't sure if it was Thera speaking to him or the protective instincts that had surged up in defense of Sienna days before. But he *knew* on a spiritual level that it was right.

Sienna clearly wanted to join in, too. Leaning forward, she dropped kiss after kiss on Arthene's neck just below where Koda's hand gripped it, whimpering quietly as she pressed herself into the bigger woman, and Koda could feel the rhythmic grinding of her hips as Sienna ground herself onto Arthene's thigh.

Arthene finally pulled back, her eyes hooded with lust as they shared one last stare while he squeezed her throat gently before releasing it and turning towards Sienna. It was all the cue that the excited wolf girl needed, and she lunged forward, bodily crawling up Arthene to steal Koda's lips in a kiss.

"Oh, you are going to be trouble, sweet Sienna," Arthene laughed while steadying the other woman with hands on her hips. "So much trouble, but worth it, I'm sure."

Rather than answer verbally, Sienna released Koda's lips with a loud *pop* before turning to claim Arthene's in a kiss with equal vehemence. The bear woman gave a brief laugh in the kiss that transferred into a moan as Sienna's hand dove between her thighs. Koda joined her in that groan when the wolf beastfolk's fingertips stroked over the soaked head of his cock as well as the folds of Arthene's sex.

"Let's get you officially added to the family, mighty Arthene," Sienna murmured with a giggle, her ears flicking excitedly after they ended their kiss. "You suitably impressed both of us, and you've earned a good pounding from our mate."

"Oh, has she now?" Koda said teasingly. "And what does my mate plan to do while I'm administering her reward?"

Sienna's bright blue-green eyes twinkled with a mixture of arousal and lust as she held one hand up, her fingers wet with Arthene's arousal, and licked her fingertips lightly before she responded.

"Why, I plan to help. After all, she did impress both of us. And I know my mate will save some for me."

With that statement, Sienna slid down from her spot, half-climbing Arthene's front. She only paused in her trip downwards to lay a kiss on top of each of Arthene's fat nipples, making the big woman coo happily at the stimulation before Sienna's knees hit the ground between Arthene's thighs.

"Sweet Sienna, you don't need— Oooh!" Arthene moaned, shuddering in Koda's arms and leaning back into him.

Koda felt rather than saw what was going on as Sienna's tongue lashed over the head of his cock and then up over Arthene's slit. A moment later, he felt gentle fingers take him and adjust the angle of his grinding until he caught in Arthene's steaming sex and sank into her in one long thrust.

Both he and Arthene groaned in pleasure as he drove up into her hot, wet sex. Koda shifted slightly to give himself the best angle while his hands returned to Arthene's breasts, cupping those jiggling mounds firmly while he began to thrust up into her, the wet clapping of their coupling slowly rising in volume in the clearing.

Sienna bent to her task with gusto. Koda could tell from how broad licks crossed his balls and up his shaft before continuing on to make Arthene moan and squeal. The big woman did her best to remain upright, but it only took a handful of seconds before her legs and body were trembling with the effort.

"Lean on me, Arthene," Sienna said, pausing in her licking for only a moment before diving in after Arthene's clit once more and making the big woman yelp at the sensation.

A bit of shuffling followed, and soon Arthene was hunching forward, leaning forward slightly to rest her arms on Sienna's shoulders to steady herself while Koda shifted his grip to the big woman's hips and began to pound her more firmly from below.

"Oh... gods..." Arthene gasped. The sweaty clapping of Koda's hips into her full bottom was echoed a moment later from her large breasts slapping together as the impact traveled up her body. "I am going... to owe... you both for this!"

A squeal of pleasure heralded a sudden rush of warm wetness as Arthene came hard on Koda's cock, bathing his crotch and Sienna's face in her juices as the big woman came undone.

Koda didn't slow down, even though Arthene's body tightening rhythmically on him did its absolute best to hold him in place. He could feel the orgasm rising in his body, his balls tightening in response to the stimulation as even more shudders racked Arthene's form. This was further aided by the delicate lapping touch of Sienna's tongue as she nuzzled into their sexes and lathered her love on them as well.

"Do it, Koda," Sienna panted from below them, her voice muffled. "Come in her. Fill Arthene with your seed and claim her as your mate. You deserve a mate as powerful as this and more!"

"Yes..." Arthene hissed again, her head rolling on her neck to look back over her shoulder. "Claim me, my mate. And know that there will be more, so much more."

Koda stared down at the sweat-streaked face, the yellow eyes, and the thick, bouncing mane of brown curls. For a brief moment, he imagined those eyes shimmering to a bright silver and her curls darkening to a pitch black before Arthene's features firmly reasserted themselves.

His climax surged, and Koda came, bellowing as he slammed his cock into Arthene and came hard, filling her with his seed as if he was trying to fill her very soul with it. Arthene let out another loud moan that ratcheted up into an orgasmic yelp when Sienna latched onto her clit again with her lips while the wolf-woman's fingers stroked Koda's shaft and balls gently, coaxing them to pour as much of himself into Arthene as possible.

That climax continued for the better part of a minute or more, with the continued stimulation from Sienna serving to prolong it for them both. When Koda's body finally had nothing more left to give, he was allowed to descend from that place of pleasure so strong it verged on pain.

Prying his fingers free of Arthene's hips, it surprised Koda to not see bruises left behind. He moaned again when he pulled free of Arthene, only to have his cock caught by Sienna's lips and rapidly cleaned before the wolf-eared woman did the same for Arthene, moaning happily as she did so.

"Oh, sweet Sienna. That... I will be repaying you for that and more," Arthene moaned, still clinging to the smaller woman as she swayed.

Koda watched the two of them together with a grin for a moment while his own legs steadied. When he was confident of his balance, he wrapped himself around Arthene from behind and gently guided her down to lay on her back on the floor of the clearing.

Arthene sprawled onto the soft grass with a sigh of exhaustion, but Koda saw that there was still a twinkle of arousal in her eyes. Arthene was finished, but only for the moment.

"Why don't you repay her now? Sienna, on top. It's your turn for the two of us to look after you," Koda suggested.

Sienna, who hadn't stopped bathing Arthene's lower lips in licks yet, glanced up in surprise with wide eyes.

"Yes, bring that beautiful bottom and your fluffy tail over here, Sienna. Come, let me return that affection while our mate recovers... well, it looks like he's already ready for you," Arthene said the last part with a laugh as Koda got to his knees over her head, his still-hard shaft bouncing in front of the big woman's face.

Sienna's astonished look transformed into a lusty one, and she scrambled into place, settling her sex over Arthene's lips while Koda gripped her hip with one hand and her fluffy tail with the other.

As his two mates settled together like this, Koda was treated to another vision of a different beastfolk woman on her knees in front of him. Again with hair the color of midnight, with faint spots in it and eyes of twinkling silver.

A blink of his eyes and Koda was again greeted by the entwined bodies of his two lovers as the vision of Thera vanished like smoke in the wind.

What was that? Koda thought, but before he could delve into the vision more, a soft set of lips kissed the underside of his shaft.

"Give it to your mate, Koda. I want to see our sweet Sienna impaled on this cock that wrecked me earlier," Arthene husked. "Let us see what sort of beautiful sounds we can get her to make in the time we have."

With Arthene's urging and the reminder that they did have a time limit, Koda pushed the worries and the visions to the side. He had two visions of loveliness in front of him that he intended to savor. The fight was not over yet, and he needed as much motivation as possible to get through the battles to come.

Author's Note

If you enjoyed this, please leave a review. Reviews are how indie authors get visibility and also what helps spur us on to keep writing. Even if it's just a quick message or a comment. Positive feedback is always welcome.

If you want a hub for my work, try my website.

http://www.mtresswrites.com

Other places you can find information on my works and support me:

http://www.patreon.com/user?u=121448296

If you want more Harem content, find people of like minds to talk to, and get the heads-up on new content, come join us on Facebook.

Harem Gamelit -

https://www.facebook.com/groups/HaremGamelit

HaremLit Readers -

https://www.facebook.com/groups/HaremLitBooks

Haremlit - https://www.facebook.com/groups/haremlit

If you want more Monster Girls (and be honest, you know you do!) come join the rest of us in mischief:

Monster Girl Fiction - https://www.facebook.com/groups/
MonsterGirlFiction/

Other Books by this Author

Steelforged Legacy

Book 1 - Defiant Hand - My Book

Monster Girls in Space

Book 1 - To Valor's Bid - My Book

Book 2 - Honor's Challenge - My Book

Book 3 - Duty's Reward - My Book

About the Author

I've been a voracious reader for as long as I can remember. According to my parents, that started really young. Apparently, my mother found me in the living room teaching myself to read with the book she'd been reading to me only an hour previous at around the age of four. Apparently, I wasn't done at the same time she was.

Since then, I've been fascinated with the written word. Everything from lore heavy games to literature to tabletop gaming as well. I wrote for the enjoyment of it and spent a fair amount of time in various pen names writing fan fiction, since those stories ended before I was done with them as well.

Now though, I can appreciate a good ending when the time comes. Especially since, as the author, I'm the one who gets to choose when the story wraps and the curtains close.

It is a good feeling!

Check This Out !

Check This Out !

https://www.facebook.com/groups/haremlitbooks

https://www.reddit.com/r/haremfantasynovels/

Made in United States
Troutdale, OR
12/29/2024

27249589R10286